WE ARE
THE ORIGIN

Wrath of the Gods: Book 1

C. M. Lockhart

WRITTEN IN MELANIN

Established • 2019

MAP OF THE REALM

Scan the QR code to view the map for the book!
Or visit WrittenInMelanin.com/wato_map

PRAISE FOR WE ARE THE ORIGIN

"Lockhart's electrifying debut gave me everything I need in an epic fantasy novel—fickle gods, intrigue, a badass heroine, and a unique world to get lost in. You need this book in your life *ASAPtually*."

— *Amanda Ross, Author of The Witchkind Series*

"The assassins, the worldbuilding, the gods, this book hits on every level. These characters aren't nice, they're savage, and I love it."

— *Celeste Harte, Author of the Dragon Bones Trilogy*

"A gritty fantasy world with lovable characters and one show-stopping heroine!"

— *C. C. Wilde, Author of Matching Mirrors*

"The more I read, the more I want to keep reading."

— *Aran Lee, host of the Blxxk Anime Podcast*

"I loved this. Beautifully written and detailed."

— *Ashley D.*

"A world crafted with beauty and darkness comes alive in 'We Are the Origin,' and I loved it! Magic, technology, love, and hate are all woven together to create a refreshing take on political intrigue and elite assassins. I can't wait for the next installment!"

— *Ashleigh Davenport, Founder of Final Beat Comics*

For the Black girls who aren't all that nice.
This one is for you.

PROLOGUE

She was as broken as the world we lived in, but even so — she stood as a
goddess among mortals, beautiful in her destruction.

— Freya and the Power of Incarnation | Lindl's First Holy Academy

---

ASARI'S DOMAIN — 6 MONTHS AGO

"Come on Lena, tell the story!"

"Again, Kinley? I've told it four times already," Lena complained.

"It's my favorite," the little girl pleaded. "Come on. One more time."

"Kinley," their mother said, her daughter's name a warning. Her eyes
never lifted from the paperwork she scribbled on and sorted behind her
desk. "Leave your sister be."

"But…" she whined, her bright eyes darting from her sister to their
mother across the room.

"I'd like to hear the story too," a voice chimed in from the side. Lena
turned and let a grin slip across her face at the green-eyed stranger. It
was rare for guests to migrate to the sitting area after the final meal, and
she usually sat in silence with them when they did, but the presence of
another often lent a soft warmth to the room that the dark blue sofas,

thick white rugs, and flickering flames of the fire couldn't emulate. It was a small thing that helped to ease her exhaustion, and though she had no desire to recount the story for Kinley, who made her tell it a thousand times a day, she had no problem entertaining a stranger.

"Okay," Lena conceded, reaching out to pull the younger girl into her lap, "but this is it. And only because our guest asked so nicely. So, go to bed after this."

"Okay," Kinley said, squirming around to pull a nearby blanket on top of them. Lena rolled her eyes at the theatrics but waited with patience as her sister got comfortable. She settled down and closed her brown eyes before forcing them open again to look up at her sister. "Go."

Lena sighed as Kinley snuggled further down into her blankets, but started the story, nonetheless.

"Long, long ago," she began, her voice soft, "when our world was new, before there existed a sun and a moon and all the people, there existed a goddess."

"A beautiful goddess," Kinley corrected.

"Quiet, you. Or I won't tell the story," Lena warned.

"Sorry," Kinley whispered.

Lena smiled and smoothed her sister's brown curls before continuing. "But yes, the goddess was very beautiful and kind. She was also very powerful. She was born of the soil and the trees, the flowers, and all the plants that cover our world. Her name was Freya and with a single drop of her own blood mixed in with the soil, she created the animals, the birds, and the fish. And with her breath, she blew life into all things." Lena paused to blow past her sister's ear and the girl giggled before

2

sinking deeper into her blankets.

"There were also four gods. Rothe, Lindl, Carna, and Asari. They were as different as different would allow, but they all had one thing in common."

"It's the goddess," Kinley whispered to the stranger, her sleepy eyes clashing with her grin and rosy cheeks.

Lena bopped her head with a gentle hand to remind her of her promise to stay quiet and Kinley pressed a finger to her lips before hiding a yawn behind her tiny hand.

"And one by one," Lena continued, laughter hidden beneath her soft tones, "they all fell in love with the goddess. Rothe was the first to ever meet her, and at the time, she was trying to tame a dangerous and rebellious creature of the night."

"A shader," Kinley mumbled.

"That's right," Lena nodded, satisfied with her sister's slowed words and drooping eyes. "It had no eyes and fur blacker than the darkness they were in, but the goddess was unafraid. She bested the creature in a battle of wills and rode the creature without fear. But when Rothe appeared, the creature was startled and threw her from its back. Rothe rushed to her aid, catching her before she had a chance to hit the ground. Once he found her unharmed, he suggested they kill the beast, but the goddess became angry with him. She told him that life was precious and not to be taken lightly. Her passion lit a spark in him and his love for her birthed the sun, bathing them and all her creations in light."

Sensing her sister drifting, Lena glanced at the stranger, who had taken up residence in the lone wingback chair opposite them, and nodded in her sister's direction. The stranger returned the nod in understanding, knowing the rest of the story would be truncated to satisfy the little girl and put her to bed.

"Soon after, the other three gods also met and fell in love with the goddess, Freya," Lena continued, her voice even softer now than the glow of the fire. "Lindl, who gave us the ocean when he realized Freya's compassion ran deeper than his seas; Carna, who gave us the sky when he opened his heart to all of Freya's love; and Asari, who gave us the moon so he could be Freya's guiding light whenever she felt lost.

"The gods loved Freya and she loved them back. In return, she gave Asari the stars; Carna, the birds of the sky; Lindl, the creatures of the sea; and to Rothe, she gave her very own heart. We are all their children, descendants of the descendants of gods. And to this day they watch over us, protecting us, and giving us their blessings until the end of time."

Kinley said nothing in return as Lena lifted her into her arms, her eyes were closed and her head rested against Lena's shoulder. Lena smiled over at the stranger and offered a nod before disappearing up the stairs to carry her sister to bed. Their mother watched them go and leaned across the counter to speak to the stranger as she rose from her seat by the fire.

"My girls have always loved that story," she said, her voice as soft as her daughters but with a huskiness to it they hadn't grown into yet, "thank you for listening to it."

"The story is a favorite of mine as well," the stranger said, making her way toward the long hallway, just to the right of the stairs, that led to the guest rooms. "Thank you again for the lodging. I appreciate it."

"Ah," the innkeeper grinned, shrugging off the thanks, "it's no problem. I'm glad we had the space for you. You heading to bed?"

The stranger nodded. "I've got a long ride ahead of me."

The innkeeper hummed under her breath in understanding. It was the nature of running an inn. People came and people went. Some were interesting and told stories of their lives and what brought them to the outskirts of Asari's domain, but others — like the stranger before her now — kept their own secrets, and she didn't pry. She knew better than to try and mind business that wasn't her own.

"There'll be a hot breakfast come morning," she said, sitting back down behind the counter. "Checkout is after that. If you need to leave before then, hand off your key to me or my oldest, Lena — she was the one telling the story. And should you need to leave in the middle of the night, leave your door unlocked and the key in your room. We'll find it. Just be sure to close the front door behind you."

"Understood."

"May Asari keep your night," the woman said, already turning back to her paperwork.

"And bless your dreams," the stranger returned before disappearing down the hall and into her room.

Three hours later and the inn was as quiet as it would get. The only sounds that filtered through the walls were snores, moans, and the sighs of an old building as it settled into its foundation a bit more. Once

Brandi had bid the proprietress that Asari bless her, she'd locked her door and slipped out the small window of the room she'd rented. She'd offered the blessing half-heartedly, but she knew the weight her words carried behind them — knew that Asari had heard her and would comply with her wishes.

The thought of what the woman would dream of that night made Brandi smirk beneath her cloak and mask. She doubted the innkeeper had ever known anyone truly blessed by the gods and would be in a daze when she woke in the morning. Whatever she dreamed of, it would be the best night of her life. It was unfortunate it would only be for a single night, but considering what she was about to do, allowing the woman pleasant dreams for a night was the most she could offer her. She didn't make a habit of taking pity on people, but living in the outskirts was no easy task, especially with two girls to protect in an inn full of strangers. But the woman at the *Starry Inn* carried the weight of her responsibilities well — her daughters were well mannered, and her inn was successful, despite it being so close to Asari's barrier. It was unfair, but she would have to continue carrying the weight of her burdens, even as Brandi added to her misfortunes.

The pity she felt for the innkeeper was short lived though. Asari's night was dense and her thoughts were focused on traversing the narrow path from the inn towards the main road with the small bit of moonlight that snuck through the clouds. The overgrown walkway was unpaved and littered with muddy sinkholes at every dip in the path and it made her miss the carefully bricked sidewalks that branched out in every direction around the Queen's Tower. As the road curved through the clumps of trees, she suppressed a sigh of irritation as she sidestepped another deceptive puddle of murky water.

It wasn't until Brandi heard footsteps on the path that she waded into the underbrush. She'd resigned herself to waiting at least another hour for her target to come strolling down the path, but she was relieved to know that it wouldn't take as long as she'd anticipated. Of all the things that were required of her, waiting was always the worst part for her.

"***Bless me, for I am the wrath of the gods***," she whispered into the night. She grinned as she felt the warm double pulse of magic saturate her blood and tickle her spine. Her bow manifested in her hand, as weightless as always, heat rising within it at the pace of her own heartbeat. No matter how many times she did this, it always excited her. Without thinking, she pulled back on the string of her bow, knowing the arrow would be there as she swept through the motions, and that if she let go, her arrow would fly as far as it needed to hit her mark.

But it was too soon.

The order had been to confirm the intel they had on this man before sending him to the gods. She'd always thought it was poor taste to play with her targets before ending them, but this time her interest had been piqued. Joyson Meys was a researcher of the gods — and though he wasn't rumored to be a particularly religious man himself, he had an obsession for the lore — the myths and the obscure stories time had forgotten. Like most who grow up in the outskirts, just inside the barrier of a gods' domain, he married local. Meela Meys was the daughter of an innkeeper and had inherited the business. So, as most saw it, Joyson married up, evident in the fact he gained a family name through his wife.

Other than his obsession with the gods, he was a rather unextraordinary man and Brandi didn't care to remember all the details about him. But, he had the misfortune of garnering the attention of some powerful people when he'd started proposing there was another god — one more powerful than all the others who had been left out of the stories and forgotten through the generations. Within a week of his first public lecture, Brandi had gotten the order and she'd had no reason to refuse.

As he neared, Brandi stepped from her hiding spot and back onto the path in front of the man. Before he had time to jolt backwards and stumble away from her grasp, she'd circled his body and looped the scarf hanging at his neck around his head twice — once to cover his mouth, and the other to cover his eyes. With the scarf secured and his hands trapped in her iron grip, she guided him to the edge of the tree line.

"Walk with me," she said, her voice gentle. "It's not far."

He tripped over his own feet and whimpered the entire time, but Brandi had expected that. Fear was a tangible thing. It made even the bravest and burliest men quake in the face of it and Joyson Meys was no different. The fact he hadn't pissed himself impressed her to a certain degree.

Once they'd walked a short distance and she was positive that even if he tried to run, he'd never make it back to the main road, she released him.

"Who are you?"

Brandi rolled her eyes. That was everyone's favorite question. It's why she hated jobs where she had to get information first. She had never been known for her patience, but a job was a job.

"We both know the answer to that," she responded.

"I'll scream," he threatened.

"No one will hear you. No one will care. But in case you doubt me and want to try something," she shrugged. "I can always make sure Lena and Kinley replace you."

Even in the intermittent light of the moon, she could see that her words had hit their mark. His eyes were wide, his fists clenched, and his shaking legs were locked in place. She could almost see his mind trying to rationalize a way for him to save himself and his daughters, but it was a futile effort. Joyson Meys would not live to see another rising of Rothe's sun.

"Why?"

"Your research," Brandi shrugged. "You seem to have blasphemed against the origin of the gods."

"I haven't!" Brandi tilted her head and he lowered his voice. "I-I haven't," he repeated, nerves shaking his voice. "I just believe we've overlooked one."

"Why do you think that? I'm curious."

"W-well, the basic idea of something coming from nothing is absurd. So, my-my theory is that our gods govern this world. That there are more worlds with different gods and a s-s-supreme god who watches over them all — who brings them all into existence. My research suggests that we've forgotten the supreme one."

"That is interesting," Brandi conceded. "But it's all fiction. There are only the gods."

"But…"

"Your girls seem to know their history," Brandi interrupted him. "I listened to Lena recount the story to Kinley tonight. You know the one, right? Where all the gods fall in love with Freya and live as one big happy family?"

"I-I know it."

"Then tell me, Joyson," Brandi said, "why is that they don't know the whole story?"

"About the other god?"

Brandi narrowed her eyes. "There was no other god, Joyson. Keep up!"

"Y-yes! Then you mean…?"

"What the gods actually do."

"I don't know what you mean."

"No one seems to," Brandi sighed. "And I'd held out hope that you, at least, would be on the right track. But you'd rather ramble on about some non-existent supreme being," she shook her head. "What you know and taught your daughters is only half the truth. Yes, Rothe gave us the sun and Lindl the sea, Carna the sky and Asari the moon," she gestured to the parting clouds above them where the full moon shone down on them. "But Asari has a darkness to him, one that thrives on the pain of mortals, so he strikes them with blindness and disease. Carna is detached and cruel, ignoring every prayer from those who beg for his protection," she explained, stepping forward. "Lindl is the god of knowledge, but even with all that he knows his emotions are volatile and he's been known to drown humans in his fits of rage. And Rothe is the embodiment of pride and destruction — he would let the fire of his sun burn this entire realm just to remind the people that he alone can withstand it and is a god."

"You blaspheme against them," he said, his brown eyes darting around as if he expected the gods to appear and strike Brandi down where she stood.

Brandi smirked. "They love me."

"Who…" he whispered, backing away from her, "who are you?"

"The executioner of the gods. Or did your research not tell you that?" Brandi questioned, letting her prayer slip beneath her breath. And as before — as always — her bow appeared in her hands and she relished the heat of her blessing coursing through her veins. Her green eyes — the same vibrant color as her goddess' — finally registered with Joyson as she stood before him, ready to end his life.

"You're blessed by Freya," he whispered, shaking his head. "That's impossible. Freya doesn't give out blessings."

"Seems you wasted your research, Joyson." Brandi pulled her bow back, the arrow humming beneath her fingers, ready to be released. She'd expected him to run — most who saw her like this tried — but he seemed entranced by what he was seeing. A true researcher of the gods until the very end.

"When you stand before the gods, tell them Brandi sent you."

His life was gone before his body hit the ground.

CHAPTER ONE

Shaders are known to be the living nightmares that stalk the realm, but they are also Freya's first beloved creations — born of a darkness that existed before light, they are a manifestation of her own heart and will heed her call, always. Tread lightly before them, for they do not tolerate disrespect.

— Shaders, A History | Lindl's First Holy Academy

CARNA'S DOMAIN — PRESENT DAY

"I'm not doing this anymore."

Brandi never thought uttering those words would lead to her lying in a cave in the Asarna Mountains. It was the shortest route to Asari's domain from the queen's tower, and the trek up the sharp cliffside had been less than ideal, but it hadn't been anything outside of her capabilities. Even the windstorm with its dusty air and flying debris had been manageable until her legs gave out beneath her. Now, she was struggling to breathe as Tiki paced around her.

I warned you this was too dangerous.

13

Brandi glanced at her shader as it nagged and wanted to point out that she hadn't had much of a choice. Freya's demand to locate Asari's vessel wasn't something she could just ignore. But she didn't have the energy to argue — the breath. Tiki could slip its thoughts into Brandi's mind, but it was a one-way street. So, Brandi settled for rolling her green eyes at the beast as it nudged closer to her.

Where is your mate?

"Jack," Brandi forced out, "should be... here soon."

Do not speak.

"Stop... asking... questions... then..."

Tiki huffed and circled the cave once more. It was larger than most shaders — bigger than a small house — and hated tight, enclosed spaces, but leaving Brandi anywhere else was out of the question. The mountains were dry, windy, and cold. Without protection, Brandi's skin would be ripped from her bones with every pebble and stone that flew by. Her body would be shredded into tiny pieces before Tiki could get her somewhere safe and breathing would no longer be one of her worries. Tiki considered hiding her in its black fur and sprinting down the mountains. If she laid flat, it would be just enough to cover her from the worst of the wind, but Brandi had insisted they wait — that Jack would be meeting them there. Tiki understood her desire to meet with him but was beginning to wonder if Brandi's mental capabilities had been compromised.

Your mate will be displeased if you die.

"I... won't."

I'll go find him for you.

"No," she gasped.

Brandi.

She shook her head, adamant about not sending Tiki out to find Jack. Shaders were dangerous.

Even trained shadows like them were taught to run from them on sight. With the height of a horse and the build of a wolf, they were the fastest creatures on land in the gods' realm and were the natural predator of every living being. Born of the darkness that existed before Rothe created the sun, they had no eyes, but they were Freya's own creation and connected to the realm. They saw things in a way natural sight could never allow, so hiding from them was impossible. They were a true thing of nightmares and Freya was the only god to never fear them, so Freya was the only god they ever obeyed.

Even though he knew about her blessing, she'd never told Jack about Tiki. So he'd have no reason to believe that a shader would be protecting her, that it would be trying to lead him to her location. Jack would see Tiki as just another shader and, at best, he would avoid it. At worst, he'd attack, and Tiki would devour him.

She grinned at Tiki, her sight blurring as the shader's wordless anxiety slipped through her mind. She tried to sound confident while she focused on forcing oxygen into her aching lungs.

"This isn't... where... I die. Trust... me..."

ROTHE'S DOMAIN — 10 YEARS AGO

"That's him."

The first time Brandi ever laid eyes on Jack, she was eleven and he was in the middle of a street punching in the face of a grown man. She stood between Noble and Najé near the center of a crowd that had gathered around to watch. They'd travelled for three days to reach fragment 10811 in the eastern outskirts of Rothe's domain, near the border of Carna's wasteland. The picturesque neighborhoods of the inner ring, where pristine streets and red brick sidewalks led up to multi-domed homes with gilded solar bikes parked in expansive garages, had long since given way to squat wooden houses and crowded dirt roads. And the quiet hum of chatter that seemed to thrum in the air of the inner ring was replaced with the shouts of kiosk owners in the market and the clang of coins exchanging hands. Sweaty bodies were pushed against each other and Brandi bit back a growl of frustration as the crowd jostled her forward and she was forced to listen to the screams of a little girl as her exposed toes were trampled over. The thought of helping her crossed Brandi's mind, but survival of the fittest was the only law that ruled in the outskirts.

And it was clear to Brandi that Jack would be the one to survive. She saw it in his eyes and in the way he moved, even while caught in an obvious fit of rage. This wasn't his first time doing something like this and he would die before admitting a loss — probably to anyone.

She was never sure what incited him to rearrange the man's face in broad daylight like that — had never cared to ask. In her world, violence was merely another currency. Blows were exchanged as often as coins. So, if it had nothing to do with her, she kept it that way.

But Jack was different. The moment Najé pointed him out to her, he became her business. So, her eyes never left him as he pounded the will to resist out of the man.

"Are you sure?"

Najé chuckled, the sound alien among all the gasps and jeers surrounding them. "Do you think I would make a mistake like that, Green?"

Brandi didn't respond. She knew that Najé wasn't looking for a real answer to that question. Besides, she wouldn't be happy to know how much confidence Brandi had in her ability to overlook important details.

They had been tasked with forming a small squad of capable fighters by Queen Leia herself — a squad that would answer only to her. She'd created the shadows when she ascended the throne, a quiet way to remove all the whispering voices that questioned her validity to rule when her younger sister had been the favored successor. But now, with her throne secured and preparing for when her own children would come of age, the shadows were being reorganized. They were becoming more of an elite task force for the royal family, and it was only natural that the queen wanted the best for herself.

It was for that reason that Najé and Brandi had been chosen. Groomed for the position, they had been trained by Glenn MelForth — the queen's former blade. During the height of what became known as "the silencing", Glenn had disposed of more than half the dissenters herself, earning her the nickname "Grim Reaper". She'd disappeared a year ago though — the day after their training finished, she was nowhere to be found. A few reckless soldiers whispered that either she or Najé had offed their mentor, but Glenn was the original shadow — she wasn't someone who would be sent to the gods by someone else's hand, especially not by one she had trained. And it was it clear that if Glenn didn't want to be found, she wouldn't be.

They'd kept an ear out for any rumors that she'd resurfaced, but they weren't surprised when nothing came back. Even so, Najé was proud to be a student of the Grim Reaper and would never do anything that could hurt her reputation. So, despite her impulsiveness, Brandi made the choice to trust that Najé had done her homework on the boy they were looking for — a young, disciplined, street fighter in the outskirts of Rothe's domain with no reservations about sending someone to the gods. If the rumors about him were true, he would be a natural fit among the queen's shadows. But with the amount of rage she was witnessing, she had to question whether or not the boy Najé had described was the same boy in front of them. But she knew better than to argue with Najé in a place like this, so as the boy drove his bloody fist into the unconscious man's face, Brandi decided to follow her orders instead.

"I know where to find you," Brandi said, maneuvering her way closer to the center of the crowd.

With those words, Noble and Najé melted into the crowd, leaving Brandi standing alone to watch the end of the spectacle. It wasn't long before the majority of the crowd dispersed. They were no longer watching a fight, they were watching an execution. And something about watching the arrival of death forced most people to avert their eyes. As if not witnessing the end of a life would make it less heartbreaking for them.

Brandi never looked away though. Instead, she stepped further into the thinning crowd, drawing more attention to herself than she felt comfortable with. They watched with renewed interest as she approached the scene, being careful not to step into the gore splattered around them.

"He's unconscious."

The boy looked up at her, blood splattered across his face and dripping from his fists.

"He's still alive."

Brandi looked at the man beneath him, struggling to breathe. Even if the boy were to stop now, the man wouldn't last more than another day or two, at best. She crossed her arms and frowned. She had no aversion to death, who she was and how she lived her life didn't allow for delicate sensibilities, but torture disgusted her. Suffering was not a necessity as death was, and she hadn't yet lived long enough to find a reason to inflict it.

"Then send him if you're going to do it."

He glared at her. "And who are you to be giving me orders?"

"I'm me," Brandi retorted. "And this show you're putting on is messy," she said, wrinkling her nose at the carnage around them. "There are cleaner ways to send someone to the gods."

He snorted. "Like you would know."

"More than you, actually," Brandi stated. "Finish up with your little theatrics and come with me," she said, sinking her hands into her pockets. "We need to talk."

"And if I refuse?"

"I'll come find you. And trust me," before anyone still watching could blink, she'd pulled a throwing knife from her pocket and launched it at the beaten man, ending his suffering and sending him to the gods, "you don't want that."

"Alright," the boy said, letting his eyes roam around the abandoned bakery he'd followed Brandi into. Every surface within sight was caked in dust, and the glass display case separating the entrance from the rest of the store was shattered. Brandi kicked the shards out of her way and the tinkling sound of glass filled the space between them as she moved to look out the dirty window on their right. When her gaze never shifted back to him, he crossed his arms and angled his body towards the door they'd walked in through. "You said we need to talk. What do you want?"

Brandi shrugged. "The queen wants you."

The boy stared at her before shaking his head and turning for the exit. "You're cracked," he said, dropping his arms to his side in defeat. Brandi could tell her words had convinced him that he'd followed the worst kind of person to a secluded location, and he was now beating himself up over his decision to follow her. His was an eat or be eaten kind of world and he seemed the type to make sure he kept himself well-fed — he hadn't survived as long as he had by putting his blind trust into a stranger. But she knew how she came across to people, how the power of Freya's soul enticed them.

She wasn't like anyone else he'd ever met in the outskirts.

Even as accustomed as he was to surviving under merciless conditions, surrounded by people who held no reservations about sending someone to the gods, it was unlikely he'd ever witnessed the kind of calculating precision she possessed. She was trained as a shadow of the queendom and Freya's incarnation — life and death were exchangeable to her.

"I know more than you think I do," she said, leaning against the wall and letting her gaze bounce between him and the window. This was the meeting spot she'd scouted out earlier with Noble and Najé, but neither of them were anywhere to be found. She wanted to be surprised about it, but she couldn't even pretend she was. It was too on-brand for them to disappear and leave the hard work to her — Brandi couldn't even be irritated by it. She expected this from them at this point. Najé was always nowhere to be found at the most inconvenient moments, and Noble had a weakness for pretty people in fragments he never planned to return to.

"You're just a ringer trying to pull a con on a skirter," the boy said, annoyance coating his words. He angled his body back to face her, but his brown eyes were already shifting toward the exit — his mind no doubt moving on to his next challenge. "I don't understand what you people from the inner rings get out of coming here. Do you thrive off the high of feeling superior or something?" He snorted and turned his back on Brandi as he walked towards the exit.

She'd heard rumors whispered at the queen's tower of bored
Rothians visiting the outskirts, promising the people who lived there
a chance at a better life just to vanish into thin air once it was time to
follow through on it. It was a sick game that inner ringers enjoyed,
offering hope to a skirter just so they could wrench it away and watch
them be crushed under the weight of devastation. She never saw what the
appeal was for them, but just because she didn't understand it didn't mean
it wasn't a real thing. She understood his wariness of her but a small part
of her was offended that he'd lump her in with that kind of low-life.

Brandi rolled her eyes. "You assume too much."

"Tell me I'm wrong then," he challenged.

"I'm not from the inner ring," Brandi stated, looking away from the
window and over to him. "I was born in Freya's domain."

"You're Freyan?" He asked, taking a closer look at her skin that was
several shades darker than his own. "And? That just makes you a common
merchant, doesn't it? Is that meant to impress me?"

"Who in the gods names would want to impress you?" Brandi
snapped. "Besides, do I look like I have wares to peddle in the market?"

Their eyes locked as he stared at her, a disinterested frown pulling
at his lips. He seemed reluctant to admit that she carried nothing but the
clothes on her back and the weapons in her pockets, but it was obvious
that she was the furthest thing from the wandering nomads who traveled
between the gods' domains peddling technology schematics and rare
items.

"So, you're not a merchant," he conceded. "Still doesn't make sense
why you'd be here. If you were born outside the barrier, there's no good

reason for you to be here in the outskirts during the hottest part of Rothe's summer."

"You don't think you're a good enough reason for me to be here?"

"I think," he countered, "that if I could leave, I would never come back. So, I don't see why you would ever come here by choice."

They stared at each other in silence and Brandi tried to keep her cool as the sweltering heat closed in around them. Even in the shade of the building though, she felt the oppressive heat against her skin, and it left her patience in tatters.

"It's not fun outside," Brandi said evenly, her eyes leaving his to focus on the dwindling foot traffic outside. "There are shaders everywhere you look, Carna's skies will drown you without warning, and Asari's nights get so dark you can't see your own hand in front of your face." Brandi scoffed and shook her head. "It makes Rothe's outskirts look like a paradise. But, by all means," she said, rolling her eyes, "continue enlightening me on why I shouldn't be here."

The boy studied her for a moment before squaring his shoulders to look at her and shoving his bruised knuckles into his pockets. "Fine," he said. "You've got my attention."

"Do I?"

When he didn't say anything in return, Brandi smirked and turned away from the window. Noble and Najé would get there when they got there — or they wouldn't, and she'd run into them days later. Her job wasn't to babysit them, it was to make sure this boy agreed to go with them by the time they left, whenever that may be. "I was serious when I said the queen wanted you," she said. "I'm sure you've heard of her "shadows?"

"The soldiers who do the bidding of the crown? Everyone's heard of them, but they're just myths."

"We're not soldiers and we're not myths."

"Are you trying to tell me you're one of them?"

Brandi nodded. "And rumor has it you'd fit right in with us. So, we came to get you."

"We?"

"I'm not here alone," Brandi said, unwilling to tell him more than that. Najé and Noble would meet him on their own terms.

The boy studied her. "Let's pretend I believe you. Why me?"

"Why not you?"

Her counter question seemed to have stalled his brain because he just stared at her, his face giving away all his secrets. He'd never considered that he would be special — that he should be someone of importance to someone important. Surviving in the outskirts didn't allow him the luxury of dreaming bigger than his circumstances. But that one question had opened the floodgates.

Because, really, why not him?

"I'm not here to beg you," she said, pushing away from the wall, her eyebrows raised in surprise as Noble approached them. "Come with us or die here."

She could tell that he had more questions for her, but she was done with the conversation. She'd delivered the message and done what she could to recruit the next member of the queen's shadows. Noble could take over from there. Or they could leave him to die in Rothe's outskirts and never look back, it didn't really matter to her. Talking to people drained her and all she wanted now was a quiet room and a decent bed.

"Wait," the boy shouted, following behind her after a moment of hesitation. "I'm coming with you."

"I don't slow down," Brandi said, keeping true to her word, "so keep up."

He jogged the few steps he needed to catch up and fell into step behind her as she left the building and followed Noble back towards the more populated areas. The crowds were beginning to thin out as people sought out shelter to hide from the intensity of Rothe's sun at its peak. Sweat crawled down Brandi's neck and shoulders, pooling in the curve of her elbows and lower back. She pulled at the form-fitting fabric of her black shirt, wishing a fresh breeze would make its way through the market as the musty stench of sweaty bodies overwhelmed her. She could see Noble glancing over his shoulder trying to catch her eye, but she looked away from him, not speaking a word to him or the boy behind her along the way. Noble led them to a small motel that had two stories and faded yellow paint before draping his arm around Brandi's shoulder and dropping a set of keys into her palm.

"I got you a room upstairs," he said. "We leave in two days."

"Where's Najé?"

He shrugged. "I'm only your keeper, Green."

Brandi rolled her eyes before meeting his gaze. "Are you coming back?"

He smirked. "Someone else has requested I keep them company in their bed, and I just couldn't turn them down."

"Of course, you did," Brandi sighed.

"Jealous, Green?" Noble teased.

"Ew." Noble laughed at the disgust on her face and Brandi shook his arm off. "And what about him?" Brandi asked, jabbing her thumb in the direction of the boy who stood a few feet away from them. He hadn't said anything since they'd met up with Noble, but she doubted he'd just walk away and agree to come back in two days — he was too skeptical to trust something like that, not that she blamed him. That skepticism had probably kept him alive, but she also didn't want to be left in charge of babysitting him.

"He can't come with me, so he's your problem now," Noble shrugged. Brandi glared at him before stomping up the stairs. She was less than enthused to be left in charge of a stranger while Najé and Noble got up to gods know what, but she didn't have the patience to argue. They could do whatever they wanted for all she cared.

The boy moved to follow her up the stairs, but Noble shot out a hand, grabbing him in a firm grip by the back of his neck. Brandi slowed her steps and watched as the warm and playful demeanor he had seconds before disappeared, replaced with the icy glare of her protector. She'd seen the look cross his face countless times over the years whenever anyone tried to get close to her and wasn't surprised when he dragged the boy over to him.

"Green is mine," he warned. "Lay one finger on her and your soul won't survive to meet the gods. Understand?"

The boy jerked his head in a quick nod, his brown eyes wide in shock. It was the second time that day he'd been threatened with being sent to the gods. Brandi choked back a giggle as his dark brows drew together in confusion as the hypocrisy of Noble's warning registered with him, but he seemed to recognize that this wasn't the time to argue his point. Besides, even if his intentions had been less than wholesome, she would send him to the gods before she ever kissed him.

"Good," Noble said, releasing the boy and taking a few steps back before turning on his heel. "Hope Rothe shines down on you, or whatever." He tossed the words over his shoulder and in a heartbeat, he was gone, disappeared around a corner and out of sight.

The boy shook off the trance he'd been left in and followed Brandi up the stairs and through the door of room seven. It was a tiny room, big enough to house an old bed with fresh sheets on the right, a short wooden bench at the foot of it, and a plain wooden dresser to the left of the headboard. There was a narrow door that led to a bathroom in the back and a tiny window behind steel bars near the ceiling that let in just enough light to keep the room from being a pit of darkness. A small fan near the door blew cold air into the room and Brandi sighed in relief as she moved to stand in front of it. It wasn't the height of luxury but it was more than enough for the moment.

"Shut the door behind you," Brandi commanded.

He did as he was told and watched as she fell onto the bed, exhausted from things he seemed to know better than to ask her about. He hesitated for a moment as if he was going to ask her permission before copying her movements, but she understood how the pull of a soft mattress could be too much to ignore and said nothing as he flopped down onto the cool sheets beside her. Instead, she turned her head to face him and quirked an

27

eyebrow.

"So, what's your name anyway?"

"Jack," he answered, a small grin pulling at the corners of his mouth.

She studied his face, taking the time to consider his dark brown skin, warm brown eyes, wide nose, full lips and dimpled cheeks. She hadn't given his features much thought before, but now that she knew he would be joining them at the queen's tower as one of her shadows, she committed them to memory. And she decided that she liked his face. There was something about the easy grin he offered her that made her feel comfortable. When he looked at her, she felt less like a weapon and more human. She nodded and offered half a smile in return before turning her back to him.

"I'm Brandi."

CARNA'S DOMAIN — PRESENT DAY

Someone is coming.

Brandi opened her eyes to focus on Tiki and tilted her head towards the exit. She needed Tiki to hide. Only Jack would be bold enough to climb the mountains in the middle of a windstorm and she needed to explain why a shader was with her before he tried to rescue her from it. As dangerous as it was, she knew Jack wouldn't hesitate to fight Tiki with his bare hands if it meant protecting her.

I will not leave you.

"Just… for a few… minutes…" Brandi wheezed.

Tiki nuzzled closer to her, its warm nose pressed into the side of her face. Brandi leaned into it, trying to let it know she would be alright. She was far more resilient than she looked and they both knew that. Besides, she'd meant what she said. She had no plans to die in some nondescript cave bordering Asari's domain.

Three minutes. That is all I will give you.

Brandi nodded. That would be plenty of time. Tiki huffed a bit of warm air into her face and Brandi smiled. It was something Tiki had done since she was a child, lost in Freya's domain, to comfort her. Despite their monstrous looks and ability to devour most living creatures whole, Freya had blessed them to smell sweet, like the maple fruits that grew year-round in the heart of her domain. Most people feared the syrupy scent as a distinct harbinger of death, but Brandi loved it.

With one more huff of sweet air in her face, Tiki disappeared. And as expected, Jack was stumbling in a few moments later, the windstorm nearly sending him tumbling down the cliff-side.

"Jack."

"Brandi!" He rushed over to scoop her into his arms. "Do you know how hard it was to find you?"

"No."

He chuckled as he held her tighter. "Let's just say, it would have been easier for Rothe to be humble." He pulled back to look at her, two lines forming between his brows as he watched her shivering in his arms and struggling for breath. "You've got the bite."

She nodded and he cursed under his breath, panic rising in his chest. He didn't have the slightest idea of how to help her and the windstorm would make it impossible to get down the mountain to find help — simply finding her had been a feat of sheer will. He started to pull his jacket off to place it over her, a futile effort to keep her warm in her thin clothes, but she placed a hand on his arm.

"I need… to tell you… something…"

"Can it wait till I get you down the mountain?" He asked, shaking her hand off to wrap the jacket around her. "You shouldn't be talking right now."

Brandi could've laughed at how alike he and Tiki sounded. She never would have imagined that two natural-born predators like them would worry over her so much. But she held his gaze and shook her head. She could feel her mind slipping away from her, desperate for the oblivion of rest. She fought to hang on to it, knowing that her words couldn't wait.

"I… have… a… shader…"

"You have a what?"

"Shader…" she repeated. "Tiki…"

Jack's eyes widened and he rushed to pick her up, not bothering to respond to her words. The bite had a wide range of symptoms, but he looked at her now as if she were delirious. Though she couldn't blame him. She knew how her words sounded, and if she'd heard him claiming to own a man-eating shader as a pet, then she'd be trying to get him down the mountain as fast as she could too.

"Listen…"

"No one can tame a shader, Brandi. Not even you."

Time's up.

She felt the words slip across her mind before she saw Tiki, its form moving to block the entrance and its sweet scent filling the cave. Jack instinctively tossed Brandi behind him and scrambled backwards, using his body to shield them both. His brown eyes narrowed on the giant, blind beast as adrenaline poured into his system like a burst dam. Shaders were the monsters rumored to live beyond the protection of the gods' domains, the legends of children's bedtime stories to keep them in line and warn them away from the mythical dangers of the outskirts. Having been born in the outskirts though, Jack knew the gods' protection covered them too and he'd been adamant in sharing his belief that the monsters weren't real. His reality had been enough of a warning for him on its own — but the fear sending tremors through his arms as he shielded Brandi from the beast in front of them was proof enough that the stories were true.

Did you not tell him?

"Tiki…" Brandi coughed out. "Jack…" His eyes darted to Brandi for half a second when she squeezed his arm with the little strength she had left, but his eyes weren't able to stay away from the shader for long. "Tiki…"

She fell forward, coughs wracking her body and Tiki moved towards her on instinct. Jack wrapped her in his arms, turning to show his back to the shader and once again putting himself between her and it. He knew shaders were ruthless and expected to feel the jaws of the beast closing around them at any moment, but instead he heard the distressed whining

31

of an animal. He lifted his head and lost all trust in his own eyes when he saw the shader pacing the cave. It sank to its belly, nose facing them, and ears drooped in its best effort to show that it wouldn't harm them.

Brandi reached for the shader and it nuzzled her hand.

"Tiki…"

"Holy Rothe," Jack whispered. "You actually tamed a shader."

Without another word, Brandi went limp in Jack's arms, the bite finally getting to be too much for even her. Jack tensed and called her name, shaking her, but it didn't take long for him to realize she wouldn't be opening her eyes anytime soon. He turned frantic eyes onto the shader with panic, fear, and desperation volleying through him at painful speeds.

"Can you get her down the mountain?"

He didn't know why he assumed the shader would understand him, but it nodded its black head and huffed, the sweet scent that had always promised death, enveloped him. He glanced down to Brandi, her breathing shallow, and realized he didn't have the luxury of hesitating. He'd have to trust her — her, and her shader. It would take him days to get her to Asari's domain on his own, maybe even longer if the windstorm didn't let up. But a shader… it didn't need eyes to see and if the rumors were true, with its speed, it would take only a few hours.

"I'm going to trust you," Jack whispered, approaching the beast. He lifted Brandi onto its back as gently as he could, surprised by how soft the fur was against the bare skin of his arms. He pulled himself up behind her and held tight to the animal as it stood, leaning over Brandi to cradle her between his arms and protect her from the slicing wind and flying rocks as best he could.

"I'm going to make sure she doesn't fall, so go," Jack told it. "As fast as you can."

Tiki huffed, then took off out of the cave, sprinting as if it was trying to outrun the gods.

CHAPTER TWO

He was the dichotomy of nature — the problem and the solution — the builder and the destroyer — the all-consuming darkness and the light that guides out of it.

— Asari, An Introduction | Lindl's Fifth Holy Academy

ASARI'S DOMAIN — PRESENT DAY

"Help her."

These were the only two words Jack managed to force out through his teeth before his knees gave way and sent him crashing into the uneven stones beneath them. Brandi was cradled in his arms, still shivering and barely breathing — but barely was enough for him. As long as she didn't stop.

His shirt was ripped and his back was battered, bleeding, and bruised from the ride down the mountain. Tiki was faster than anything he could have imagined, and Jack would be forever grateful to it for making a trip that would have taken him three days in four hours. But that meant every rock caught in the windstorm, no matter how small, became a battering ram on his back. He knew his wounds were gruesome, but he didn't care. Brandi was flirting with the gods in his arms and he'd been forced to leave Tiki behind and carry her the rest of the way himself because shaders weren't allowed inside the gods' domains.

His sister, Jaquelyn, had raised him and his brothers on the legends of the gods. Alongside their daily prayers to Rothe, she'd taught them about the other gods and how, despite Freya's love for the creatures, they'd raised barriers around their domains for the sole purpose of keeping shaders out. Jacquelyn had always chuckled under her breath when she told them of Carna and his refusal to erect a barrier out of spite towards Asari and indifference towards the people, but her favorite part of the story had always been when she spoke of Freya and how the goddess adored the beasts, giving them names and inviting them to make her domain their home. His sister had never used the threat of shaders to frighten them to bed as most parents seemed to do, but that hadn't kept him from wondering what could entice any sane person to leave the protection of the gods of their own volition.

He could almost laugh at himself now. When Brandi told him that she'd abandoned the shadows and to meet her in the Asarna Mountains, he hadn't hesitated. Her reasons for leaving the queendom and wanting to meet in Carna's wastelands didn't matter to him.

He would do anything Brandi asked of him.

And now that he knew about her pet shader, he understood. She'd chosen the mountains because of Tiki. But the base of the Asarna Mountains ended in Asari's domain, and Tiki could go no further once they reached the barrier. So Jack had carried Brandi two miles to the nearest fragment on his own.

It had been a struggle to navigate through the dense undergrowth at the base of the mountain with Brandi unconscious in his arms. Even with his blessing of strength from Rothe, he would have bled out long before he ever laid eyes on the massive stone walls surrounding the fragment had it been any further away from the edge of the barrier.

He'd thought it strange there were no guards at the gate as he stumbled through it, but as he looked up at the people surrounding them, he understood. They were at the base of the Asarna Mountains on the furthest edge of Asari's domain — the people here probably weren't accustomed to outsiders. Looking at all the near-identical faces with brown curls and wide eyes that stared at the two of them in shock, he guessed that he'd stumbled into some skirter fragment where everyone was born there and no one ever left. He swallowed his pride and frustration as he scanned the crowd for anyone who looked like they would be willing to help, but they were all frozen. They'd been stopped in the midst of their daily activities by his plea for help, but not a single person took a step toward them.

"Please," he begged. "She's got the bite. Can someone help her?"

When no one responded, his anger flared and he bit back a shout of frustration before struggling back to his feet. Rothe would be a beggar before he bled out and let them die in a place like this.

"Wait!"

Jack's head snapped up, his short locs dancing around his head as he studied the two people stepping toward him. The first was a man with the same brown hair and eyes as everyone else, though a bit taller than average and better dressed, Jack guessed he probably ran some type of business funded by the monarchy if he wore a suit in a fragment like this. It was the other person who caught his attention though — a blonde-haired girl with pale blue eyes. Though the surprise on her face was the same as everyone else's, it was obvious that she was the other among them. It was her voice he'd heard, and it was her who took a step toward them now.

"I can help her," she said.

His eyebrows raised at the confidence in her words. He watched her delicate hands reach for Brandi and he hoped the girl wouldn't offer them more than disappointment.

"I'm blessed," she said gently when Jack tightened his grip on Brandi. "Asari has given me the gift of healing."

Those words piqued Jack's interest. Like the other gods, Asari was known to give out blessings according to his own whims, but it was rare for him to give anyone the ability to heal. Only once every century or so, if the rumors were to be believed. But if what the girl spoke was true, then he'd have to be cracked not to allow her to help.

Jack nodded at her and she rushed forward, her hands pressing into Brandi's chest. His mind didn't register the words she spoke, but he saw the pale blue glow beneath her hands and felt the stilling of Brandi's shakes. It only took a few moments before Brandi was cracking her green eyes open to look up at him.

"Hey," she croaked out.

He smirked down at her. "Hey. You had me worried the gods might be wanting you back."

She coughed out a laugh. "I would never let them take me that easily."

As they exchanged looks with each other, the girl stepped back and cleared her throat. Jack looked up at her with his eyebrows raised and she gestured to his back.

"You can come to my house and I can do something about that," she offered. "But it would probably be best not to linger here," she said, her voice lowered and her blue eyes darting to all the curious ones still watching them.

Jack nodded and rose to his feet, with Brandi still cradled in his arms, to follow the girl down the path she led them on.

It was a short walk through what Jack guessed to be the main square, but it was long enough for Jack to confirm his suspicions that whatever fragment they were in, they didn't get visitors often and they wouldn't be welcomed with open arms. The countless pairs of eyes watching them with unwavering stares as they followed the blonde girl made his senses jittery. He'd been a shadow long enough that open scrutiny put him on edge now. But he couldn't blame them for staring. Things were no different when he'd lived in the outskirts of Rothe's domain. When you lived close to the border of the gods, it was never a good sign when new people showed up, because if they didn't come through the main gate, they'd come from outside the gods' barrier. And nothing good ever came of that.

"This way," the girl said, her voice soft as she pointed to a path off the main road, "my home is a little farther out."

Jack nodded and followed her, feeling more at ease as the shade of the trees covered them and the unwanted gazes of strangers fell away. He made a mental note of the way they'd come in, and he saw that the path, though obscured enough to hide its entrance, was well worn. The undergrowth had been cut back, and small lights had been strung through the branches of the trees at regular intervals along the way.

Their walk down the path wasn't a short one, but the girl moved with a sense of urgency in her steps. After walking what Jack guessed to be a little less than half a mile, they reached a small green house nestled in a clearing. There were flat gray stones pushed into the ground that began at the end of the dirt path they were on and led up to a painted white door. The girl's steps slowed as she stepped on the stones, her movements becoming more intentional as if she were wary of slipping on them. Jack held no such reservations as he met the girl at the door and followed her inside. She directed him to place Brandi, who'd fallen asleep in his arms, on the couch as she locked the door behind them. It made him curious as to who she thought would bother her as far out as she was, but he didn't bother asking. People carried their own burdens and he had no desire to pick up hers — even if she was being kind enough to help them.

"Come sit over here," she said, pointing to a stool she'd placed in the middle of the room. "And remove your shirt, please."

He did as he was told, though he didn't have much shirt left to remove. After being shredded to pieces on the ride down the mountain, it fell apart in his hands with one swift tug. His mind had long since numbed itself to the pain, focusing only on keeping Brandi alive. But as he sat down and he heard the blonde girl gasp from behind him, his mind began to focus on all the sensations he'd been blocking out.

The girl placed a cool cloth against him, and he winced, sucking in a sharp breath between his gritted teeth as the water felt like acid sliding down his back.

"I'm sorry," she whispered. "I have to clean this at least a little so I can see what I'm healing."

Jack grunted as she placed the cloth back to his skin but said nothing. If that's what she needed to do, then so be it. He was still wrapping his mind around the fact they managed to find a healer. And if this healer was who he thought she was, he'd have several questions for Brandi when she woke up. But he couldn't pretend to be too surprised — the nature of Brandi's blessing made her a magnet for those touched by the gods.

The gods loved her and so did those blessed by them.

She pulled the cloth away from his skin for a final time and placed her palm against him as gently as she could. He flinched, but she remained steady, unwilling to move her hand as she began whispering the words to heal him. When she'd healed Brandi, he hadn't paid much attention to her words, but now, in the dead silence of the room, he realized that he couldn't understand the words. It seemed like another language that slipped from her lips. Though her tone was soft and her voice soothing, confusion filled him the longer he listened and some innate part of him understood that she was speaking the language of the gods.

He knew that shouldn't be possible, but before he could contemplate it, she fell silent and stepped away from him.

"Alright," she said. "I'm done."

She walked around to face him and offered him a plain white shirt. He reached for it and was almost surprised when he didn't feel the agony from earlier screaming across his back. He rolled his shoulders and rose to his feet to catch a glimpse of his reflection in the mirror mounted above her fireplace. His back didn't look as if he'd been healed — it looked as if he'd never taken any damage in the first place.

"This," he said, twisting to see as much as he could without a second mirror, "is incredible."

"Thank you," she said, smiling as she watched him.

In the reflection of the mirror, he saw her eyes dip to the muscles of his chest and abs, and the newly healed ones in his back. He guessed that she wasn't unfamiliar with the male body. Being a healer, he didn't imagine that she'd have time to be shy when someone was hurt, but if she'd never left Asari's domain, then this was probably the first time she'd ever seen someone like him. He stood almost a head taller than most people and his sister had always complimented his brown skin with its rich golden hues, telling him it was almost as if the rays of Rothe's sun were trapped beneath it. It was the exact opposite of the milky tones that were common in Asari's domain. Even his black hair was styled in a way that was unique to Rothe's domain. Asari's children either had brown floppy curls, brown buzz cuts, or brown hair straight as bones. He'd never seen an Asarian with black hair like his or blonde hair like hers.

Her blue eyes roved over his body with a greediness in them he recognized. He'd always been confident in his looks for good reason, but as a light blush crept across the girl's cheeks, his stomach knotted in distaste at whatever thoughts she might be having about him. He shot a quick glance over to Brandi and was grateful to see that she still slept. She was a possessive woman with little patience. So, before the girl had time to get any ideas in her head that would get her sent to the gods, Jack pulled on the shirt she'd given him, breaking her trance.

"You may feel fine, but you'll still need rest," she warned, bending to pick up the bloody cloth and water she'd used to clean him. "You lost a lot of blood and carrying her all this way didn't help."

Jack shrugged as his gaze settled on Brandi. "If I was sent to the gods saving her, then meeting them would've been worth it."

She paused her movements and looked back to him. He wondered if his conviction had surprised her. Not many people would speak with such nonchalance about meeting the gods, but he'd meant what he said.

"We haven't been introduced," she said, turning to face him. "I'm Sarah."

He studied her, his experience as a shadow making him hesitant to give away anything more that could be used to identify them later, but he figured it was too late for that. She'd already gotten a good look at them — if she wanted to describe them to someone, she'd have no problem. Neither would half the fragment who'd seen them in the main square. Instead of dwelling on the possibility of having to send the entire population of a fragment to the gods, he decided to let things play out as the gods wanted them to and moved to take a seat on the floor by Brandi. Even unconscious, she instinctively reached out for him, and he took her hand before turning back to Sarah.

"I'm Jack," he finally answered. "And this," he said, nodding his head towards the couch, "is Brandi."

"Her, I know," Sarah said, returning to her task. "We've met before."

ASARI'S DOMAIN — 14 YEARS AGO

Most people do not have life-altering experiences at the age of eight and three-quarters. However, most people are not born Sarah Rothens, first daughter of the second princess of the queendom. And although she knew that to be her family name, she also knew better than to claim it — to even speak it. So, when anyone asked, she was just Sarah. Things were simpler that way, and she preferred simple.

So, when the girl with the same dark brown skin and bright green eyes as the goddess was found at their doorstep on a rainy afternoon like a waterlogged rag doll, Sarah was not enthused. She'd never been the type of girl who longed for an adventure — who waited with hope in her heart and wonder in her eyes for a sign that she was to embark on some kind of grand journey. Quite the opposite, in fact. Sarah prayed for mediocrity. She hoped that anything even remotely interesting would avoid her. Her mother was the one with a heart for the unexpected, and though Sarah loved her mother as much as the gods loved Freya, she had seen where her mother's desire for an interesting life had landed them — exiled from Rothe's domain, renounced by the monarchy, and hunted by the queen and her shadows while living under a false name in fragment 42617, the furthest outskirts of Asari's domain.

There were times Sarah wished their quiet life was more comfortable, but she knew better than to desire more from the gods than what they were willing to give.

So, she wanted nothing to do with the girl who, no doubt, already had their attention. Her presence in their home would be enough to drag her family under the gods' scrutiny, inviting nothing but chaos into their home. But her parents were kind and trusting people and could never leave a child like her to her own devices. And much like she would be fourteen years later, the first time she met the girl she'd come to know as Brandi, she was already flirting with the gods.

A fever raged through her body and steam rolled off her in waves that could have burned them all, but her eyes were clear and focused on things only she could see. Sarah didn't know what to think of her, but in that moment, she was afraid. And it wasn't the kind of fear she felt when she ran to her bed after flicking out the light, but the kind that unsettled her core and made her want to cling to her father. Because when new things aren't fascinating, they're terrifying.

For days Sarah kept watch over the girl from a distance as her parents worried over her. But they weren't blessed by the gods, and their medical knowledge, while better than most, was still limited. Nothing they tried seemed to bring her fever any lower. For three days, all they could do was ply her with water, wipe her free of sweat, and keep her covered in as much ice as their little freezer could make. Sarah and her little brother, Jamie, weren't allowed near her for fear they would catch whatever the girl was suffering from, but it soon became apparent that whatever the girl had was unique to her.

On the third night she was with them, the anxious whispers of her parents floated through Sarah's door. Normally, she would simply turn towards the wall and ignore the sounds. Their small house didn't afford them much privacy and she'd already learned the hard lesson that eavesdropping could ruin lots of things. But that night, she knew she would get no rest. Her parent's growing anxiety had permeated the house. Dinner had been silent and even Jamie had lost some of his boundless energy, the silence creating shadows in the corners of their home that seemed to creep in closer with every passing minute. Even the glow of the full moon, drenching her room in its pale blue glow, made her heart race with paranoia when it had always brought her a sense of peace and comfort before. It was as if Asari himself were watching her.

Sarah wrapped her blanket around her shoulders and pulled it behind her as she tip-toed across the room, careful to avoid the creaky floorboard just at the edge of her bed. She sat down with her back pressed to the door and huddled into her orange blanket, the only protection she believed kept her safe from the man-eating shaders her mother warned would come after her if she was caught out of bed past her bedtime. She was willing to risk facing a shader if that meant finding out what was going on in their home, and from her seat by the door, she could hear everything.

"What are we going to do?" Her mother whispered, a frustration in her voice Sarah had never heard before. "We can't afford to take care of another child."

"I know," her father said, his voice heavy, like he'd been tasked with carrying a burden meant for the gods. "But what would you have us do? Abandon her like some stray animal we lost interest in?" He gave a deep sigh before he spoke again, his voice thick with an emotion she couldn't quite place. "She's Temari's daughter, Vee. If she's here, then…"

"I know," her mother whispered.

"Temari and Ross are probably with the gods now," he said, a slight crack in his voice. "Which means Glenn is probably looking for her."

Sarah wondered who Glenn was and why they would be looking for the sick girl down the hall, but knew she could never ask her father. They could never know there was a third set of ears listening to their conversation.

"I know that," her mother whispered. "And may Freya have mercy on their souls. But Mark. If you ask me to choose between her and our family, I'd abandon her in a heartbeat."

"You can't mean that…" he said, pausing as if waiting for her mother to apologize for her words. "Vee! We owe them the greatest debt of our lives. If they hadn't helped us escape the tower, we wouldn't even be here," he pointed out. "Once Leia announced the execution of both you and Sarah, Ross had been the only one willing to help us leave Rothe's domain. And he gave us shelter in his home for weeks even though his wife was sick, and they'd just had a baby. They were like family to us, and now you're talking about leaving their daughter to fend for herself? Are you cracked, woman?"

"I take no pride in knowing this about myself," she admitted. "But we've already risked everything once. Risked the lives of our children. I won't do it again," she declared, her voice stronger than it had been before. "Not even for the gods themselves."

"Venetia!" His hand slammed against the table, and Sarah jumped at the sound as his chair scraped across the tile. "That's blasphemy."

"Then let the gods punish me as they see fit," she snapped. "But any god that would have me save a stranger and risk the death of my own children is not a god worth serving."

"I do hope she's prepared for that."

It was in that moment that Sarah noticed the pale white mist flowing into her room. She tried to scream but her voice was gone, and when she turned to reach for the doorknob — to race towards her father — the door was gone, replaced with a black emptiness that made her cower back into the mist. The only light she saw was the circular reflection of the moon on her bedroom floor — bright and blinding, as if it hovered over her head.

Her eyes darted around the familiar space, now shrouded in a darkness that transformed everything into something foreign to her. Too shocked to even shed tears, she couldn't move away when she realized she was no longer alone.

"Ah," a gentle voice, soft like clouds, whispered across her ears. "Your mother does not fear me, but I see that you do."

Sarah whipped her head around to find the voice, and her eyes met the gaze of a blue pair that matched her own and towered above her. She wasn't sure if he was tall enough to reach out and touch the stars, or if the stars had simply followed him down into her room, but he was larger than her entire world. Pale blue hair fell in waves down his back and over the white suit he wore, as if he were the groom in a lavish wedding. He was breathtaking and blinding in his beauty, but it was his smile that made Sarah quake under her blanket. As gentle and warm as it was, it felt devious. It belied his fickle nature. He was being kind to her now, but she sensed the sinister ruthlessness that churned just beneath his tranquil surface, and as he hiked up his pants leg to bend down to her level as a parent would to speak with an errant child — she instinctively fell to her knees and pressed her head to the floor.

She'd never met a god before, but there was no question that she was in the presence of one now.

"Your mother is bold to speak against me when my beloved rests in her home," he said, "and in my own domain no less." He shook his head, his hair falling over his shoulder and casting a shadow over the left side of his face. "You children of Rothe," he said, his lips curling in disgust, "have too much pride."

Sarah wanted to puke from the sheer amount of fear coursing through her at his words. There was so much loathing in them. He spoke in a language she had never heard, but even so, she understood him. It sent her young mind spinning and she wanted nothing more than to cry and run to her father. Or wake up to find this was all nothing more than a terrible nightmare. But when he reached one pale, elegant finger out to lift her chin, she knew he was real. Her body was numb, and in the face of absolute fear, there was nothing she could do.

"I came here to punish your mother as she requested," he said with an air of disinterest, using his finger under Sarah's chin to turn her head to the left and then to the right. "But you," he hummed. "I find you to be intriguing." He smiled, a warm thing that chased every chill from Sarah's body as she looked on him. "What is your name, child?"

With a pulse in her throat that jolted her forward, her voice returned just long enough for her to utter her name. "Sarah."

"Sarah," he repeated, making her name sound like a melody as the stars shimmied in dance above him. "Your hair is the color of Rothe's treasured sun, but your eyes," he leaned closer to her, shifting slightly so the light fell onto her flushed cheeks, "your eyes carry the moon."

He chuckled, and Sarah shivered as the sound danced over her skin and played on her spine. It was both painful and delightful — terrifying and addicting. She didn't know whether to scream or laugh. But as quickly as the sensation came, it melted away — a memory, just seconds later, she couldn't be sure was real. Her legs began to ache as she kneeled on the hard floor and he studied her. He watched her as if he were watching a movie of her life, and she didn't dare move from under his gaze as the grin on his face grew wider.

"I do believe I've taken a liking to you, Sarah," he said, a gentleness in his voice that felt comforting — like he'd taken the black velvet between the stars and wrapped every word inside them. "So this is what I shall do," he said, removing his hand from her chin. "I shall overlook your mother's transgression," he paused and looked at her. "Do you know what that word means?" Sarah shook her head, and he adjusted his wording. "I will forgive your mother this once. So, you'll do me a favor in return for not taking her with me, won't you?"

Sarah nodded, stricken by how little the god cared about taking her mother's life. It seemed as trivial to him as brushing his hair away from his face.

"Good girl," he whispered. "There is something I need you to do, but first," he gestured to himself, "do you know who I am?" Sarah nodded again, and he shook his head. "Speak my name, child."

"Asari," she whispered, "god of the moon."

"And do you know whom I love more than anyone?"

"Freya," Sarah answered. "Goddess of life and judger of souls."

"Very good, Sarah," Asari praised. "Right now, my beloved is incarnated in the little girl next door to you. The one with the beautiful green eyes." Sarah felt an envy like nothing she'd ever felt before overtake her at the god calling the other girl beautiful. She'd never felt insecure — didn't know the feeling just yet — but in that moment, she wished Asari had carried the same kind of wistfulness in his voice when he'd said her eyes carried the moon. But she pushed the feeling aside. As he said, the gods loved Freya more than anyone else. It didn't seem to matter what form she was in.

"I will give you power," he promised. "Power to heal anyone you wish. I shall teach you the words," he smiled, "then you need only call on me and I shall aid you. In exchange," he continued, "when Rothe raises his sun, you must heal my beloved. Do you understand?" Sarah nodded and he beamed, almost blinding her with the brightness of his joy. Without warning, he leaned forward and placed a gentle kiss on top of her head.

She melted into his soft touch before her body convulsed, and what felt like liquid fire pulsed through her veins. She tried to scream, but as he had before, Asari had taken her voice. Tears leaked out of her eyes as every sense and nerve ending in her body raged against the heat the flood of magic caused. She fell on her back and clawed at her chest, the burning inside her lungs suffocating her as it spread. Sarah threw her hands in front of her, clutching at anything that might save her from the agony flowing through her as Asari watched.

"Hang in there," he encouraged. "It's almost done."

Sarah wanted to believe his words, but as the heat reached her stomach, she knew she couldn't trust them. A wordless scream tried to rip free of her throat as she gasped and curled in on herself, but she still had no voice. Her stomach churned and acid bubbled up the back of her throat, but it felt like only flames would eject from her if she threw up now. She heaved but got no relief. She slammed her head against the hardwood floors, her instincts urging her to seek the void of unconsciousness any way she could, as voiceless screams continued to escape her. She didn't know how much longer she could bear the pain of sinking into what seemed to be an endless pit of fiery lava.

As the heat enveloped her toes, she was sure she was at her end. She'd trusted the god of the night and had fallen for his ploy. This was the punishment she'd endure for her mother's blasphemy.

But then, it was gone. Like cool water on molten steel, she felt a relief so deep in her bones she could have screamed in joy. She cracked her eyes open to see she was surrounded by clouds and Asari was cradling her small body in his hands. The same hands that had carved out every phase of the moon and placed every one of the stars Freya gifted him into the night sky. She looked up into Asari's deep blue gaze and felt as though she were sinking and floating at the same time.

"You know the words now?"

She nodded and closed her eyes, no longer having the strength to keep them open or respond to him.

"You are no longer a daughter of Rothe, but a vessel of mine," he whispered to her as he placed her back in her bed. "Keep your promise to me, Sarah," he warned as he pulled her blanket up around her and his mist faded from the room. "I am not a god who forgives twice."

CHAPTER THREE

His thoughts were as scattered as the stars and his moods as shifting as the moon — his only constant was her.

— Asari, An Introduction | Lindl's Fifth Holy Academy

ASARI'S DOMAIN — 14 YEARS AGO

Sarah was groggy when she woke up the next morning.

Her room was dark. The stars and moon that normally lit it up were already gone to make way for the coming morning. She rubbed at her eyes, thinking the previous night might have been nothing more than a terrible nightmare, but as if to mock her hope, the memories of meeting Asari flooded her mind until she could think of nothing else. But it was the quick pulse of magic that left a lingering heat in her blood that ruined any plans she had of feigning ignorance. Everything had been real. Still unfamiliar with the sensation that wasn't quite pain or pleasure, her fear ran rampant, wild and unchecked. And with her voice finally returned to her, she screamed for her father.

"Sarah!"

Her parents barged into her room, her father nearly taking the door off its hinges as they rushed in. She clung to her father and wailed into his chest as he scooped her up and wrapped his strong arms around her, rubbing soothing circles into her back. She tried to tell them what happened last night, but nothing she was saying made any sense — even to her. She couldn't stop rambling about stars and blue hair and burning. She knew her parents must have thought she'd simply had a nightmare, but it was more than that.

Sarah had always taken pride in being mature and level-headed. She had her tantrums and rebellious moments as any child did, but they were short-lived and far between — like her father, she didn't care to be the center of attention. But now, her voice was thick with tears and her words rattled and fell over each other as she struggled to tell them everything that happened last night. They nodded and soothed, but they didn't understand her — they couldn't. Having never met a god, what she was trying to tell them was beyond their comprehension.

When her wails settled down into nothing more than hiccups and sniffles, she thought the worst of it was over and she could finally tell her parents something coherent. But as the first rays of the sunrise began to light the room, her body went rigid in her father's arms, almost as if she'd been possessed.

"The gods are real," she whispered, the first clear words she'd spoken all morning. She pulled her face from her father's chest to turn her blue eyes onto her mother, "and they're watching you."

Then, without another word, she jumped from her father's arms, stumbling to her feet as she bolted out of the room and sprinted towards the end of the hall where the girl was resting. Sarah heard her parents call after her, but she didn't slow down. Even when Jamie came stumbling out of his room looking for the bathroom, she jumped over him rather than risk running him over in the narrow hallway.

Sarah didn't know how literal Asari was when he told her to heal the girl when Rothe raised the sun — whether she had to do it the minute the sun entered the sky or if she had time — but she didn't want to test his patience or risk angering him. Honestly, she never wanted to see the god again, but she didn't have any hope of getting away with that. She was his vessel. And though she'd never agreed to his terms and conditions — didn't even know what they were — she knew there would be no escaping Asari until the day she stood before the gods.

She came to an abrupt stop in front of the girl's bed and took a deep breath into her burning lungs before she placed her hands on either side of the girl's face. She was distracted for a brief second by the contrast of her creamy skin next to the girl's dark melanin tones, but refocused on the urgency of her task when she flinched at how hot her skin was to the touch. She wanted to yank her hands away, but Sarah knew better than to do that, and the pain she felt now was nothing to what she'd felt last night. If she could live through receiving the power of a god, she could tolerate a little heat.

The words Asari etched into her soul last night lit up inside her, and a heat similar to what she'd endured from his blessing, rose in bursts from the palms of her hands. A searing heat spread up her arms followed by an icy chill that made her shiver. Over and over again, the new magic bubbling within her surged through her body until her senses were numb

57

and she was convinced she would never feel anything again. She closed her eyes and focused on controlling the sensation — on giving voice to the foreign words living inside her as if she'd spoken it every day of her life.

"Hear me Asari, the plea of your chosen. Light the way for the wounded. Guide them out of their darkest nights."

She could feel her connection to Asari strengthen as he heeded her call, and power bloomed beneath her palms — the heat in her blood calming from a searing pain to a simmering wave with every breath as the ice she'd felt before pooled in her hands like a cooling mist. She closed her eyes and clung to the feeling, pushing it into the girl she was trying to save and forcing her fever to break like a twig beneath her fingers. When the magic receded back into her palms, she opened her eyes and almost jumped out of her skin when she saw bright green ones staring back at her. They weren't clouded with fever this time and the girl gave her a weak smile.

She didn't say anything, but something in Sarah's spirit shifted in the brief moment their eyes connected. Her chest tightened and she could feel Asari's obsessive love for Freya taking over her mind. His desire to please the goddess at any cost convoluted her own sense of right and wrong — like up and down were now the same thing and somehow the difference between them was irrelevant. Her head spun as she sank to her knees beside the bed, exhausted from the use of her blessing. She looked over to the girl and watched as she drifted off into sleep — a peaceful one this time. Her head was pounding and she wanted to go back to her own room, but something stronger than her own desires compelled her to stay. Even when her parents tried to coax her from the room, she screamed and fought her father's grip to stay by the girl's side.

Sarah couldn't understand why she wanted — needed to stay, but she also knew that it was beyond her to resist the urge. She knew it was Asari's doing, but it felt unnatural for her to be anywhere else now. So, she spent the entire day curled up on the floor next to the girl's bed, waiting for her to wake up. She didn't want to even imagine what Asari would do to her if she'd failed in her task and the girl never recovered.

It was the middle of the night when she finally came to.

"Are you awake?"

Sarah cracked her eyes open at the question and turned to look towards the bed. When she saw green eyes looking back at her, instead of being startled this time, she smiled and nodded. "Yeah."

"What's your name?"

"Sarah."

"I'm Brandi," the girl whispered back. There was a slight pause before she said her next words and Sarah wondered if that would be the extent of their conversation. "You met Asari?"

Sarah gulped and looked away. Even remembering her interaction with the god unsettled her. But she nodded anyway. "Yeah. I did."

"So, you know who I am?"

"Yeah."

"Are you scared of me?"

Sarah looked up then and for a fraction of a second, she understood why Asari loved the girl. She no longer questioned why he'd been willing to kill her mother for disrespecting her or why he'd warned her that he wouldn't be forgiving if she forgot her promise. She wasn't some all-powerful goddess like the stories told. Well, she was, in a way, but she was also just a little girl and probably just as overwhelmed by everything as Sarah was. She could tell that Brandi was anxious about what her answer would be. She didn't know where the girl had come from or why her house had been the one she'd been left at, but Sarah felt the same fierce determination to protect her that she felt for Jamie. She reached out and clutched the girl's hand.

"Of course not. Why would I be?"

"I'm not a good person," she whispered.

She thought to question what Brandi meant by that, but instead, Sarah laughed. The sound was unexpected, but she embraced it and smiled at the girl, releasing her hand to fold her arms against the mattress and rest her head on them. She glanced at the moon shining through the window and shrugged.

"Neither am I," Sarah said, knowing that she spoke the truth. Whoever she had been before she met Asari, that wasn't who she was now and that wasn't who she would grow up to be. She was someone new, someone who would do anything Brandi asked of her without question, even if that meant sending her own family to the gods. And that realization terrified her, but it also made her stomach jitter with excitement. She turned back to the girl resting in her home and grinned at her.

"We can be terrible people together."

ASARI'S DOMAIN — PRESENT DAY

When Brandi finally opened her eyes again, the moon had already risen in Asari's domain and she didn't recognize anything about the place she was in — not the gray couch she slept on, the threadbare quilt pulled across her, or the blonde girl on the floor, nodding off under a ragged orange blanket. She glanced around the small room, taking in the dark hardwood floors and the neatly stacked bookshelves. It was an immaculate space that felt both cozy and empty at the same time.

"About time you woke up."

Brandi's green eyes darted over to Jack and he gave her hand, where their fingers were still entwined, a gentle squeeze. She sat up then and pulled her free hand over her face as she tried to collect herself and ground her senses.

"How long have I been out?"

"About seven hours," Jack responded, his eyes darting over to the other side of the room. "She healed you." Brandi followed his gaze to take a closer look at the girl and let out a sharp breath as recognition slammed into her. Before she could open her mouth to say anything though, Jack kept talking.

"I'm not going to ask how or why you know Sarah Rothens," he said, holding Brandi's gaze as he leaned forward. "I don't even really care why

61

we're here. All I need to know is what you want me to do now."

"That's it?"

"That's it," he said with a nod of his head. "You are where I am. We can talk about the rest later," he said with a smirk.

Brandi let a smile ghost across her lips before she answered him. "Get us some transportation," she said. "And wait for me at the southwestern edge of the fragment. We're leaving with Sarah tonight."

His eyebrows shot up in surprise at her words, but he didn't question her. Instead, he simply leaned forward and captured her lips with his own and she welcomed his touch. She held his face in her hands, melting into his featherlight kisses until he pulled her into his embrace. His arms tightened around her, and he buried his face in the crook of her neck before raising his head to rest his forehead against hers.

"Whatever you want," he whispered. "Just don't take too long."

"I won't," she promised.

He held her gaze for another moment before pressing another soft kiss to her lips and one to her forehead, before rising to his feet and disappearing out the door to do what she'd asked of him.

Sarah snapped awake at the sound of the door closing and raised her head to look at Brandi. Her blue eyes darted over her body as if she were concerned Brandi might be in pain. The bite was a simple enough infection to cure, but it was resilient. At the queen's tower those who caught it were prescribed a healthy dose of antibiotics to fight off any lingering effects, but Brandi knew those would take days to get access to in the outskirts. But when Sarah realized that her breathing was fine and her strength appeared to have returned, her body melted into the chair.

She ran her fingers through her long hair with a sigh and gave a weak smile.

"So," Sarah said, "Asari brings us together again."

Brandi almost laughed at the thought of someone remembering her. Aside from the family she'd found with Najé, Noble, and Jack in the shadows, most people didn't live long enough to hold onto memories of who she was. Her lips twitched upward as she swung her legs over the side of the couch to place her feet on the floor.

"I'd give more of the credit to Freya," Brandi joked, looking around the empty room and focusing on the lopsided drawing hanging above the stone fireplace. "How's your brother?"

"Jamie's fine," she answered. When Sarah didn't offer anything more than that, Brandi let it go. Fourteen years was a long time to not see each other, and she didn't know what had changed since she last saw them. And if she were honest, she didn't much care to know the details. Sarah had only crossed her mind a select few times in the years between them, but now that she sat in the same room with her, Brandi was relieved to see she was still alive and well.

They sat in silence for a while, thinking on the brief time they spent together as children, the few days they believed they ever had a chance at being both blessed and normal. Brandi stood to her feet and stretched. Sarah watched her move and let out a sigh of relief before closing her eyes, ready to doze off as she stared into the crackling fire across the room.

She didn't look any different than Brandi remembered her. She was older and had grown into her looks. She resembled her mother now

with the same thin frame and blonde hair down to her hips, but her pale
blue eyes hadn't changed in the slightest. Brandi had always found Sarah
interesting to look at and doubted she was the only one who thought so.
Blonde hair was unique to the children of Rothe, a trait he gave to those
who found his favor. But the same could be said of Asari and blue eyes.
The gods only blessed their own children, and it was rare for people to
ever leave the domain they were born in to cross into another. It was rarer
still for them to stay and have children with someone who wasn't a child
of their own god. But even if a child was born to a union like that, it was
unheard of for a child to be born with traits that displayed the favor of
one of the gods, let alone two of them.

It was always thought that Rothe was too prideful — and Asari too
selfish — to let a child born in their domains be blessed by another god,
but Sarah was living proof that everything the people claimed to know
about the gods wasn't true.

Her brother had been fortunate enough to have the same brown eyes
and brown hair as their father, but Brandi doubted that Sarah had known
a single day of peace since leaving the secluded home her parents had
built further out in Asari's outskirts. But then again, she wasn't in such a
different situation when she had the green eyes of the goddess. She was
the only person in the world to possess them and it made her think about
how the researcher, Joyson Meys, had claimed the goddess didn't give out
blessings.

He was only half right.

Freya didn't give out blessings — she incarnated.

But if Brandi hid her eyes, she could pass for any other person born in Rothe's domain. It didn't take her long to realize that fact as a shadow. Her skin was several shades darker, but whenever she spun the story of growing up with Jack under Rothe's unforgiving sun in the outskirts, people didn't think anything else of it. It would take a lot more if Sarah ever wanted to go unnoticed though. She'd never pass as a child of Rothe with skin as pale as hers — and it would be near impossible to hide all that golden hair of hers. If she did, she could probably convince a few people she was a daughter of Asari. But, looking around her home at the neatly stacked shelves of books, the hand-woven rugs, and the framed pictures of her and Jamie, Brandi doubted Sarah had ever considered leaving this place — of hiding who she was to convince others she was anything else.

"Seems like you turned out alright," Brandi said, drawing Sarah's attention back to her. "After everything that happened, you're lucky to have found some peace."

Sarah opened her mouth to say something, but before she could, three loud knocks landed against the front door. Brandi tensed and turned to Sarah who had surprise and confusion etched onto her face. Whoever was on the other side of the door, she hadn't been expecting them.

"Do you still speak the language of the gods?"

It was a simple question, whispered under her breath at a rapid pace, but Sarah met her gaze and nodded. That was enough for Brandi and she moved across the room to peek out the window. Not a single floorboard in the old house creaked under her weight and Sarah watched her with wide eyes, reminding them both that they had lived two different lives when they'd parted ways. Brandi wasn't the same girl she'd saved when they were kids. Sarah had no idea of what she was capable of now.

"*It's a man in a suit.*"

Sarah sighed and dropped her head in her hands, her shoulders drooping under an invisible weight as she realized who was on the other side of the door. It was clear from the way she rubbed at her face and pulled at her hair, that she had no desire to speak with the man outside. She squared her shoulders and took several deep breaths before clearing her face of any unpleasant emotions and moving across the room to wrap her fingers around the handle.

"It's okay," she whispered to Brandi in her natural tongue. "I know him."

Brandi raised an eyebrow but moved to stand back from the entrance, moving across the room to lean against the wall near the fireplace as Sarah pulled open the door. Brandi couldn't see her face from where she stood, but she noticed how Sarah blocked the narrow entryway with her body.

"Kyle," she sighed. "What can I do for you so late in the night?"

"I came to check on you," he said. "You led two strangers back to your home and I didn't hear from you. I wanted to make sure they didn't hurt you."

"I'm fine," she affirmed. "So, if there's nothing else, I'm exhausted," she said, her words dripping with honesty. "I'd like to go back to sleep."

"Can I come in for a bit?"

Sarah paused and glanced behind her at Brandi, her brows pulled together in thought as she seemed to weigh the option of denying him.

Brandi could tell from the man's tone and the way he shifted his weight from foot to foot with impatience that it would be Asari's plague trying to deal with him if she didn't let him in. But it was also clear that Sarah had no desire to let him in, and Brandi couldn't shake the gut feeling that he would be an insufferable man she would not get along with. However, it seemed Sarah's exhaustion was getting the better of her and she lost all will to argue with him since he'd invited himself in after she'd made it clear his company was unwanted. So, she took a step back and widened the door.

"Why not?"

Chapter Four

He was not the first to love her, but it only took an instant to know his heart would never be his again.

— Asari, An Introduction | Lindl's Fifth Holy Academy

ASARI'S DOMAIN — PRESENT DAY

The moment Sarah let Kyle inside the house and he no more than glanced at Brandi after she introduced him, she knew things would not end well. Whatever had brought him to her house in the middle of the night, it wasn't good. She read it in the worry he tried to hide on his face, but she couldn't muster up the energy to show him any empathy — she was too irritated and exhausted to care.

"Why is she still here?"

Sarah glanced at Brandi before returning her gaze to Kyle, annoyance and confusion combating for dominance on her expression. "Where else would she be, Kyle?"

"There are plenty of rooms in the main square."

"And you're suggesting that Clara would rent them a room?" Sarah scoffed. "She won't even speak to me."

"She's just hesitant to trust strangers."

"I've lived here for ten years," Sarah sighed. "How long am I supposed to be considered a stranger?"

"Time has nothing to do with how well someone knows you," Kyle retorted. He sighed and shook his head, as if trying to remember why he'd trekked out as far as he had. "But I didn't come here to argue with you."

"Then what did you come here for?"

His eyes darted over to Brandi, who hadn't moved from her spot. She was resting against the wall with her arms crossed. Her eyes watched the fire, but there was no way for her to disguise the fact that she was listening to them. The space wasn't big enough for her to even feign otherwise. Kyle lowered his voice when he turned his attention back to her.

"Can we talk in private, Sarah?" His eyes drifted in Brandi's direction again, unable to keep from stealing glances at her. Sarah wasn't surprised. Brandi was the type of person you wanted to look at — the kind of person you wanted to see you. It was nice to not be the object of the overt attention he normally gave her, but as the night grew longer, her patience shortened in equal measure. She sighed and Kyle drew his eyes back to her.

"Please," he added. "Just for a few minutes."

"She's a guest here," Sarah stated. "I'm not going to ask her to just go wander the fragment until we're done talking. It's the middle of Asari's night."

Brandi lifted her head at those words and straightened up away from the wall. "I'll step out," she said, moving to slip back into her black boots. She wasn't sure when they'd been removed for her, but she guessed Jack had done it sometime while she'd been asleep. "I'll do a lap around the main square or something. You two should be done by then, right?"

Before Brandi could reach the door, Sarah reached out and grabbed Brandi's wrist, her heart pounding as she was overwhelmed by the same compulsion to stay with her she'd felt when she was eight. Brandi glanced down at her hand and back up again, but Sarah didn't release her.

"Will you come back?"

"I didn't risk getting the bite just so I could drop by for a nap, so yes," Brandi answered, peeling Sarah's fingers from her skin. "We have a few things to discuss, but," she took a step back toward the door as her eyes darted over to Kyle, "I've better things to do than be witness to some domestic dispute."

Kyle frowned and Sarah shook her head, her chest clenching at the thought of Brandi disappearing into the night. She had never taken much issue with Kyle in the past — had even liked him to a certain extent — but there was nothing he could say to her right now that would take priority over her staying by Brandi's side. That fact overwhelmed her mind as she stared at the door Brandi had her hand on.

"You need to go."

No one in the room had been expecting that, not even Sarah herself. But she refused to take back the words. Even as a cold panic spread through her and her heart pounded in time to her rapid-fire thoughts, she turned to face Kyle, steeling herself for whatever was to come. She'd been careful to always stay on Kyle's good side so she could reap the benefits of being close to him, but she had never truly invested any emotions into him or their relationship. She'd learned a long time ago though that she had the kind of looks that drew attention — whether she wanted it, or not. It had been a hard and fast lesson — that jealousy and desire often ran in tandem with each other and birthed an obsession.

It drove people to do unreasonable and hateful things.

But for every person who would mock her — threaten her — ostracize her — there was always someone like Kyle — someone who would fall for her subtle curves, long hair, round face, and soft voice. Someone who would decide all on their own that she needed protection. And she used that to her advantage.

Kyle was the guardian of district 29, and had been groomed from the time he could talk to succeed his mother in the role. He had been born into power, had countless connections, and an unwavering influence over the people. A single word from him could change the course of entire lives of anyone under his jurisdiction. And she had needed to make use of that when she and Jamie wandered into the fragment, both of them on the verge of meeting the gods after weeks of navigating the outskirts on their own with no one to protect them. Kyle had been the one to offer them aid, and so Kyle had been the one she'd befriended — the one she'd played at being in love with.

It had been a long game, but it was over now.

If she had to choose between him and Brandi, there would be no hesitation in making her choice — the years of work she put in be forsaken by the gods. She'd always known that her blessing from Asari was what compelled her to stay with Brandi, but understanding it did little to change her overwhelming need to be with her. Kyle was not her priority. He never was.

"You can't mean that," he said softly, his hands reaching of her.

"I absolutely do," Sarah affirmed. "Get out."

"I'm leaving," Brandi interjected. "You can argue without me."

"No," Sarah pleaded, reaching for Brandi again. She smacked her hand away and narrowed her green eyes at her, but Sarah didn't pay attention to it. "Stay. He's the one who needs to leave."

"You can't just kick me out," Kyle fumed. "I'm the one who gave you this house!"

"A gift means it's not yours anymore," Sarah retorted, whipping back around to face him. "It's mine, and I'm telling you to leave."

"No."

"No?" Sarah repeated. "You can't just refuse!"

He sighed, his anger gone as quickly as it came, and he waved a hand as if to dismiss hers as well. "I just did. And if you would listen to me, I'd be gone by now."

"Then speak."

He glared at her tone and straightened his back. "I came to inform you that some people came asking after you in the main square," he said, his voice clipped. "They said they were looking for a Sarah Rothens."

Sarah froze at that name and her eyes grew wide. As far as she knew, only she, Jamie, and Queen Leia herself should know of that name. Brandi looked as shocked as she felt, but where Sarah was stunned into stillness, Brandi moved with intention across the room to stand in front

73

of Kyle.

"What did they look like?" Brandi demanded.

"I wasn't speaking to you," Kyle said, his voice cold.

Before he could even attempt to move past her, Brandi had grabbed him by the collar of his shirt and swept his feet from under him, sending him crashing to the floor and forcing him to kneel before her. She grabbed a fistful of his brown hair and yanked it back until chin snapped up and his gaze met hers. She held no weapon in her hands and was careful not to leave him with any lasting damage, but she made it clear that any further disrespect would not be tolerated.

"You're speaking to me now," Brandi said.

He tried to keep his fear from disrupting his composure, but Brandi heard the tremor in his voice and saw how his pupils dilated. "There were two of them I saw. Both of them looked to be children of Carna — straight silver hair and black eyes with sandy skin. They wore all black clothes and carried weapons I'd never seen before." When Brandi didn't let him go, he held up his hands with his palms facing her. "That's all I know."

"What did you tell them when they asked for Sarah?"

"I told them she was staying with a friend on the opposite side of the fragment. I came here to warn her as soon as they left."

Brandi released him and walked over to the window to peek out once more. She didn't see any movement outside from where she stood, but that didn't mean anything. If they were the shadows she thought they were, they'd have no problem blending into the night. After all, it was the first skill every shadow was required to master — disappearing.

"How long did it take you to get here?"

"Not more than fifteen minutes," he replied, standing back to his feet. He brushed his hands against his pants leg to knock the dust off before he turned back to Sarah. "You told me you didn't have a family name."

"I don't," Sarah whispered.

He scoffed. "There's no point in lying now, Sarah. They described you as if you stood in front of them." He took a step forward, his hands reaching for her as if to pull her into his arms while his brow furrowed in concern. "That makes you Princess Venetia's daughter, doesn't it? Why didn't you tell me?"

Sarah avoided his gaze, shifting her weight back so his hands only grazed her, and looked out at the moon. "It wasn't something you needed to know."

"I was going to share my life with you!" Kyle shouted, his use of the past tense not lost on Sarah. "Does that not warrant at least a bit of faith in me?"

"No," she gave him a weak smile. "You loved me, Kyle. The feeling was never mutual."

He recoiled as if she'd punched him in the chest. They'd been together for years — since they were children. He probably thought she'd been falling in love with him that whole time, but he couldn't be further from the truth. His look of distress almost made Sarah feel guilty as he shook his head at her.

"What?"

"You were convenient, but I didn't trust you," she admitted. "I couldn't. I've seen how far trusting others will get you in this world."

She pulled a hand through her hair, the stress of the last few hours weighing on her as the reality of what would come next began to make itself clear. She glanced behind her and when she saw Brandi was still there, her eyes searching the darkness and her attention off them, she felt relieved. When her gaze returned to Kyle, her relief wasted no time in turning to guilt. She could see the pain playing out across his face as he pulled a hand through his own hair and kept his gaze on anything but her as he straightened his shoulders, fixed his suit jacket and tried to compose himself.

Her stomach flipped as she considered what the repercussions of her words would be, but she made no effort to take any of it back — she was done pretending. She had no more secrets to keep. No more opportunities to manipulate him. No more time to waste.

"How can you say that?"

"Because it's the truth," Sarah told him, brushing by him to her bedroom. She picked up the black bag she kept packed and ready by the door, and she shrugged on the dark blue jacket hanging on the hook. It wasn't a large backpack — a nondescript thing she'd picked up in the marketplace of fragment 40100 when Kyle had taken her and Jamie to visit Asari's temple — but it was waterproof and sturdy, filled to the brim with all of her essentials.

Since the night her parents were sent to the gods and she'd been forced to run away with nothing more than the clothes on her back, dragging a crying Jamie behind her, she'd kept one packed. She would always be prepared, ready to leave in an instant. She'd started to believe she'd never need the bag, had even considered unpacking it as she'd started moving her things into Kyle's home little by little. But every time she'd gone to unpack it, Asari lit up her soul, warming her from the inside out until she felt as if her blood boiled in her veins and she repacked it — double checking that she had every item she could need.

Sarah pulled her hair back into a ponytail and looped it around itself until a messy bun rested at the back of her head, then zipped up the jacket before sliding her arms through the loops on the backpack. She offered a weak smile towards Kyle, but her words were directed at Brandi, who had returned her attention to the room.

"After the first time, you stay prepared."

Brandi nodded. "What about Jamie?"

"He'll have to come with me."

"Does he know who he is?"

"I'll explain it to him on the way," she said, moving to douse the fire. "He knows our family name but that's all. I didn't want him to have to live with the worries I do, but he'll catch on quick."

"Leave him here," Kyle said.

Sarah scoffed as she finished her task, leaving only the dim moonlight to highlight the cold resolve on Kyle's face.

"I can't just leave without him."

"Why not?" Kyle challenged. "Your feelings for me may have been as fake as Asari's smile," he grimaced, "but I loved you. And I care about Jamie too. Besides," he pointed out, "you didn't even think about taking him with you until she said something," he glanced at Brandi, who stood silent again, watching the exchange.

"You were always an outsider, but he looks like the rest of us. And without you around, he'd fit in. Not a single person would question him." Sarah flinched at the words, and the smirk that flitted across his lips gave her the sense that Kyle took some sense of joy in knowing that he would be able to inflict some wounds on her heart before she left. "He may be a prince of the queendom, but it's not like a man could ever place a bid for the throne. And aside from the three of us, no one knows he's your brother. They were only looking for you."

"He'd never forgive me."

"Maybe not," Kyle agreed. "But he'd be alive to hate you. That's something, isn't it?"

Sarah paused, her eyes dropping to the ground as her mind worked overtime to make sense of what Kyle was suggesting.

Jamie had just turned sixteen — it would be hard enough escaping the fragment on her own even as prepared as she was, but it would be a near impossible task with Jamie. He'd been too young to fight her before, but the same couldn't be said of him now. He wouldn't want to leave, and she didn't have the time to explain things to him. Even if she did, though, what kind of life would he have? Kyle made valid points, the most important one being that the people who wanted to send her to the gods didn't even know Jamie existed.

He'd be safer without her.

She knew that, but the idea of leaving him behind ripped her apart. She'd never considered not taking him with her, but she couldn't afford to hesitate. All she wanted right now was more time, but no matter how long she had to mull it over, her options wouldn't change. If she stayed in the fragment, she'd be sent to the gods and if Jamie came with her, he might get sent with her. Her eyes were bright with unshed tears when she looked up at Kyle, but the choice she had to make was clear.

"You promise to take care of him?" Sarah asked, her voice thick. "Swear it. Right now."

"I swear it," Kyle said. "Asari's plague devour me should I lie."

"Fine," she whispered. "I'll entrust him to you then."

Kyle nodded and headed towards the door. "I'll contact the Asarna family and make the arrangements tonight. By morning, no one will ever mention his name with yours again."

"Thank you," Sarah forced out.

"Don't thank me," Kyle snapped. "Just," he paused at the door, his voice shaking as he gripped the handle, "don't ever come back."

"Okay."

He looked more hurt at her acceptance of his words than anything else she'd said that night, as if he'd wanted her to fight back. Wanted to believe her words earlier were a lie to create distance between them because of what she had to do. But the truth was transparent — she hadn't gone to him for help, or asked him to go with her. Her plans had never included him and she knew that would break his heart in ways he would never recover from.

"I loved you," he whispered. "But you're not who I thought you were."

"No," Sarah agreed. "I'm not."

He didn't look back as the door shut behind him, and Sarah swiped at her eyes before turning to Brandi. Her attention was still focused on searching for something outside the window, but Sarah had her concerns to deal with. Her mind jumped briefly to Jack and his whereabouts, but she was more concerned with Jamie and if she'd be able to say goodbye to him. She'd moved into her own place when she'd turned sixteen, and he was almost an adult now, but not seeing him for a few days was nothing like the possibility of never seeing him again.

Her heart raced in terror at that possible reality, and she shoved the thoughts aside, focusing instead on what took priority in that moment. Brandi had seemed to know the people Kyle had described. And if shadows were looking for her, then it wouldn't be long until they found her if they didn't leave soon. Kyle had only mentioned two people, but she wouldn't dismiss the possibility that there were more of them lurking in the darkness.

She'd managed to get her and Jamie away from them once before because of their parents sacrifice, but even with the good fortune afforded to her in Asari's domain, she knew there was no chance in escaping them twice.

"Let me come with you," Sarah said, turning to Brandi.

"Sure," Brandi said with a quick glance in her direction. "I did come here to get you after all. Although," she shook her head with a sigh, "I don't know why you would be so trusting of me."

"*I know who you are.*" Sarah said in the gods' tongue, never once looking away from Brandi.

"And that should frighten you," Brandi told her, meeting her gaze. "I serve as the Queen's Blade. I've sent more people to the gods than you could possibly imagine," she stated.

"I know who you are," Sarah repeated, unfazed. *"I have always known you're a terrible person."*

Brandi cracked a smile at her choice of words and Sarah smirked, glad to know that Brandi remembered their time together, same as she did. Brandi tied her own braids back to keep them out of her face as she opened the door to venture into the night.

"Then let's be terrible people together."

Brandi hadn't taken two steps beyond the threshold before she realized the situation they were in.

"Mother Freya!"

The words slipped from Brandi's lips as she shoved Sarah back through the door and slammed it behind them. Almost as soon as she did, seven hard knocks landed against the door, splintering the wood at the hinges. Brandi rushed over to the wing chair and used all her strength to push it in front of the door. It wouldn't hold forever, but any time was better than none.

"What's happening?"

"Get down!"

Brandi tackled Sarah to the ground as a tiny steel marble shattered the window Sarah had just been standing in front of. Sarah yelped as her head bounced against the hard floor. Her vision blurred and her ears rang as her senses rushed back to her. She reached a shaking hand up to her temple, and paled when she saw the blood on her fingers, but Brandi couldn't waste time forcing out an apology for her actions. She was too focused on keeping Sarah still beneath her as several more projectiles came crashing through the window. Sarah flinched and turned her face away from the shattering glass, but Brandi watched as the tiny missiles lodged themselves into the sofa.

They were nondescript things, the size of a thumbnail and black as a night without Asari's moon. Sarah's blue eyes grew wide at the sight of them, but Brandi recognized them as Yuri's weapon of choice — a handheld airgun that had been one of Adam Bertanal's toys. As the only consort to the queen who couldn't give her children, he had far more time available to him than the others, and Brandi would never accuse him of spending it wisely. He was a scholar who studied technology in Lindl's domain before he became a consort to the queen, and rather than using his knowledge to help advance the queendom, he preferred to conjure up weapon ideas for shadows without blessings. His ideas were heresy, but the queen favored him, so the order never came to send him.

Yuri was the type of shadow obsessed with power and infuriated that the gods never blessed her, so she never hesitated to volunteer to test out his prototypes and Vanna, who loved Yuri to a fault, was always right behind her. The airgun was a tiny metal appendage that clung to the inside of her left palm and shot steel marbles. Brandi was never sure exactly how it worked, but it was an inconspicuous and near silent weapon. If it weren't for the whistling of the steel ball in motion, no one would ever know Yuri was armed.

"Stay down," Brandi whispered. "She's a terrible shot but anyone could hit a standing target."

Brandi glanced around her, realizing that keeping Sarah alive and helping her escape was going to be more trouble than she was worth. It had been less than five minutes and she was already regretting every choice that brought her to this moment. She had her own reasons for not wanting to see Sarah sent to the gods, but it was still preferable to being sent to meet them herself. She pointed to the bedroom Sarah had pulled the backpack from earlier.

"*There*," Brandi whispered. "*Hide there until I give the signal. Then run.*"

Sarah frowned at Brandi's words, no doubt wanting to ask what the signal would be and where she was supposed to run to, but Brandi was grateful when she kept her mouth shut and began scrambling across the floor to the room. They would both just have to trust that she would figure it out when the time came.

A barrage of steel came raining in through the windows and Sarah covered her ears against the sound. Her movements were clumsy and uncoordinated, slower than before her sudden collision with the ground, but anyone would prefer a raging headache over a steel ball embedded in their skull. So, she grit her teeth against the sound and continued crawling on her stomach over to the bedroom — a dark room with no windows that was completely out of Brandi's way.

Once she was in the room, Brandi darted over to the wall. She slammed her back into it and slid down until she was able to crouch under the shattered window. With Sarah out of the way, she felt more composed — her fighting instincts flared to life, and she closed her eyes, whispering her favorite words.

*"**Bless me, for I am the wrath of the gods.**"*

In an instant, her empty hands were filled with the green bow and arrows she always craved. She took a deep breath, losing herself to the feel of her blessing pulsing beneath her skin and relishing in the heat it brought with it. She focused on controlling the warmth beneath her palms as it spread up her arms and through her chest. It crashed through her like comforting waves breaking against her shores. It lulled her into a sense of peace like no other and filled her with all the confidence of Freya herself. She let a grin play across her lips before shouting into the void outside.

"I know you're out there, Yuri." When she got no response, she glanced at the window on the other side of the splintered door. "Vanna! You too. I know you wouldn't let Yuri come to meet the gods on her own."

"Bold of you to assume we're meeting the gods tonight!"

"No! Don't respond to —" Yuri's words were cut off as Brandi stood and let her arrow fly through the same opening in the glass they'd created. She ducked back down before Vanna could get off another shot at her, but the loud, gurgling crash and the subsequent scream of rage let her know that she'd hit her mark — though she hadn't been concerned about her accuracy. It was the nature of the power lent to her by Freya.

She never missed.

"I didn't think you were the type to let Yuri go places on her own like that, Vanna," Brandi taunted, summoning another arrow to her hands. "Are you really going to let her meet the gods alone?"

Vanna didn't say anything else. The harsh lesson Brandi had just delivered embedded in her mind. Yuri had been Vanna's best friend — more than that. Even from the outside it had seemed as if their souls had been a perfect match for each other. They'd left Carna's domain and joined the shadows at the same time, albeit for different reasons. Yuri joined to become stronger, but Vanna joined because she had no other choice if she didn't want to die in the wastelands or be eaten by a shader. But they'd had each other. Through every slit throat and silent headshot, they'd always had a family to return to, no matter that it was just the two of them.

But now Yuri was gone.

Brandi could imagine the gaping hole that would be left in her neck once her arrow dissolved into mist. Her blood would seep into the ground and stain her silver hair before pooling around her unseeing eyes — black orbs that gaped at a moon that refused to give them any light.

Brandi could sense the rage and sorrow that rolled off Vanna in waves as her choked wail broke into a sob. She'd lost all her composure and couldn't hide the sound of her fumbling movements as she reloaded her air gun — the palmender, as she'd heard Bert call it — with shaking hands as she tried to contain it all. Brandi knew Vanna would never want to give her the satisfaction of lashing out with uncontrollable emotions, but it was obvious to both of them who the victor of this fight would be. Brandi took a deep breath as she imagined Vanna swiping at the tears that were no doubt streaming down her face. Her focus would be on mourning Yuri and cursing Carna for ever allowing them to leave his wastelands if their fate had only been to be shot down in Asari's outskirts.

Her mind would be tripping over itself, trying to understand how she'd landed herself in a standoff with Brandi, and recognizing that her fight had become a lost cause the moment she lost focus on her target.

There was no way Vanna would see morning without meeting the gods first.

Brandi felt no sympathy for Vanna though — it was her own fault for picking a fight with her. Brandi was, without question, the best of the shadows. Everyone had idolized her, fueling the rumors that claimed she could shoot a man from a fragment away and that she would even send a newborn child if those were her orders. Rumors of her ruthlessness had spread faster than the light of Rothe's sun when she'd sent one of her own informants to the gods. It wasn't even six months later that she'd found herself fighting off the bite in the Asarna Mountains.

She wasn't surprised they'd tracked her to Asari's domain with such little effort — outskirters were always quick to sell out strangers to the monarchy, and Brandi had her suspicions that the innkeeper in town had been no different. She wasn't even surprised that the queendom had issued an order to silence her, she knew it would come the moment she decided to leave. No, what surprised Brandi the most was that anyone had been willing to accept the order. Even Najé, the only person who had ever proven herself to be Brandi's equal in fight, had made it a known fact that she would refuse any order to send Brandi if the queendom ever tried to force her hand. And her reason for declaring that had been simple.

The gods didn't want Brandi.

Everyone knew that. And facing her alone was the dumbest thing

Yuri and Vanna could have done. They would have been better off walking into the gods' realm on their own terms. At least then, they would have been able to go together.

But they'd forfeited that option the moment they'd followed her to Asari's outskirts, so Brandi listened for the sound of Vanna trying to choke back the sobs that threatened to leak out and summoned another arrow. She flexed the fingers on her right hand and let the heat build in her palm until it almost burned, then closed her eyes and took another steadying breath.

Visualizing a target was one of the first things Glenn had taught her and Najé when she'd started training them. She'd been unyielding on the idea that if they could imagine their target in their mind, even when their eyes couldn't physically see them, they'd never fail a mission. They'd been forced to practice for hours until it was second nature for them to be able to predict where a target was, what they were doing, and what they would do next. It was because of that practice that Brandi heard the laughter floating on the wind long before she heard Vanna's yelp of surprise.

She hissed in pain as Brandi heard the rustle of leaves as she fell — first against the trunk of the tree and then once again to the ground. There was a tiny clink of metal against rock as her breathing became labored. Her grunts of pain as she shuffled about in the leaves confirmed Brandi's suspicions.

Vanna had been poisoned.

Brandi could only think of one person who would do something like that, so she let the magic of her blessing dissipate as she heard another lighthearted giggle ring through the trees.

"You know," the girl said, stage whispering just loud enough for Brandi to hear, "Brandi really hates surprises."

CHAPTER FIVE

People will remember their mother and not their executioner — a shame
when, in all instances, she is both.

— Adage of the Gods | Lindl's Five Holy Academies Compilation

ASARI'S DOMAIN — PRESENT DAY

"Holy Freya!"

Brandi shouted, covering her head as sharp pieces of glass rained down on her and a body came barreling through the window. It groaned as a much smaller body jumped through, landing beside it. Brandi watched as the person standing turned in a slow circle, looking at the absolute wreckage of the house. But when a pair of hazel eyes landed on Brandi, the figure pulled down their mask and yanked off their hood with a grin.

"I figured that laugh was yours, Pine."

Brandi started to climb to her feet, but the tiny woman threw herself at her, wrapping her arms around Brandi's neck and sending them both to the ground with a thud. Brandi cringed at the sudden contact, but knew

Pine wouldn't relent until she gave in. So, she returned the hug for a brief second before pushing her away and standing to her feet.

"What are you doing here?"

"You know you wouldn't have a clue what to do without me, raindrop," Pine smirked, nudging the body on the ground with her foot, "so, I'm never too far away."

"Sure," Brandi said, rolling her eyes and dismissing her banter. "And now the reason you're really here?"

"A little corpse told me you'd left the queendom for," Pine glanced at the books scattered across the floor with torn pages, the broken glass, and the couch littered with holes before giggling again, "greener pastures."

"Which one?"

"Does it matter?"

They locked eyes before Brandi smirked and shook her head. Pine wasn't a shadow, but she was dangerous in her own right and liked to keep her secrets. Trying to pry information from her was like trying to outsmart Lindl — impossible. She was a vault of classified information and would never talk to Brandi about anything worth knowing unless it was in private. And Brandi could tell from the way Pine watched Sarah, appraising her through narrowed eyes, that she'd already formed an unfavorable opinion of her.

Brandi wasn't surprised though. It was rare for Pine to take a liking to anyone. Even though she was beautiful with bright hazel eyes, dark wavy hair, honeyed brown skin, and was adept at giving away smiles and making anyone feel like they were her bestest friend, she was a creature of isolation who gave her time to few people and her trust to even less.

When you got below her surface, Pine was irritable and violent, cold, distant and flighty — likely to be gone as soon as she came. But to those who she let into her world, she was loyal like no other.

They were alike in that way.

But she didn't let her attention stay on Pine and Sarah for long, and instead Brandi shifted her attention to the body lying in the middle of the floor. She needed to make the most of Pine's gift, and since Pine never made an appearance without reason, she didn't want to spend any more time interrogating Vanna than she had to. Brandi moved to the center of the room to get a better look at her and saw that her hands and feet were bound. She was silent other than a groan every now and again, no doubt suffering at the hands of whatever Pine had dosed her with. The woman was little more than a mad scientist when it came to crafting poisons. Her unorthodox experiments were one of the many reasons she'd been expelled from Lindl's School of Science, Technology, Mathematics, and Engineering and rejected by the polite society of the Lindlian elites. Pine was resilient though, and she always remembered the faces of her enemies. And it was that aspect of her personality that made her more dangerous than anyone cared to realize.

The woman on the ground in front of her would have been more successful if she'd embodied a few of those some traits, but she'd never been committed to anything other than Yuri. Brandi let her green eyes drift over Vanna's cropped silver hair and black eyes. She looked just as Kyle had reported, but she also had a light dusting of freckles that he probably hadn't been able to see in the dark. She was a few years older than Brandi, but she'd joined the shadows with her best friend three years ago and Brandi had been the one to train them on long distance sniping. Vanna had been patient with a natural talent for it, but her friend, Yuri, hadn't been able to hit a sitting target three feet in front of her. She remembered them because instead of getting angry, Yuri had laughed and claimed Vanna balanced her out. That had been the end of it and Brandi only saw them in passing after that, but they'd always been together — always giggling about something.

The only thing that seemed different about Vanna now was the little white stud pierced through her left ear. It was a common practice for couples to get their left ears pierced together when they were serious about each other — a simple way of letting others know they were in a relationship. Some people had three or four piercings running up the side of their ear like Queen Leia and her consorts, but other people, like Brandi and Jack, were adamant about only ever having one. And Brandi didn't doubt that if she went outside to look at Yuri's corpse, she'd have her left ear pierced as well.

Their love story would have been beautiful if not for their tragic end, but it was nothing for Brandi to dwell on. Instead, she squatted to meet Vanna's eyes.

"Why are you here?"

When Vanna only glared at Brandi in response, she looked over to Pine. "Before I get indignant, I guess I should ask. Can she speak?"

Pine looked away from where she and Sarah were having a staring contest. Sarah, for her part, had stayed in the room and not moved a muscle. Brandi had to give her survival instincts credit for that. With Pine in the room, the shadows looking for her were not the most immediate threat on her life, and she liked that Sarah wasn't dumb enough to forget the orders she'd received — Brandi hadn't given her a signal yet.

Pine glanced at the body before returning her gaze to Sarah and nodded. "There's nothing preventing her from speaking with you," Pine answered. "She's only being stubborn."

"Is that so?" Brandi sighed and looked down at Vanna. "Look," she began, "I don't want this to be any more painful for you than it's already going to be," she said, pulling her favorite curved blade from her pocket. Forged by the queen's best smithy from one of Tiki's baby teeth, it was pitch black, indestructible, and sharp enough to cut both paper and steel with ease. It had four holes drilled along the lower edge that she slid her fingers into. She curled them into a fist around the grip and displayed it to Vanna. "But we both know I'll get the information I'm looking for," she warned. "The only thing up for discussion is whether you volunteer it," she used the tip of the blade to force Vanna's chin up to meet her gaze, "or I make you beg me to listen to it."

Pine giggled again, an angelic laugh that disguised all her ill intentions. Pine's light-footed steps brought her over to where they were, and she draped herself over Brandi as she smiled at Vanna. It was a warm smile, one so deceptive that even though Vanna knew it shouldn't, it calmed her. Brandi watched the struggle play out on her face as she glanced between them. Her survival instincts raged under Brandi's stare and fought against her desire to trust the warm, smiling gaze of the girl beside her. The confusion on her face was clear, and rightfully so — Pine had Lindl's blessing of coercion. Her smile was enough to make anyone feel at ease, even with their limbs bound and facing the wrong end of a shadow's blade.

"I would give her what she wants," Pine cooed. "You really don't want to see her angry."

"I can't," Vanna finally whispered. "He'll send me."

Brandi raised her eyebrows at Vanna's words. "You're in this position and more afraid of what someone else will do to you?" She glanced up at Pine. "You know just about everyone worth knowing," Brandi said. "Is there someone who incites more fear than me?"

"I haven't met them, no," Pine said with a quick shake of her head.

"Hm," Brandi hummed under her breath. "Tell me," Brandi said, turning back to Vanna, "who is this 'he'?"

"Saya," Vanna whispered. "He's the one who talked Yuri into taking this job. Into finding you."

"And why would you listen to him? Did I seem like I wanted to be found?"

"No, but," Vanna licked her lips, "the pay was good. Enough to leave the shadows."

Brandi laughed. "You thought money would solve your problems? That the queen would simply let you go because you wanted to run off with Yuri?"

Vanna narrowed her eyes at Yuri's name on Brandi's tongue. The heartbreak was too fresh — the emotional wounds ran too deep for her rational side to remain in control.

"Keep her name out your mouth," she screamed, lunging forward, doing her best to take a bite out of the exposed skin on Brandi's wrist. But Brandi was unfazed and slammed her right fist into Vanna's jaw.

Her neck snapped violently in the opposite direction as two of her teeth clattered across the floor and Brandi shook her hand out. When Vanna groaned, she used the flat edge of the knife to force her swelling face back towards her.

"Sorry about that," Brandi said, feigning remorse. "My natural reaction when someone bares their teeth at me is to knock them out," she explained. "Now, back to the matter at hand," she said. "Who is this Saya person? What does he look like?"

"He's a child of Rothe," Vanna said, her words slurred as blood, snot, and tears dripped down her lips. "One of Bert's shadows. Nothing special."

"Why would he be looking for me?"

"I don't know."

"Did he come with you?"

"No."

"Then who's your third?" Brandi questioned. "You wouldn't come here with Yuri alone. You're impulsive, not stupid."

Vanna winced, biting back another scream of rage. "Najé," she answered.

Brandi froze. If Najé was their third, then she'd played this all wrong. She didn't have time to be interrogating some shadow who was probably only giving her half the truth. Najé was a formidable force, even for her to deal with. The gods loved Brandi, but Najé thrived under the light of Rothe's sun. She was skilled, intuitive, and her punches carried behind them the literal fire power of Rothe. Brandi scanned the darkness as she stood to her feet, half expecting Najé to walk out from one of the dark corners with a smirk on her face for having outsmarted her.

Yuri and Vanna had been distractions.

Brandi sucked her teeth as her mind raced to come up with another plan. Vanna smirked in the darkness at Brandi's visible unease. The mirth in her bubbled up until her body shook and a wet, broken laughter bounced against the floor. Brandi looked down at her, her face blank as she watched the girl.

"And what's so funny?"

"You walk around like you're a god," Vanna chuckled. "But even you get nervous when someone's hunting you."

Brandi laughed at that and grinned down at Vanna. "I guess no one told you," she said, letting some of Freya's spiritual power slip through her restraints. "I am a god."

Vanna's eyes widened, frantic as she searched the room for relief from the spiritual pressure. She wheezed as Brandi took a step forward, letting more of her power free. She took her time crushing Vanna under the invisible boot of her unrestrained presence.

"And I'm tired of the disrespect I'm getting tonight."

"That's not what I—" Vanna started, her words silenced with a glare from Brandi.

"No, no," Brandi shushed her denial and put her blade away. "You meant it. Just let the gods know that's what got you sent to them."

Brandi raised her foot and stomped it into Vanna's face, breaking her nose and crushing her skull inward. Her scream filled the night for a brief second before only the sound of her blood dripping out on the floor remained. Brandi turned her green eyes to Pine, all traces of lightheartedness gone as she gestured for Sarah to come to her.

She didn't hesitate and was careful to sidestep the blood spreading on the hardwood floor as she stopped at Brandi's side. She didn't say anything, and Brandi didn't look at her as she spoke.

"*Wait for me outside,*" she directed. "*And pray to Asari. Tell him I need him to light the way out of this fragment.*"

Sarah nodded and moved to follow her instructions. Her skin flushed under Pine's unwavering gaze, but she moved with quick steps through the kitchen and let herself out the back door. Brandi watched her take a deep breath of the cool night air before she sank to her knees, facing the moon, and began whispering in the gods' tongue to plead for Asari's help.

With Sarah gone, Brandi returned her attention to Pine, who was seething across the room. Pine was accustomed to being everyone's favorite. It was the way she'd been raised and the nature of her blessing — she was infectious. She got into people's lives and they obsessed over her, but Brandi was different. She didn't care how Pine felt about her and that made Pine want Brandi to like her. And not because of her blessing, but in the genuine sense.

The problem was, her skills were for manipulating people, not befriending them.

That didn't keep her from trying though, and Brandi had to admit that Pine had worked hard to earn her trust. Aside from Jack, Noble, and Najé, there was no one she trusted more than Pine. But she could see the envy twisting across her face as she'd spoken to Sarah in a language she couldn't understand. She stood now with her fists clenched and her jaw tight and, for once, Brandi wished she could offer her some comfort.

"Do me a favor, Pine," Brandi finally said. "There's a fresh corpse in Lindl's domain at his First Holy Academy. I need you to find it and deliver a message for me."

Pine scrunched up her face. "Is that a request I can refuse?"

"Of course it is," Brandi said, crossing her arms against the breeze drifting in through the window. "Is that what you would like to do?"

The question was innocent enough, but it hung in the air as Pine thought it over. She never wanted to disappoint Brandi, but going back to Lindl's domain always put Pine on edge. She much preferred to spend her time in Rothe's sunny domain rather than Lindl's rainy one, but even as she chewed on her bottom lip considering her answer, they both knew a decision had already been made.

"You know I'd do anything for you, raindrop," Pine admitted with a sigh, pulling her mask and hood back up.

"Thank you," Brandi said.

She wasted no time giving Pine her message, and when she repeated it back to her with perfect recall, Brandi smiled.

"I knew I could trust you," she whispered.

"Always," Pine grinned, winking at Brandi. "I'm heading out, raindrop. But if you need me," she started.

"I know how to find you," Brandi finished.

They bumped fists and Pine was gone through the same shattered window as quickly as she had come through it, the dark night swallowing her in an instant. Brandi wasted no time going out the back door and meeting Sarah by the far corner of the house, where Asari's moon shone down on her. When she called her name, Sarah looked up from her prayers, her blue eyes glowing with the light of Asari's power inside of her. Brandi searched her face for any signs of trepidation at what she'd witnessed inside, but if Sarah felt uneasy about any of it, she hid it well under a beaming smile.

"I'll lead the way."

It took over an hour for them to fall into a reasonable stride. Brandi had no problems navigating the undergrowth of the trees, but she was following Sarah, who seemed to trip over every branch and root in existence. She didn't even bother to show her annoyance as she, once again, caught Sarah's arm and pulled her back to her feet. Sarah whispered her gratitude, but Brandi paid no attention to it — the words held no meaning at this point.

It wasn't until Sarah stopped dead in her tracks that Brandi lost the tentative grip she had on her patience. They'd been moving at a pace that children could easily outrun, but at least they had been making steady progress. Now, Sarah's blue eyes were wide as she stared at a cluster of small houses on the furthest edge of the fragment and Brandi could no longer temper her frustration. Gripping Sarah's wrist and pulling her around to face her, she broke Sarah's trance with an angry glare.

"What in Freya's name do you think you're doing?"

"That's the Asarna house," Sarah said, pointing to one of the older houses in the cluster. "The sisters there, Mya and Myrna, are the ones who took me and Jamie in. Gave us a home," she explained. "Even when no one else in the fragment would speak to me, they were kind and treated me as part of their family. I can't just leave them," she said, shaking her head at Brandi. "I can't just leave Jamie."

"You can," Brandi said, tightening her grip on Sarah, "and you will."

"You can't just decide that for me!"

"If you want to be sent to the gods tonight, I can help you with that," Brandi snapped. "But I was under the impression you wanted to live. Or did you forget the reason you kept that bag packed all this time?"

Sarah huffed and snatched her arm away from Brandi, her wrist red from the grip. She rubbed at it and looked around the trees. The night didn't allow them to see far, and Brandi prayed for Freya's mercy if Sarah brought up taking the main path again. When they'd first arrived at the edge of the trees, Sarah had tried to convince Brandi that no one else would be willing to go traipsing through the undergrowth just to find them and that taking one of the less used paths out of the fragment would be easier to navigate in the dark. Brandi had pointed out to her several times that Asari hadn't led them that way, but now that they were only a few steps away from Jamie she wished he hadn't. They didn't have time for Sarah to waver in her decision now that it was time to see it through.

"You don't forget hearing your parents be sent to the gods," Sarah said, her voice flat as she clenched her fists at her side. "But that's exactly why I can't leave without saying something to him. I'm all he has."

"He has Kyle now," Brandi pointed out. "You trusted him with your brother, so let him do what he promised to and stay out of it."

Sarah rolled her eyes. "Kyle will probably tell him I'm abandoning him."

"You are," Brandi said. "Or do you think leaving in the middle of the night is something else?" Sarah sucked in a sharp breath, but said nothing and Brandi shook her head. "This isn't some kind of game, Sarah. There are people hunting you," she explained. "You may not understand what that means, but understand that if they see you talking to Jamie, they're going to send him."

"They wouldn't—"

"I would," Brandi cut her off. "Because the fastest way to break someone is to take away what they love the most. Why do you think Kyle was so willing to let you go?" Brandi scoffed. "For a guy who claims to love you, he didn't offer once to go with you."

"I didn't ask him to come with me either."

"Does telling yourself that make you feel better about it?"

Sarah glared at her, her face and neck turning a bright red beneath the moonlight.

"What does it matter to you?"

"It matters because Asari has made you his vessel," Brandi said, pointing to the dimly lit path before them. "And I'm under strict orders to keep you on this side of the gods' realm, but you're making that task far more difficult than it needs to be."

"How so?" Sarah questioned. "Because last I checked, all I've done was cure your sickness, give you a place to sleep, and follow every order you've given me!"

"Keep your voice down," Brandi warned.

"Why? No one is even out here!" Sarah shouted, fed up with the whispering and the arguing. "We're the only ones making any type of noise!"

Brandi's movements stopped at that.

Sarah was right. She'd been focused on keeping Sarah moving, but the forest was too quiet. Even if it was just the two of them, there should have been wildlife — foxes, crickets, snakes. But the forest wasn't moving — wasn't breathing. She whipped around to look behind them as if she would be able to see their tail, but she knew it was a hopeless task. Even with her eyesight, it was too dark. She took a calming breath and grabbed Sarah's wrist again.

Sarah looked down at Brandi's hand and almost snapped at her to let go, but when she saw the focus on Brandi's face, she bit back her retort and tensed. Her eyes darted around as well, but if Brandi couldn't see them, there was no chance that Sarah's untrained eye would spot anything.

"Remember that signal I told you about earlier?" Brandi whispered.

"Yes."

"This is it," she whispered back, shoving Sarah away from her and towards the path of light as a projectile came flying between them.

"*Run!*"

CHAPTER SIX

The gods are loving, kind, and patient with their children — but do not test them, for their wrath is swift, fierce, and unforgiving.

— Adage of the Gods | Lindl's Five Holy Academies Compilation

---

ASARI'S DOMAIN — PRESENT DAY

"Well, ain't Carna a bastard," a husky voice crooned from the darkness. "I missed."

Brandi looked up from the mini javelin lodged in the ground into a pair of brown eyes she'd never seen before.

"Who are you?"

"Ain't nobody introduced me?" He grinned, his perfectly aligned teeth glinting in the dark. "Names Saya."

"Oh," Brandi said, straightening her stance and wishing she could send Vanna to the gods twice for lying to her. She pushed her anger aside though and gave the man standing in front of her a good once over. The starless night hid most of his features, but she could see that, while it was clear Saya was no slouch when it came to his training, he hadn't been doing it long and hadn't put on much muscle yet. His black hair was shaved close to his scalp — but he wasn't bald — and she spotted a scar trailing across his forehead that split his left eyebrow.

He was as Vanna described him — nothing special.

"So, you're the one who thought he could send me to the gods," Brandi said, a smirk playing at her lips.

"More'n just a thought, sweetness."

Two more javelins came flying in her direction and Brandi spun out of their way, sinking into the shadows of the trees and undergrowth. It was clear that he had the advantage in a head on fight, but no one — not even Najé — was a match for her when she was out of sight.

"Now, don't be like that," he drawled, retrieving the projectiles and moving through the dark without much thought of hiding from her. "I came all this way to see you, and this is the greeting you give me? That hurts."

Brandi rolled her eyes at his poor attempts to bait her and retreated through the trees, moving with a silence honed from her years growing up in Freya's domain. Nature was her home, and the night was her cloak. She felt invincible as she settled into a spot just outside of Saya's range. She couldn't see him, but that wasn't necessary.

"Bless me, for I am the wrath of the gods."

The words slipped from her lips and into the breeze that whispered through the trees as she narrowed her green eyes in focus, a light sweat breaking out across her skin at the sudden rush of power that filled her. She inhaled once, and released her arrow, trusting it to hit exactly where she needed it to. Saya had been cocky, but he was still mortal. She counted the seconds it would take for her arrow to hit, listening for some sound of confirmation that she was used to — a scream, a thud, a gurgle — or some combination of the three.

But there was only silence.

She took in a sharp breath as her instincts screamed at her, forcing her to lunge behind the nearest tree just in time to hear five solid thuds land against the bark. The tree shook from the force of the impact, fluttering leaves down around her as she listened to the wood splinter and crack. Her eyes searched the dark, expecting to find another enemy, but they widened in shock as Saya's drawl came drifting back towards her.

"Come on, sweetness," he said, his arrogance coating every word. "One shot is all I'm worth?" He sighed, reloading his weapon. "I thought I'd be at least worth two. I gave you five."

Brandi kept her mouth shut and pulled her bow back, releasing another arrow. This time, she heard a fizzle, like the sound of a campfire doused in water, and a rumbling laugh as Saya walked into her line of sight. He had a dumb grin on his face and she narrowed her eyes, firing off another shot.

He didn't dodge it.

Instead, she watched as her arrow dissolved in front of him where it should've pierced his heart. She clicked her tongue, refusing to show him anything other than her annoyance. But her heart raced as her mind tried to make sense of what she was witnessing. Her arrows didn't work on him, and that should be impossible. No one was immune to the powers of a god.

She gripped her bow tighter and lifted it again, refusing to back away from his slow approach.

"Go head, sweetness," he taunted. "Fire off as many of those pretty shots as you want. It's true that you're a dead aim," he nodded, "but it don't mean nothing if your arrow can't hit me."

"How?"

She barked the word out through her teeth, angry at herself the moment she gave in to his game. His grin spread as he laughed and held his arms out wide, as if he were a god — or impervious to them.

"Wouldn't you like to know?" He did a quick little spin in the night, the dead leaves crunching beneath him as he showed off something she couldn't see in the dark. "I'll give you a hint, though. Bert made it custom for me."

Bert.

"Of course, it would be Bert," Brandi scoffed under her breath, rolling her eyes.

Bert had resented the gods since the day the queen became pregnant with her firstborn son, Liren, and his resentment had only grown with each child she bore. He may have been the queen's favored lover, but he was far from the only one.

As with every queen before her, Queen Leia had four lovers — one from each domain of the gods' realm. The practice had been shaped after Freya's own relationships with the gods, and it ensured that each domain had a representative in the queen's royal court. And with each child she gave birth to, the gods blessed the child and their father accordingly. But Bert was sterile and that made him useless as a consort in the eyes of the queendom. It didn't matter that the queen loved him the most or that he was vocal in advocating for the people — the will of the gods was absolute in all things and the personal favor of mortals meant nothing. So, without a child and without a blessing, Bert dedicated most of his time to creating weapons that could rival the blessings from the gods.

He was obsessed with the notion of putting mortals on the same playing field as the gods and Brandi had always blamed him for the rise of dissenters in the queendom. His wording was clever and he was never explicit in speaking against them, but Bert didn't shy away from speaking on his displeasure with the gods. It's why Brandi believed that people like Joyson Meys and his ridiculous ideas had taken root and spread like Asari's plague among the masses. It had been her job to cure the queendom of the individual symptoms, but the infection in the queen's court was still spreading.

Saya and his arrogance towards her were evidence of that.

"Aw, come on, sweetness," he smirked. "That's all you got to say?"

"You shouldn't be so arrogant in Asari's domain, Saya."

Brandi and Saya both turned to see Najé walking into the small clearing they occupied. Brandi watched Saya narrowed his eyes and take several steps back as Najé made her way over to Brandi. It put her on edge to have Najé that close, but Brandi didn't move away. If she was taking her side, then — at least for the moment — Najé wasn't a threat to her.

"Why are you here?" Saya questioned. "Ain't you supposed to be securing the perimeter?"

"There wasn't much need to," Najé shrugged, leaning her elbow onto Brandi's shoulder and replacing it when Brandi shrugged her off. She'd been doing that since they were kids. Two years older than Brandi, Najé had always been taller than her and now stood at six feet. Brandi huffed in annoyance and felt Najé's body shake in silent amusement at her expense.

"It was already done," Najé told him.

"By who?"

"Me."

Saya turned around in time to take an uppercut to his jaw. Without further introduction, Jack pounced on Saya, taking advantage of his surprise to straddle him and pound on his face. The scene reminded Brandi of when she'd first met Jack, but the outcome was much different now. Though Jack was bigger, stronger, and faster, his opponent wasn't some random person who thought he could use his age as a weapon. Jack was fighting another shadow — one who had come prepared.

He grunted under the force of Jack's blows, but it was clear that whatever Bert had created for him, it was taking the brunt of them. It protected him from getting his teeth knocked out, but he still struggled to get his arms up in front of him to block Jack's barrage of punches, and it wasn't until he managed it that he was able to shift his weight and shove Jack off of him. But Jack recovered faster than Saya did and landed a solid kick to Saya's chest before he was able to regain his composure. The light barrier flashed around him again, but he stumbled back, winded and clutching his chest.

When Saya was able to catch his breath, he rose to his full height of five-eleven with his chest heaving and his face already starting to bruise — only to find himself surrounded. Najé had moved to stand behind

him, off to his right. With Jack in front of him and Brandi covering
the left, they'd formed an inescapable triangle. His eyes darted around,
looking for an opening, but they'd worked together in the shadows longer
than he had even known they were real. There was a reason they were
untouchable, even among the elite, and he saw that now.

Najé had already called forth her blessing, and unlike Brandi and
Sarah, she didn't need words to do it. Hers wasn't as powerful as theirs,
but it was more than enough to accomplish her goals and little rings of
fire encircled her wrists in the dark. She used it to give the clearing a
small amount of light as she glared at Saya. He held her gaze and smirked
before letting his eyes dart over to Jack and Brandi.

"Y'all really think y'all won, huh?"

"It's more than just a thought when it's reality, isn't it?" Najé joked.
"You might be the leader of Bert's personal guard, but there's no way
under Rothe's sun you could hope to fight all three of us and win."

His smirk fell, and he glared at Najé. "You think just cause the gods
picked favorites outta y'all that I can't win?"

"I don't need my blessing to send you to the gods," she said, her
voice flat. "None of us do," she clarified. "But even if we did, that little
trinket around your neck won't hold out forever."

Saya sucked his teeth and looked away. He probably didn't want to
admit the truth, but it was obvious to all of them that she was right. The
light surrounding him had diminished with each blow he'd taken. And if
that was any indication of its durability, it wouldn't be long before he was
completely unprotected.

"What even is that thing?" Jack questioned. "Felt like I was punching some kind of bouncy wall."

"It's a defensive shield that Bert's cooked up," Najé answered. "It's supposed to protect against attacks that use the gods' power, and he's very excited about this one," she sighed with a roll of her eyes. "He's been calling it the Gods Anti Approbation Retaliation Armor and he won't shut up about it. Every meeting of the council is GAARA this and GAARA that."

"You're allowed into those meetings now?" Brandi asked.

Najé nodded. "Father announced me as his successor a few days after you left. You're now looking at the future director of shadows!"

"Bert must have been pleased with that," Jack chuckled.

"He was absolutely thrilled," Najé laughed. "Probably why he gave impossible orders to baby shadows," she said, shaking her head and smirking at the way Saya bristled at her casual insult. "I mean, really. My first mission to oversee as director and he orders the shadows we personally trained to send you to the gods?" She shook her head and threw her hands up in exasperation, "I don't know what the man could've been thinking. There was absolutely no way they were going to succeed at that! They wouldn't even have been able to find you if I hadn't guided them every step of the way."

"Now, hold on a second. We —"

"Shut up, Saya," Najé snapped. "You failed and no one is interested in your excuses."

Brandi's eyebrows raised when she saw Saya bite his lip in frustration and dig his nails into his palm like a scolded child, but he didn't retort. "Oh. So, this is your doing?"

"Unfortunately," Najé said with a shrug. "Father requested I train him personally but, as you can see, he's not the brightest star in Asari's sky. And since Bert issued that ridiculous order, my first assignment as director was to ensure that GAARA was tested effectively."

"So, what?" Brandi questioned, narrowing her eyes at Najé. "You're just going to run back to the tower and report everything to Bert?"

"Something like that," Najé shrugged. "And, I'm going to need you two to let the Saya come back with me."

"What?"

The question came from Jack and Brandi in unison, but Najé looked at Brandi when she answered.

"I'm going to take him back to the queen's tower with me. Father did put me in charge of him after all."

"Or, better idea," Brandi said, pulling her arrow back. "We send him now and you can go back to the tower about two hundred pounds lighter."

Najé laughed. "You never were good at seeing the bigger picture, so that would be your idea. But I can't let you do that." She shrugged, stepping in front of Brandi's shot. "Sorry, Green. I've got strict orders to make sure he goes back alive.".

"You saying you were sent to babysit me?"

"I was sent to account for your incompetency, yes," she snapped at Saya, clearing up his lingering confusion as to why she'd come with them when she'd never had any intention of sending Brandi to the gods.

"I'm glad to see you're doing alright, but this is still a job and I already let you get away with sending Yuri and Vanna," Najé pointed out, returning her attention to Brandi. "And don't forget you went rogue. You have a target on your back as big as Glenn and Sarah Rothens now. I'll let you go, but every shadow is going to be waiting for you to let your guard down and this will be the first and only time I ever let a target walk away from me. So take the win." When Brandi refused to lower her bow, she narrowed her eyes. "Come on, Green. Or do you really want to fight me?"

"Brandi," Jack said, moving towards her.

"Fine," Brandi conceded, taking a step back.

"Thanks, Green." Najé said with a smile before moving to grab Saya by his forearm. He'd used it to block Jack's fist and from the way he winced and hissed, Brandi didn't doubt it was broken, but Najé didn't let up on her grip.

Brandi glanced around, expecting Sal to come strolling out of the trees now that the altercation was over. He was never too far from Najé, but he wasn't a fighter like they were. He could hold his own against the average person, but he led the shadows' informant network and leaned into more covert work since he was one of the weakest among them. When he was nowhere to be found, Brandi glanced at Najé.

"Where's your puppy?"

Najé chuckled at the question as she began to drag Saya away with her.

"With yours, I'm guessing."

CHAPTER SEVEN

*Freya gifted the gods many things — creatures and stars, affection and
children — but it was only to Rothe that she gave her heart and her soul.
And it was only Rothe who stood at her side as her true equal.*

— Love: A Study of Rothe, Freya, and Creation | Lindl's Second Holy Academy

ASARI'S DOMAIN — PRESENT DAY

The moment they were alone and out of earshot, Jack reached for
Brandi's hand and pulled her to a stop. She turned her green eyes onto
him with a single eyebrow raised.

"What is it?"

"Talk to me real quick, Bee," he said, stepping closer to her. "Why are
we helping Sarah Rothens?"

"I thought you said you didn't care about how or why I knew Sarah?"
Brandi teased, taking another step in the direction they'd been headed in.
Sarah had left a clear trail of footprints and trampled leaves in her wake,
so tracking her hadn't required much effort. But Jack wanted answers
and her flimsy attempt at keeping things light wouldn't work. She knew

that. But she also didn't know how she could answer his question without sounding crazy — it would be easier to admit that she held conversations with shaders in her down time.

"I care about you," Jack stated, keeping a firm grasp on her hand and refusing to budge from where he stood. "I don't need to know the how or why of your past with her. I just need to know why you suddenly want to help her."

"Maybe I'm just a nice person," Brandi sighed. "You ever think of that?"

Jack snickered in the dark at her joke, and she couldn't help but crack a smile too. When he caught his breath he squeezed her hand and took another step towards her, his brown eyes gentle and serious at the same time.

"Talk to me, Bee," he said again.

"Can't you just trust me on this one?"

"I always trust you. But Sarah is number one on the SOS list," Jack pointed out, and Brandi scoffed thing about the queen's send on sight list, and didn't want to point out to him that they were probably on it now too. "So why is the queen's blade trying to keep her alive instead?"

Brandi chewed on her bottom lip as she tried to think of a better reason to give Jack that sounded better than the truth, but she didn't want to lie to him. That was something she'd never done. No matter what the circumstances or how harsh it was, they'd always given each other the truth. So, she sighed and shook her head.

"You're going to think I'm insane."

"Too late for that," he snorted, making her laugh.

"Freya told me to protect Sarah," Brandi admitted. "So, technically speaking, we're defying the queen but we're also carrying out the will of the gods."

"I'm sorry," Jack said, shaking his head. "I'm going to need you to make that make sense."

ROTHE'S DOMAIN — 10 DAYS AGO

It was never Brandi's plan to leave the shadows.

Since the time she'd been forced to join them when she was seven, the shadows had overtaken her world. Sending people to the gods had been her only responsibility, and she was good at it. She'd been trained by Glenn "Grim Reaper" MelForth, the best shadow to ever be in the queen's service, but she also carried the soul of Freya — the goddess of life and judger of souls, and her spirit thrummed in pleasure with every soul Brandi sent back to the gods.

And for fourteen years, she was the best weapon the queendom had ever crafted. She was efficient and completed every mission without question. It didn't matter who her target was, whenever she reported back to the queen, they were no longer a problem. Even when her targets became other shadows who were incapable of doing the job or buckled under the weight of what they'd done — Brandi didn't hesitate. She wasted no time harboring guilt or thoughts of remorse and mercy. She buried her feelings and carried out her job as Glenn had taught her to do from the beginning.

There was no room for sympathy in her line of work.

She was the myth that haunted nightmares by the time she was ten and a walking legend by the time she was fifteen. She'd accepted her role in the queendom and became known as "The Queen's Blade," and she was, without question, the unyielding wrath of the gods.

But she was still a mortal and the day she and Najé were called into the tower to meet with the council, instead of with Queen Leia, her instincts warned her that something was wrong.

Under normal circumstances, her team of shadows never interacted with anyone other than the queen herself. There was no one better than their elite team, so the orders they received always came straight from Queen Leia's own lips. The council, though, was a different matter.

It was comprised solely of the men of the throne. Because the crown, which held the most power and absolute authority throughout the realm, could only be passed down to its daughters, the sons were relegated to the council. It was a far less brutal rite of passage than competing in a bid for the throne, but it came with a limited form of power that left the more ambitious men on the wrong end of a shadow's blade. The current council was made up of the queen's brothers: Kinri Rothens, Casin Linser, and Zenin Canton, her consorts: Rinn MelForth, Sam Sentera, Adam Bertanal, and Krim Taren, and her son, Liren Taren.

Rinn MelForth was the leader and organizer of the shadows. Along with his wife, Mina, they trained and delivered jobs for the shadows.

It was under their guidance that the tower developed training grounds and housing for new shadows, as well as the protocol for inducting new members — and the protocol for removing traitors. So, it came as a surprise to both Najé and Brandi when they'd entered the meeting room of the tower and found that the only member of the council that was present was the queen's consort — Adam "Bert" Bertanal.

"What are you doing here?"

The question had been blunt and Najé cut her eyes over to Brandi. Brandi met her gaze, but kept her mouth shut. Between the two of them, Najé was their de facto leader. She was two years older and had started training with Glenn from the moment she could walk, but she was also the third daughter of Rinn MelForth. Her youngest sister, Riné, was the third daughter of the queen and Najé would one day be tasked with protecting her if she won her bid for the throne. So, her training as a shadow had also included lessons on how to carry herself as a member of the queen's highest court. That meant there were certain things she couldn't allow, even from Brandi. And that included being disrespectful to the queen's favored consort.

"My apologies for my sister's rudeness," Najé offered with a half-bow of respect. "She's not as familiar with the etiquette of the high court as I am."

Bert smiled and waved one of his wide hands through the air to dismiss the subject.

"Do not worry about it," he said. "The question is warranted as it is a bit unorthodox for me to meet with you without the rest of the council present."

"Yes," Najé said, a gentle smile ghosting her lips. "But we are the shadows, and as such we serve the queendom as we can. What is it that we may do for you?"

Bert smiled again, and it made Brandi's stomach roil in discomfort. Some people would find Adam Bertanal to be a handsome man with his light brown skin, dark curly hair, and full lips. He was well dressed in a rich purple suit that did nothing to hide the bulky muscles he carried underneath, with a small purple stud in his left ear to signify his relationship to the queen. He was a man of average height with a gentle nature — but something in his hazel eyes always seemed to put Brandi on edge. They held no light in them, as if his soul wasn't resting inside his body. It often made Brandi wonder if slitting his throat would even send him to the gods.

"I have a request to make of you," he said, sliding his hands into the pockets of his suit. He was attempting to feign an air of casualness, but there was nothing casual about this meeting. Rather than meeting in the throne room, which she and Najé were both accustomed to, they were meeting in the council room, where the lower ranked shadows received their orders.

The room was small with barely enough space for all the adults normally required to be in the room. There was one round table bolted to the center of the floor and eight chairs surrounding it. With no windows, the manufactured lights were bright to the point of blinding, and there was only one door that allowed them to enter and exit from the room.

It was the kind of space that Brandi didn't like being in, but they hadn't had a choice. She stood a half step behind Najé now as she spoke with Bert, but her fingers itched for her bow. She wanted nothing more than to summon Freya's power to protect herself from whatever negative energy resided in Bert's body. But she couldn't do that without causing an uproar, so she bit her lip and took deep breaths to try and calm her raging pulse.

"I would like for you to send a girl to the gods for me," he said, sliding a folder that he seemed to pull out from nowhere across the table to them. It was thin and when Najé opened it, there was only a single notecard-sized photo of a girl with blonde hair and blue eyes. It was a candid photo of her carrying vegetables in a basket while talking to some Asarian boy who walked beside her, but with a single glance, Brandi knew who she was even before Bert uttered her name.

"That is Sarah. She's currently living in Asari's domain."

"Why do you want us to send her?" Najé asked, studying the picture.

Bert chuckled. "I wasn't aware that shadows were in the habit of asking questions of their orders."

Najé smiled and closed the folder, setting it back down on the table. "Well, Sir Bertanal," she began, "this isn't an order, it's a request," she pointed out, a chill to her tone as she explained the basic tenets of the court to him. "Without the queen present or the majority agreement of the council, we're under no obligation to send anyone."

"I am aware of how the court operates, my dear," he said, his voice clipped in irritation. "I'm making this request in private so that it may be handled with discretion."

"Oh?" Najé asked. "Then why contact us? We serve the queen directly. Are you not concerned that we would slip your secrets to her?

What is it, Sir Bertanal?" Najé jested, a false smile on her face as her brown eyes searched his. "Did you have an affair with this girl and now she carries your child?"

"You should tread lightly, Najé MelForth," Bert warned, his tone dark as he took his hands from his pockets to stand to his full height. He was a few inches shorter than Najé's six-foot frame, but his presence filled the room as he met her gaze. "You may be Rinn's daughter, but I will not tolerate disrespect."

"You misunderstand me," Najé said, her voice gentler. "I tease with pure intentions. I would simply like to know what this girl, Sarah, could have done to have garnered such animosity from you. You are requesting the aid of The Queen's Blade after all."

"The question is not what she has done, but who she is," Bert answered. "But that is all that I am willing to share. You may speak like a member of the court, but you're still nothing more than Leia's attack dog," he said, straightening himself and pulling a black card from his pocket. He set it on the table and Najé stared at it before returning her gaze to him.

There were only ever five black cards in circulation at one time, and they were reserved for the queen and her consorts. It gave them access to the endless amounts of wealth the monarchy had accumulated over the course of nearly thirty centuries. If Bert was placing it in front of them, he was making it clear that there was no limit on the price he was willing to pay for the job.

Najé passed her watch over it to scan it, typed in an exorbitant amount and smiled once the payment went through. She picked up the folder again and circled the table towards the door. Brandi followed close behind, anxious to get out of the room and the queen's tower altogether. Najé paused in front of Bert, though, and placed a hand on his shoulder as she leaned in to whisper in his ear.

"You speak boldly for a man I could send to the gods with a simple flick of my fingers," she said, "but don't you forget, Sir Bertanal, that no matter how obedient it may seem, a beast with teeth will always bite." With those words, she summoned her blessing just enough to cause Bert's suit to singe under the flames she created. It was a tiny flame that would have flickered out long before reaching his skin, but she laughed anyway as he jumped back from her, doing his best to shrug out of his suit jacket.

"Don't worry about the girl," Najé said, opening the door and smiling in the face of Bert's angry glare. "We'll handle it."

It wasn't until they were standing outside the queen's tower, heading back to the training grounds, that Brandi finally stopped trailing behind Najé. They were in a secluded walkway, one that didn't get much traffic since they'd built out the tunnel network. Rinn MelForth had insisted that there needed to be some way for the shadows to move inconspicuously throughout the domain and the council hadn't disagreed.

So, they stood in the light of Rothe's dipping sun, staring at each other with questioning looks on their faces.

"You don't really plan on completing this job, do you?"

The question made Brandi sound foreign to her own ears. In her fourteen years of being a shadow, she'd never questioned the validity of an assignment — not once. She'd never had any need to. Every person was just a target to her, a nameless, faceless being who offended the gods and caught the attention of the crown.

This time was different, though.

She knew this girl, and she knew the gods didn't want her.

Queen Leia had a reputation for being a heartless woman, that the ice in her soul was the only way winter would ever come to Rothe's domain, but as cruel as she was, she wasn't unjust. Every order she gave was for the life of someone who had blasphemed against the gods — people who taught against the teachings they left behind in their temples or those who proclaimed that they weren't real. The kind of people who scoffed at believers and claimed the gods couldn't love them because they allowed pain to exist in the mortal realm. Queen Leia had no tolerance for people like that, and neither did Freya.

But from the moment Brandi had seen her picture and heard Bert's request, Freya's spirit had been in an uproar. Brandi's chest burned at the idea of Sarah being sent to the gods. Even if it wasn't by her own hands, it was clear that Freya didn't want her. But that wasn't something she could explain to Najé, so she had no words when Najé looked at her in confusion.

"What are you talking about, Green?" She laughed. "Of course, we're going to complete it."

Brandi shook her head, the ends of her braids brushing against her bare shoulders as she curled her fingers into her palms and looked away from Najé. They'd been together from the moment she'd joined the shadows, and Najé had always been adamant about being by Brandi's side. She'd refused her father's request to be put on another team in order to train the next generation as Glenn had done for them, and she'd never wavered in her conviction that should Riné win her bid for the throne and Najé become her right hand, then Brandi would be hers. They'd been a package deal from the first day of their meeting and Najé had told her on multiple occasions that Brandi felt more like her sister than any of the other three people she shared blood with.

Brandi had no desire to cause friction between them now. She'd only met Sarah briefly as a child, and she wasn't half as important to her as Najé, but there was no avoiding it. She was doing her best to fight off the heat rising in her throat as Freya warned her against acquiescing to Najé's plan for the sake of keeping the peace.

You cannot let that girl be returned to us, Freya whispered into her mind.

Brandi sucked in a sharp breath at the pinpricks of pain that lingered behind at the injection of Freya's thoughts into her mind. It wasn't the first time it had happened, but bearing the sensation of having a needle pulled through the center of her skull never got any easier. Brandi focused her green eyes on Najé's brown ones and shook her head again.

"We can't send her," Brandi said.

"We absolutely can," Najé smirked. "It's not like we lack the ability to. But," her sharp eyes searched Brandi's face she wished she could hide the discomfort and apprehension rolling off of her in waves, "what's got you so stressed about this? It's not like you to refuse a job."

"You don't understand," Brandi said, emphasizing her words as her throat and tongue burned with all the might of Rothe's fire as she spoke. "That girl is Sarah Rothens," Brandi said, fighting to maintain her voice as Najé's eyebrows shot up in recognition of Sarah's family name. "We absolutely cannot send her. The gods don't want her."

"And how would you know that?"

"Because I—"

You know better than that, Brandi. You can't tell her, Freya warned.

Brandi clenched her teeth together and broke away from Najé's gaze as she bit back a grunt of pain. Her head pounded in time to Freya's silky words and the fire building in her chest made her wish for the gentle touch of Asari's cooling hand. But she knew praying to him in Rothe's domain would be pointless — he'd never show up.

"Brandi, what's going on with you?"

"It's nothing," Brandi huffed out. "I just don't like taking orders from Bert. It doesn't feel right."

"Yeah," Najé agreed, "but we can't exactly turn him down. Even if the protocol was all wrong, he's still the favored consort of the queen. His power and influence is more than enough to make it impossible for us to refuse."

"We have to," Brandi demanded. "We can't send her Najé."

"You keep saying that," Najé huffed, losing her patience. "But like I just said," she emphasized, "we don't have a choice. It's just one girl."

"The gods don't want her," Brandi repeated. "If we send her, you'll have to face the true wrath of the gods."

"Is that a threat, Green?"

"Of course not," Brandi said. "It's a warning."

"Warning received and ignored," Najé said, waving her hand through the air. "We don't get to pick the targets, Green. You know that. And I don't see why this one girl should be any different."

"I'll protect her," Brandi whispered, hating herself for speaking the words but almost whimpering in relief at the receding heat in her lungs.

"What?"

"If you insist on sending her," Brandi said, "I'll stop you."

"Is this truly the path you want to choose for yourself, Brandi?"

Najé asked the question with narrowed eyes and Brandi couldn't blame her. She'd never spoken out so vehemently against sending someone — not since the first job they had back in Carna's domain where she'd refused to send the target and had escaped from Glenn and Patches. They'd found her hours later with a light-skinned boy who insisted on coming back with them. But since then, Brandi hadn't uttered a word against the queendom and her required duties. So, she understood why Najé couldn't understand why she was drawing a line in Lindl's metaphorical sand now.

"I've never chosen any path for myself," Brandi told her. "I'm little more than a pawn for the gods."

"You're more than a pawn," Najé countered, taking a step forward. "You're my sister. And you can decide for yourself which path you'll take because you're the only one who has to walk down it." She took another step forward, her brown eyes searching Brandi's face again. "I don't know what's going through your head, but I don't think you understand all the options you have available to you. You don't have to stand against me, Brandi. I don't want you to."

"I'm sorry," Brandi whispered, taking a step back. "I can't do this anymore."

"So, you're leaving?" Brandi nodded and Najé glanced at the soft, glowing sun on the horizon. "Forty-eight hours," Najé whispered. "That's the most lead time I can give you to get away from here. After that," Najé released a deep sigh and turned sad eyes onto Brandi. "After that, my father will add you to the SOS list and every shadow you've ever trained will become your enemy."

"Just the ones I've trained, huh?" Brandi smirked at the ground before giving Najé a quick nod. "I understand."

Brandi turned on her heel and sprinted across the open fields to the dorms. She and Jack didn't live there anymore, but there were a plethora of shadows who did and still owed her favors. She planned to call most of them in, starting with Mara.

"So, you're not going to tell her about the rebellion?"

The words came from Sal as he sidled up to Najé's side. He'd been in love with her since he first laid eyes on her when he was ten. When he was twelve, he'd given up being Risal of Sentera, second prince of the crown, to be just Sal, Najé's favorite person.

"She wouldn't have listened."

"You might have changed her mind," he offered. "Saved her from all the heartache headed her way."

"Maybe," she agreed, turning to continue down the walkway into the shadow's headquarters, "but she didn't give me the chance."

ASARI'S DOMAIN — PRESENT DAY

When Brandi finished her story, Jack looked like he had more questions he wanted to ask, but they shifted their focus to the task at hand. They continued following Sarah's trail until they found her sitting on the ground, glaring up at Sal as he leaned against a tree. He grinned as they approached. Asari's path still surrounded Sarah and soft moonlight lit up the small clearing.

"Took you two long enough," Sal teased. "I thought you would've gotten here much faster. She's been waiting this entire time."

Brandi sighed. "Uncompell her."

He glanced over his shoulder to wink at Sarah and she tumbled sideways with a yelp. Sal's blessing was from Asari and was the gift of compulsion. With a single word, he could get anyone to do just about anything, as long as his will was stronger than theirs. His ability didn't work on most shadows who completed any level of their mental conditioning, but it was a powerful tool against everyone else. Especially the simple commands he'd used to train the dogs in the queen's tower. Those were powerful enough to work on almost anyone and it's what made him so great at gathering information — he could simply tell someone to speak, and they would spill their secrets without hesitation.

So, Brandi couldn't help the snicker that slipped through her at seeing Sarah — who'd felt bold enough to raise her voice at her earlier when she'd been doing her best to keep her from seeing the gods — sprawled on the ground, the energy she'd been exerting to try and fight against Sal's compulsion, used against her. She jumped up as if she'd never fallen over, brushing her jeans off and picking dead leaves out of her hair. But Brandi smothered the sound as quick as it came, and she turned back to Sal.

"If you're here instead of with Najé, I'm assuming you have a message for me."

"A gift actually," he smirked. "Najé had your access code removed from the EREN. You won't be able to use any of your resources until you find another way to access it, but at least you're invisible to big sister now and won't be able to be tracked. We couldn't do anything about the ERIS though, you're going to need to find a proper engineer for that."

"Who are Eren and Eris?" Sarah asked, walking over to them.

"Not 'who'," Sal said with a chuckle, "but what. Not many people know of the entire realm's internal systems. Only the queen's court has access to it. But have you really never heard of the entire realm's external network — the EREN?" He asked, looking at her with eyebrows raised.

"She's never left Asari's outskirts," Brandi explained.

"Ah," he said, looking Sarah up and down as if she were a foreign creature. "The fickle god does hold a particular disdain for Lindl's technology."

"What does that mean?" Sarah asked, her blue eyes darting between their faces.

"It means you've been living in a technological desert," Sal laughed.

"What about Jack?" Brandi asked, bringing the conversation back into focus. "Did you get him removed from the EREN too?"

"Mara only owed us one favor," Sal answered with a shrug. "But Najé did send me with a message that may be of use to you."

"Out with it, man," Jack said, scanning the area. "Asari's night isn't going to last forever."

Sal frowned. He was a head shorter than Jack and stood closer to Sarah's height of five-seven than Jack's six-two, but he didn't hesitate to throw a glare in his direction. He swiped at the brown floppy curls that fell into his face but bit back a retort. Sal was usually the one trying to keep the peace between them since Jack was known to have the pride of Rothe at times and a much shorter temper. The two of them had never gotten along well, but that could be said of most shadows — they weren't known for being friendly and forging bonds with others. But they weren't impervious to them either, and when shadows worked together as long as Sal and Jack had, they usually felt more like family than anything else. It didn't always work out that way, but that's how it was for Brandi and Najé.

Brandi had been born to a pair of nomads in Freya's domain, and Najé born to Rinn and Mina MelForth, the leaders of the shadows, but they'd been raised together and had fought back-to-back more times than either of them could count. They were sisters, whether blood ties said they were, or not.

And, by extension, that made Jack and Sal in-laws of sorts.

"You never were the patient one," Sal sighed. He turned toward Sarah and draped an arm around her shoulders. "Listen well, cousin. I'm not much for repeating myself, and you should hear this as well."

"Cousin?" Sarah asked. "Who's cousin?"

"My cousin," Sal clarified. "Or could you not tell I was Asarian, too?" He held his arms out wide for her inspection and when Sarah stared blankly at him, he dropped them and held back a laugh, "I am Risal of Sentera," he introduced himself with a nod, a half-hearted imitation of a polite greeting. "Second son of Queen Leia. Pleased to meet you."

Sarah sucked in a sharp breath, and she glanced between them all. Her face flushed bright red as the fact sunk in that not only did they know who she was, she was meeting a blood relative for the first time — a blood relative whose mother was responsible for destroying her family. Her knees shook with the shock, but she locked them and lifted her chin. She struggled to hide the flood of overwhelming emotions that played out across her face, but it was obvious that she had no desire to be laughed at again.

Sal watched her torment herself for a moment before smirking at her.

"It is generally considered polite to give your name in return when one introduces themselves," he quipped. "Or have you never been taught that, although you're considered to be a proper princess of the crown?"

Sarah narrowed her eyes at him but refused to speak. She knew who she was better than anyone else standing there. She also know that because of who she was, she was being forced to abandon her home in the middle of the night for the second time in her life, leaving behind the only bit of family who loved her to crawl through the depths of Asari's night with strangers who took no issue with sending people to the gods.

She hated who she was and refused to feed into Sal's little game. Instead, she looked him over once with disdain and removed his arm from her shoulders. "Sarah," she said, purposefully leaving off her family name and a proper introduction. "Pleased to meet you as well."

Sal faked a shiver and chuckled. "With that mastery of the cold shoulder, you are a proper princess indeed. I've got chills," he teased, rubbing at his exposed arms. "Well," he said, turning back to Brandi and Jack, "we could indulge in small talk all night, but let's get down to business, shall we?" He motioned towards Brandi. "There are a great many people who would like to see you returned to the gods. And Adam Bertanal is at the top of the list."

Brandi rolled her eyes. "Yeah. And what's new about that?"

"This time," Sal said, getting serious. "He seems to be getting some help."

"I'm not worried about anyone born into the gods' realm," Brandi said, confident that she could handle anyone who was bold enough to come after her.

"And therein lies the problem," Sal said. "This person may not have been born a child of the gods."

"How would that even be possible?" Jack asked, looking at Sal with narrowed eyes.

"And how am I to know that?" Sal shrugged. "I'm just a messenger, and that's all I've got you."

"Lot of help that is," Jack scoffed.

"It's more than nothing, so be grateful," Sal shot back. "Also," he said, turning to Brandi, "my informant said a wanderer was looking for you. Said you two go back further than the gods?"

"That mean something to you?" Jack questioned with raised eyebrows.

"Yeah," Brandi nodded. "Where?"

"Lindl's domain," Sal answered. "Five days from now."

CHAPTER EIGHT

Kissed by the sun, loved by the sea, cherished by the sky, and adored by the stars, beauty has no meaning without her.

— Words of Worship for the Goddess | Lindl's First Holy Academy

REALM OF THE GODS — PRESENT DAY

"So, we meet again."

Brandi turned around, both surprised and annoyed to find herself no longer with Jack in Asari's domain, but in the throne room of Freya's temple. It was a big, open space with dark wood floors and stone walls covered in tapestries depicting Freya and the gods creating the realm. From Rothe and the sun, to Asari and the moon, the tapestries covered the entirety of the walls and made the room feel warm — safe. And though there was no ceiling, Brandi had never known even a single drop to fall inside.

Her green eyes danced around the familiar room. Her childhood had been far from easy, but Freya's domain — her temple — was home for Brandi. It didn't matter that she hadn't been back since the day she left.

The large rug on the floor still reminded her of all the nights she'd spent surrounded by Tiki and the others, their soft fur keeping her warm on Asari's coldest nights and filling her dreams with sweet maple scents. Tiki had been her first real friend and was never far from her — it had been the one to keep her safe from the dangers that lived in the depths of the forest when her parents were sent back to the gods, and she was left alone.

She was five the first time she met Freya here.

The memory was bittersweet, but returning to the temple now still filled her with a sense of comfort. And the first thing she noticed was how still everything was. The incense wasn't burning, the little aquamarine birds that lived in the temple were stuck in mid-flight, and the constant breeze that flowed through the temple was gone. More than anything else though, Brandi noticed the only color in the space was the goddess herself as she stood in the center of the room.

She wore a dark green halter dress that stopped at her knees. It hugged every curve of her body and her dark skin gleamed in the non-existent sunlight. Her long locs matched the color of her dress and were pulled back into two low ponytails that hung over her shoulders and stopped at her hips. Her feet were bare, and her thick glossy lips pulled into a smile as Brandi met her green gaze with her own.

"Why'd you call me here?" Brandi asked, walking further into the temple.

Freya shrugged, a simple movement that she managed to make elegant as she walked toward her altar. It was situated in front of the mural depicting Freya sitting in her throne with the gods surrounding her.

Rothe stood by her left hand, his fingers intertwined with hers as his sun lit the realm. Lindl stood to behind them, his arms crossed on the top of her throne with the books that held all his knowledge stacked beside him. Carna leaned casually against the other side of her throne, opposite from Rothe with his arms crossed and a smirk on his face while Asari kneeled in front of Freya, her fingers pressed to his lips. The entire image was painted on the wall behind her actual throne, so whenever Freya took a seat, she completed the picture.

"It's time for me to tell you the story of creation."

"You've told me that story already," Brandi pointed out, thinking of the time when she was seven and first met the other gods. At the time, she hadn't realized just how much strain meeting the gods had put on her body. She'd only realized how bad it had gotten when she'd woken up in a strange bed with a blue-eyed girl staring down at her and Tiki nowhere in sight. But she remembered every word they'd told her. It's why she'd felt confident enforcing the queen's mandate of silencing blasphemers. Brandi had gotten the story of creation from the gods themselves. It wasn't just some myth that was passed down to her.

"I'm glad you remember," Freya said. *"But there is now more I must tell you."*

"More?" Brandi questioned. "How can there be more?"

"When you're eternal as we are, there is always more," Freya answered, her voice gentle and patient as she faced Brandi who was shaking her head.

"Okay, but why didn't you tell me before?"

"You were barely more than an infant," Freya told her. *"You*

were hardly ready to even meet us then. How were we to tell you that the mortal understanding of creation was simplistic?

Brandi paused, her eyebrows pulling together as she watched the goddess watch her. Freya was the most revered of the gods, but also the one Brandi felt most comfortable around. They were two sides of the same soul, after all.

"Simplistic?" Brandi repeated. "What do you mean?"

Freya took a seat on the dusty floor of her temple, foregoing her throne to sit with her legs crossed in the center of the room. She looked up at Asari's moon before gesturing to the spot across from her. Brandi met Freya in the center of the room and mimicked her movements, but as fluid as hers were, they were nowhere near as graceful as Freya's. They sat with their knees touching and Freya reached forward to grab Brandi's hands, making Brandi feel more like her little sister than the mortal vessel she needed to manifest her soul in the living world.

"There are some things we left out when we first told you the story," Freya started. *"You were just too young for us to tell you everything. But you're older now and the reality of what you're going to have to face soon is becoming apparent."*

"That sounds daunting," Brandi warned.

"Yes, well," Freya sighed. *"It's no easy task make this request of one of my children. Even if you are my favorite vessel."*

"I'm your favorite?" Brandi asked, her grin cracking her face at the compliment.

Freya laughed. *"Of course you are."* She smiled and leaned forward a bit. *"Of all the lifetimes I've witnessed, yours is the most exciting.*

My other vessels were simple people," she mused, staring at something beyond Brandi's sight and getting lost in her thoughts. "*Gentle. Their souls were not as strong as yours. I loved them all, of course,*" she glanced at Brandi with a smile, "*but I would be lying if I said I was not having the most fun with you. You accept the responsibility of housing my soul and use the gifts I've given you,*" she nodded. "*I am both excited and grateful for you.*"

Brandi didn't know what to say, so she simply dropped her eyes to the ground and beamed.

"*But let us keep to the matter at hand,*" Freya said, giving Brandi's hand a light squeeze. It was a gentle reminder that she had not called Brandi to her simply to give her praise. "*I'm sure your lover and Asari's vessel are worried about you. And the longer you're with me, the closer you become to staying with me.*"

Brandi nodded and straightened her back. She'd completely forgotten that while her soul was with the gods, it wasn't in her body. And that meant she'd fainted somewhere and was probably driving Jack and Sarah crazy with anxiety over what happened to her.

"Right. Tell me what I need to know."

Freya smiled and nodded before letting her expression become serious again.

"*You've been told of how I created this realm with Rothe, Lindl, Carna, and Asari. You know that story as well as anyone,*" Freya said, and Brandi nodded. The story of creation was a popular children's story and she'd always enjoyed listening to it. And now that she knew the whole story, she loved it even more when the less than

137

desirable sides of the gods weren't left out. *"But as I said earlier, there is more. There was a time between creation and the beginning of the mortal realm."*

"I don't understand," Brandi said, interrupting her. "How could there be something between those two points?"

Freya paused, then held up her left hand. *"Let's say I want to punch someone,"* she said, choosing an analogy she was confident Brandi would understand. *"In order to do that, I must first create a fist, yes?"* Brandi nodded and Freya continued. *"But I have not punched someone simply because I made a fist,"* she explained. *"So, it is the same with creation. We had created the world, but the movement forward,"* she moved her fist toward Brandi to tap her shoulder, *"is what makes a punch. What counts as the beginning."*

"So," Brandi said. "You're trying to say… what? Time hadn't started yet or something?"

"Exactly," Freya said. *"And we are powerful,"* she said, referring to herself and her lovers, *"but we do not control the flow of time."*

"So, who does?"

"That would be Zareal," Freya answered. *"He is a being who exists outside of our realm, beyond the reach of the gods, and outside of time itself."*

REALM OF THE GODS — BEFORE THE BEGINNING OF TIME

138

The day that Zareal arrived in their realm was the day that everything began to change. In hindsight, Freya understood that was the nature of who Zareal was. He controlled time, and with time, everything changed.

He's arrival had taken them all by surprise. They'd been chatting by the gazebo centered in Freya's everlasting garden, and rather than enjoy the beauty of her lush fields, bountiful trees, and blooming flowers, Rothe and Asari chose to argue with each other. Her green eyes danced between them in amazement as she pondered on how they could be at odds with each other and yet somehow manage to remain in agreement whenever it came to convincing her that she shouldn't spend so much time with the shaders she loved.

They were opposites in every way. From the way Rothe's muscled body, dark brown skin, curly golden hair and eyes, was a direct contrast to Asari's slender form, creamy skin, blue eyes and silky strands — to the way Rothe was the god of the sun and Asari was the god of the moon. The only thing they had in common was their love for Freya and their hatred of the shaders she'd created. They didn't see any purpose in their existence and had caught her ire on more than one occasion when they suggested she destroy them. And though Lindl was never direct in speaking against them, Carna had been the only one willing to allow them free reign in his domain.

"I don't understand why you insist on making this an issue," Freya sighed.

"Because, my love, it is one," Asari said, pulling a hand through

139

his blue hair as he tried to reason with her. "*Your shaders are a menace.*"

"*They are not,*" Freya snapped.

"*I hate to agree with him, Freya,*" Rothe shrugged, "*but he's right.*"

"*You,*" she said, emphasizing the word, "*are agreeing with him?*"

"*I have no other choice,*" Rothe said, his face deflated.

"*Do not say that as if I've destroyed something precious to you,*" Asari snapped. "*I am simply right about this.*"

"*You are not,*" Freya shot back. "*My shaders just don't like you.*"

"*And is that not reason enough to be rid of them?*" Asari challenged. "*Or do you mean this to be an elaborate ruse to imply you don't love me anymore?*"

"*Don't be dramatic. Of course, I still love you.*"

"*I wish to see you prove it,*" Asari smirked.

"*If it doesn't involve destroying my shaders, I'd be more than happy to prove it to you however you like.*" Freya said, taking a step forward into the moonlight surrounding Asari and batting her green eyes up at him. "*I can be negotiated with.*"

"*No,*" Rothe said, stepping between them and pulling Freya into his own arms and into the light of his sun. "*You won't be batting those beautiful eyes of yours and getting what you want this time.*"

"*So, you're saying,*" Freya said, trailing her fingertips up his forearms and gazing up at him, "*that you won't give me what I want? I promise to ask nicely for it.*"

Rothe was at a loss for words and Carna chuckled beneath his breath from the cloud he drifted on above them. His arms were folded behind his head and he let his left leg dangle over the edge. His silver hair was pulled back from his face just enough to see his dark gray eyes glinting in amusement.

"*You two are fools for arguing with her,*" he laughed.

"*I agree,*" Lindl offered, breezing into the garden on his ocean's breeze and pulling Freya from Rothe's grasp into his own. "*This one is a master at getting what she wants. Trying to deny her is like trying to stop the tides,*" he stole a quick kiss from her lips, "*utterly impossible,*" he finished, a smirk on his face as he released her back into Rothe's waiting arms.

"*No one asked for you to inject your opinion,*" Asari snapped.

"*And no one asked for you to bring this up again, and yet here we are,*" Lindl shot back.

They glared at each other for a moment, but before another argument could break out, two solid knocks on a door that appeared at the edge of the garden silenced everyone.

"*Has that door always been there?*" Lindl asked, giving voice to the question that had pushed its way into everyone's mind.

"*No,*" Freya said, curiosity lighting up her face, "*but clearly it's here now. Let's go see who's on the other side.*"

The four gods shared a look with each other, none of them enthused by the idea of there being another god to fall in love with their goddess, but they followed her through her fields anyway and stood behind her as she opened the door.

The first thing Freya noticed was that the stranger on the other side had black eyes like voids. He had no pupils, just an infinite darkness contained within his sockets. He wore a black monochrome suit, his skin was gray, and his bald head glinted in the light. He dropped his head in a show of respect and she took a step back, bumping into Rothe's chest. He steadied her with a hand on her shoulder, but his eyes were focused on the being in front of them.

"**Who are you?**"

Freya cut a glare at Rothe, his displeasure at their guest apparent by the set of his square jaw and the firm grip he still had on her shoulder. She glanced behind her to ask one of the others to lead Rothe away, but they were all in similar states of irritation. She took a deep breath, prepared to tell each of them to dismiss themselves if they were just going to be rude, when their guest spoke.

"**I am Zareal,**" he introduced himself. "**A being of time.**"

Freya faced him again and offered a smile. "**Why don't you come in?**"

After a few warning looks shot at each one of them, she stepped around Rothe and allowed Zareal to enter the garden. She led them back to the gazebo and Zareal studied all the gods in turn, but Freya felt his focus continue to return to her. She was the first to take a seat in the center and the others filled in around her as Zareal straightened his shoulders in front of them.

"**Well,**" Zareal said, clearing his raspy voice. "**I've come here on two separate matters. One is purely business, the other is a personal request that I hope you will consider.**"

"**That's an unusual way to start a conversation,**" Carna said, his eyes narrowed in suspicion.

"*I like to be direct,*" Zareal said, unfazed. "*Now, business first,*" he said, pulling out a pocket watch. "*Your realm has been created and fully recognized by the Galaxiers — watchers of the universe. As such, I have been sent here to begin the passage of time in your realm. It will continue until I, or another time being, come to stop it. You, as gods, will not be affected, but the mortals you have created will begin to age and die, and their realm will begin to change. As gods, you may guide them as you see fit. Whether that is directly,*" he looked at Rothe, "*or indirectly,*" he said, glancing at Carna, "*is up to you.*" He glanced around the room. "*Are there any questions?*"

They shared a look, but it was Lindl who spoke. "*We understand. Continue.*"

"*Very well.*" Zareal clicked a button on his pocket watch and put it away. "*Once I leave, you will be able to witness the beginning of time,*" he said, reaching into his pocket and pulling out a card as black as his gaze. "*I am your official time guardian. Should you need to contact me for any reason, my information is here.*" He extended the card to them and Lindl accepted it.

"*Now, for the personal request,*" he said. "*If I may ask, I would like Madame Freya to take on a mortal form and live in the lower part of the realm.*"

Silence spread through the garden before Rothe, Asari, and Carna began shouting all at once.

Freya could only stare at Zareal in shock. She couldn't discern any clear words from the others, but they made their displeasure known. She'd expected Rothe and Asari to be livid — they were always the most vocal about their emotions. But even Carna, who tended to be the most unbothered of them all, was on his feet with balled fists and his narrowed eyes. Dark clouds filled the realm and lightning flashed as Rothe and Asari struggled to keep their composure. The temperature of the peaceful garden fluctuated in uncomfortable pulses as the leaves were ripped from the trees in swirling winds. Lindl was the only one who managed to keep a lid on his rage at Zareal's suggestion, but he was also the most practiced at it. Unlike the others, if he lost his control, he'd drown everyone in both the mortal and god realms.

So, instead, he threaded his fingers through Freya's and brought her hand to his lips. She broke her staring contest with Zareal then and instead focused her attention on Lindl. She blinked a few times, trying to wrap her mind around the request Zareal had dropped on them, and Lindl kissed her forehead. It was a soft moment and all he could do in an effort to comfort her. She relaxed a bit under his gentle touch and took a deep breath.

"*Alright,*" she finally spoke, her voice cutting through all the other noise in the room. "*You asked that I hear your request and I'm willing to do at least that. What do you need from me?*"

"*No!*" Rothe roared. "*You're not becoming mortal!*"

"*Rothe,*" Freya said, her voice gentle. "*Let him voice his request. I don't think we should dismiss it before we even know why he would ask this of us, love.*"

"*The reasoning behind his request doesn't concern us,*" Asari snapped. *"And I must agree with Rothe. You becoming mortal,"* he scoffed. *"It's an absolutely absurd idea to even suggest!"*

"I'll go," Carna said, drawing the eyes and surprise of everyone in the room. Carna loved the freedom he had as a god, his offer to take on the restrictions that came with living in a mortal vessel didn't go unnoticed by any of them. *"Freya can stay here. It just has to be one of us, right? It doesn't have to be her?"*

The question was directed towards Zareal, and he nodded.

"In theory, yes. However," he hesitated and glanced around the room. *"Enlighten me if I am not aware, but can anyone besides Madame Freya manipulate the ability of incarnation?"*

No one spoke, and Freya sighed. *"No,"* she answered. *"I'm the only one."*

"Then I'm afraid it must be you."

"She can't just incarnate one of our souls?" Rothe asked. *"She's able to manipulate the souls of mortals. Surely it can't be that different for us."*

"I'm not familiar with the exact limitations of your realm, but based on what I've seen elsewhere, should you be willing to give up your godhood, then yes. She would be able to incarnate you in her place," Zareal nodded, accepting of the idea.

"What?"

"Her ability works because she created them. They are mortals and she is their goddess," Lindl spoke up, attracting all eyes as he explained. *"In order for her to be able to manipulate your soul, you would need to become one of them and stop being a god."*

"*And I won't let you do that,*" Freya told Carna. "*Or any of you,*" she said, looking around the room. "*If it's going to be anyone, it has to be me,*" she said, turning back to Zareal. "*Why would you ask this of me?*"

"*In three thousand years, I will need you to incarnate into your realm and stop my apprentice, Azinne, from destroying it.*"

"*I'm curious as to why we have to deal with this when you are already aware of the problem,*" Asari said, the chill in his voice forming ice crystals along the glass panes of the gazebo. "*This is your apprentice, no? Should you not be dealing with him yourself?*"

"*The authority to do that is beyond me.*"

"*Explain,*" Lindl demanded.

"*I am a being of time,*" Zareal expounded. "*I stop time. I start time. I watch time. That is the totality of who I am and what I can do. My apprentice is the same, but his ambition is wild. Unchecked. And the Galaxiers have refused to grant me the authority to stop him. They fear that the power to do so will corrupt me as well and, unfortunately, I am not a god who may act upon my own free will,*" he sighed. "*I am required by the Galaxiers to start his time and to teach him. But I see a time in the future when he will bring chaos to the universe. Should he succeed in his goals, he will destroy this realm and continue on a path of destruction in a futile effort to become a god. I do not wish to see this realm, or any other, destroyed. But I cannot stop him. So, I must ask you to.*"

"*And why must I incarnate for this?*" Freya asked. "*I have more power as I am now."*

"Yes," Zareal nodded, *"but like me, he is a being of time. Therefore, he is beyond your reach of power as a god."*

"So, we can't stop him, but mortals can?" Carna scoffed.

"Mortals are beings of change," Zareal said. *"It is the only constant for them, and it makes them powerful in unexpected ways. I'm sure you will see that for yourselves as the gods who watch over them."* When no one spoke to deny his words, he continued. *"My apprentice is no different. He is immune to your powers, but he can still fall prey to the whims of the mortals he wishes to have worship him."*

"So, you need me to become one to lead a rebellion to stop him?"

"Yes. I wanted you to have time to prepare, so I came to you now."

"Alright," Freya nodded. *"I'll do it."*

Zareal bowed deeply. *"Thank you."*

"I don't care for this outcome," Lindl said, *"but if this is what you wish, then we shall help you."*

Asari nodded. *"If we each choose a mortal vessel, we should be able to teach them how to harness our powers when you are with them. Then it will be almost as if we are there by your side. It will not be the same, but it will be better than doing nothing and watching you undergo this task on your own."*

For once, none of the others argued against him. This wasn't a matter of slight bickering anymore. This was a matter of protecting their children, their realm, and their beloved goddess. If it meant getting along, that was the least of what was being asked of them.

"*So,*" Carna said, his gray eyes still narrowed at Zareal as he lowered himself to sit on the edge of his cloud. "*What can you tell us about this apprentice?*"

REALM OF THE GODS — PRESENT DAY

"Okay. But why are you telling me about this apprentice now?" Brandi asked, her eyebrows pulling together in confusion.

"*You would question my actions?*"

A searing flash of heat shot down Brandi's spine at Freya's question and she immediately shook her head. "No," Brandi said, anxiety speeding her words. "No, I just meant that I want to understand."

"*We gods are not meant to be understood by mortals. There are limitations to what your mind can process, even for a vessel as strong as you are,*" Freya quipped. "*But to explain it in a way you may comprehend, I have brought you to me now so that I may warn you of what is to come.*"

"Warn me?" Brandi repeated. "Of what?"

"*Of Azinne,*" Freya answered. "*Like Zareal, he exists beyond our realm in a universe too vast for me to explain to you. But unlike*

Zareal," Freya said with a sigh, "*he wishes to upend our realm by destroying us and claiming it as his own.*"

"But why?" Brandi whispered, her eyes wide and unblinking at the thought of Freya being destroyed.

"*Because not all children are content with who they are,*" Freya said gently. "*You are fortunate to not know that frustration, but there are many who are unhappy with the course of their lives. They blame us,*" she said, her eyes dropping. "*We want to help them, but there is only so much we can do. If we controlled everything, they would have no free will, and what would be the point in that?*"

Brandi didn't have an answer to her question, so she ignored it.

"And this apprentice? There's nothing you can do about him?"

"*No,*" Freya said with a slight shake of her head. "*Not as the goddess of this realm. But that is why I have been incarnating for so many centuries.*"

"You've been building up to this," Brandi said, amazement coloring her voice as she studied the goddess. Her heart pounded as her mind raced to keep up with all the possibilities that Freya's words had suggested. "For how long?"

Freya laughed, the lightness of her voice a welcome change to lessen the gravity of the situation as she watched Brandi with patience, waiting for her to answer her own question.

"Since the beginning of time?"

"*Since before then,*" Freya corrected with a smile, squeezing Brandi's hand in confirmation. "*Once we knew of this threat, we began to prepare.*"

"And the other gods?"

"*They have vessels as well,*" Freya confirmed. "*Although they do not incarnate as I do, so they do not forfeit their godly forms for corporeal bodies as I do. As such, their vessels are not as powerful as mine.*"

"That's why…" Brandi trailed off, her mind racing to connect all the dots she'd never thought were related until now. She understood now why it was rumored that Asari only gave out the ability to heal once every generation. He wasn't being stingy in his blessings, he was connecting his power to a mortal vessel.

"Wait," Brandi said. "So, if you've been incarnating since the beginning of the realm, did you create the monarchy?"

Freya nodded. "*In my first lifetime. Each of my consorts was a vessel of the gods. In my second lifetime, we spread the rumors of creation. We'd hoped that warning people there were no other gods would discourage them from trusting anyone aside from us. In my last lifetime, I planted the idea of creating the shadows in Queen Leia's mind in an effort to remove those who would speak out against us.*"

"So, that means…"

"*I was Madame Jelane,*" Freya nodded. "*The wandering nomad Leia met as a child.*"

"My head hurts," Brandi sighed, pulling her hands away from Freya's to massage her temples. "I can't even…"

"*I warned you that it would be a lot for you to comprehend,*"

Freya teased. "*But we are eternal. Time does not mean to us what it does to you, so take your time.*" She moved to her knees and pulled Brandi into a warm embrace and Brandi sank into it, wrapping her arms around Freya's waist. "*Now that you know this, I must ask that you defeat Azinne.*"

It was Brandi's turn to laugh. "You don't truly expect me to do something that you can't, right?" She squeezed Freya and buried her face in the velvet of her dress and the sweet scent of her domain that reminded Brandi of better — simpler — days. "We are one and the same, after all. If it is impossible for you, then it's definitely impossible for me."

"*That is not true,*" Freya said gently. "*We may share a soul,*" she rested her head on top of Brandi's, "*but we are also different.*"

"Where do I even start?" Brandi asked, forcing the question out over her fear of the answer.

"*Find the other vessels,*" Freya told her. "*You will need their support in the battle to come.*"

"And how many of your children cover the face of the realm? How am I supposed to find four specific people without a face or a name?"

"*You are resourceful. You'll figure it out.*"

"No pressure," Brandi sighed.

Freya laughed. "*None at all,*" she teased. She pulled away from Brandi, her hands on her shoulders as their green eyes met.

"*Your time with me is almost up,*" she warned. "*But there is something I would like to give you.*"

"Will it be like last time?" Brandi asked, her voice skeptical as she recalled the searing pain in her chest that had lingered for weeks the last time one of the gods had blessed her.

Freya had taught her the words to summon her power when she was seven, shortly after her first meeting with the gods. Then over the next few weeks, each god had given her a blessing and taught her how to use it. Asari how to see through his night, Rothe how to enhance her physical abilities, Lindl how to read and speak the language of the gods, and Carna how to hide her presence from others. It had been a torturous experience that involved her passing out and catching a fever, only to wake up in a strange place with Najé worrying over her. Glenn had never been far, but she was never the one fussing over her, and not once did she go easier on Brandi because of it. She'd forced her to push through the pain and become an elite shadow. And Brandi was grateful for it, but she wasn't excited at the thought of receiving another blessing from the gods.

"*It won't,*" Freya smiled. "*I shall give you the power needed to request an audience with us beyond our temple walls. But,*" she warned, "*this still will not be comfortable.*"

"Of course, it won't," Brandi sighed, rolling her eyes before closing them and laying back on the temple floor, knowing if she didn't, she'd simply bang her head against it later.

Freya laughed and moved to situate Brandi's head in her lap. She pushed Brandi's braids out of her face and smiled down at her.

"*Just relax,*" Freya soothed. "*This one won't be so bad,*" she said, leaning down to place a kiss on Brandi's forehead, who sucked in a hiss of air as the fire sprang to life within her. "*I promise.*"

152

CHAPTER NINE

He was the originator of light and of love — the giver of joy, deliverer of laughter, and the constant reminder that the gods exist beyond the reach of mortals.

— Rothe's Realm of Light | Lindl's Second Holy Academy

ASARI'S DOMAIN — PRESENT DAY

Brandi groaned as she tried to force her eyes open.

No matter how often she met the gods, having her soul returned to her body was never an easy thing. Her blood pounded with the heat of Freya's power and her nerves were raw from the sensation of her mind adjusting back to having a physical body. She shivered at the cool breeze that felt like ice against her burning skin. She clung to the warm body holding her on instinct but immediately pushed away as a searing pain shot through her senses. She hissed in pain and bolted upright, breathing a sigh of relief when she was finally able to pry her eyelids apart.

"You awake?"

She looked up into Jack's concerned eyes and her face softened.

"Yeah," she nodded. "How long was I out this time?"

"A few hours."

She took a deep breath of the cool air as she took in their surroundings. They were crammed into the back of someone's wagon and it reminded Brandi that Asari's domain was always slow in adopting new technologies. She'd grown accustomed to the innovative metropolis that existed in Rothe's domain and wished they were crammed into one of the cushy transport pods that shot through the skies, or even the side car of a solar bike, instead of the wooden wagon that tossed them in the air with every bump in the road. She sucked in a sharp breath and looked to the sky as they hit another bump that landed her on her hip.

Asari's moon was still out, but the sky was starting to lighten with the arrival of Rothe's sun, and one quick look around made it clear that they were nowhere near where she last remembered them being. She glanced around the small space and noticed Sarah sitting across from her, her knees pulled to her chest and her blue eyes focused on Brandi.

"Welcome back," she offered.

"Thanks," Brandi said, adjusting herself beside Jack and hissing in pain as the wagon rocked, slamming her back into the unforgiving wood.

"You okay?" Jack asked, reaching out to steady Brandi against his own body as she tried to regain her equilibrium. "Sarah can heal you if you need it."

"You could just ask me instead of volunteering my services," Sarah said, rolling her eyes. "I'm literally sitting right here."

"And yet somehow, I still wasn't speaking to you," Jack shot back.

Sarah huffed and the two glared at each other, neither of them willing to be the first to look away. It wasn't until Brandi raised an eyebrow at them that Sarah broke their staring contest and looked away to watch the passing scenery.

"What was that all about?"

"I don't like Asarians," Jack answered, shifting his body to give her more room.

"Figures," Brandi snickered. "No one would ever doubt you were a genuine child of Rothe."

There wasn't much leg room, so Brandi crossed hers and gave a slight nod to the driver, who had turned around to look at her. He returned the gesture, his loose brown curls bouncing around his shoulders, before returning his focus back to the road in front of them.

It was a narrow path with tall trees on either side of it. The tops of the trees grew together in dense patches that blocked out the sky and their roots knotted together at the bottom, suffocating anything that might have grown there. Wherever they were, the forest she saw now was wild. No one had tamed it, and depending on how close they were to the border, she doubted few would ever be brave enough to try. But with the trees as tall as they were, they reminded her of Freya's domain, and she wouldn't be surprised if there was an oasis hidden somewhere deep inside the forest.

She looked away from the trees and back over to Jack.

"Where are we headed?"

"An inn on the other side of Asari's domain."

Jack paused and glanced at the driver before lowering his voice. The man hadn't given any indication he was listening to them, but none of them believed he wasn't. "What happened back there? You were standing next to me one second, and then…" his words trailed off and his eyebrows drew together in a pained expression.

"I," Brandi paused.

Freya had always forbidden her from telling anyone she was her incarnation and human vessel. There were rules the gods set forth that even she couldn't break, so she couldn't be casual in admitting that Freya had summoned her soul to her temple, or that, to her, only an hour had passed because time moved slower in the god realm than it did in the mortal one. Even if she could form the words, he would look at her the same way he had when she'd told him about Tiki. There were just certain parts of her life that were difficult to explain to others if they'd never experienced meeting the gods for themselves. It's part of the reason she was glad to have Sarah around, even if she was reluctant to admit it. Sarah understood the things that were impossible to explain.

But looking over at Jack and seeing the concern in his eyes, she realized she would have to try. She'd always let him believe what everyone else had about her, that she was just a rare case of being blessed by Freya. She'd let him hold onto the idea that she was the same as every other person who received a blessing from the gods. But she wouldn't be able to keep the truth from him anymore — especially not if she was going to fulfill Freya's request. But more than that, she wanted him to know who she was. Brandi didn't want to keep any secrets from him, not even the ones Freya had entrusted her with. She'd kept them for the past sixteen years and had sworn to take them with her when she returned to the gods, but she wasn't a broken child anymore and even Brandi had her limits.

"It would be easier," she said, reaching for his hand, "if I just show you."

"Show me what?"

Brandi turned her green eyes to Sarah, her hand extended and eyebrows raised in a silent question. Sarah shook her head and hid her hands, making it clear she wanted no parts of what Brandi was about to do.

"I'll watch over you from here," Sarah said.

Brandi nodded and held Jack's gaze with her own. She summoned Freya's power forward, her palm heating in Jack's. His muscles tensed as a green glow blossomed between their palms. His eyes danced between Brandi and the growing light between them, but he didn't pull away. Instead, he tightened his grip on her and a smile ghosted across her lips. She hadn't imagined that she would be using Freya's gift so soon, but nevertheless, she whispered her next words in the god's tongue.

"*Hear me, Rothe, giver of light. You were the first to love this soul I carry, and I beseech your heart now. Show him what you have always known.*"

REALM OF THE GODS — PRESENT DAY

"Where are we?"

Jack looked around, his brown eyes narrowing as he took in the vastness of the gods' realm. It was an ever-shifting plane of existence that morphed into whatever display suited the god in control. When they were all present, a garden atop a rolling green hill appeared, and it was the most beautiful place Brandi had ever seen. She hadn't seen it since she was a child and felt a twinge of disappointment when it didn't appear now. Because, unlike the realm Freya created that mimicked her temple in the real world, Rothe didn't bother with such comforting niceties.

The realm they stood in now was one of his own creation. An endless sea of white clouds drifted in every direction around them, swallowing their feet. The sky was a golden hue above them, as if the vibrant tones of Rothe's sun had soaked into every inch of it, and the breeze surrounding them was warm, meandering across their dark skin as if it was in no hurry to get anywhere else. Brandi closed her eyes and took a deep breath, letting herself drown in the feeling of sunlight on her skin and the warm air in her lungs. She forgot for a moment why they were there until Rothe's deep, rumbling voice drifted across to them.

"You have asked me to bring you here, and so I have. What is it you desire, vessel of Freya?"

Brandi and Jack both spun around to find Rothe sitting on his throne. He wore black dress pants with a fitted red pullover. The three buttons at the top were closed around his thick neck. His muscles strained at the fabric, but he still managed to look comfortable with his left ankle crossed over his knee and his arms resting on the edges of his throne as he leaned back in his seat. He watched them with an eyebrow raised,

158

curiosity twinkling in his golden eyes.

Jack's snapped his eyes shut and sank to his knees in worship, as he'd been taught to do all his life. Each domain had its own rituals for things like praying to the gods, but Rothe's children were the most devout. Jack lowered his head, pushed the palms of his hands together, and began whispering the words of Rothe's prayer under his breath.

"Our father who resides in his realm, may your name be exalted in every domain," Jack muttered. "May the knee of every child bow in respect of your awesomeness and may every command of yours be followed in the realms you helped create. Please look kindly on your children as they serve you. Show them favor as they move about beneath your sun. Have mercy on those who do not revere your greatness and strike down all who would disrespect you. Give strength to your servants and all those who would worship you."

Rothe listened to Jack repeat his prayer twice before pulling his voice away from him. His body stiffened, but instead of clawing at his throat as Rothe was accustomed to seeing, he kept his head lowered and waited.

Brandi stood to Jack's right, watching the exchange. When Rothe turned his attention to her, she bowed her head in respect. She and Freya may have shared a soul, but Rothe always saw them as separate. There was Freya, and then there was Freya's vessel — after the first few, he no longer bothered to remember their names. They were temporary and never lasted even a century.

"*I have come to ask a favor of you.*"

"*Oh?*" Rothe smiled and lowered both feet to the ground. "*I have already brought you to see me. Allowed this mortal to gaze upon*

159

me. And you would still ask for more?"

"*I would,*" Brandi said. Having met the god on multiple occasions, she was no longer fazed by Rothe's arrogance. She would have to stand firm under his gaze, otherwise, things would not go in the way she wanted.

"*And if I tell you I have no wish to hear whatever else it is your greedy soul could want?*"

"*You would think me greedy, Rothe?*"

They both turned to see the goddess standing next to Brandi. Her dark green dress was white for the occasion, making her dark skin stand in stark contrast to everything else in Rothe's part of the realm. Everything Brandi could see was almost too bright to look at, but even his sun dulled in comparison to the grin that split his face when Freya appeared. He stood to his feet and opened his arms wide for her.

"*Freya.*" Her name was a promise on his lips, enough heat in that single utterance to melt his sun. He walked towards them and pulled Freya into an embrace. "*You,*" he whispered, "*could never be greedy in asking anything of me. All that I have is yours.*"

"*Then why would you deny my vessel as you have?*"

"*She is not you,*" he said plainly. "*She is mortal. Carrying your soul or not, I do not cater to her whims as I cater to yours.*"

"*You can be so unreasonable.*"

"*If that is what you would call impartial and consistent towards mortals, then yes,*" he released her and led her back to his throne, where he took a seat and pulled her into his lap. "*I am unreasonable.*" He turned to look at Brandi once more, who matched his golden, fiery gaze. *"But for you, I will hear her request."*

He waved his right hand at her, sending sparks from the small rings of fire encircling his fingers floating her way. *"Continue then,"* he said.

"I would ask that you choose this man as your mortal vessel," Brandi said, her voice clear and her words concise. She wanted to let her eyes drift over to Jack, but she knew that he didn't know the language of the gods and, more importantly, if she looked away from Rothe now he would only perceive it as a sign as disrespect. So, she kept her gaze focused on the gods in front of them until Rothe spoke again.

Rothe narrowed his eyes at her. *"That is a bold request. Mortals do not dictate who the gods choose for themselves. Not even Freya's own vessel."*

Brandi dropped her gaze from his. The warm air that had felt comforting just moments before, now scorched her throat as she tried to take another breath to calm her racing heart. She knew she was asking a lot. But there was no one in the world she trusted more than Jack, and keeping him away from the other part of her life — the other part of herself — was becoming too large a burden to bear. One great enough that she would dare ask the most prideful god, who cared the least for her, to do something he had no intentions of even considering.

"I mean no disrespect with my request," Brandi said. *"I only offer it as an option to you. This man is skilled in many things. He is one of your devout children and you have already blessed him once."*

"I know who he is," Rothe said, the edge in his voice showing his waning patience. *"I am not a god who needs reminding of who my*

own children are."

"*No, you are not,*" Brandi agreed, chiding herself for sounding as if she were demeaning Rothe as she raised her head. "*I only meant to share his good points with you.*"

Rothe studied Brandi and his golden eyes narrowed at her. He took in the brown skin a few shades darker than his own, the dark braids parted into neat boxes, her perfect posture, and her dark clothes. She was both the spitting image of Freya and still nothing like her. But it was the green eyes avoiding his gaze that shook something loose in him — a willingness to hear her out he'd never felt for any of Freya's previous vessels.

"*Vessel of Freya,*" Rothe said, shifting Freya to the arm of his chair so that he could lean forward to rest his elbows on his knees and speak without distraction. "*Speak freely. Why do you wish for me to choose this man? Who is he to you?*"

"*He is the man that I love,*" Brandi answered. "*I'm making this request of you because I don't want to keep secrets from him anymore.*"

"*And you realize the totality of what you are asking of me?*" Rothe asked. "*I have not chosen him because he loves you. You have seen for yourself how our love for Freya changes the way our vessels interact with hers, have you not?*" Sarah's immediate and unwavering trust in her despite the years between them flooded Brandi's mind and Rothe's eyes danced over her face, searching for any hesitation that might exist there. "*He will be compelled to obey you, even if he wouldn't otherwise. Is that the kind of man you wish to have at your side?*"

Brandi took a deep breath, her mind trying to come to terms with what Rothe was saying. She'd never considered that there could be a reason why Jack hadn't been chosen by the gods. She just knew what Freya had taught her — that the gods expected their vessels to support Freya's for the entirety of her incarnation. But it was because Jack had already chosen to remain with her that Rothe hadn't made him into his vessel. In his own way, he'd done his best to honor the love they already shared rather than choosing him and risking Jack's heart being swayed by emotions that weren't his own, forcing him to become someone who couldn't disobey her. In that moment, Brandi understood more of why the goddess had fallen in love with Rothe. He was a romantic and there was much more to Rothe than the myths gave him credit for.

Knowing that made her smile.

"*I believe,*" she said, "*that he loves me enough that your love for Freya won't overshadow that.*"

Rothe studied her, then threw back his head and laughed. It shook the entirety of his chest and throne, forcing Freya to stand to her feet. His voice echoed like thunder in the clouds and Jack closed his eyes against the sudden noise, but he remained still. Brandi wanted to reach out to him, knowing he hadn't understood a word of the conversation they were having, but she couldn't. For now, he would have to trust her to have this conversation with the gods.

"*You hear this, Freya?*" Rothe chuckled. "*This mortal believes this man loves her more than I love you.*" Saying the words aloud sent him into another fit of laughter. "*You have a boldness to you that I can't say I don't appreciate.*" He turned to Freya. "*What do you think? Does this man love her more than I, you?*"

"*It is silly to compare,*" Freya answered. "*But if I am to be truthful, it would be impossible to say. It is unusual for mortals to love as deeply as the gods, but this one comes close.*"

Rothe's face stilled as he listened to his goddess. The laughter that had echoed through the realm faded to silence and he was slow to look away from Freya. But instead of looking to Brandi, his eyes settled on Jack.

"*Stand.*"

Rothe gave the order, and it tickled Jack's brain as the foreign words untangled themselves in his mind. He didn't meet the intense gaze of the god as he rose to his feet, but his posture was straight — rigid — proud. He wasn't a man who slouched, not even under the immense pressure of a god.

"*Look at me,*" Rothe demanded. Jack complied and his brown eyes widened in awe as he truly looked upon the gods for the first time. He wanted to glance at Brandi, to confirm that she was seeing what he was seeing, but he knew better than to look away when Rothe had given him a direct order. Besides, Brandi had been speaking to them this entire time. Whether he'd understood their words, or not, he knew that what he was experiencing was real. Rothe waved his hand and Jack felt his voice return. He gasped at the sensation but promptly clamped his jaw shut.

"*These two claim that you love the woman standing next to you. Is this true?*"

"Yes," Jack said. His voice cracked with its return to him, but he spoke with confidence and cleared his throat before speaking again. "It is."

"If I were to choose you as my own vessel, would you be able to remain in love with this woman? Or would you let my love for Freya overtake you?" Jack hesitated in his response and Rothe nodded at him. *"Speak freely."*

"I love Brandi more than anything in the realm. Mortal or god. Nothing could change that."

"You border on blasphemy with your words," Rothe pointed out. *"But I respect them all the same."* Rothe paused and studied Jack, as he had Brandi earlier. *"If I were to threaten your beloved. What would you do? Would you raise your hand against me?"*

"Without hesitation," Jack said with a nod. "I would destroy this entire realm if it meant protecting her." Jack paused and bowed his head. "With all due respect."

Rothe smiled, a laugh bubbling up in his chest again at the boldness of Jack's statements. Brandi had been one thing, but for a common mortal to speak to him with such blatant words — it tickled his soul. He let out another rolling laugh before leaning back on his throne.

"I like your resolve, mortal," Rothe said. *"However, I cannot honor your request."* He glanced up at Freya, who gave him a tiny nod, before he returned his attention to the two mortals standing in front of him. *"I can give you the gift of knowledge as your beloved has requested, and of the gods' tongue,"* Rothe said to Jack, *"but I cannot choose you as my vessel until the contract with my previous one is broken."*

Brandi's brows drew together as she glanced between Freya and

Rothe. "*What do you mean?*"

"*Under normal circumstances, the contract would be broken when the soul returned to our realm after completing its natural course in the mortal one. However,*" Rothe said, "*seeing as how my vessel is no longer by your side, I feel exceptions can be made to acquiesce your request.*" Rothe leaned forward once again on his throne and reached to pull Freya back to him. "*I made my choice of vessel before any of the other gods,*" Rothe explained. "*When you were a child, you were vulnerable and needed someone to take care of you. Someone to bring you into the fold of the shadows Freya had worked to create in her previous lifetimes.*"

"*But who...*"

"*Have you never thought it odd,*" Rothe smirked, "*that the people who hunted you decided to take you in as one of their own?*"

Brandi froze as Rothe's words and the meaning behind them sunk into her mind. She shook her head, her fingers fitting into the grooves between her braids as if physically holding her head would help keep her mind from being overwhelmed. Jack reached over to her, but for once, she didn't fall into his embrace.

She stood rigid and unmoving. Her eyes darted through the shifting clouds they stood on, her memories replaying through her mind at a rapid pace as the meaning behind everything she'd known shifted with her new perspective. They all stood silent as they waited for what would come next. It was minutes later when Brandi finally took a deep breath and steeled her heart against the answer to her next question.

"How do we break the contract?"

"Sending her to me is the easiest way," Rothe answered. *"But that may be an impossible task, even for you."*

"If that is what must be done," Brandi said, her voice razor sharp. One of the first things she had ever been taught as a shadow was the art of caging her emotions. No matter how big they were, her life didn't afford her the space to give in to them or have her actions be governed by them. Being a shadow meant sending people — sometimes good people — to the gods at the behest of the queen. She was raised to be a weapon, a tool forged in blood for the sole purpose of being slipped across the throats of her enemies and pressed into the backs of those who would betray her.

And weapons did not have emotions.

"Again," Rothe nodded. *"I respect your resolve. But there is another way. Simply request to bring her to me, as you have brought this one,"* he nodded to Jack. *"If she is here, I can free her without harm. Once that happens,"* he looked at Jack, *"I can bestow my full blessing onto you. In the meantime,"* Rothe said, standing to his feet, *"you will need to prepare yourself."* He looked toward Brandi. *"He will be unable to move for three rising cycles of my sun. This will be his second blessing and as you have experienced for yourself,"* he smirked, *"the more power you are gifted, the more difficult it is to receive it."*

Brandi remembered the searing pain that had coursed through her body with more intensity every time she had met with the gods. They were generous beings, but the reality was that mortal bodies were not meant to carry their power. If the body wasn't strong enough, it could degrade their brain, atrophy their muscles, or even return them to the gods who had been trying to bless them. It's why they refused to give blessings out to every mortal who wished for one.

The gods had no desire to inflict unnecessary pain on their children or to bless them with abilities that would take more away from them than it would give. Jack was different, though. He would survive whatever he needed to if it meant being able to protect Brandi — to be able to continue standing by her side — so he nodded his head and squared his shoulders.

"You should sit down," Brandi whispered to him. "Trust me."

Jack's eyebrows shot upwards for a quick second before he obliged. He kneeled on the ground as Rothe approached him. He didn't say anything as he took a knee in front of Jack and placed a hand on the back of his neck, placing a kiss on his forehead like a father would his treasured son.

Jack grunted from the heat that flowed through him, and Brandi watched as literal sparks of flame exhaled from his mouth with each breath. He did his best to hide the extent of his pain from her, but she knew firsthand how difficult it was to accept a blessing from Rothe. She wanted to rush to him, but knew better than to lay hands on him. As well-meaning as it would have been, she knew any physical touch would feel like a unique form of torture. There was nothing she could do for him except watch with a pained look on her face at every flaming breath he took.

It wasn't until Freya walked over and touched Jack's shoulder that

Brandi felt the tightness in her chest ease. Jack slumped into Freya's touch and the tension in his shoulders disappeared. Freya winked at Brandi, who sighed in relief as Jack's breath returned to his normal pace, before returning to Rothe.

"*It's time we go, my love.*"

"*It is always too soon when you must leave,*" Rothe said, sadness clouding his face and darkening the realm.

"*I know,*" Freya whispered. "*I know.*"

Rothe framed Freya's face with his hands and brought his lips down to meet hers. Freya leaned into it and Brandi watched as the clouds rolled faster and the sun rose higher in the sky, blinding her with its light. She shut her eyes against it and turned away, giving Rothe and Freya their moment together.

Freya only ever saw the gods when they were in the gods' realm together, and Brandi's soul couldn't stay there for long, otherwise, she would never be able to return to the mortal realm. So, their moments with Freya were always passing ones, but they never failed to surprise Brandi with how deep their love for her ran. When she was young and missing her parents, Freya began sharing some of her memories with Brandi to help assuage her pain and show her who the gods were as she knew them. And Brandi had loved watching the happiness and the laughter that flowed between the gods and Freya. Even with months and years and decades apart, they always welcomed her into their arms like she was returning home.

She'd only ever loved Jack — would only ever love Jack — but she was amazed by how much Freya loved them all. It wasn't a competition between them. She loved them differently — Brandi felt that. But it was also the same. Aside from Rothe, who she'd gifted her heart, all of them took up the same amount of room in Freya's soul.

It wasn't until Brandi felt Freya's arms drape around her that she turned. Freya smiled down at her and Rothe flopped back into his seat, a smirk on his face as his throne and clouds began to slide away from them into the endless sky and he sent their souls back to the mortal realm.

"It has been interesting to see you, again vessel of Freya. I shall be waiting for you to call on me again."

CHAPTER TEN

*Love is not big. It is not all grand gestures and exuberant confessions.
It is a collection of small moments that mean bigger things — gentle
touches that spark fires — an unwavering desire that cannot be altered by
anger, jealousy, or malicious forces outside of those who share it. It is a
magnificent thing, and though it is not the solution to every problem, there
does not exist a problem that it cannot solve.*

— Of Light and Love | Lindl's Second Holy Academy

ASARI'S DOMAIN — PRESENT DAY

"Why didn't you tell me?"

That was the only question Jack had when he finally woke up. After
spending three days trapped in the fiery inferno that was Rothe's memory,
Jack's head pounded and he wanted nothing more than to melt into a
tub full of ice, but his anger forced him up and out of bed. Brandi had
snapped awake at his sudden movements, and her face lit up when she
saw his brown eyes open for the first time in days. Although Rothe had
warned them that he wouldn't be waking anytime soon, she hadn't been

able to stop the incessant worries that paraded through her mind that he might never wake up again. She'd been ready to throw herself into his arms the moment he was awake, but her face fell when her mind caught up to his question. She dropped his gaze, and he glanced around the room. It didn't take long for him to realize they were at the inn Grady had been headed to when Brandi was unconscious.

Jack had secured the wagon and the driver earlier in Asari's night when Brandi had asked him to, but it had been Sarah who convinced the man they were harmless. Jack wasn't ashamed to admit that her ability to talk the man into letting them ride in the back of his wagon had impressed him. The driver was an older Asarian man — long brown hair and round eyes, with a belly that hung over the belt of his creased pants. His sharp eyes had given them all a once over and, despite the fact that Jack towered over his five-four stature, carried an unconscious woman in his arms, and had enough muscle in his left arm alone to strangle the man's old horse, he'd introduced himself as Grady and invited them into the bed of his wagon. He'd seemed hesitant to at first, but the old man kept his word and took them to the inn in fragment 43205.

Grady had spent the first part of the ride explaining that he worked making deliveries for most of the smaller companies in the fragments that surrounded the inner ring and sent clothes to the outskirts. The supply chain usually didn't go out that far, so he'd spent the better part of the last forty years making contracts with the guardians of the outskirts and running a delivery service for their goods. He had no problem bragging about how he had over six hundred drivers and reminding them how lucky they were that he'd decided to leave the office for a change and do one of the delivery routes himself. He'd mumbled about being nostalgic for the roads and how the younger generation of merchants only wanted to use the fancy new rail technology the Lindlians created instead of a horse and buggy.

The rails hadn't made it as far as the Asarna Mountains yet, so traditional transportation was still required to make the deliveries. He'd considered sending one of the younger people he'd hired, but he'd decided to do the route himself for the sake of nostalgia. Sarah had played the part of an avid listener well, nodding and encouraging him — asking questions when it was clear he was waiting for one. She had the man wrapped around her little finger in under an hour, so much so, he hadn't batted an eye when Sarah mentioned that her friend needed silence to rest. He'd given her a sympathetic pat on the hand and turned his attention to the road. They'd ridden in silence until Brandi woke up.

Jack didn't know what happened after that, or how he'd managed to wake up in a bed at the inn — but he knew everything else. From the truth about creation, to the request Zareal had made of the gods before the beginning of time, to the pain Rothe had suffered at being apart from Freya as she lived her lifetimes in the mortal realm. His heart yearned for the goddess as he was forced to watch over her from a distance with the other gods and the feeling was overwhelming for Jack. His mind still raced as it tried to sort out the memories he now had that he knew weren't his.

He grabbed at his head, the sudden motion of sitting up in bed catching up to him. He grit his teeth and closed his eyes, taking in deep breaths. His head kept rhythm with his pulse, but it wasn't anything he couldn't handle. He'd always been a devout believer of the gods and had been blessed once already — what he endured now was worse than the first time, but it was worth it to have met Rothe.

It was worth it to know everything that he knew.

Now he stared at Brandi. He tried to get a handle on all the emotions flashing through him, but he couldn't. She watched him with concern shining in her beautiful green eyes and he couldn't decide if he was grateful that they were both okay, or pissed that she'd kept so much of her true identity a secret from him.

"Answer me, Bee," he said. "Why didn't you tell me?"

Brandi opened her mouth to speak, then closed it. She glanced across the room to the other bed, where Sarah was snoring softly, and Jack followed her gaze. Brandi had slept sitting upright on the bed beside Jack, so she was the first thing he'd seen, but they weren't alone. Jack's irritation doubled the moment he saw Sarah sleeping in the bed across the room but he also understood the necessity of her being with them. Aside from the fact that Sarah was defenseless without them, both he and Brandi were locked out of accessing their funds in Rothe's domain. As annoying as it was, even he could admit that paying extra for the added benefit of privacy wasn't the best way to spend their limited amount of coins.

Besides that, Jack was still connected to the EREN. Brandi had been removed from it but what remained in her accounts was no doubt frozen and monitored now. Not that it mattered. Using anything other than physical coins in Asari's domain would be impossible. Asarians hadn't adopted the tech to accept payments from the EREN, but it wouldn't be worth the risk even if they could. Najé and Sal may have their ways of

174

finding out where they were at, but he doubted anyone else possessed Najé's tracking skill or Sal's connections. And without a digital trail for them to follow, finding them would be like trying to find the end of a rainbow. But it was a pain and a half to not have access to the resources they were accustomed to.

A quick glance around the room was enough for Jack to analyze the space. It was far from anything luxurious. Jack's feet hung over the edge of the narrow bed and there was barely enough room for them to move around, but the place was clean, quiet. The menu displayed on the nightstand between the beds advertised two meals a day for its residents and names of the three hosts on duty for the week.

Brandi climbed over Jack to make it off the bed and moved to shake Sarah awake. She groaned and rolled over but didn't wake up. Brandi sucked her teeth at how heavily Sarah could sleep. She'd always been a light sleeper. Shadows didn't have the luxury of having delayed reactions, even when they rested, so Jack hadn't needed to do much to get her attention when he'd woken up. It was just another reminder of how different Sarah was from them. Brandi shook her head and gave Sarah another shake.

"What?" Sarah asked, bolting upright in bed. Her blonde hair swung from side to side as her eyes searched the room for impending danger. "What's happening?"

"Nothing," Brandi said. "We just need the room."

Sarah blinked a few times and rubbed the sleep out of her blue eyes. She looked around the room in surprise as if she had forgotten they weren't in fragment 42913 anymore. They were at *Carol's Inn*, a rest stop on the opposite end of Asari's domain. She pulled a hand across her face and then through the roots of her tangled ponytail as her face grew pink and her blue eyes narrowed at them.

"Did you really just wake me up so you guys could bang?"

Brandi narrowed her own eyes and scoffed at Sarah's tone. "No," she said, "I didn't. But even if I did," she yanked Sarah from the bed and shoved her towards the door, "that wouldn't be any of your business. Now, get out."

Sarah stumbled at the abruptness of being thrown to her feet. She crashed into the door, catching herself with a hand on the little blue dresser pushed against the foot of her bed. She hadn't hit the ground, but adrenaline now poured into her system at having just avoiding that outcome. Her head whipped up, strands of her blonde hair stuck to her face and forehead as she glared at Brandi.

"Father Asari! You are hard to like," she huffed as she stormed out of the room, slamming the door behind her.

Brandi ignored her and turned back to Jack. He was alert and watching her, his thick legs slung over the edge of the bed with his elbows resting on his knees. He was still dressed in his black pants and the white shirt Sarah had given him, and he leaned forward to meet Brandi's gaze, searching her face for answers to questions he didn't know how to ask as she stood by the door.

"Why didn't you tell me?" He shook his head, anger and hurt competing for dominance on his face. "Did you think I wouldn't want to know?"

"It wasn't that," she said with a shake of her head. "I couldn't."

"Why?" He demanded. "What would have been so hard about telling me that you're…" he trailed off, his hands sliding through his short locs as he tried to wrap his mind around the facts he already knew to be irrefutable, "you're the goddess," he forced out.

"I'm not," Brandi whispered.

"Brandi," Jack snapped, her name a warning. "I've just been through three days that made being hunted by shaders, sound fun. Do not choose this moment to try and split hairs with me."

"I'm not trying to do that," she said. "I'm trying to explain why I couldn't tell you. You asked me why, didn't you?"

He studied her. It was clear she didn't want to argue with him — the fact that she stood by the door with her hands shoved into her jacket pockets and her shoulders relaxed proved that. But she wasn't one to back down from a fight. Not with him. Never with him. He was the only person she trusted with anything important enough to argue over — the only person she felt comfortable being herself with.

It's why her secrets had eaten at her with a relentless ferocity. He had accepted her for who she was, from the day she first met him. Even before she'd fallen in love with him, back when he was just another member of the shadows she went on assignments with, they'd sworn to always be honest with each other. And now that he knew everything that Rothe knew about her, she wasn't surprised that he was pissed. He had every right to be. But even so, there had been so many things outside of her control, and she had the right to explain herself.

"Are you going to listen?" Brandi asked. "Or do you just want to be mad at me for things I had no say in?"

He looked toward the small window between the beds, clearing his mind of the static that clouded his mind whenever he stared at her for too long. A part of him did just want to be mad — to stay mad. They'd been together for eight years and not once had she mentioned being the incarnation of the goddess — of having met the gods — of being blessed in some capacity by all of them. Part of him felt like there was nothing she could say that could explain why she'd let him believe she'd just been one of the rare people Freya took the time to bless. But another part of him knew she had to have a good reason. He wasn't blind enough to miss the way her eyes bore into his, waiting for him to give her the chance to share her side of the story.

He sighed and gestured to the bed across from him for her to take a seat. "I'm listening."

Brandi walked over to the other bed and took a seat. The room wasn't big and their knees almost touched as she sat down across from him.

Almost.

She could feel the heat radiating off of him. Whether that was because of his new blessing or because being close to him never ceased to make her heart race, she couldn't tell exactly. His dark skin, muscled arms, thick lips and deep brown eyes were always the distraction that was her undoing. Either way, she felt every bit of the distance between them. Instead of closing it like she wanted to, though, she pulled her bare feet up on the bed and crossed her legs, growing the distance between them.

"I couldn't tell you because the vessels of gods aren't allowed to tell people who don't already know who we are."

"That makes no sense," Jack said.

"I don't make the rules," Brandi shot back. "But I've tested it," she admitted. "I've tried to tell you so many times. But the closest I've ever managed to admit to anyone is telling them that I'm a god. And that only made me sound like I had the arrogance of Rothe. Besides," she paused and shook her head, "that isn't even true."

"What are you talking about? You literally have Freya's soul. That makes you the goddess," Jack said.

"We aren't the same like that," she told him. "She has her own thoughts and feelings, and I have mine. We are similar in a lot of ways and her soul is part of mine," she admitted relishing the feeling of finally being able to tell him the truth. "But she's still separate from me. You saw it for yourself," she pointed out.

"I definitely saw something," Jack said, pulling a hand through his short locs. "What even was that?"

"That was the gods' realm," Brandi told him. "Anything is possible there." She waved her hand at him. "I mean, you met Rothe. And Freya. And then Rothe gave you a second blessing."

"Yeah, but…" he shook his head again, letting his rebuttal fall. The room was silent as Brandi waited for him to process everything. She knew it was a lot. It had been a lot for her the first time, too. She could only imagine what it must feel like to have the person she'd always loved and believed she knew better than herself, be someone completely different.

"How long have you known?"

"Since I was five," Brandi told him. "Freya's been a part of me since the day I was born, but when my parents were sent to the gods, she made herself known to me. Protected me with her shaders. That's how I met Tiki."

"And how long have you been able to just... visit the god realm whenever you want?" Jack huffed out a puff of air, not quite believing his own words and what he'd witnessed. "Because if you had a direct line to them like that, I can think of a few times that would've been useful."

Brandi narrowed her eyes at Jack.

"I get that you're pissed off," she said, "but you need to tread carefully."

"Or what?" He snapped, jumping to his feet. "You'll call Rothe down here to deliver some divine punishment?"

"Is that what you think I'd do?"

Her voice was soft, but her eyes never left his. Her chest tightened at the thought that all the anger in the eyes looking back at her were the same eyes that had looked at her like she held the entire realm in her palms. And just thinking that she might never see them look at her that way again made her want to bolt from the room. She couldn't stand to see Jack looking at her as if she had just cheated him of the most important thing in his life.

"I don't know," he said, breaking away from her green gaze to pace the floor. "You watched me pray to Rothe every day but never mentioned that you'd already met him in the divine realm. Multiple times."

"And what if I had?"

"What?" Jack asked, pausing his pacing to look at her.

"What if I had?" Brandi repeated. "What if I'd told you the day I'd met you that I was Freya incarnated? That her soul was mine, and that

I had powers no one person should be able to wield? That they'd taken me to their realm as a child and I'd walked through the endless fields of Freya's garden? Would you have believed me if I told you I'd listened to Rothe and Asari argue in her gazebo while Lindl read me stories and Freya braided my hair? That I had been uniquely blessed by each of them by the time I was ten?" She shook her head. "You didn't even want to believe the queen, a mortal being, wanted you to be one of her shadows. How were you going to react if I'd told you I had a pet shader waiting for me just outside the barrier, and had been raised by them in Freya's temple until I was taken in by the people who sent my parents to the gods? That, since the time I was seven, I had been raised to be nothing more than a weapon of the queendom? Hm?" She raised her eyebrows again and looked at him with daggers in her eyes. "What would you have done with that information, Jack?"

Brandi did her best to remain calm, but her voice still rose with her frustration. He was acting as if she'd crafted this situation with the intention of deceiving him — as if she'd withheld information from him for no other reason than to keep something from him. She shook her head at him and shrugged.

"If I'd told you all of that when you were thirteen — or fourteen, or eighteen, or twenty — when would you have believed me?" She scoffed. "You didn't even want to believe me four days ago when Tiki was right in front of us."

When he didn't answer right away, they stared at each other. He wanted to say that he would have believed her right away, but they both knew that would have been an unbelievable lie. Even now, had he not

181

met Tiki and ridden on the back of the shader himself — had he not met Rothe and received his gift of knowledge, he wouldn't have believed her now. Her words sounded like they were flowing out the mouth of someone who had lost their mind long ago and had no respect for the gods — a blasphemer of the worst degree.

But her words were true. She was the goddess incarnated and had been raised in Freya's temple by shaders. She'd been taken in by the queendom to become a shadow because that is what the gods had planned for her before she was ever born. It didn't matter to them that it was her — it only mattered that she was compatible with Freya's soul.

She was just as much a victim of their whims as he was.

"So," she said, her voice still soft, "what would you have had me do?" She swiped at her eyes, the pain in her chest excruciating as the thought of Jack not loving her anymore, now that he knew the truth, forced its way into her mind. "I wanted to tell you so many times, but Freya wouldn't let me. Only the gods can reveal their vessels to mortals. And despite what you may think, I am not one of them," she said, taking a shaky breath. "I took you to see Rothe because I didn't want to hide this from you anymore. But if you can't forgive me for keeping this from you, then…" she shrugged.

There was nothing she could do. Her options had been exhausted. She'd told him the entirety of her truth. All she could do now was hope that it was enough.

Jack pinched the bridge of his nose between his fingers, took a deep breath, and stood still. He prayed to Rothe for the patience to deal with her before he opened his brown eyes to meet her gaze again. A softness returned to them, though the anger in his face hadn't left yet.

"It's not that I can't forgive you, Bee," he finally said. "This is just a lot to process. I get that you couldn't tell me, I do," he shrugged, "but it still makes me feel like I've been lied to this whole time. I mean, I thought I knew you better than anyone." He shook his head, his jaw tightened. "Turns out some Asarian girl and Noble knew you better than I ever could."

"Noble? What's he got to do with this?"

"Are you trying to tell me you didn't know he's Carna's vessel?"

Brandi's green eyes grew wide. "No," she whispered. "I didn't."

"Well, now you do," Jack huffed, taking a seat back on his bed. "And if I can tell you that, apparently mortals can tell others if they know," he barked out a laugh. "Now, there's a loophole for you."

"It doesn't matter," Brandi said, placing her feet on the floor and leaning forward until their knees touched this time. "Noble and Sarah aren't you. And you do know me better than anyone else."

"How can you say that when they knew who you were, and I didn't?"

"They knew about my connection to Freya," she said firmly. "They didn't know me. They don't," she emphasized, "know me the way you do." She reached up and held his face in her hands. "I never want them to know me the way that you do."

Jack sighed before letting a smirk slide across his face. "Definitely not Noble."

Brandi laughed. "Yeah, no. Definitely not him."

The room fell silent as they locked eyes with each other, a million silent words and emotions flowing between them. Jack sighed and reached out for Brandi, and she went to him. He cradled her in his lap and nuzzled his face into the soft warmth of her neck. His grip on her was tight, but she didn't mind it. She just closed her eyes and let herself feel safe, the way she always did whenever he wrapped his arms around her.

"You remember what I told you? Back when you first told me you loved me?"

"You're mine," Brandi said, a smile pulling at her lips as she repeated his words.

He nodded his head and placed a kiss at the base of her throat, sliding his hands under her shirt to place them against the bare skin of her waist. "Go lock the door," he said, easing her off his lap, "so I can make sure you don't forget that."

Sarah froze in her tracks, her blue eyes wide as she approached the door to the room.

She'd been gone for over an hour and had done her best to ignore the side glances she received from the other guests when she'd taken up residence in the lobby after storming out of the room. But she'd huffed out without grabbing a change of clothes from her bag or even a pair of shoes. She looked so much like a homeless hitchhiker, she couldn't even form a proper rebuttal when the youngest host of the inn — Carson — had suggested she return to her room to become presentable before joining the other diners for breakfast. She'd come back, ready to demand entry to at least get a pair of shoes and what she needed to take care of her hair, but all the fire in her spirit left when she heard the sounds drifting through the door.

"Woah," she whispered under her breath, backing away from the door as if it could burst into flames at any second.

She glanced down both ends of the narrow hallway, unsure of whether she wanted to be sure no one saw her, or if she wanted someone to confirm that they heard the same things she did. When she saw no one, though, she turned her attention back to the door. She knew that she should leave — that eavesdropping on Jack and Brandi was the worst decision she could ever make, especially if she got caught — but her muscles were beyond her control. She was stunned that Brandi — the girl who had crushed the skull of someone she knew beneath her boot without a second thought — could sound so soft and agreeable. More than that, Sarah couldn't believe that there was anyone in all of the mortal realm who could make her sound that way.

What she heard now painted a very different picture of the two people inside that clashed with the reality she'd already come to expect from them.

Part of her was pissed that she had been right about their reason for forcing her out of the room, but another part of her was curious. She wasn't innocent enough to be ignorant as to what happened behind closed doors — she'd spent plenty of her own time behind them with Kyle. But she'd never heard — or made — the kind of sounds she heard now. Her face flushed a darker shade of pink with each passing second as she listened to them and she wondered what it would be like to have someone be as forceful and possessive over her as Jack clearly was with Brandi.

"I wouldn't have guessed you'd be into this type of thing."

Sarah jumped out of her skin and tasted blood in her mouth as her teeth caught her tongue between them in surprise. She winced and turned around to meet the gaze of the handsome stranger she'd met the other night.

"I…" she started, shaking her head, ready to deny everything his dark eyes seemed to be accusing her of. "I just—" she glanced at the door again, breaking away from his scrutiny. "My shoes," she forced out, gesturing to her feet. "I came back for them. I wasn't—"

He chuckled under his breath as he leaned against the wall next to her. His pink lips were pulled into a knowing smirk as he watched her stumble over her words. He took his time looking her up and down, and she ached for her hairbrush, a fresh change of clothes, and a hot shower. Sarah had no doubts that she looked every part of the mess she felt like. And under normal circumstances, that wouldn't bother her — she'd never been the type who needed validation from anyone, let alone the lustful eyes of a man who knew nothing about her. But there was something about the dark gaze in front of her — the way he watched her — that made her want him to find her attractive. She couldn't keep her eyes from roving over him and appreciating the way his sandy brown skin seemed to glow under the gentle lights in the hallway and the way his lean muscles fit snugly under his dark blue sweater as he shoved his hands into the pockets of his black jeans.

He was just standing there and it made her heart pound in places it shouldn't, letting her know that she definitely enjoyed looking at him.

Despite her best efforts not to, she tried to pull a hand through her tangled hair. It was a silly decision because she was forced to give up on the effort a few seconds later when her fingers caught on several knots. So, instead, she pulled both her hands behind her back to keep them from giving away her nervousness any further. She studied the blood-red rug that ran the length of the hallway for a moment, and she took a deep breath before forcing her blue eyes up to meet his.

"I didn't catch your name the other night when you helped us bring Jack in," she said, trying to sound calm and in control of the situation despite the fact that the sounds inside were getting louder and she was doing her best to pretend she didn't hear them.

"That's because I didn't give it to you," he said. "But I will if you ask me for it properly."

His words sounded as if they carried another meaning behind them and Sarah felt her ears burn as she tried to keep her thoughts of him as pure as she could, but she was failing miserably. Her eyes darted around the hallway, searching for something harmless to focus on so she could avoid undressing him with her eyes. It wasn't an easy task, though. He was almost as handsome as Asari himself and he watched her like he knew the effect he had on her — the effect he probably had on anyone with at least half a working eyeball.

She clenched her fists behind her back and shrugged at him, trying to remain nonchalant. "I don't really care if you don't tell me."

"You don't?" He chuckled. "How about you tell me your name

instead?"

"Do you really want to know?"

He laughed then — actually laughed, and Sarah's face grew pink for an entirely new reason. He had the most addictive laughter she'd ever heard. It was rich and deep as it echoed down the hall. It sent jitters through her stomach and made her want to keep him laughing. He calmed down and smiled at her, a glint in his eye that hadn't been there before.

"I do now," he said. "What's your name?"

"Sarah," she relented. "And yours?"

"Never said I would give you mine," he said, winking at her as he pushed off the wall to walk by her.

Her mouth fell open, and she narrowed her eyes at him. "That's hardly polite. Or fair."

"Did I give you the impression I was either of those things?"

She sighed. "I'm clearly a fool for assuming you would be."

He laughed again and draped an arm around her shoulders to lead her away from the door they'd been standing in front of. She didn't protest, but her face turned as pink as the wildflowers that grew in Carna's western domain. He leaned into her as they neared the stairs.

"I'll let you in on a little secret," he whispered into her ear, biting back another chuckle as her face went from pink to red. "They're going to be a while, so I suggest you find something better to do. Perhaps with me?"

She barked out a laugh and shoved him away from her, causing his eyebrows to shoot up. He'd seen plenty of people — men, women, and everything in between — melt at just the idea of him being that close to them. He'd encountered a few who liked to play at being immune to his charms, but it was all a game. They'd pretend they didn't want him in their bed and he'd pretend he'd still be there in the morning. But this was the first time he'd been pushed away from a girl he could see was seconds away from becoming an indecent puddle in the middle of the hallway.

"You misunderstand me completely," Sarah huffed, trying to hear herself over the blood rushing in her ears, "if you think I'd simply walk off with someone I don't know to do gods know what."

"And what did you think I was implying?"

"I honestly don't care to guess," Sarah shot back at him.

He grinned and held out a hand to her. The first genuine gesture she'd seen him offer her.

"My apologies. I went too far with my teasing. In truth, my offer was only to escort you to breakfast downstairs. On my honor, I promise I meant to imply nothing more than that." He glanced over her appearance and smirked. "And I can procure you some shoes. Since that is what you came back for, after all."

"And your name," Sarah prodded, deciding not to ask how he would get them for her as she reached out to shake the hand he offered her.

He grinned. "It's Noble."

CHAPTER ELEVEN

The sky does not trust the moon, so it keeps it close — away from its horizon.

— Boundless: An Introduction to Carna's Realm | Lindl's Fourth Holy Academy

ASARI'S DOMAIN — PRESENT DAY

Sarah followed Noble down the stairs to the dining area after he delivered on his promise of procuring her not only a new pair of shoes but a complete change of clothes. Now that she was freshly showered, dressed in a knee-length wool dress the same color as her eyes, with her hair properly brushed and braided down her back, and her feet snug in a warm pair of cream-colored ankle boots, she felt much more confident walking into the dining room.

She turned a few heads as she followed Noble outside to the deck, but he broke necks as every eye turned to watch him as he moved through the room. She couldn't blame them, though. There was something about him that was mesmerizing, transfixing anyone who crossed his path and making them want to have their presence acknowledged by him. Even the waiters lost the natural rhythm of their movements as he passed by them. Sarah could almost feel her skin catch fire as Noble pressed his palm into the small of her back to guide her toward the seats that would give them the most privacy.

She stole a glance at his handsome face as he led the way and almost wished he hadn't made such a show of being kind to her. Almost. But she couldn't deny that there was some pleasure in the twisted sense of superiority that snaked through her as he pulled out her chair. The same people who had recommended she excuse herself from their company only an hour earlier now stewed in jealous spite as they watched Noble treat her with the utmost respect.

The day was warm for Asari's domain and the double doors to the deck were opened wide to let in the drifting breeze, but she and Noble were the only ones who'd taken a seat at one of the wrought-iron tables. They were surrounded by giant evergreens that seemed to dominate the sky. Sarah sat facing Noble and the woodlands beyond the inn, but she could feel the unrelenting gazes from inside boring into her back. It made her want to run back inside and have her meal somewhere she felt safe, where she'd neither be seen nor overheard. But that wasn't an option available to her, so she rolled her shoulders back and straightened her spine. She refused to buckle under the weight of their stares, and eyed Noble as he leaned back in his seat, seeming to not a have a single care in the world.

A waiter appeared by their side in no time at all. He was tall and lanky, like his arms were too long for his body and the breeze would knock him over without much effort, but he still managed to set their table with an ease that contradicted any idea he was frail and ungraceful. He wore his curly, brown hair short with the right side shaved close to his scalp, giving Sarah a clear display of all his piercings. There were dark blue studs going through both of his dimpled cheeks and through the center of his bottom lip, right above his chin. He wore a ring going through the septum of his nose and had two more in his right eyebrow. But it was his blue eyes that Sarah found hard to look away from him.

"Welcome to Carol's Inn," he greeted them, offering them a gentle smile and pulling two menus out from beneath his arm. "I'm Carol's fifth son and my name is Asta. I'll be taking care of you this morning. May I start you off with something warm to drink?"

Sarah glanced over the menu, scouring it for the cheapest thing and doing her best to keep her eyes from growing wide at the double digit numbers that accompanied every item. She had the coins on hand to get whatever she wanted, but the problem remained that what she had was finite. She'd saved up plenty working as a medic in the outskirts, people had come from several fragments over to have her treat them, but given her current circumstances, she didn't know when she'd have the opportunity to work again. So, she wasn't big on the idea of burning through the bulk of her stash before she had a plan to replenish it. Now that the queen's shadows had found her, she had no idea how long she'd be running from them or if she'd ever be able to stop.

She gave her head a quick shake, trying to dislodge the unsettling thoughts that had crept into her mind. When she glanced up to see both men waiting for her to place her order with questioning looks on their faces, a blush crept up her neck and she forced a smile while handing the menu back to Asta.

"I'll just have water," she said. "I'll decide a bit later if I want something to eat."

"As you wish," he said with a nod, "and you?" He asked, turning to Noble with a flirtier smile. "Can I get you anything?"

Noble gave him a once over and smirked. "Depends," he said, "what do you recommend?"

"Our apple cider is the best," he suggested, moving closer to Noble to point it out on the menu and letting the long side of his hair fall forward. "It's hot and sweet."

It could've been Sarah's imagination, or her temper flaring, but Asta's words seemed to carry a double meaning to them. And the way he angled his body closer to Noble and used his hair as a curtain to block Sarah's view of his face made her feel slighted. And even though she knew having breakfast with Noble was nowhere close to what anyone would consider a date, the blatant disrespect for her presence was enough to make her roll her eyes.

"That does sound tempting. Maybe I'll try some later when I have the time to really enjoy it," he said, winking at Asta before turning his attention back towards Sarah and choking back a laugh at her poor attempts to hide her irritation. "But for now, we'll both have water and whatever today's special is," he said, handing his menu back to Asta. "Just add everything to my tab."

"Of course," Asta said again, a satisfied grin on his face as he straightened away from the table. "I'll be back shortly."

"Thank you. And Asta," Noble said, catching the waiter's attention before he got too far away, "if you wouldn't mind closing the door behind you. We'd like a bit of privacy."

Asta's blue eyes darted between them before he dropped his gaze and gave them a slight nod. "Of course."

He left them on the deck and closed the doors behind him, but it felt like the staring became more blatant behind her once he did, and Sarah felt as if she'd been placed in a glass case on display. It put her on edge to have so many eyes on her at once. Fragment 42913 was tiny. The occupancy of the inn alone could rival the entire population of where she'd spent most of her life, and she was uncomfortable with so many strangers watching her. She hadn't realized how accustomed she'd grown to being isolated and ignored by the people around her.

She brushed her hand along her arm before locking her gaze onto Noble's. Focusing on him was easier than allowing her thoughts to run wild, but he wasn't much better than the strangers inside. He stared openly at her too, but with him, she felt bold enough to return the gesture and didn't shy away from his dark eyes. He was relaxed in his seat, both his arms spread along the back of the wooden bench that lined the far edge of the deck. He looked comfortable under everyone's gaze, like this was his show, and they'd come just for a chance to see him. She scoffed under her breath at the thought, and he raised his eyebrows at her.

"Something wrong?"

"Not at all," Sarah lied, looking around at the trees clustered together and surrounding the inn. "I was just curious as to what would make you bring me out here."

"Maybe I just thought you were cute and wanted to treat you to breakfast?"

Sarah's face flushed at the casual compliment, but she rolled her eyes anyway. "Somehow, I doubt your motives are that simple."

Noble chuckled. "What? You think I'm above romancing someone I find attractive?"

"With the options you clearly have available to you," Sarah said, giving a half-hearted wave towards the myriad of people inside who were devouring him with their eyes over their meals, "I don't see why you would bother 'romancing' anyone," she scoffed. "Let alone someone like me."

"And what's that supposed to mean?" Noble asked, raising one silver-haired eyebrow. "Is there some reason I shouldn't be attracted to you?"

"I've been told my looks are disturbing," she said. "The blonde hair of Rothe and blue eyes of Asari tend to frighten most people away."

"And do I look like 'most people' to you?"

Sarah studied him and his casual demeanor as he spoke to her. It was true that he hadn't once backed away from her, avoided her gaze, or done anything to suggest that he found her features to be unnatural. Her lips gave a soft quirk upwards as she sat back in her seat, giving Asta room to place their drinks and meal.

"No," she said, placing the napkin from the table over her lap. "You don't," she admitted. She hadn't realized she'd been inching toward him the entire time until Asta set the steaming plates in front of them. There were two bowls of sweet potato hash mixed with spinach, chickpeas, and bell peppers with two poached eggs on top. It smelled delightful and Sarah had to remind herself that she was in the presence of polite company as she resisted the urge to start eating right away, but she could do nothing to stop her stomach from growling.

Asta grinned at her. "You two are lucky. My mother is working the kitchen this morning and made this special for you two." He turned his gaze towards Sarah and smirked. "Delicious food and company. What's it like to be Asari's favorite?"

"You tell me," Sarah quipped. "He's shown favor on you too, hasn't he?"

"I wouldn't say that, but I'm sure hoping he shows me some favor when I get off," Asta said, lowering his voice as he glanced over to Noble. "But," he said, his enthusiasm returning, "I hope you enjoy your food. Is there anything else I can get you?"

"No, we're fine," Noble said.

"Excellent. I'll be back to check on you, so if you do need anything, let me know then."

Asta disappeared and Sarah wasted no time digging into her food once they were alone. They ate in silence and Sarah struggled to keep herself from groaning at how amazing everything tasted. The food was the perfect match of salty and sweet, every bite more satisfying than the last. When her plate was clear, she began sipping on her water. When she chanced a glance up at Noble, she found that he had set his emptied bowl aside as well and returned to the same leisurely position he was in before, but his eyes focused on something in the distance.

"So," Sarah said, ready to have a real conversation with him, "are we going to continue beating around this bush, or are you going to tell me what it is you actually want from me?"

"You're assuming I want something," Noble said, shaking his head. "I'm being nice to you because I enjoy looking at you and because I find you interesting," he said with a shrug. "My motives are purely selfish ones driven by my basest desires. But I've made that known already, and it seems like you're looking for a different answer."

"It's too simple," she said. "If that were the only reason, wouldn't you be doing your best to convince me back to your room with you right now?"

"Depends," he said, turning his focus back to her. "Would you be willing to go with me?"

"I'm not inclined to at the moment," Sarah said flatly.

"I didn't think so," he said with a light laugh. "So, why waste my time trying to convince you to do something you have no interest in?"

"If you knew that, your actions make even less sense than they did before."

"Why are you stuck on this?" He asked, his eyebrows pulling together. "Is it so rare an experience for someone to be kind to you?"

"Yes," Sarah shot back. "It is. And I know expectations generally accompany unwarranted behaviors. So," she said, setting her cup back on the table and forcing a smile onto her face, "I'd appreciate it if you'd be straightforward with me. What do you want?"

He studied her for a moment before laughing again and straightening in his seat. She could tell that he'd thought she'd be simple to charm. From the way Asta had reacted to him, it seemed like every person who found themselves alone with him was, so it made sense. Even the suggestion of his undivided attention was enough to make her want to tell him any and everything he wanted to hear.

But she knew better than do something like that.

She was not the kind of person that people were kind to. Knowing that about herself meant her survival instincts had to be sharp, and he gave her the feeling of someone who wasn't kind to others unless he was getting something out of it. Everything about her conversation with him put her on edge, if only because showing her any level of attention triggered all of her warning signals and she distrusted anyone who would approach her without reason.

He placed both hands on the table, lacing his long fingers together before locking his eyes onto her. An amused smile played at his lips and his demeanor shifted as he seemed to abandon any plan that included seducing her secrets away from her. He leaned forward and smiled at her, a gesture that felt genuine like the handshake he'd offered her in the hallway.

"I was telling the truth earlier," he admitted. "I do find you enjoyable to look at, and I am the kind of man who indulges himself in simple pleasures. But, I'm also here because I've been informed that you've been hanging around Brandi," he narrowed his eyes slightly, "my Brandi," he emphasized, "and I don't like that."

"Hanging around?" Sarah scoffed, her mind wondering how he would have gotten that information in the first place. "If you think I'd be here with her without proper motivation, you're mistaken."

"Am I?"

"Yes," Sarah nodded.

"Then why are you still with her?"

"I don't see how my interactions with her would be any concern of yours."

Sarah studied the man in front of her with narrowed eyes. The air around them shifted from something light, even flirty, to something much heavier. Something dangerous. It was the same feeling that had colored the background of her entire life and kept her mindful of why she kept a backpack ready to go at all times. She never knew when she'd need to run again.

"You'd be surprised," Noble shrugged. "Everything Brandi does is a concern of mine."

Sarah quirked her eyebrows upward in surprise at the declaration in his tone. The look in his dark eyes made it clear that he understood the weight those words carried and he meant them. Whatever Brandi was to him, it surpassed everything anyone else could ever possibly be to him. And Sarah tried to make sense of the rivaling emotions of jealousy, surprise, curiosity, and apprehension that roiled inside of her. She'd never met anyone who could be so bold in staking a claim on another person — especially when they both knew the person in question was tangled up in the arms of someone else as they spoke. She searched Noble's face for any sign that he might be hiding the truth as she asked her next question.

"Are you in love with her or something?"

Noble frowned. "That's a disgusting suggestion."

Sarah shook her head, unable to keep up with the conversation while battling her own mind. Relief washed through her that he had no romantic interest in Brandi — and she had no intentions of dissecting that feeling anytime soon — but she was still confused by his earlier words. If it wasn't romantic or sexual attraction he felt for her, then what could possess him to go so far as to track her down in the outskirts of Asari's domain just to find out who she was traveling with?

"If you're not, then how can you sit there and claim that she's every concern of yours?"

"She's my responsibility. I look after her," he said. "So, when she decides to defy the queendom to protect some Asarian girl, I have questions."

"You honestly think she would reject the queendom for me? That's insane."

"It's a rare thing for the truth to make sense with her," he said. "But facts don't change under an unfavorable judgment. She left to protect you."

"If you know that," Sarah questioned, leaning forward, "then what issue could you possibly have with me for being with her?"

"I don't know you," Noble said. "And your existence has already proven to be problematic for multiple reasons. So, I want to know why it was you she drew the line at and why it's you who's traveling with her now."

"I would have never guessed she had a keeper telling her who she could spend time with."

Noble laughed. "I may be her keeper, but I can't stop her from doing what she wants. You, on the other hand," he said, lowering his voice and every ounce of amusement slipping from his face, "I can stop you without issue. So, answer the question. Why are you with Brandi?"

Sarah studied his face and decided to be honest with him.

"Where else would I go? I have no home to return to and the place I've lived since childhood just gave me a not-so-subtle boot to the back." Sarah shrugged. "I'm here because she offered to let me come with her."

"Why would she do that?"

"Your guess is as good as mine, Keeper."

"So, you have no idea?"

Sarah searched his face but kept hers still — a skill she'd mastered through years of verbal abuse and living as an outcast in fragment 42913.

"None," she lied. "Do you?"

"Why would you accept her offer, then?" Noble asked, ignoring Sarah's question. "If you don't even know why she would offer to keep you safe, why would you believe her?"

Before she could answer, two swift knocks came from the other side of the door, separating them from the dining room. Jack stood there, in a fresh pair of clothes with his short locs retwisted and tied back from his face. Both Sarah and Noble had their attention jerked over to him, but instead of stepping outside to meet them, he pointed to the stairs, no doubt indicating that their presence was required elsewhere. Sarah gave an awkward wave and a nod to acknowledge the request and Jack returned the nod before turning and striding back through the dining room.

Sarah's blue gaze shifted back to Noble and she offered him a soft smile. People like him didn't know what it was like to live a life like hers — outcasted, ignored, and ridiculed, with no way to protect herself other than to rely on the strength of others. It was a frustrating existence that few understood unless they had lived it for themselves. But he had his

WE ARE THE ORIGIN

own strength and could therefore live by his own rules, move through
the world with a confidence that she wasn't allowed to have. He wouldn't
understand it any more than Jack or Brandi would. And explaining it to
him in hopes of any sort of empathy would be a wasted effort.

She wasn't part of their world, and they weren't part of hers. The
rules they governed themselves by were different on fundamental levels.

"You've met me," Sarah said, with a slight shrug of her shoulders.
"I'm not especially talented at anything, and I don't have the skills needed
to survive on my own. Brandi does." She searched his face for a glimmer
of sympathy or a shred of understanding. "So, when it was requested I
depart from the fragment I'd been living in, and she agreed to help me,
what do you think I should've done? Ignored her offer and seen how I
fared on my own?"

"It was an option," Noble shrugged.

Sarah laughed.

"You've clearly never been weak or you would understand that's
not how we survive. When you're hungry," she said, standing from the
table, "you don't bite the hand trying to feed you. Now, you have my
apologies if this current arrangement makes you uncomfortable, but," she
shrugged, "I have no intentions of starving."

CHAPTER TWELVE

*As different as they may be themselves, the gods love all the children born
of Freya and watch over them with care — whether the mortals want to be
seen by them or not.*

— Adage of the Gods | Lindl's Five Holy Academies Compilation

ASARI'S DOMAIN — PRESENT DAY

When Sarah made it back up the stairs and to the room, the door was
open, along with the little window situated between the two beds.

Jack and Brandi stood by the door and out of the way while Carol's
oldest daughter, Cara, moved about the room, changing sheets and
replacing the linen. She didn't spare much attention to Sarah as she
walked in at first, nothing beyond a quick upward flick of her eyes. But
she did a double take when she noticed Sarah wearing the outfit she'd

abandoned in a guest's room last night and her face flushed a crimson red.

She didn't say anything though, only bit her tongue, averted her eyes, and finished her tasks with an efficiency that made it clear she'd done them a hundred times over and could do them in her sleep. In just a few moments, the room was back in perfect condition, with fresh sheets on the beds, clean towels on top of the dressers, and a light lemony scent in the air. Cara mumbled a simple nicety as she tried to exit the room, but before she could make her swift escape, Noble came strolling in with a grin on his face, blocking the door.

"I see you two are finally ready for decent company," he joked as he leaned against the opened doorframe.

"What are you doing here?" Jack asked, with raised eyebrows.

"Green is here," Noble said, shrugging. "Where else would I be?"

Jack stared at Noble for a brief moment before shooting a glance over to Brandi with a raised eyebrow and she sighed.

"He tracked us down on the way here," Brandi explained. "You were unconscious when he showed up, but apparently Sal tipped him off on where to find us."

"Wasn't too hard," Noble admitted. "Asarians tend to remember the buff Rothian traveling with a girl who has green eyes."

"You know I would've been fine," Brandi said, moving toward the beds once Cara finished her tasks "I was with Jack."

"And that is what worries me," Noble said, shaking his head. "You expect me to leave my precious little sister in his care?"

Jack glared at Noble, but before he could say anything to defend himself, Noble's attention fell on the housekeeper. She was trying to make a discreet exit by squeezing past him with a large trolley of dirty laundry on squeaky wheels, and a sly grin crept across his face.

"Hey, Cara."

She glanced up at him, her face flushing all over again, and nodded. Cara didn't speak as she finally moved past him and hurried off to the next room, and it wasn't lost on Sarah how Noble watched her go. She'd thought their server at breakfast had been an anomaly — someone he would have been interested in had she not been there — but what she witnessed now was beginning to paint a clearer picture of who Noble was. But she refused to give him any more space in her mind, despite the jealousy and irritation that flared to life at his attention being on someone else. Whether she liked the totality of who he was or not, it was of no consequence to either of them. Her heart could make up whatever irrational emotions it wanted for him — it changed nothing.

So, she directed her attention to Jack and Brandi, who had moved the small nightstand that had been sitting under the window to the center of the floor between the two beds. Brandi took a seat on their bed next to Jack as he spread out a thin sheet of paper on it.

"If you plan to be part of this conversation, I suggest you come sit down," Brandi stated.

Sarah moved to the far side of her own bed to take a seat, leaving plenty of room for Noble to take one beside her once he'd closed the door. The scent of rain wafted in from the open window, overtaking the gentle smell of lemon Cara had left behind in the room. Brandi's green eyes darted to the window before refocusing on the sheet of paper in front of them.

Sarah followed her gaze and her blue eyes grew wide as she stared at the map in front of them. She lifted her in disbelief to search the faces of everyone else, but they were unfazed.

Most maps were created for people within a specific domain and didn't contain information for anything that existed outside of the barrier because it wasn't a necessary thing to know for common folks. So, every map she'd ever seen had only been for Asari's domain. Her mother had told her stories of Rothe's domain and the royal tower that stood in the center of his inner ring, reaching high enough into the sky that the top floors were hidden beyond the clouds. That was the extent of her knowledge beyond Asari's domain, though.

She'd never spent much time imagining what Carna or Lindl's domains would be like — and looking at the map, she began to understand just how small her view of the realm had been. She studied it, trying to commit every detail of the map to her memory.

Freya's domain was the smallest and in the heart of the map — the direct center of the entire realm and it wasn't divided into districts and fragments like the rest. Only the capital existed where her temple was, and her lands connected to every other domain. It was Carna's domain that Sarah found fascinating, though. Rothe, Lindl, and Asari all had barriers around their domains, but they didn't overlap because Carna's domain cut between each of theirs. Instead of one extensive area like the others, his domain was split into three. There was a western domain between Rothe and Lindl's, an eastern domain between Rothe and Asari's — the one Brandi and Jack had crossed through to reach the Asarna mountains and her little fragment in the outskirts — and a southern domain that existed between Lindl and Asari's.

Seeing her world put into perspective shook the foundation of everything she thought she'd known about the realm. Knowing there were other domains, and seeing them laid out for her, were different things and it made her hungry for more information. She wanted to know everything she'd never known about the realm. She looked at the others with shocked excitement in her eyes and realized with startling clarity that they didn't have to imagine what the realm outside of the barriers was like — they'd already seen it for themselves.

She knew Brandi was from Freya's domain already, and that they'd come from Rothe's. And with his silver hair and dark eyes, Noble couldn't disguise the fact he was a child of Carna. She'd known those facts, but now, seeing that not only were they unfazed by a map of the entire realm, but treated it as if it were nothing special, she wondered what other information they'd had access to as part of the queen's shadows. She was overtaken by the urge to see the queen's tower. She wanted to see for herself all the things she'd never imagined before and immerse herself in all the knowledge she should have been entitled to. Her mind began racing through all the possibilities of what her life could have been like had she not been denied her birthright and an anger she'd never experienced bloomed inside of her. For the first time in her life, she resented Queen Leia with her whole being. But her attention was drawn from her own emotions to Brandi's slender finger, pointing to another destination on the map.

"We're here," Brandi said, pointing to fragment 43205, "and we need to get over here," she said, moving her finger west, "to Lindl's domain."

"So, we're leaving Asari's domain?"

"Did you think we'd stay at this inn forever?" Noble asked. "Of course we're leaving."

"That's not what I meant," Sarah snapped, turning her attention to Brandi. "I just never considered it," she admitted, her excitement over seeing the map waning in light of the apprehension that came with traveling to another domain. "I've never been outside the barrier."

"What shocking information that is," Noble teased.

Sarah rolled her eyes, her mind too focused on what it meant to be leaving Asari's domain to snap back at him, and Brandi shot him a glare that forced him to shut his mouth and avert his eyes from hers. Noble didn't appear to take many things — or people — seriously. But he seemed to take Brandi at face value, and Sarah could understand that. Brandi wasn't the type of person who would be persuaded by his manipulative tactics and she'd be more than willing to ignore anyone who managed to piss her off. Being on her bad side wasn't something she would wish on anyone. So, when Noble chanced a glance back in Brandi's direction and saw her still glaring, he held up his hands in surrender. When he did, Jack turned his attention to Sarah and tried to be patient as he explained things to her.

"We've already been in Asari's domain for nearly a week. We stay any longer and the shadows looking for you will catch up to us. We bought some time by having Sal feed them some false information back in fragment 42913, but they'll see through it eventually and we'll lose any lead time we have."

"But why Lindl's domain?"

"Oh, I'm sorry," Brandi quipped. "Was there some other domain you'd rather go to? Maybe Rothe's where the queen and her shadows live? Or perhaps one where there's no barrier?"

"I see your point," Sarah murmured.

"I agreed to keep you alive, so let me do what I said I would. We don't have a lot of time," she said, pointing to the map again as the breeze blew through, billowing the sheer deep red and bringing another powerful scent of rain with it. "We need to get here, to fragment 20311. I have a few contacts there I need to meet up with."

"In person?" Noble asked, his eyes narrowed. "That's unlike you, Green. Why not have them send you whatever information you need like normal?"

"I'm not connected to the EREN anymore. But even if I was," Brandi emphasized, "I'd still go. I don't want big sister knowing I'm in contact with this person."

"Then let's head here," he said, sliding his finger over to fragment 30303 in Carna's domain. "I know a girl who would be willing to help us."

"Us? Are you coming too?"

Noble barked out a laugh. "You know good and well that Carna would become a militant god before I let you out of my sights again."

"Then that'll help us out," Brandi nodded, glancing out the window at the darkening clouds. "We'll exit Asari's domain here," she said pointing to fragment 43206, just south of the inn, "cross over into Carna's domain here," she said, sliding her finger west and pointing to fragment 30305, "head north until we meet your people," she said directing her words to Noble who nodded, "and then cross over into Lindl's domain here," she finished, pointing even further west to fragment 21121. "It'll take three days total to get where we're going if we leave now."

"Wait," Sarah interjected, pointing to the map herself. "Why are we going south in Asari's domain just to head north again once we enter Carna's domain? Why don't we just cross here and save ourselves some time?"

"You can only cross through the barrier at certain points," Noble explained.

"But how do you know where the points are?"

"How do you know where a bridge is to cross a river?" Noble shrugged. "You just have to find it."

"Or," Brandi interjected, "you make one. But making a pathway through a barrier takes time. Years. And we don't have that. So, we're heading south, where one already exists."

"Right now?" Sarah asked, looking out the window at the dark clouds rolling towards them in ominous waves. "You realize that the rains are about to begin?"

"Exactly why we can't wait around," Brandi said, refolding the map along its creases and sliding it into one of the many pockets on her cargo pants. "Before we go, though, we need to make some things known."

"Like what?" Sarah asked.

Brandi turned to look at Jack, who leaned forward.

"So, apparently there are rules keeping y'all from telling each other, but there are none stopping me," he said. "All of you are vessels of the gods," Jack said, looking at Noble, whose eyes darted to Sarah as she turned to look at him. "You already know Brandi is the incarnation of

Freya. Sarah's the vessel of Asari, and Noble," he said, turning to Sarah, "is the vessel of Carna."

"That explains a lot," Noble said, looking at Sarah.

"Hm," Sarah hummed, giving Noble a squinty smile that held no joy in it. "What about you?" She asked, looking at Jack. "You went to the god realm, didn't you? Did Rothe make you his vessel?"

"Yes and no," Jack said.

"Explain," Noble demanded.

"That's another reason we're headed to Lindl's domain," Brandi answered for him, rising to her feet as thunder rumbled through the room. "In order for Jack to be chosen as Rothe's new vessel, we have to find his current one, force them into the gods' realm, and have Rothe revoke his power," she explained. "I have a contact in Lindl's domain who should have a lead on where to find our target."

"I get why you want to find this person," Sarah said, "but why do we have to search for them right now?"

"Because on my first trip to the god realm, I met with Freya," Brandi answered. "And she warned me that the gods made us vessels us for a reason. That they've been gifting their power to mortals for centuries to prepare for a fight with a being that's beyond the reach of their power. An apprentice of time who wants to destroy the gods and this entire realm."

"That's crazy," Sarah said, shaking her head. "If the gods can't do anything, what do they expect us to do?"

"I don't know," Brandi said with a shrug. "But we weren't given a choice in the matter. So, if you plan on defying the will of the gods, it would be best to make it known now," Brandi suggested, another rumble of thunder punctuating her sentence. "We can leave you here in Asari's domain, but we're not turning back."

"As if that's an actual choice," Sarah scoffed. "I'm going. This just sounds impossible."

"Who are we looking for, anyway?" Noble asked.

"The Grim Reaper."

"What are you planning to do all the way out here?"

The question came from Grady, the driver who Sarah had somehow managed to talk into giving them another ride. He'd raised his eyes at the request, but had still rolled off his barstool at the inn to drive them to the last intersection on the south side of Asari's domain. The rumbling thunder that had been in the distance twenty minutes ago, was close now, and lightning split the sky above them at quick intervals. The rains hadn't started yet, but it was clear that they didn't have much time before they arrived.

Sarah was squished into the back of the wagon with the rest of them, Noble's right side pressed up against her left as the wagon jostled them around with every rock and bump in the path. She pushed away from him to lean closer to the seat where Grady sat driving the horses. His hearing wasn't as good as it used to be, and with the thunder rolling over them, she didn't want to have to shout to be heard.

"We're visiting a friend," Sarah lied. "She lives as far out in the outskirts as she can without actually leaving Asari's domain."

"That's not very wise," Grady grumbled. "Too far out for any decent person to live."

"Well," Sarah offered with a weak smile, "she's not like most people. That's for sure. But we wanted to get there before we got trapped at the inn by the rains."

"You just be careful," he said, glancing behind Sarah to her companions and lowering his voice. "A girl like you?" He shook his head, turning his face back to the road. "I just don't want to see you get hurt and think I had some part to play in it." He reached down to give her hand a gentle pat. "You need a ride to some other fragment? You just let old Grady know. I'll get you there."

Sarah smiled at the gentleness of the old man. She knew it would be a hard ride back to the inner ring of Asari's domain without her. The only reason the rains had held out this long was because her blessing gave her favor within Asari's domain. Once they parted ways, Grady would likely be caught in the worst storm of his life. And with Asari's fickle nature, even though Grady had helped her and Brandi when they needed it, Asari would still be indifferent to his plight. She didn't want that for the man who had been kind to her, but she wasn't bold enough to think she could sway Asari's moods. So, she only thanked him for his kindness and promised she would be fine before situating herself back into the wagon. She did whisper a quick prayer for Grady to make it back to the inn safely, but she didn't feel the pull of her connection to Asari like she normally did. She wasn't surprised though, if she wasn't healing someone Asari tended to ignore her pleas.

It wasn't long after that they arrived at the intersection. The road didn't end, but the fuzzy haze caused by the gods' barrier was within sight. Grady took one look at it and shivered, soothing his horse as he turned his wagon back in the direction they had just come from. They all piled out of the wagon, and Sarah walked up to Grady's side to smile up at him.

"Thank you for the ride."

Grady grunted and glanced over her head once more to Brandi, Noble, and Jack. They'd already started walking down the last stretch of road toward the barrier. They were too far away to hear their conversation, but they moved without apprehension at nearing the barrier. It was clear that they were people who felt more comfortable on the move than they did behind the safe walls of the inn. Noble was joking with them about something, and while Jack laughed, Brandi only shoved him in the arm. Grady looked at Sarah from his driver's seat and offered her an escape, one last time.

"Are you sure you don't want to ride back with me, girlie?"

"I'm sure," she said. "But thank you, Grady. You really have been a huge help to us."

He grunted. "I hope our paths meet again, should Asari allow it."

"Should Asari allow it," she nodded. "And Grady? You should head back to the inn as quick as you can. I don't think the rains will hold out for much longer."

He frowned at the sky with the dark clouds rolling on top of each other and at the winds picking up and bending the tops of the evergreens.

Another crack of thunder and flash of lightning lit up the sky, almost at the same time, and she could see the pulse jump in Grady's neck. Even his horse was getting skittish, and he gave a slow nod in Sarah's direction.

"I think I'll take you up on your advice."

Sarah gave a smile of relief and waved to him as he took off back towards the inn. With his load lighter and her warning in his ears, Grady's wagon took off at a much faster pace than it had before, kicking up dust that swirled in the wind as his horse ran as fast as it could down the path. When she was sure he wasn't going to be turning around, she adjusted her bag and hustled to catch up to the others.

Sarah had never experienced life outside the barrier — not that she could remember anyway. She knew that she'd been born in Rothe's domain and that her mother was the second princess, Venetia — the only sister of the current ruler, Queen Leia. But she'd escaped the domain shortly after Sarah's second birthday. The only domain Sarah had ever truly known was Asari's, and with her blessing keeping her close to the fickle-natured god, the apprehension she felt now at leaving caused her chest to tighten and her palms to sweat. With every breath she took, it was like a fresh wave of nausea and reluctance washed over her, warning her away from the barrier.

But she couldn't stay.

She knew that.

Asari had been clear from the day he'd first blessed her that her role in this life was to help and serve Brandi. Even through her nerves, she felt an unbreakable connection to Brandi that compelled her to follow her wherever she went.

Sarah took a deep breath and ran even faster. She was winded by the time she caught up to them, and they all looked at her with amused pity.

"Did that jog from the intersection actually wind you?"

"Don't judge me," Sarah huffed, straightening the straps of her backpack and looking away from them to hide her reddening cheeks. "I'm not trained to send people to the gods like the rest of you."

"That's obvious," Noble snickered. "But it's okay. We'll get you into shape in no time."

"What?" Sarah asked, her eyes darting between them. "What does that mean?"

"It means," Jack said, "that you need to keep up because we're not going to slow down. Right?" He asked, looking down at Brandi and sliding an arm around her shoulders.

"Right," she laughed, leaning into him.

Sarah turned her head to watch them as she and Jack drifted further behind her and Noble, moving at their own pace with some private conversation spilling from their lips as he leaned closer to her ear. An incomprehensible desire to rush over to them and listen to what they were saying overtook her, and she surprised herself with how hard it was to keep her emotions in check.

But she'd never heard Brandi laugh, not really.

Whenever they were together, it was always something dire that made their paths intersect. But she realized now that there were lots of things she didn't know about Brandi. And that made her chest tighten with an irrational flare of jealousy, but she squashed it. Her mind understood that it was Asari's desire to be close to Freya and not her own desire to be close to Brandi. But her emotions were a different matter. They weren't governed by her mind, so she looked away with an indignant huff, deciding to not even bother trying to sort every contradicting emotion she felt. They would settle on their own soon enough.

Even knowing that, though, when she caught Noble's dark gaze on her, her face flushed a deep shade of pink.

"Don't look at me like that," Sarah mumbled.

"Like what?"

"Like you know what I'm thinking."

"I do though," he said, the left side of his mouth quirking upward and softening his face. "I've been there. You hear her laugh for the first time and it's like your whole chest seizes up. It makes you want to both laugh with her and destroy the person who made her do it because it wasn't you. Sound about right?"

Sarah huffed, but she refused to agree with him.

"Don't worry," Noble said, nudging her shoulder with his. "It gets easier. You'll get used to him."

"Get used to who?"

"Jack," Noble said. "And seeing her be in love with him. Watching that when you're a vessel of the gods can be hard, even when you know the emotions aren't yours." He raised his eyebrows as he looked down at her. "Who did you think I meant?"

Instead of responding to him, Sarah shook her head and focused on matching his pace. She wasn't short, but his long legs took him further than hers did and it was clear that the swift pace they set wasn't a challenge for any of them. She sucked in a deep breath through her nose, and Noble glanced down at her.

"Keep your breath even," he coached. "You lose your breath and you're going to pass out before we get to the other side."

Sarah frowned and tried to keep her breathing under control with even inhales to match her exhales, instead of sucking all the air down at once and huffing it out. But it was a challenge. She was never the kind of girl who indulged in a lot of physical exercise. She wasn't heavyset by any means, but she was soft and didn't have much muscle to speak of.

"How far is the barrier, anyway?" Sarah asked. "It seemed like it was just a few feet away at the intersection, but," she glanced behind them and the intersection was too far to even see now, "I guess I was wrong?"

Noble laughed. "You're not wrong. It's an illusion the gods create," Noble explained. "You ever seen a mirror reflected in another mirror?"

"Of course."

"Imagine walking through it," Noble offered. "It gets confusing because it seems like the same image is repeating forever. But if you keep walking," he grabbed her hand and tugged her forward the last few steps, making her yelp as she struggled to keep her feet under her, "you come through on the other side."

She gasped as she took in the scenery around her.

Moments ago, they'd been in Asari's domain — a quiet little place full of dirt and cobblestone roads, tall trees, quaint houses, and an inn every fifty miles or so. Now, though, they were in Carna's domain and she felt like she'd stepped into a different world. Gone were the beautiful trees and the gentle breezes, now she stood in a valley full of lush grass and rolling hills with dense copses of trees topping them and trailing down the sides. Everything was nestled between two massive cliffs on either side of them that had vines crawling down them. Sarah's eyes grew even wider as she realized the cliffs were farther away than she first realized. It would take them days to cross over the narrow strips of paths that led up to them.

"This," Noble said, looking at her with a grin on his face, "is Carna's domain."

"It's beautiful," Sarah whispered.

"That's because Carna doesn't favor his people over the land," Brandi offered, walking over to them as she and Jack crossed through the barrier behind them. "He treats nature with the same respect as Freya," she explained. "So it grows thick and wild in his domains."

"And it's why most of my people tend to leave," Noble added. "It's beautiful, but it's not easy to live here. Especially with the shaders."

Sarah's heart began to race at the word. She'd never met a shader, but her parents hadn't shied away from using the terrifying creatures to warn her and Jamie to get to bed on time and stay there throughout the night, especially since they'd lived so close to the outskirts. They'd told stories about how some of the strongest shaders were able to break through the gods' barrier to munch on disobedient children. Or, with Asari specifically, her mother told of how he would change his mind at times about keeping them out and, every once in a while when Freya pleaded with him, he'd drop his barrier to allow them through. Sarah had never believed any of the stories though. What kind of monster only preyed on disobedient children?

But seeing the way Noble narrowed his eyes now and how all of them scanned the area with a preemptive caution, she knew better than to believe everything her mother had told her was a lie. She took a deep breath and let her eyes dart around the area.

"Should we…" she started. "Should we be worried?"

"If you were by yourself," Brandi said, walking further into the domain with the boys following close behind, "then I would say yes. But you're with me, so you'll be fine."

"What does that mean?"

"It means," Brandi said, pausing to place two fingers to her lips and release a high-pitched whistle that made Sarah wince at the sound, "I'm more dangerous than anything in Carna's realm."

"How can you say that," Sarah whispered, her eyes darting around as if a shader would pop out from one of the thickets at any moment to prove her wrong, "when you just said that shaders roam freely here?"

Brandi didn't bother acknowledging Sarah's question and kept walking forward on her own, smiling at something only she could see in the distance. Before Sarah could tell what it was, a black shadow that seemed to devour all the light from the Rothe's setting sun appeared. The sweet scent of maple overtook her and Sarah's heart raced as a monster, bigger than any horse she'd ever seen, nuzzled its faceless head into Brandi, who giggled and hugged it back.

Noble took a step back and Sarah fell to the ground in complete shock. Jack was the only one who didn't move, and Noble narrowed his eyes at him.

"You knew about this?"

Jack shrugged. "Only since we crossed the Asarna mountains."

"But you knew," Noble insisted.

"I knew," Jack confirmed, walking up to Tiki and placing a tentative hand against its long fur. Tiki huffed a puff of warm air in his face as a show of affection, but it directed its thoughts towards Brandi.

I like this human. He doesn't fear me as the others do.

"He knows you," Brandi giggled, burying her face in Tiki's fur. "But he was definitely terrified the first time you met."

As are most humans. But he is conquering his fear. I like this one, Tiki repeated, huffing more air into his face, and Jack smiled.

"I'm going to take this as a sign that Tiki approves of me."

I do. But he should be wary of Lia. She has come to help carry your companions, but she is not as gentle as me.

Brandi laughed and looked over to Jack, gesturing to the others.

"You should probably take a step back."

Before he could adhere to her warning, another black shadow appeared beside them. It stopped to the left of Jack and he whipped his head around. Before he could do anything, it opened its gaping maw full of razor-sharp teeth and let out a deep roar, stomping its front paws with enough force to send tremors through the ground beneath them. Jack froze and didn't move until Brandi gave his shoulder a slight nudge. Once she did, he took measured steps back to where Noble stood, walking backward and never taking his eyes off the new shader.

Brandi reached out to Lia and, like Tiki, she nuzzled into the side of her face.

Tiny Human, Lia hummed in Brandi's mind. *It is good to see you well.*

C. M. LOCKHART

"You too, Lia," Brandi laughed, before turning to face Sarah, Jack, and Noble, who all had expressions of shock and awe written on their face.

"This is why I'm not worried," Brandi said to Sarah. "Because the shaders are mine."

224

CHAPTER THIRTEEN

*He was the breeze that flowed through the realm — as free as the birds
and as uninhibited as the clouds — the only thing that grounded him was
the horizon.*

— Boundless: An Introduction to Carna's Realm | Lindl's Fourth Holy
Academy

CARNA'S SOUTHERN DOMAIN — PRESENT DAY

Brandi gave short introductions, pointing each of them out to the shaders
in turn. Tiki and Lia both kept their distance, but Noble, Jack, and Sarah
didn't have long to get accustomed to them. Tiki approached the group
with caution, wanting to give the humans as much time to adjust as it
could, but the crack of thunder above them was a reminder of how short
on time they were. They may have crossed through the barrier before the
storm started, but Carna was the ruler of the skies and he wasn't fickle
like Asari — if his skies promised rain, then rain would come.

"Come on," Brandi said, hauling Sarah to her feet and pulling her
closer to Lia. "Lia won't hurt you."

Lia opened her mouth as Sarah got closer, showing off the double row of black, razor-sharp teeth embedded in her jaw. She gave a low growl and Sarah burst into tears as Brandi applied pressure to her back, moving her forward.

"No!" Sarah screamed, digging her heels into the ground and shaking her head, her blonde braid swishing from side to side. "No!"

"She's only teasing you," Brandi snapped. "And you're making it too easy!"

"I don't care," Sarah cried. "I'm not getting anywhere near that thing."

Lia roared again, and Brandi glared at her. "Lia! You're not helping."

This human is weak. Leave her.

"That's not your call to make," Brandi shot back in the god tongue, no longer needing to hide it from the others.

Lia took a step toward Brandi and Sarah screamed, stumbling through the dirt to hide behind Jack and Noble. They'd been standing back, waiting for Brandi to give the okay for them to move closer, and watched the exchange between the women in silent amusement. Jack shifted to move to Brandi's side, but Tiki stepped in front of him to block his path. It shook its faceless head once and Jack stopped. He knew Tiki, but it still felt counterintuitive to have it be so close to him. He couldn't hear Tiki in his head as Brandi could, but he understood that it wanted them to let whatever was happening between Brandi and the other shader, play out.

"Fine," he muttered. "But if things get rough…" he trailed off and Tiki gave a quick dip of its head in agreement.

You would ask me for a favor and then presume to command me? Lia hummed into Brandi's mind. Brandi felt the indignation in Lia's words, she didn't budge from her stance on the matter. Lia stomped her paw in front of Brandi, shaking the ground once more. *I do not require your consent to deny you.*

"*No,*" Brandi agreed, "*but you came when I sent for Tiki. Did you come here only to disobey me and slow us down?*"

I came to see you. Lia stated. *But only the goddess commands me, Tiny Human. Do not forget that.*

"*I would never forget that,*" Brandi said. "*But it wasn't the goddess who called you here. And it wasn't the goddess you came to see.*"

That is true.

"*So, help me,*" Brandi said, reaching a hand out to Lia. "*She is weak, but she is Asari's vessel. We cannot leave her behind.*"

Lia turned her head toward Sarah, who whimpered behind the boys, clinging to Noble's arm. He looked at her with a frown and shook her off.

"Have some dignity," he muttered, moving out of her grip.

Sarah looked at him with her tears in her blue eyes but refocused them back on Lia as the shader approached. She tried to scramble back, but Lia was faster. Two of her giant strides were enough to close the gap between them and she used her paw to pin Sarah to the ground. Sarah wept genuine tears of fear as the shader leaned its head closer to her face as if observing her.

This is who the god of the moon has chosen? I disapprove.

"*You'll have to take that up with him then,*" Brandi said, looking

227

back to the sky as she felt the first raindrop slide down her cheek. *"But she is the one who saved my life when Tiki first brought me to Asari's domain."*

Lia leaned her head closer to Sarah, who had gone still and quiet in a near catatonic state of shock. Lia huffed air into her face, the scent of maple fruits flowing over Sarah as she mumbled a nonsensical prayer to Asari that the gods would have mercy on her soul when she met them. She squeezed her eyes shut and turned her face away from Lia.

This girl?

"Yes."

Then I am grateful to her. For what she has done in the past, I shall allow her to ride me.

"*Thank you*," Brandi said, turning to look at Tiki. "*I should have asked, but do you have any objections?*"

Of course not. But I desire to carry this human, Tiki said, moving to nuzzle its head against Jack. He laughed and petted Tiki's head in return, already comfortable with the deadly creature. *I like this one.*

"*Me too*," Brandi agreed. She clapped her hands together and gestured for the shaders to come to her. Tiki moved away from Jack without hesitation, but Lia snapped at Sarah once while she still had her underfoot, eliciting a high-pitched scream from her. Lia howled in laughter before stepping away from her and returning to Brandi's side. They both kneeled on the ground, making it easier for the humans to climb onto their wide backs.

"Let's get moving," she said, hauling herself up onto Tiki's back as Noble helped Sarah back to her feet. "Jack's with me. Noble and Sarah,

228

you'll ride Lia."

"How can you tell them apart?" Jack asked, pulling himself up behind her.

"You can't?" Brandi asked with raised eyebrows.

"They look identical."

"Not really," Brandi said with a shake of her head. "Tiki's bigger, and its fur is shorter. The leader of their pack. Lia is leaner and shorter, with curlier fur. And she's a girl."

"So, Tiki's not?"

"Tiki is Tiki," Brandi said, glancing over to the others.

Sarah avoided her gaze and rubbed at her swollen eyes and tear-stained face. She took deep breaths and tried to swallow her anxiety as she neared Lia. She wanted nothing to do with the creature, but still, she reached out a hand to the beast with tentative caution. When Lia dipped her head with a low, gentle hum, and pushed her nose into Sarah's palm, Sarah stamped down whatever fear was trying to hold her back. She took a deep breath and copied Brandi's movements to climb on top of the giant beast. It was easier than she expected, and she marveled at the view she had from so high up. It was unlike anything she'd ever experienced, and she let a small smile ghost across her lips.

Only Noble was left on the ground and he took a few slow steps forward to stand in front of Lia. And before she could refuse his advance, he placed his right hand behind his back, and his left fist over his heart, his thumb pointing outward, and bowed low. Lia considered him before dipping her head in return and huffing air into his face. He stood up with a grin stretched across his lips and joined Sarah on Lia's back.

He took a seat in front of Sarah, who wrapped shaking hands around his back as the shader rose from the ground.

Noble glanced over his shoulder at her, ready to tell her to ease up on her grip, but when he saw the fear and wonderment on her face, he was reminded of his first interaction with a shader and swallowed his comment. He turned back around to place a gentle hand against Lia's shoulder to let her know that they were ready and she moved to stand beside Tiki.

"You could've mentioned that you knew how to tame shaders," Brandi said, amusement coloring her words.

"And you could've mentioned that you kept a few on call," he shot back. "But here we are."

"Here we are," Brandi grinned. "You ready?"

"Of course," Noble said, leaning forward so he wouldn't be thrown from Lia's back when it took off. "Let's go!"

CARNA'S WESTERN DOMAIN — 14 YEARS AGO

Noble was eleven the first time he met a god, and it was nothing like what he had imagined.

In all actuality, he had never expected to meet a god. Not before his time in the mortal realm was done anyway.

He'd heard stories about the gods all his life from his skymother — his mother's mother. Like all of Carna's children, she'd been born without a family name to pass down. So, she was known only as Sage among their people. Everyone treated her as if they were a part of her lineage and she'd welcomed them all.

She'd made sure they'd known the legends and the stories of the gods like they knew their own names, and every night she told them a different story of Freya and Carna, the god in whose lands they lived. And every year, without fail, once they had harvested their crops after the final rains, everyone below the age of twelve — the age of requirement — made a trip to the central border of Carna's western domain to visit his temple.

It sat a hair's breadth away from Freya's lands, which they were warned to treat with the utmost respect. Skymother Sage always warned that Freya resided in the heart of her lands and walking into her domain was akin to being in her embrace, and that leaving the presence of the goddess was enough to drive grown men mad with longing — until they took their own life just to meet her again.

It wasn't an easy journey though. Unlike the other gods, Carna never erected a barrier around his lands to keep the shaders out and he allowed them to roam free in his lands the same way Freya did. Because of that, despite having the most beautiful lands of all the gods, with green rolling hills, lush valleys, crystal clear waterfalls, and plains that stretched for days under a perfect blue sky, his people almost never stayed in them. They often migrated to Rothe's or Lindl's domains once they became of age, preferring the safety of the protected fragments to the wilderness of Carna's lands.

But Sage was one of the few who had lived her entire life in Carna's domain. She had ventured to Rothe's domain once when she was younger, following behind her friends who couldn't wait to leave, but she was never able to find the peace they'd promised would be behind the barrier. She always claimed that Carna's domain carried a breath of freedom in the air that didn't exist in other domains. And it was in Carna's temple that Sage would tell them the stories of his exploits and his great love with the goddess Freya. Even as she aged and walking became more laborious, she never failed to guide the young ones through the halls, explaining the stories behind the images carved into the walls.

It was on his eleventh — and final — trip with skymother Sage that Noble met Brandi and Carna made himself known to him.

They'd arrived at the temple a few days prior that year. It was a weathered stone building with sharp angles that stood out against the open plains behind it. It was larger on the inside than looked possible from the outside, with long, wide hallways paved with ancient stones and lined with tall columns that led to the sanctuary inside. Skymother Sage was getting older and making the four-hour trek from their little village on the hill in one day was beyond her capabilities now. But as she showed the youngest children around the temple, leaning her slim body onto the cane Noble's father, King, had crafted for her, Noble wandered outside.

He'd seen the carvings and heard the stories more times than he cared to count. He could tell them in his sleep if he had to. And that was a good thing because he knew that skymother Sage wanted him to take over her role as an elder of their community one day. But he didn't love the stories like she did. He didn't know if he even believed them anymore. Royal would've been the better pick, but Noble hadn't heard from his older brother since he'd turned eighteen and left the village. He hadn't gone to Lindl's domain like the rest of his friends had. He'd shrugged and waved to them as he headed off in the opposite direction with his shader, Crown.

Royal had been the only person Noble knew who wasn't afraid of the shaders. He'd tried to convince his younger brother that they weren't monsters like the stories made them out to be, that they were gentle creatures that hunted for food and formed families together, bonding with each other for life. Where one went, there were usually many more close by. Royal had been fascinated by shaders and had even taught Noble the proper technique to get close to one.

"Shaders are proud creatures," he'd said, showing Noble the greeting. "They're the only creatures who were directly created by the goddess. So, you have to treat them with respect."

"I thought we were all children of the goddess?"

"We are," Royal responded, reaching out to correct Noble's fist that curled over his heart. "But shaders were created by her," he said, emphasizing the words. "They carry her blood, her breath, inside of them. And no god but her can command them. Don't you think that's amazing?"

"If that's true, they'd have to live forever."

Royal laughed. "Maybe they do. We can barely tell them apart, so we wouldn't know, would we?"

They'd practiced until Noble got it right and then they never talked about shaders again. Not until Royal told Noble he'd bonded with one named Crown, and that he was going to explore the realm with him. He'd talked about wanting to find out more about some truth he'd found hidden behind secret doors in Carna's temple and Noble had always wondered what it was that Royal had found, but he knew better than to wander the temple alone. Skymother Sage hated that, always warning them that they were in Carna's home and it was rude to wander around uninvited.

So, he wandered in the tall grass outside instead. This would be the last year he'd be forced to come to the temple and was jealous of Terra and Russ who'd gotten out of coming by going with their mother to visit their older brother Shian in Lindl's domain. He'd wanted to go with them, but skymother Sage had refused to give him permission and he felt lonely without his two best friends. He sighed thinking about them and how he couldn't wait to turn twelve and be old enough to make the decision for himself. There were some older folks, like skymother Sage, who were devoted to Carna and his ways, and a few parents who came with their youngest children on their first few visits, but most people stopped coming when it was no longer required. He hadn't decided yet if he would or not, but he knew that he was bored out of his mind now that Royal was gone.

Noble had been lost in his thoughts and hadn't realized how far he'd wandered from the temple until he heard the low growling of a shader and the high-pitched screams of a girl.

His heart jumped into his throat and he sprinted in the direction of the sounds without thinking. His brother had promised that shaders were gentle, but Noble wouldn't believe that until he saw it with his own eyes. He trusted his brother, but he'd heard the stories that adults whispered around the main hall at night when the children had all been put to bed. He'd listened to the murmured stories of shaders devouring entire villages, not even leaving behind the bones of their victims for the mourning to bury. It's why everyone kept the children close and warned them against straying too far whenever they played in the fields. They didn't want to give the shaders any reason to prey on them.

Most of the time, it worked.

Sometimes, it didn't.

And Noble had no idea how he would protect anyone from a shader, but he didn't want to be responsible for letting a little girl get sent to the gods because he had trusted his brother's words over his own intuition.

He was sprinting toward the river as fast as his long legs would take him. The river split the valley down the middle and he hoped the girl was on his side so he could help her. But before he could even catch a glimpse of the girl, thick white clouds descended upon him, surrounding him until he completely lost his way, and he tripped over his own feet and went crashing into the hard ground. He shivered as the icy droplets soaked into his clothes and he looked for a way out of the endless sea of white mist. His heart raced as his dark eyes darted around the empty space — no longer searching for the girl he'd been trying to protect, but watching in amazement as the clouds dispersed and revealed an endless field of tall grass. The cold mist was blown away by a warm breeze and his clothes were dried in an instant.

Noble rubbed his hands along his arms, trying to understand what was happening. His knees were still buried in the tall grass when he heard footsteps walk up beside him. He looked to his left and his body stiffened as his eyes traveled upward, taking in the bare feet, dark blue jeans, fitted white shirt, long silver hair and piercing gray eyes focused on him.

Without missing a beat, Noble pressed his head to the soil, bowing in respect and going through the same motions his skymother Sage had forced him to perform in Carna's temple before his empty throne. His body trembled with nerves and he wanted to look up, but he kept his eyes downcast as the god looked upon him.

"Straighten your back, boy," Carna said, reaching down to place a hand on Noble's back. "I wish to speak with you."

It took Noble a few seconds for his mind to catch up with the reality of what was happening. He clambered to his feet to stand before Carna, the god his skymother had revered and worshipped her entire life. Just a few moments ago he'd been questioning whether or not the stories his skymother told him were just that — stories.

And now Carna stood with a hand on his shoulder.

He raised his head and stood straight as he'd been told, but he kept his eyes on Carna's feet. He couldn't bear to look the god in the eye a second time, and he worked to keep his body from quaking under his gaze, but his body still trembled.

"You know who I am?"

"Yes," Noble whispered with a nod.

"Then this won't take long," Carna said. "But raise your head and look at me, boy. I don't make the effort to appear before many and when I do, I like to be seen."

Noble did as he was told and stood in awe of the god. He looked exactly like the carvings in his temple depicted. His long silver hair was pulled back into a ponytail at the base of his neck, and his sandy brown skin matched Noble's. With the exception of his gray eyes, Noble could've been his twin — his son. Carna smiled down at the boy and clapped his hand on his shoulder once more.

"Don't be afraid, boy," he said with a gentle laugh that sent a breeze flowing through the tall grass of the plains they were standing in. "I won't hurt you. I am only here to speak with you. Nothing more."

"Okay," Noble said nodding. "But there was a girl," Noble said, pointing in the direction he thought the river to be in. "She was in trouble. Screaming. Can you save her? Please?"

Carna smiled and waved his hand through the air, bringing the girl and the shader back into view.

He could actually see the girl now and Noble stood there, stunned, unable to look away from her. He'd seen images of the goddess on Carna's temple walls, but — like meeting Carna himself — he never imagined that someone that beautiful could exist. Yet there she was. With the darkest brown skin he'd ever seen, big green eyes, and a smile wider than Carna's skies. Her braids were black, and she was younger than him, but those were the only differences Noble could find between her and the images of the goddess depicted in the temple.

He watched her in wonderment, and as she continued running around, Noble realized that she was playing with the shader. The scream he'd heard was one of merriment. She hadn't been in any danger at all and his mind raced as it tried to process that fact.

His brother had been right. Shaders weren't inherently evil creatures.

Not his brother's shader, Crown, and not this one either. It seemed like they bonded with humans who discarded their fear of them, and coming to that understanding forced a crack in the foundation of everything Noble thought he knew about the realm. What else had the elders been wrong about? What else was there to know about the realm that the gods created?

Noble looked to Carna with a million questions swimming in his dark eyes, and the god smiled down at him.

"You would like to know more, yes?"

Noble nodded his head and Carna started walking through the field. He said nothing to him at first, but Noble followed behind him just the same. His dark eyes were glued to Carna's back as he trailed behind him through the endless sea of grass. As they walked, Carna waved his hand, shifting the winds until images appeared in the clouds.

"I know you must have many questions for me," Carna said, pausing at the first image he'd created. "But you should listen first." He pointed one slender finger towards the image he'd created of himself standing with Freya and the other gods. "You know the story of creation as it has been taught in the realm. I know that the stories of my own accomplishments are etched into your heart. Now, it is time you see the entire picture."

He continued on and, again, Noble followed behind him. His amazement grew with each passing image that Carna created. He was rendered speechless by how beautiful the goddess was in Carna's memory. She was stunning in his temple, but Noble was beginning to understand why his skymother had always said that human hands would never be able to capture the totality of who the gods truly were. Standing in Carna's presence now and seeing the gods as he did, Noble understood the ancient carvings in his temple to be little more than the scribbles of a child.

"Once we created the world," Carna told him, "time was gifted to us."

"So, you didn't create it?"

Carna smiled, pleased that Noble had finally found his voice to speak with him. "No, boy. We didn't. We are powerful, but we do not control the flow of time. It marches onward without our intervention." Carna paused in front of an image with an endless stream of faces in front of him. "Because we do not control time, we cannot control when the chaos will come."

"Chaos? What's that?"

"It would be the end of the realm as you understand it," Carna said, the amusement in his voice gone. "And we alone cannot prevent it. That is why we gift our power to you mortals. Every generation, we relinquish some of it to you so that you may have the power to do what we cannot," he said, turning around and showing Noble a myriad of faces that looked similar, if not identical, to the girl he saw playing in the field. "And our goddess," he whispered, his gray eyes softening as he looked upon an image of Freya smiling up at him, "she is devoted to protecting you mortals beyond anything we gods can understand. She sends her own soul to this realm in every lifetime to help guide and protect you."

"The goddess is here?" Noble asked, whipping his head around to try and spot the goddess with his own two eyes.

"She stood before you, and you did not notice," Carna pointed out, annoyance lining the edges of his voice and chilling the breeze that drifted through the plains. "Look again," he said, waving his hand to reveal the girl and the shader from earlier.

"She's the goddess?"

"Her current incarnation," Carna corrected with a nod. "She carries the soul of Freya within her."

Noble stared at the girl, committing her face to memory, though it didn't take much effort. The girl was beautiful. She sat on the ground now, leaning against the shader and plucking leaves off the plants surrounding them before letting them drift on the wind toward the river. She smiled over at the shader and Noble felt something in his heart twist as her smile faded into a dark grimace.

She stood to her feet and stepped in front of the shader as if to hide it from view. Noble searched the area for what could have caused her demeanor to change so quickly, but Carna's image revealed nothing to him.

"What's happening?" Noble asked, turning to look up at Carna. "Why is she so angry now?"

"Time marches onward," Carna repeated. "She is being pulled into a world of violence that she wants no parts of."

"Violence?" Noble whispered, his eyes wide as he thought about what that meant.

His life was a peaceful one. They faced the constant threat of shaders and the reality that they were only one bad harvest away from being forced from their home, but his existence was a peaceful one. He had friends — Terra and Russ — and a family that loved him. The hardest part of his days was listening to skymother Sage tell him the same stories of Carna, over and over again. He'd never thought of what the realm was like beyond the small part of it he lived in.

"Yes," Carna said, turning to look the boy in his eyes. "She will become a weapon used by your queen," he said. "She will be forced to destroy every emotion inside her and send people to the gods at the command of another. She will train until her body is exhausted and her spirit is broken and she is little more than a shell of herself."

Carna's eyes narrowed as he spoke the words, and the temperature in the realm dropped with his tone. Noble shivered as his breath formed before him in the sunny plains and he crossed his arms against the icy chill in the air. It was almost always sunny in Carna's domain, and even when it wasn't, the breeze was always warm and gentle on his skin. He had no resistance to the cold and standing next to Carna made that apparent to him.

"I don't want that for her," Noble whispered, the urge to protect her blooming in his soul. He wanted the smile he'd seen just a few moments ago to return to her face and for her to never have to worry about anything ever again. He knew he didn't have the power to make that happen, but he wanted it. He wanted to be able to put her at ease and protect her, the same way Royal had always looked out for him.

"No?"

Noble shook his head. "She looked so beautiful when she was smiling," Noble answered. "I want her to stay smiling." He lifted his eyes to Carna's. "I want to protect her."

"Good," Carna said, his face stretching into a grin and the plains warming fast enough to send chills up Noble's spine. "Then I shall give you the power to do just that."

"You will?"

Carna nodded, waving his hand through the air to lock Noble's legs in place as he walked toward him. "And in exchange," Carna said, his gray eyes glowing bright with power as his clouds swirled around him and his body began to dissolve into the fluffy white mist, "you will protect the incarnation of my goddess with your life. You will see that no undue harm comes to her. Can you promise me that, boy?"

"Yes," Noble said, his voice strong despite the fear that snaked through him at Carna's shifting form. "I will protect her."

"Then I will choose you as my vessel in this realm and gift you a portion of my power," he said, stopping in front of Noble and allowing his clouds to spread out around them. "This will hurt. More than anything you've ever experienced," Carna warned, "but you will have to endure it. When her master returns to take her back to Rothe's domain, you must go with her. You will not have another chance."

"I understand," Noble said, gulping down his fear.

He wouldn't have time to tell skymother Sage he'd met Carna. That he believed her and knew that all of her stories were real and that he was sorry for having ever doubted her. He wouldn't be able to tell her that he would miss her or say goodbye to his friends — to his father. His world was shifting, moving forward, and from now on it would revolve around the girl that Carna brought back into view.

Carna placed a hand on top of Noble's head, his misty form sending shivers down his spine. He quacked under Carna's intense stare, but his eyes never drifted away from his. He held the god's gaze, and Carna smiled at the boy.

"Should you ever need me, simply call on my name and I will aid you," Carna said, bending to place a kiss to Noble's forehead. He sucked in a sharp breath, his mind reeling at how Carna's icy touch could spark fires in his blood. Noble's legs gave way under the oppressive heat, but Carna caught him and placed him back on his feet, returning him to the mortal realm. He placed a cool hand on Noble's back and gave him an encouraging push forward that sent Noble stumbling down the small hill toward the river and the girl.

"Be well, my son."

Carna's words echoed in Noble's head and when Noble came to a stop at the bottom of the hill, his ears rang and every bone and muscle in his body screamed in agony. He felt like the entirety of Rothe's sun had been forced into his bones and he wanted to scream with every breath he took, but he couldn't stop — couldn't forget Carna's words.

This would be his only chance.

The girl stood in front of him now, her eyes focused on something in the distance he couldn't see yet, but he could tell from her growing apprehension that it was getting closer. She turned her green eyes onto him and Noble sucked in a breath at the surprise he felt at seeing her close up. He'd never seen someone like her before and couldn't get over how dark her skin was. He'd never been to any other domain, so he'd only ever seen people with skin tones a shade or two different from his own. Noble couldn't keep himself from staring as he stood in front of her now, trying to figure out what to say. He hadn't had time to think of anything before he'd left Carna's presence and his mind tumbled over itself now, rushing to figure something out. But before he could utter a single word, she glared at him and took a step back.

"Who are you?"

His heart dropped at the question, but he knew that it only made sense she would be wary of him. He'd spent the last however long with Carna explaining who she was to him, so he felt like he already knew her. But he was a complete stranger to her, some random boy who had come stumbling down the hill out of nowhere.

He sucked in another shaky breath, his chest heaving as he tried in pointless desperation to keep his breathing under control. His lungs burned like fires raged within them and he held back tears as sweat beaded on his forehead. His vision was beginning to blur around the edges and he silently begged Carna to keep him conscious. He couldn't lose consciousness before he made it to wherever the girl was going.

"Noble," he forced out, answering her question.

"Is that your name?" She asked, not hesitating to fire off her next question once he nodded. "Why are you here?"

"Carna…"

His eyes went wide as his voice seized up. He'd meant to tell her that he knew she was the incarnation of Freya and that he was going with her. That he'd been told by the god of the skies to protect her, no matter what the cost, and he planned to do just that. That he hadn't hesitated to agree to leave behind his family, friends, and everything he'd ever known to be with her. But the words wouldn't come, and the burning in his chest intensified.

He groaned and clutched at his chest, bending over to rest his free hand against his knee. He swayed on his feet and bit back a cry of pain as the fire flared at the base of his spine. He shot up and turned his eyes toward the sky as the girl watched from a distance, her narrowed softening in understanding. She'd experienced the kind of pain he was in, the kind that stole your words, your breath, and your sanity.

"You've been blessed," she said, piecing together his mention of Carna with the condition he was in now. "What are you doing here? How are you even moving right now?"

"Had to…" Noble grunted, "go… with you…"

"With me?" She huffed. "You don't even know me."

"Doesn't… matter…" he heaved out. "Protect."

"Protect me?"

He nodded his head and reached out for her — anything — to help keep him on his feet as the fire spread up his spine and he lost his balance.

She scoffed but still reached out to catch him. She staggered under his weight but managed to maneuver herself under his arm and pull it over her shoulders. She didn't believe he would be able to protect her from what she knew was coming for her, especially not in the state he was in now. But she could tell that he believed his own words. Besides, if Carna had just blessed him and he was managing to stand in front of her now, he was much stronger than he looked. Not knowing his reasons for wanting to protect her made her apprehensive, but she couldn't leave him behind. She wasn't in the business of denying the gods, even if she didn't understand them.

"No one can protect me," she whispered.

"I will," Noble grunted again, his body cooling a bit as he leaned against her. "I promised," he sighed.

"You're not making any sense," she said, looking into the distance and tensing under his arm. He looked up from the ground he'd been staring at and followed her gaze. He saw now that she'd been staring at a small group of people moving toward them.

"They're not going to be happy with me," she warned.

"Why?"

"I left without telling them," she answered. "But I don't want to fight anymore..."

She didn't say anything after that, and Noble didn't have the strength to comfort her. All he could do was lean on her and force his eyes to stay open as they approached. When they did, he saw three people. A man, a woman, and a girl about his age — all children of Rothe. They rode on two-seater solar bikes that hovered a few feet off the ground, and Noble was amazed at what he saw. He'd never witnessed anything like it before, but he'd heard stories that Rothe and Lindl's domains were far more advanced than anything they possessed in their simple lives. His stomach flipped in awe as they stopped in front of them. The woman on the first bike jumped off first, and an angry glare marred her face as she stomped toward the girl.

Even in her anger, though, the woman was stunning in her own way with the golden brown skin and eyes that all children of Rothe had. She had thick black locs pulled back into a bun and the muscles in her arms were on full display as she clenched and unclenched her fists by her sides. She wore simple clothes, jeans and a nondescript gray shirt with combat boots, but the air around her felt dangerous. Even though she looked as harmless as one of the mothers from his village, he understood from the way his gut clenched and how he straightened his back as she approached that this was not someone he wanted to anger.

"Where up Rothe's ass have you been?" She snapped. "I look away for two seconds and you're gone!"

"I don't want to fight anymore."

"'I don't want to fight anymore'," the woman mocked, reaching out to snatch the girl by the arm and drag her forward. Noble stumbled as his support was pulled away from him and the girl yelped from the force the woman used. Noble narrowed his eyes at the woman, but he was unable to move forward, and she paid no attention to him. "You don't get to make that choice," the woman said, her tone icy as she bent forward to look the girl in the eye. "Either you fight, or you get sent to the gods."

"Send me then," the girl shot back. "I didn't want to be with you, anyway!"

"You ungrateful…!"

Before Noble could move, a sharp slap rang out across the plains and the girl he'd sworn to Carna to protect, screamed and fell back into the dirt. She pressed her palm to her left cheek as tears streaked down her face and she glared up at the woman who towered above her.

"I don't care what you think of me," the woman said, her brown eyes cold as she looked down her nose at the girl, "or whether you want to be with me or not. But don't you ever speak of giving your life to the gods without a fight. You may be too selfish to realize that there are people in this realm who want you here," she said turning on her heel to walk back toward the bikes where the older girl sat, "but that doesn't mean they don't exist." She jerked her thumb in the direction of the girl on the ground.

"Go help her up, Najé. Patches and I are going back to finish what we started since you two seem to be completely incompetent today," she said, her frustration sharpening the insult. She slung her leg over the side of her bike and started the silent machine, letting it idle a few feet off the ground, before turning her gaze back to the girls. "Just stay here until we're done and meet us at the top of the river when Rothe puts the sun to rest."

The older girl — Najé — climbed off the bike where she had been riding behind the man and crossed over to the girl on the ground without hesitation. She crouched down and pulled the girl into a tight hug. The girl tensed at first, but then gave in to it, and Noble breathed a sigh of relief.

"And what hole did you crawl out of?" The woman asked, her brown eyes narrowed as Noble whipped his head around to meet her gaze.

"I'm Noble."

"I didn't ask you your name," she said. "What are you doing here?"

"I'm going with her," Noble forced out, doing his best to keep his back straight.

The woman's eyebrows shot up at the confidence in his words and she let her eyes rove over him as she appraised him. She didn't seem particularly impressed with the person standing in front of her, but Noble guessed that she sensed some type of potential in him. Maybe it was his budding muscles, the tone of his voice, or the sheer determination it took to make eye contact with her without fear, but she began nodding her head as she gave him another once over.

"You know who we are?"

"I was informed," Noble coughed out.

"Informed, huh?" The woman smirked and put her bike into gear. "Alright, kid. You can come with us. I'm Glenn. That's Patches," she said, hooking her thumb over her shoulder to the man who sat on the other bike. "And that pain in the ass is Brandi," she said, pointing to the green-eyed girl he'd sworn to protect. "And from now on, you belong to us."

CHAPTER FOURTEEN

Freedom comes with a price, as does love — take heed lest you wind up in debt with both.

— Adage of the Gods | Lindl's Five Holy Academies Compilation

CARNA'S SOUTHERN DOMAIN — PRESENT DAY

Lightning shot through the dark skies over fragment 30305 as Tiki and Lia sprinted towards their destination. Noble led the way with precise instructions, but even as fast as the shaders were, it still took over an hour to reach the hill that overlooked a two-story patchwork house and the rain hadn't waited for them to get there.

Tiki and Lia brought them as far as they could, but Brandi had warned against riding them up to the front door since most people wouldn't react well to shaders appearing at their home. So, they'd trekked up the hill on foot for the last leg of the journey and arrived at the painted blue door soaked through to the bone and covered in every type of nature Carna's realm had to offer.

The downpour had made for a slow journey and none of them could see more than two inches beyond their own nose. That was frustrating enough on its own, but it was Sarah's lack of experience that wore on all of them when she'd slipped back down the hill as they neared the top. She'd grabbed onto Brandi's ankle when she fell in a futile attempt to save herself, dragging Brandi back down the hill with her. Jack caught Brandi before she reached the bottom, but Sarah was almost washed away by the current of the flash flood that was winding its way through the valley. Her only saving grace had been her backpack that caught on a stray branch lodged into the wet ground, giving Noble enough time to reach her and haul her out before she got truly swept away. But that meant they'd had to backtrack in the downpour to save her and climb the hill twice. By the time Noble had the chance to knock his knuckles against the door, all of them were in a sour mood.

The house sat on wide stilts that seemed to grow from the ground like tree trunks to keep the house level. It had a white tin roof that was sloped at such an angle that the water pouring off it almost looked like a waterfall. Sarah had never seen a house quite like it, but as the rain poured from the skies and rushed down the hill, around the house, and into the lowest depths of the valley, it was obvious why they'd chosen to build the house the way they had.

They didn't have to wait long before a silver-haired girl with a pixie cut swung the door open. She wore a pink crop top and old white sweatpants that were rolled up to just below her knees. Her eyebrows shot to the edge of her blunt cut bangs before her freckled face broke out in a grin.

"Well, I'll be the gods' forgotten," she laughed. "What are you doing here?"

"Getting rained on," Noble deadpanned.

"Well, I can see that," she smirked. "But why are you here?" She repeated, emphasizing her question.

"To get out of the rain for one, if you don't mind," Noble huffed, pushing past her into the house. "I didn't come all this way just to stand outside in Carna's downpour."

Brandi and Jack followed behind him without a word, but Sarah mumbled an apology as she passed the girl who shut the door behind them.

"Well, excuse me for being surprised," she shot back at Noble. "I haven't laid eyes on you in almost a year and then you show up out of nowhere." She shook her head and stared at him. "I'm in shock."

"To the point, you couldn't move aside to let us out the rain? Skymother Sage would've beat you into next week with her cane for that."

The girl moved to a closet on the other side of the room and tossed a handful of towels their way as they stood dripping on the hardwood floors. Noble caught them and passed them around to the others as he eyed the girl in front of him. His eyes roved over the soft curves in her body with a familiar shamelessness that made the others avert their gazes. She crossed her arms and returned the look before shaking her head and walking over to him.

"You haven't changed at all," she said, taking the towel from his hands and waiting for him to bend down so she could run it across his hair.

"Not true," Noble said, stepping back from the girl to pull his shirt over his head. "I've gotten bigger in some places since you've last seen me."

"I'm sure you have," the girl responded, her voice drenched in lust as her dark eyes trailed over his sculpted body in a way that made Sarah both uncomfortable and irritated at the same time. She averted her eyes from Noble's exposed skin and wondered if she was a prude for not undressing to her underwear like everyone else, since they seemed so unfazed by it. She tried to ignore them, but when Brandi pulled her shirt over her head to expose the plain black bra she wore underneath, Sarah gasped and stepped closer to her.

"Brandi! You're in a living room."

"Your point?" Brandi asked, refusing to look at her.

"It's not modest…"

Brandi snorted. "Privacy is a luxury, Sarah. Remember that."

"But —"

"Sarah," Brandi whispered, pausing her movements to take several deep, shaky breaths. "Have you no regard for your own life? Because you are about two seconds away from explaining to Asari why he has to choose a new vessel," Brandi said, emphasizing her words. "So, shut up and get away from me."

"That's a genuine threat," Jack warned her, peeling off his own clothes. "You're brave to be speaking to her after you literally dragged her through the mud."

"Sorry," Sarah whispered, taking several steps back from Brandi. Before she could think to say anything else though, the girl with the pixie cut tossed Noble's towel into his face while shaking her head.

"Talking about me and my bad manners. Skymother would have had your backside too for not introducing me properly."

The girl pivoted to look at the rest of them and smiled, her freckled cheeks pulling into a friendly greeting as she gave a small wave.

"I'm Terra. Me and this one," she said, using her thumb to point at Noble, "grew up together in Carna's western domain."

"I'm Brandi," Brandi said, peeling her pants off her legs, "that's Jack, and Sarah," she said nodding in their respective directions. Terra smiled at both of them, but her eyes didn't stay on them for long and darted back to Brandi's abs and long legs. She stood in only her underwear now, and Sarah noticed for the first time that Brandi's muscles, while leaner and not even half as bulky as the boys, were just as toned. Like with Noble, Terra didn't hide the once over she gave Brandi and Jack, appreciation shining in her eyes as they stripped down.

"You're beautiful," Terra said, her eyes back on Brandi. "I thought I was pretty, but the gods decided to make you into a work of art, didn't they?"

"Thanks. I get that a lot." Brandi shrugged. "You got a shower around here?"

"Through here," Terra said, leading the way to a sliding wooden door that opened up to a giant bathroom. There was a sink to the left, a wide shower beside it, a water closet on the opposite side of the room, and a sunken bathtub in the middle of the floor that was more like a pool than anything else. Sarah guessed that four adult people could fit into it with ease. The far wall by the shower was nothing but glass, and the storm outside almost looked relaxing as the water poured off the trees and past the windows to the valley below.

"It's not much," Terra offered, "but it's yours to use as you like. There's more soap and towels below the sink. And I'll scrounge up some clean clothes for you, so just toss yours in that chute over there," she said, pointing to the far corner of the room, where a small door was built into the wall. "It'll drop them in the laundry for you."

"Appreciate it," Jack said with a nod as he passed Terra. He grabbed Brandi's hand and pulled her inside, shutting the door behind them.

"There's another bathroom upstairs you can use," Terra said, looking at Sarah. "And you," she said, pressing a finger into Noble's bare chest, "can use the bathroom in my room. You already know where it is."

Noble smirked and caught Terra's hand as she was pulling away to hold it against his chest while he leaned forward to whisper something in her ear. Sarah couldn't hear his exact words, but whatever he said caused Terra's cheeks to flush and push him away.

"That's a promise you better keep," she warned under her breath. "No take backs."

"You know I don't make promises I won't keep," he said, biting his lip and walking backward, heading toward a hallway that Sarah could only guess led to her room.

Terra watched him turn the corner before turning her flushed face back to Sarah. "Sorry about that," she apologized, walking towards the stairs. "He's always been a massive flirt, even when we were kids."

"Oh," Sarah quipped, thinking back on how his demeanor with her had changed at the inn once he realized she wouldn't be seduced out of information. "He doesn't really flirt with me, so I hadn't noticed."

Terra paused on the landing at the top of the stairs, her silver eyebrows disappearing into her bangs once more. "He doesn't?"

"Not unless he's attempting to embarrass me," Sarah shrugged. "I guess my looks don't appeal to him much."

Terra gave Sarah an instinctual once over, but she didn't say anything as they continued walking, leading Sarah past a lounge area and a kitchen towards a wide hallway with doors lining either side. Sarah's eyes danced all over the place as she kept pace behind Terra. The house hadn't looked like much from the outside with its simple porch and tin roof, but it was clear the space inside had been created with a great attention to detail. Everything was organized and carefully placed, without a speck of dust to be found. Simple wall art hung on the walls and windows dotted the length of the hallway, along with a few more doors, each painted a different pastel shade of blue.

The hallway twisted and turned in subtle ways, enough that it was obvious that the entire house hadn't been built at one time, but not so much that it was confusing or disconcerting to navigate through. It had looked like a patchwork job from the outside, but it was a near-seamless design on the inside, and Sarah found herself amazed at the difference between her reality and her expectations.

Terra stopped by a door at the very end of the hall that was painted a dark shade of blue and swung it open to reveal another bathroom that was identical to the one below it. The only differences Sarah noticed were the direction the windows faced and the fact that they were frosted, offering more privacy than the previous one.

"Same as I told them," Terra said, pointing to the sink. "Soap and towels are below. Drop your clothes in the chute. I'll find you something to wear when you get out."

"Thank you."

"No problem," Terra said as she turned to leave, her mind clearly back on Noble as she began moving back down the hallway. "If you need anything, just shout."

With that, Terra turned on her heel and departed, closing the door behind her. Sarah listened to her almost run back down the hall and tried to push the thought of her with Noble out of her mind. It didn't matter. Noble was a grown man and whatever he did with the other grown people in his life was none of her business. She wouldn't let it bother her and would instead focus on the tasks at hand — getting clean, fixing her hair, figuring out what they would do next and where they were going to go. She told herself that there were bigger things for her to be worrying about, but when she caught a glimpse of her face in the reflection of the mirror, her cheeks flushed and blotchy, her eyes bright and on the verge of tears, she sighed and dropped her face into her hands.

"Asari give me strength," she whispered. "Why does it have to be him?"

Half an hour later, Sarah was freshly washed and wrapped in one of the light blue robes she'd found folded under the sink next to the soap and shampoo. Terra had promised to find her something to wear, but she'd never returned and the clothes she'd worn when they arrived had already been dropped down the laundry chute. She'd been at a loss of what to do when she'd finally pulled herself away from the relaxing stream of hot water.

When it became apparent that Terra wouldn't be making an appearance any time soon, Sarah walked to the bathroom door and cracked it open to peek out of it. She jumped back in surprise when she was met with another pair of dark eyes and freckled cheeks. The problem was, they didn't belong to Terra.

"Sorry to surprise you! Are you looking for my sister?"

"Possibly," Sarah said, pulling her robe tighter around her chest and edging the door closed. The man on the other side looked just like Terra, but where she had short hair and gentle curves, he was bald with black, rectangular glasses and carried most of his weight in his midsection. Sarah would've been surprised if they weren't related, but Terra hadn't mentioned that there was someone else in the house with them. Sarah's eyes darted over him, trying to assess how dangerous he could be.

He wore a loose pair of black shorts and a yellow, sleeveless sweatshirt. He offered a gentle smile as he angled his body back down the hall, as if he sensed her unease.

"Terra told me that Noble had arrived with some friends in tow, so I'm guessing you're one of them?"

Sarah rolled her eyes and scoffed. "I wouldn't exactly call us friends."

"Okay," the man laughed. "Well, I'm Russ, Terra's older brother. And you are?"

"Sarah."

"Well, Sarah," he said with a smile, "I'm going to go out on a limb here and guess that she promised you clothes and never delivered?" He asked the question while glancing at her hand that still clutched the fluffy edges of the robe against her chest. Sarah blushed and nodded, avoiding his gaze, and he pointed to one of the lighter colored doors on the other side of the hall. "Yeah, that's typical T. She forgets everyone else whenever Noble comes around. They'll probably be big on you, but I can loan you some of my clothes if you want?"

"That would be appreciated," Sarah whispered, trying to convince her mind to not get stuck on the fact that Noble had come around before. She reasoned with herself that they were his friends and it would have been stranger if he hadn't come around. "Thank you."

"Don't worry about it," Russ said, strolling down the hall. "I'll be back in a second."

Five minutes later, Sarah was dressed in an outfit almost identical to Russ's that were, as he'd predicted, two sizes too big on her. She could deal with the shirt, but the shorts were a different matter. Even with the drawstring pulled as tight as it would go, they still slipped down to her hips. She gave up on them and decided to wear the yellow shirt he'd given her as a dress instead. It hung down to her knees and covered everything, but she still felt uncomfortable and exposed. Though she had to admit to herself it was probably foolish to think anyone in the house would find the outfit sexy or suggestive. Because if she'd learned anything from Kyle and the people of fragment 42913, it was that if people didn't flock to her for how unusual her yellow hair and blue eyes were, they avoided her at all costs. She sighed and pulled a brush through her wet hair before tying it up, re-braiding it, and twisting it into a loose bun. She slid her feet into the fluffy pair of socks Russ had put out for her and left the room to go find him.

Sarah meandered down the hall, taking her time to appreciate the subtle artwork that hung on the walls before finding her way back to the kitchen. Russ stood at the counter, chopping vegetables as he hummed the words of some song under his breath. Sarah tapped against the counter to grab his attention and he paused to look up at her, the gentle smile from before spreading across his lips.

"Hey. You're dressed."

"Yeah," Sarah nodded, walking over to where he was. The kitchen was big and open, with shiny appliances and white cabinets lining the wall to her right and a sprawling island with a sink that Russ stood at to her left. It opened to a large lounge area with floor-to-ceiling windows on either side of a brick fireplace, two black couches, a coffee table, and half a dozen bookshelves that were pushed up against the wall. Each one was packed with books of varying sizes and colors, and she wanted to walk over to them and see what they were about, but she noticed that the room was empty except for the two of them. Her blue eyes darted to the stairs they'd come up from before turning back to Russ.

"Where is everyone?"

He shrugged and returned to his task of chopping peppers.

"I'm guessing they're still downstairs. I haven't seen your other two friends, but I know Terra and Noble tend to disappear for hours whenever they get together."

"Do they?"

Russ looked up at Sarah's words and searched her face for a brief moment before shaking his head. "Ah," he said. "You like him."

"Like, who?" Sarah asked, leaning against the counter.

"Noble," Russ said with a questioning look. "You're not hiding it very well."

"Because I don't have anything to hide."

"Sure, you don't," Russ chuckled. "But if you did, I would say I pity the person who finally does fall for him. He's a rolling stone if I ever did meet one."

"Is he though? Seems like he's got eyes for your sister," Sarah offered, making Russ laugh.

"Noble has eyes for absolutely everyone," he said. "There might be someone out there that could make him want to change his ways and reign himself in, but it's not Terra. That's for sure."

"And how do you know that?" Sarah asked, chiding herself for allowing her curiosity to continue the conversation and for letting the smidgen of hope she felt blossoming in her chest sneak its way into her voice. She shouldn't have such a visceral reaction to the failure of someone else's relationship, but she couldn't stop herself from hanging onto Russ's every word.

He didn't look up from his chopping, but his lips did pull upward as he finished the peppers and swept them into a baking dish of chopped mushrooms, onions, noodles, and sauce. He stirred everything together and sprinkled some cheese over the whole thing before sliding the pan into the oven he'd preheated. Once he'd set the timer, he turned his dark eyes to Sarah and held her gaze.

"I know that because Noble is more complex than anyone gives him credit for," Russ said, sliding his hands into his pockets as he mimicked Sarah's posture and leaned against the opposite counter. "He's always been good looking, always had his pick of whoever he wanted, whenever he wanted them. That kind of freedom," Russ shrugged. "When you're loved that openly, it's hard to know who's being genuine with you and who's not. It weighs on you after a while."

Sarah scoffed. "It must be so hard being everyone's favorite."

Russ's smile fell and his dark eyes studied Sarah, searching for the meaning behind her words. She felt the casual air in the room shift as Russ looked at her, but she refused to look away this time. Instead, she stood up straight and stared back at him.

"What? You expect me to have sympathy for him?"

"I don't know you well enough to expect anything from you," Russ said, the light tone still in his voice. "I just think it's cute how you have the audacity to be jealous of my sister when it's clear you haven't been bothered to get to know him at all."

"What's there to know?" Sarah asked, listing Noble's traits off on her fingers. "He's handsome, charming, and can smooth talk anyone out of anything and he knows it. He's arrogant and self-important and yet people flock to him as if he were Carna himself. He's clearly one of the gods' favorites," she laughed mirthlessly, "but he's never been ridiculed or outcast because of it like I have. So, forgive me," Sarah said, rolling her eyes, "if I can't muster up any tears to cry for him."

"And that is why you're up here with me, instead of downstairs with him."

"That's rude."

"It's the truth," Russ said, shrugging. "You're no different from anyone else who falls in love with the idea of him. You make your assumptions about him because he plays to his strengths, but you haven't stopped to think about why he is the way he is," he said, pushing off from the counter to stand in front of her. "But let me ask you this. Would it make you feel better if he pretended to be humble? If he feigned insecurity and ignored all the people throwing themselves at him everywhere he went?" When Sarah was at a loss for words, Russ nodded and winked at her. "Never thought about the alternative, did you? Let me answer that for you — it wouldn't be better. And he can't do anything about the way people react to him any more than you can. So, he embraces it instead of fighting it. And you can't stand it because people fall over themselves to get him to notice them, but what you fail to realize is that," Russ pointed at her and shook his head, "that has nothing to do with him or who he is."

"Your real problem," Russ continued when she didn't speak up, "is that the gods fought over you and Rothe gave you yellow hair, but Asari gave you blue eyes and people have never seen that before. The gods loved you, but people fear what they don't know. It's why they avoid you. And it makes you so desperate for anyone to love you that you can't stand Noble because he doesn't love anyone except for the girl with green eyes who looks like Freya." Sarah looked away from his gaze and he took a step back. "I'm just saying," he said, "don't take your issues out on him. He's got his own problems and you," he pointed at her, "you should play to your strengths, too. If people avoid you, use that to your advantage instead of lamenting it."

"Don't speak like you know me."

"I know more about you than you think," Russ shot back. "Probably more than you know about yourself, Sarah Rothens. First daughter of the second princess, the late Venetia Rothens."

"You shouldn't know that."

Russ laughed and relaxed against the counter again. "Seriously? How many people do you think are walking around with blonde hair and blue eyes? That backwater fragment in Asari's domain may not have known who you were, but trust and believe that everyone else does."

"That will make things difficult."

"Or maybe it'll make things easier," Russ countered. "You never know."

"You're optimistic," Sarah said with a huff.

"I'll take that as a compliment," he laughed.

"What are you two laughing about in here?"

The question came from Noble as he climbed the stairs. He was shirtless and barefoot, wearing only a pair of blue sweatpants as he walked over to them. Jack and Brandi trailed behind, Brandi in a green crop top and a pair of shorts, and Jack in a blue t-shirt tight enough to split down the middle and a pair of loose shorts that matched the pair Russ wore, but Sarah couldn't pull her eyes away from Noble.

"It's nothing," Russ said, walking over to drape an arm around Sarah's shoulder. He looked away from the rest of them as he leaned into her ear. "Stop drooling. You'll give off the impression that you actually like him."

Sarah's eyes snapped to his, and he smirked. She huffed and pushed him away, but he laughed and pulled her back to him. Keeping his voice low, he turned Sarah away from them and grinned at her.

"Just trust me," Russ said.

"What are you about to do?"

"Just play along. And trust me," he repeated, winking at her before walking over to give Noble a man-hug — one of those where they shake hands and hug at the same time — before nodding in Jack and Brandi's direction. Noble gave them quick introductions before glancing over to Sarah and raising his eyebrows once he noticed she was wearing Russ's shirt and nothing else.

"I see you've already met Sarah."

"We spent some time together while everyone else was busy," Russ shrugged. "Where's T?"

"Still sleep," Noble chuckled. "She'll come up when she's ready."

"I'm sure," Russ said, glancing at him. "While we wait, go put on a shirt."

"What, you don't find this attractive?" Noble teased, flexing his muscles in Russ's direction.

"I'm sure many people do, but I'm not one of them," Russ said, shaking his head and pointing to his room. "You know the way."

"Yeah, yeah." Noble's eyes drifted over to Sarah again and her face flushed as she looked away. "You need to find something of T's for her to wear."

"Why?" Russ asked, looking behind him at Sarah with a smirk. "I think she looks good."

"Really?" Noble glanced over Sarah again. "She looks more out-of-place than anything else."

Russ raised an eyebrow at him. "Wow. Harsh, man."

"I'm just saying," Noble said, holding up his hands in mock surrender. "I think you should at least get her some pants."

"Yeah, yeah," Russ said, waving him off and walking towards the stairs. Noble disappeared around the corner and Sarah moved to the couch opposite of Jack. She watched Brandi browsing the shelves of the bookcases and wondered how many of them Russ had actually read. Just as Sarah was beginning to get comfortable though, the timer that Russ had set earlier went off.

"What's that for?" Jack asked, looking up from the book Brandi had handed him.

"Russ was making some food," Sarah said, looking behind her towards the kitchen. "I guess it's done."

"I'll grab it," Jack said, rising to his feet to walk toward the kitchen. He let his fingertips graze across the skin of Brandi's exposed back as he passed by her and paused to place a kiss against her shoulder. She looked up from the book she was looking at and smiled at him, before returning her attention back to the pages. Sarah caught the small, wordless exchange between them and averted her eyes as a small smile ghosted her lips.

The pang from before reverberated in her soul. Asari's desire to be the one to make Freya smile was a force to be reckoned with, but she wasn't him and Brandi wasn't Freya. But as Noble had mentioned earlier, it wasn't as poignant as the first time it happened. And she had no desire to be what Jack was to Brandi. She'd have to learn to live with Asari's desires as Noble, no doubt, learned to live with Carna's. Before she could spend any more time with the thought though, Noble returned wearing one of Russ's hoodies and Russ topped the stairs carrying a handful of Terra's clothes. He stopped in front of Sarah and offered her a hand, which she took.

"I'll take you back to my room," Russ said, his voice low, but still just loud enough for everyone else to hear. Sarah's face flushed a bright pink as Russ entwined their fingers to lead the way past Noble and back down the hall.

"I thought you didn't walk off with people you don't know," Noble said as they passed.

Sarah looked up at him and thought back on Russ's words. Noble was used to people falling over him left and right — the staff at the inn, Terra — and she didn't want to be like them. She wasn't naïve enough to think she liked Noble for his personality, but she had no plans to be one of many. Of that, she was absolutely sure. So, without thinking too much about it, Sarah decided she wouldn't be. She wasn't going to continue to fall over Noble like everyone else. Instead, she'd make him want her, and the idea of that birthed a flurry of butterflies in her stomach.

She'd be lying if she said her decisions were being motivated by anything other than the heat that pooled between her thighs whenever he held her gaze, but she didn't really care. She wanted him to want her and that was all there was to it. And the challenge of making that happen almost enticed her more than the man himself.

This was all a game to Noble, and she was going to play to win.

"You misunderstand," Sarah said with a small smile. "I just wasn't willing to walk off somewhere with you."

Noble scoffed and Sarah sped up her pace to lead Russ back to his room. When the door closed behind him, Sarah pressed a hand to her racing heart and turned wide eyes to Russ, who stood there smirking with his arms crossed.

"How?" Sarah asked. She shook her head, trying to contemplate how in the gods' realm Russ was able to make Noble pay attention to her.

"I told you," Russ said, handing over the clothes. "Noble is more complex than you think. Lucky for you, I know him pretty well."

"Thank you," Sarah breathed.

"Of course," Russ said, turning his back to her so Sarah could change in private. "But something you should know about me," Russ warned, "is I don't do anything without my own motivations."

Sarah snorted and rolled her eyes as she slid into the Black overalls and yellow shirt Russ had brought her. They fit much better than the oversized clothes he'd lent to her, and she felt relieved to be properly covered again.

"Surprise, surprise," she muttered. "You and everyone else."

Russ laughed as he faced the corner.

"You know what? I think we're going to get along, Sarah Rothens," he said, turning back to face her when she announced she was decent. "We're going to get along just fine."

CHAPTER FIFTEEN

Every sky must have horizons — take note of where yours are and let no one cross them.

— Boundless: An Introduction to Carna's Realm | Lindl's Fourth Holy Academy

---

CARNA'S SOUTHERN DOMAIN — PRESENT DAY

"So, now I really want to know," Terra said, leaning forward to rest her elbows on her denim clad knees, "why are y'all here?"

Brandi looked up from the book she'd been reading as Terra posed the question to the room. They all sat around on the various couches, entertaining themselves while they waited for the last of Carna's storm to let up. The winds had died down, but the rain still fell in unrelenting sheets from the dark sky. Brandi had wanted to keep moving, but Jack pointed out that unless she would be willing to leave Sarah behind or watch her drown in the flood, they'd have to wait out the storm. So, they'd resigned themselves to staying until morning and making the best of their current situation.

They'd devoured the simple pasta Russ made for them and the room had settled into the quiet sounds of clinking dishes as Russ and Sarah cleaned up, turning pages as Brandi read, and soft snores as Jack and Noble drifted in and out of sleep. Terra was the only one full of boundless energy as her eyes darted between all of them waiting for an answer to her question. Brandi sighed and snapped her book shut with enough force to wake both Jack and Noble.

They both shot up, their eyes focusing on her as the sleep left their eyes.

"Terra asked a question," Brandi said, straightening herself from the reclined position she was in. "One that I would also like to know the answer to. You said you had friends who could help us, but help us how? Why are we here, Noble?"

"The better question is," Noble said, leaning forward, "what were you two planning to do in Lindl's domain while he was still connected to the EREN," he said looking at Jack, "and she has never been on it?" he asked nodding his head in Sarah's direction.

"We would've dealt with that when we got there," Jack said.

"You're not that stupid," Noble shot back at him. "You know that once you enter Lindl's domain, you'll be connected, and the council will know exactly where we are in seconds."

"It's not like I had time to disconnect," Jack snapped. "Besides, Asari's domain doesn't even have access the EREN yet, so how was I supposed to find someone to remove me from it?"

"You should've just gotten off it before you left."

Jack snorted. "Right. Because you would've waited an extra twelve hours before leaving if Brandi had sent for you."

"Lucky for me," Noble shrugged, his eyes cold as they darted over to Brandi. "I didn't have that problem. She didn't send for me."

"What? Are your feelings hurt now?"

"It would've been a simple message," he said, holding her gaze. "I would've gone with you anywhere. You know that."

They stared each other down, and the air in the room became tense. Despite his casual demeanor, Noble was always serious whenever it came to her. He'd spent most of his life as her protector, so she wasn't surprised that it rubbed him the wrong way that she hadn't let him know when she abandoned the shadows. The only reason he'd found out about it was because Sal had left a message for him when he returned from his last job. He'd already left with Najé to track Jack and Brandi down, and Noble had taken off after them as soon as he could without looking back.

"I could only send one encoded message," Brandi said. "Mara only owed me one favor and you know how she is. She wasn't going to do something for nothing."

"The fact is, the message wasn't to me and that's what it is."

"You never seem this invested when I send for you," Terra joked while nudging Noble in his side. It was an attempt to inject some lightheartedness back into the room, but when Noble looked at her with his jaw set and all traces of amusement wiped from his face, her smile disappeared.

"Brandi's different."

"I see," Terra said, averting her eyes from him. "So, you only brought them here so I could disconnect them from the EREN?"

"If you wouldn't mind," Noble nodded.

"So earlier…" Terra trailed off, searching his eyes for an answer to the question she didn't want to speak in front of everyone. Her shoulders sagged when he gave a half smirk to her.

"Payment."

Terra flopped back into the cushions of the couch with her arms crossed and her eyes focused on the vaulted ceiling. Brandi had expected to see tears flood Terra's eyes and was somewhat surprised when they didn't come. There was usually a lot of sobbing involved whenever Noble broke a heart, but it seemed as if Terra had expected Noble's indifference towards her. It was probably an old cycle for them considering how long they'd known each other. Terra probably knew better than to expect more — to expect anything — from Noble. Brandi had expected some kind of outburst, but instead, Terra took a deep breath and straightened herself with a half smile on her face.

"I should've known that would be the only reason you'd come here," she chuckled.

"Not the only one," he said, reaching out for her, "but the main one. We could really use your expertise, T."

"I'm sure," she said, pushing his hands away. "I'm the fool for thinking you'd simply wanted to see me. But that's on me, right?" She scoffed and waved Noble's rebuttal away before he had a chance to speak. "It's not even worth discussing anymore," she said, leaning forward and focusing her gaze on Jack, "let's just get down to business, shall we? Whose child are you?"

"You're an engineer?" Jack asked, his eyebrows high.

"No, I'm just pretending to be one," Terra snapped, a frown pulling at her lips. She glanced over him before waving him off, her patience seeming to have already reached its limit. She didn't appear to be offended by his question — it was more like she didn't have the bandwidth to convince someone of her skills.

If Brandi had to guess, she probably got that question all the time. She could imagine that people would make the journey out to see them for one reason or another, following the end of a rumor that a rogue engineer could architect them exclusive gear that would upgrade their systems while disconnecting them from the EREN and getting them away from big sister's watchful eye. And with his more studious looks, it was probably a common misconception that Russ was the engineer rather than Terra in her pink crop tops and shorts.

"He clearly belongs to Rothe, but you," Terra said, her words trailing off as she studied Brandi's features more critically than she had when they'd first arrived. "You're from Freya's domain, aren't you?"

"I am."

A ghost of amusement flitted across Terra's face before it disappeared. "I've never met anyone from Freya's domain before."

"Now you have," Brandi said. "How long will this take?"

"Twelve hours," Terra stated. "Three to create the gear you'll need, six for it to replicate and delete the data from the EREN, another three to calibrate it."

"Our information is housed in the tower," Brandi warned, her eyebrows raised in surprise. "You're saying your software can infiltrate and delete Jack's information that quickly?"

"You're with Noble, so I had a pretty good guess of who you were when you arrived," Terra scoffed. "And yes. I wouldn't have said it could if it wasn't capable. You'll be out of here by tomorrow morning."

"We'll need transportation too," Noble pointed out. "So, we may be here longer than that."

"You'll be out of here by tomorrow morning," Terra repeated, the finality in her voice clear as she stood to her feet. "I'll be in my workshop. I'll need you," she said, pointing to Jack, "to give me the code you used to access the tower. I'll send for you when I'm ready."

Without another word, Terra left the room. Sarah glanced over to Russ as he dried the final dish and put it away on the shelves above them. He met her gaze and raised one of his silver eyebrows in question.

"Should we go after her?" Sarah whispered.

Russ shook his head. "This happens whenever Noble is around. Just let them do what they do and stay out of it. She'll deal with her emotions her own way."

"If you say so," Sarah whispered, her eyes still on the steps Terra had disappeared down. She wanted to go after her and offer her whatever comfort she could, but what was there for her to say? They weren't friends, so whatever sympathy Sarah showed her would only be seen as pity. So, instead of running after her, she trusted Russ and his words. Terra would simply have to work things out for herself.

When they were done, she followed Russ to the empty spot on the couch Terra had left behind and fell into the plush cushions beside him. He didn't pull her closer to him, but his thigh was pressed against hers on the cushions and she appreciated the gentle comfort he offered by just sitting next to her. She thought of stealing a glance at Noble but decided against it. She didn't know what he thought of her casual proximity to Russ, but if she didn't want to end up like Terra and Cara from the inn — with only her memories of a stolen interlude with Noble to mend the broken heart he would leave her with — she had to play the long game with him.

So, instead, she focused her attention on Brandi, who was staring at Noble.

"Why didn't you tell us you knew an engineer?"

"I didn't think it was worth mentioning until we got here," Noble said.

Brandi sighed and massaged her temples but didn't say anything else. It wasn't uncommon for Noble to withhold information until he felt like sharing it, because if there was anything he was better at than breaking hearts, it was keeping secrets.

"You're an ass, Noble," Brandi sighed. "But at least you got this figured out for us."

"You're welcome," Noble smirked. "Maybe next time you'll call me first so you won't lose access to your funds and can avoid sharing a room with blondie over there."

"Why did you have to bring me into this?" Sarah sighed. "I wasn't bothering anyone."

Noble chuckled under his breath, but he didn't respond to her question. Russ didn't look at her, but he gave her knee a gentle nudge with his own. It was a simple gesture, but it helped to ease some of her nerves.

"So, where are you guys headed?" Russ asked, changing the topic of conversation. "It's got to be a good distance away if you need transportation."

"It's not for us," Noble said, glancing over to Sarah, who flushed under his gaze. She was more than aware that her lack of skill slowed the rest of them down. She'd done her best to keep up with them, but up until a few days ago, she'd never had to walk further than the town square. It just wasn't possible for her to move like them.

"Don't you normally head back to Rothe's domain when you leave here?"

"Things are a bit complicated there at the moment."

"What did you do?" Russ asked, smirking at Noble. "Don't tell me you snuck off with one of the princesses and got yourself banned from the tower."

"Nah," Noble laughed. "I quit the shadows."

"You what?" Russ asked, sitting up to look at his friend.

"I quit," Noble repeated. "Following behind those two over there."

Russ's eyes darted over to Brandi and Jack. "Why would you quit?"

"Believe it or not," Brandi quipped, "sending people to the gods isn't as glamorous as it sounds."

"So you just got tired of it and…," Russ shook his head, trying to wrap his mind around what she was implying, "left?"

"More or less," Brandi shrugged.

"You should just tell her the truth, Green," Noble interjected, an edge to his voice as he sat up once again to look at her. "Or did I just imagine you insulting me for withholding useful information?"

"I wouldn't exactly call this 'useful information'."

"But you don't get to decide that, do you?"

"Noble," Jack said, leaning forward. "Chill."

"Tell her," Noble said, pointing to Sarah, "or I will."

"And when did you become so honest and upstanding?" Jack challenged.

"No one has ever accused me of being those things," Noble said, barking out a laugh. "But if our plan revolves around keeping her alive, she should at least know why the queendom wants her sent to the gods."

"What are you all talking about?" Sarah interjected, looking around the room. The mood that had been light and full of teasing moments ago was now tense as Noble and Jack stared each other down, and Brandi turned her intense green eyes onto Sarah. She searched her face briefly before letting out a sigh and standing to her feet.

"If you think it's so important, I'll tell her," Brandi stated. "But you have to take responsibility for whatever the aftermath is."

"I'm fine with that."

"Is there somewhere we can talk privately?" Brandi asked Russ.

"There's a balcony at the end of the hall."

"Thanks," Brandi answered, turning to look at Noble. "I'm assuming you know the way?"

Noble nodded and walked off while Brandi looked at Sarah and gestured for her to follow.

"Come on," she said. "You're the one who needs to hear this."

CHAPTER SIXTEEN

*She is the judge, jury, and executioner — she need not ask for forgiveness,
for in every decision, she is right.*

— Words of Worship for the Goddess | Lindl's First Holy Academy

CARNA'S SOUTHERN DOMAIN — PRESENT DAY

The three of them stood in a loose circle on the balcony that overlooked
Carna's valley, sheltered from the steady rain by the awning. The worst
of the storm was over and what they saw now was a breathtaking sight.
The water formed a winding river through the deepest parts of the valley
and flowed to the edge of the horizon. It would be gone like it had never
existed by tomorrow, but with the shadows that were cast across the hills
and the rhythmic tapping of rain against the roof, it was enough to make
anyone appreciate being alive in the gods' realm.

Brandi and Sarah stood by the edge of the balcony, leaning against
the metal railing and watching the valley as Brandi told her story. From
the day she'd left Sarah's family, to becoming a shadow and meeting
Noble, to what her life had been like while serving as the queen's blade, to

the moment she decided to leave everything behind to protect Sarah from being sent — she left nothing out. It was hard to listen to, but Brandi had been clear from the beginning that she wanted to make Sarah understand the full extent of who she was dealing with. The people she'd grown comfortable with over the past few days were no different from the people hunting her, and had the situation been any different, Jack, Brandi, and Noble would be hunting her too.

Sarah's shoulders grew heavier with each new piece of information, but it was Noble's reaction that Brandi seemed to be watching. He'd come outside with them and taken up a stance by the door to hear Brandi's version of the story, but his face had devolved deeper into a frown the more he heard, and his muscles tensed with every passing detail Brandi shared.

He'd asked for this, though, so Brandi didn't stop until her story was done.

Their eyes were locked when Sarah finally tore hers away from the valley below. Her mind had been racing, trying to keep up with everything Brandi told her. She hadn't appreciated how simple her life had been due to her parent's sacrifice, and her thoughts shifted over to Jamie. He was born in Asari's domain after their mother abandoned her bid for the throne. No one should even know he existed, and she prayed to Asari that no one ever came to realize that the boy in the photograph Brandi mentioned Bert having, was him. If they did, his life would be upended, just like hers.

But she couldn't worry about him now. Despite everything that happened, she had faith that Kyle would keep his word and protect Jamie from whatever dangers may one day seek him out. For now, there was only one question she wanted an answer to.

"Why me?" Sarah asked. "If he knows my face, then he knows I've been in hiding for all twenty-two years of my life. Why come after me now?"

Sarah's voice shook with the question and she tried to hold back the tears welling in her blue eyes and burning the back of her throat. She took deep breaths of the wet air and rubbed her hands against the goosebumps that had risen along her exposed arms. She shivered as the wind carried a light mist over to them from the rain and she struggled to keep her emotions under control. But with the realization sinking in of just how much her world was falling apart around her, she knew she wouldn't last for long.

"I hate to be the one to tell you this," Brandi said slowly, "but the queendom has wanted you dead from the moment you took your first breath."

"What?" Sarah asked, straightening up from the rails. "No," she said, shaking her head. "I may have been raised in Asari's domain, but I was born in Rothe's. A p-princess," she said, stuttering over the word. "Why would the queendom want to kill a princess?"

"Because you were born a girl," Brandi stated. "Your very existence posed a threat to Queen Leia's claim to the throne."

"That's ridiculous," Sarah scoffed. "I don't want the throne."

"Of course, you would think that's the issue here," Brandi sighed, rolling her eyes.

Sarah wanted to ignore the frustration that flared to life at Brandi's reaction, but her emotional dam was growing weak under all that it was trying to hold back. She hadn't chosen to be raised in the outskirts of Asari's domain, and it wasn't her fault that fragment 42617 was as far away from the queen and her tower as possible. She couldn't help that she was ignorant as to how the politics of the realm worked since she'd spent most of her life in hiding from the queendom. She liked to think that her mother had planned to teach her more, but she knew it was a wasted thought. Her parents were gone and whatever they had meant to teach her was irrelevant now.

All she knew was that she was Sarah Rothens, first daughter of the late second princess, Venetia.

"Then what is the issue?" Sarah asked, pulling at the ends of her hair. "Explain it to me so I can understand. Because, in case it wasn't obvious, I'm clearly not as well-informed as the rest of you."

"There's too much to explain the intricacies of it all, but here are the basics you need to know," Brandi said, listing off the information on her fingers. "The crown can only be passed down to its female descendants. This was a tradition created to honor Freya and it's why we call it the 'queendom'," Brandi stated, and Sarah nodded.

"Yes, I know that."

"Then you must also know that because the tradition honors Freya, and she is the goddess of life and judger of souls, those who lose their bid for the throne lose their life." Sarah gasped, and Brandi nodded. "I see you didn't get to that part of your history lessons."

"But... I don't...," Sarah wrung her hands and shook her head as she searched for words.

"That's why your mother abandoned the luxuries of the queendom to live in one of the worst outskirts in the realm," Brandi explained. "When she lost the throne, she'd also forfeited her life. But you'd already been born by the time she lost. So, instead of letting them execute you alongside her, she probably just took you and ran," Brandi guessed. "In doing so, she became one of the biggest traitors in the realm's history and with the creation of the shadows," Brandi shrugged. "Glenn and Patches made easy work of your parents."

"Don't talk about them as if they were strangers to you," Sarah snapped. "They took care of you!"

"And I protected you in exchange," Brandi said evenly. "Or did you conveniently forget that?"

Sarah locked eyes with Brandi and the tears that had been threatening, spilled down her cheeks as the complete shock of her words burst the dam holding back everything she'd been feeling.

"What?" Sarah asked, her voice cracking. "Why would you…" her question trailed off as Sarah shook her head.

The memory of her mother shoving her and Jamie out the little window at the back of their house into one of Asari's darkest nights still haunted her nights sometimes. They'd been completely blind in the dark, the unrelenting rain had blocked out every trace of the stars and her mother had screamed at her — begged her — to get away and find somewhere safe for her and Jamie. She'd heard her mother's screams and Brandi's high-pitched shrieks as strangers dragged her away from their home. She'd had to clamp a hand over Jamie's mouth to muffle his wails as they hid in the bushes, and she'd sobbed into the top of his head for what felt like hours until they'd finally been able to sneak away. She'd dragged him north for weeks, looking for anyone kind enough to let them stay in their fragment. It wasn't until they met the Asarna sisters, and they'd taken Jamie away for a hot bath, that she'd crumpled to the ground and cried for her parents like the child she was.

It had been weeks later before she'd even thought of Brandi again. So, to hear her say that she'd only become a shadow to protect her made Sarah's stomach clench with all types of guilt and regret. She met Brandi's gaze again and she gave her a nonchalant shrug.

"The night the shadows came, I tried to leave with you," Brandi told her. "Your mother begged me to help get you and Jamie out of the fragment, but Freya forced me to stay behind. She told me that I needed to go with Glenn. I tried to leave anyway, but I'm sure you know what it's like trying to defy the will of the gods," Brandi scoffed. "So, I did the next best thing. I distracted the shadows by letting them take me instead of you. It's the only reason you're alive now."

"Why would they have even wanted her?"

The question came from Noble, and something about the absolute disbelief in his tone that anyone could want her made her chest ache. She knew that she'd found favor with the gods, and she'd endured more hate and rejection than most people ever had to experience in their lifetime, but it felt like Noble's words were the ones that broke her. She looked to the darkening sky and counted the stars she could see poking through the clouds. She'd wanted to know the truth and Brandi didn't seem like she was done talking just yet.

"I'd like to know that too," Sarah said softly.

"The shadows were there to send your parents," Brandi answered. "But they were also there to force you into the service of Queen Leia."

"I don't understand."

"Should a former princess birth an heiress to the throne before her execution, that child will be considered a daughter of the throne and allowed to place a bid for it when she becomes of age," Brandi stated, repeating the words that Rinn MelForth had taught them.

"They wanted to keep you under their thumb," Brandi explained when Sarah didn't respond. "If you'd become a shadow, your existence would have been erased and no one would have believed you were a daughter of the throne. Any bid you eventually made would have been dismissed as a ridiculous claim. It was probably the queen's suggestion," Brandi pointed out. "Rather than sending her own niece, she probably wanted you brought back to the tower. You would've been a shadow, but you would have reported directly to her. You would've been untouchable."

"If that's true, then why did they take you?"

"Probably because Rothe demanded it," Brandi said, looking away from them. "He did make her his vessel to protect me after all."

Neither Sarah nor Noble knew what to say to that. They didn't know anything about Brandi's history. She wasn't one to talk about her past or where she'd come from. All Sarah knew about her was that her parents were sent to the gods by the shadows and then she'd joined them. She never got more of an explanation than that and Brandi didn't offer one now.

"That still doesn't answer why it has to be now," Sarah whispered. "If everything you said is true —"

"It is," Brandi affirmed.

"Then why send the shadows after me now? I came of age four years ago."

"I don't know," Brandi admitted. "But knowing what Freya told me, I'd guess it has something to do with stopping Azinne."

Sarah scoffed. "I'm just one girl. I can't do much against a being who controls time."

"You're Asari's vessel and you can do more than you give yourself credit for."

"Thanks," Sarah said, shock widening her blue eyes. She wasn't accustomed to Brandi encouraging her, and she didn't know how to place the feeling blooming in her chest. If she had to give it a name, though, it made her feel hopeful.

"I wasn't trying to make you feel better." Brandi shrugged. "I'm just pretty confident we're going to need all the gods' vessels to stop this time apprentice. At least, that's what Freya hinted at."

"She didn't give you more specific instructions? That's helpful," Noble scoffed, and Sarah jumped at the sound. She'd nearly forgotten he was there.

"Did you expect a manual?" Brandi asked him. "The gods are never transparent, other than when they want something." When neither of them disagreed with her, Brandi crossed her arms with a sigh. "The point I was trying to make is this — if I was Bert working for some time apprentice, I'd use my power to send one of the vessels to the gods prematurely too. And if the assumption is that we can't stop him if we're not all together, then you," she said, pointing to Sarah, "would be the easiest one to get rid of."

The hope Sarah felt blossoming in her chest earlier rotted and she sighed. There was nothing she could say to refute Brandi's words. She didn't know who Lindl's vessel was, but if Rothe's vessel was Glenn MelForth, Carna's was Noble, and Freya's was Brandi, she understood why Bert would start with her too. The others were the people who trained the shadows he'd have to send after them — and that wasn't an effective strategy. But she was just an abandoned princess in hiding. As much as she hated the truth of her words, Brandi was right. She would be, without question, the easiest one to send to the gods.

Before she could open her mouth to ask another question, though, Jack came to the door. He opened it and pointed back towards the way he'd come from.

"Terra's ready for us."

"I thought she only needed you?" Brandi responded.

"Honestly, I just don't want to be left alone in a room with her. She seems a little emotionally vulnerable," he said, looking at Noble, "and I don't want her imprinting on me or something. So, I came to get you. Come on," he said holding his hand out to her.

Without another word, Brandi pushed off the railing, took Jack's hand, and followed him down the hall, leaving Sarah alone with Noble. She realized immediately that she probably looked worse than she had when they'd dragged themselves in from the storm. With tears streaming down her cheeks, a runny nose, and red splotches all along her skin, she had to look anything but desirable. She turned away from him and covered her eyes as she lost the last of the restraint she had on her emotions and the first of her sobs broke through.

Sarah prayed to Asari that he would just leave her to her thoughts. She didn't want him, or anyone else, to see her like that. But instead, she felt his presence beside her. She looked up at him and he stood leaning against the railing next to her with his arms crossed and his dark eyes focused on some fixed point on the wall. He wasn't paying any attention to her, but her heart still skipped a beat from him being so close.

So very close.

She felt the heat radiating off his skin and looked away, back toward the valley below them.

"I'm not good with tears," he offered, "but if you need a shoulder to cry on," he trailed off, twisting his body to lean his shoulder closer to her.

She looked up again, first at his face, then at the shoulder he was offering her. It was broad and she could already feel her heart prepping to run a marathon. She glanced up to his face again, trying her best to figure out if his offer was genuine or if he was looking for another reason to tease her. Her heart wouldn't be able to handle it if he was just teasing her again, so she closed her eyes.

"If this is just you making fun of me again, I'm fine," she whispered.

"I'm not."

"I don't trust you."

He sighed and reached out for her. Without warning, he pulled her into his arms and pressed her head against his shoulder. It was a gentle gesture — one far gentler than anything she thought him capable of — and it sent her pulse flying.

"Yeah," he muttered. "No one seems to trust me these days, but you don't need to," he said. "I'm the one who told Brandi to tell you all that and I'm the one who promised to deal with the aftermath, whatever it was. So, let it out and then we'll pretend this never happened."

Sarah clenched her eyes shut and before she could stop herself, she clutched his shirt in her fists and wept.

"What do you need from us?"

Brandi had asked the question as she followed Jack into Terra's workshop. Russ had given them instructions on how to get there from the couch he occupied. He was stretched out on the black sofa with a book in his hands and had barely looked up from it as he pointed out the way. It made Brandi curious as to which book he had picked up, but she hadn't lingered to ask. She simply followed Jack down the stairs, through the living area they'd entered into before, and through a door at the end of a short hallway.

Terra's workshop was built onto the back of their house and Brandi was surprised by just how advanced everything was. Every piece of tech she'd ever seen in Lindl's domain seemed to be there in some capacity — from the watches and accessories that allowed reality to be augmented, to scale models of the pods used to navigate the skies above the city, to micro and nanochips strategically organized and placed around the room to be within an arm's reach of the workbenches. There was a door in the back of the room equipped with a traditional padlock and body scanner, and it made Brandi curious about what could be behind it that needed so much protection.

The most impressive thing to Brandi's eye though was the digital setup on the far right of the room. Five monitors were mounted to the wall, running a constant stream of numbers and codes that even Brandi struggled to keep up with. They were connected to a line of keyboards on a single desk running along the length of the wall, and Brandi couldn't look away from it. Terra sat cross-legged in a chair amid a holographic display. As she moved her fingers across the transparent keys on her armrests, the displays shifted. Her eyes were swollen, but that was the only evidence she'd been crying at some point. Now, her dark eyes moved at the rapid pace of the shifting holograms, darting over to the monitors every so often. Her chair spun in time with the displays and the glow from the blue light they emitted made her seem almost ethereal.

It wasn't until Jack rapped his knuckles against one of the workbenches that Terra seemed to snap out of her trance and managed to pull her eyes away from the displays. Brandi doubted she'd heard her original question because Terra frowned as her gaze shifted between her and Jack.

"I wasn't expecting you to bring Brandi too."

"Is my being here a problem?"

"Of course not," Terra said, waving away the question. "Be wherever you want to. It's just going to be boring watching me work." Terra turned her head to look at Jack and raised an eyebrow. "You're the one who needed to be removed from the EREN right?"

"Both of us actually," he said nodding. "And if you could get us out of the ERIS, that would be great too."

"I should've already been removed from the EREN," Brandi reminded him.

"Doesn't hurt to confirm that. I mean, it's not that I don't trust Najé and Sal but," Jack shrugged, "they lie."

"It's not a big deal," Terra said, "I can do all of it. Either way, I only need one access code to break into the ERIS," she said, turning her attention back to the holograms in front of her. "Unless your information isn't housed in the same place?" When neither of them responded, she looked up again and stopped her chair to look at them.

"Explain," she demanded.

"We're both shadows," Jack said, "but she's more important than I am."

Terra narrowed her eyes as she focused on Brandi. Brandi held her gaze, and they stared each other down before Terra smirked and relented, turning her gaze back to Jack.

"How much more important?"

"I served Queen Leia directly," Brandi said, answering for herself. "So, my information may be harder to access."

"When you say 'directly'," Terra said slowly, drawing air quotes through the air. "Do you mean…"

"I mean," Brandi interjected, "that I was a member of the queen's private court. All of the dirty work, none of the parties."

"Well, I'll be Carna's left ass cheek," Terra whistled, a grin pulling across her face. "You've got some of the highest security in the realm!"

"Is that going to be a problem?"

Brandi asked the question with a smirk and lilt in her voice that made it clear that this was a challenge, and Terra's excitement at the idea of breaking into the ERIS confirmed Brandi's suspicions that she was a genuine engineer. Anyone without the proper training would have wilted under the pressure of such a massive task, and the only place for an engineer to train was at one of the academies in Lindl's domain. The courses there were rumored to be so difficult, they could only be completed with Lindl's divine intervention. Brandi didn't know if she truly believed that or not, but she'd witnessed Lindl's intellect for herself, so she never rejected the idea that it was possible.

But, once the secrets of the EREN were learned, it was forbidden for anyone to leave the academy. If they did, they became branded as a rogue engineer, excommunicated from the EREN and the intellectual community, and sent to the gods on sight if they ever tried to return. Because of that, rogue engineers were few and far between, but they were also some of the most capable mechanics, hackers, and informants in the entire realm.

Mara was one of them, but even she had encountered struggles when trying to access locked information on the ERIS. So, Brandi had her doubts about whether a single girl from Carna's domain could handle it or not, but if Noble was willing to vouch for her skill, Brandi wanted to see for herself exactly what Terra was capable of.

Terra grinned at Brandi's question and turned in her chair to face the holograms again. With a swipe of her hand through the air, they dimmed and her chair moved her to the desk in front of the line of monitors.

She focused on the screens and moved her fingers across three separate keyboards before glancing over her shoulder.

"Access codes for the ERIS," she demanded. "Him first."

"d8N13lz1w148Ki," Jack responded without missing a beat.

Terra's fingers flew across the keys at a pace that made them blur together. Her chair moved down the line of monitors and two of the screens flashed white before scrolling through a sequence of rapid numbers and letters at twice the speed of the others. It was several moments before she looked up and nodded.

"Done," she answered. "It'll be done in about six hours, and I'll calibrate a new watch for you in the morning. Now, miss high and mighty over there."

Brandi scoffed and rolled her eyes, but she didn't say anything as Terra refocused her eyes on the screens in front of her, preparing to repeat her process.

"Access code," she demanded again.

"70cK4—"

Brandi stopped mid-sentence and hissed under her breath as Freya's thoughts invaded her mind.

Give her the one Lindl taught you.

Brandi tried to resist Freya's words, but that only made the goddess push harder, and the force of it nearly blinded Brandi for the moment.

She will know what to do with it. Tell her.

"Brandi?" Jack placed his hand on her back and she huffed, covering her face with her hands. She couldn't argue with Freya when she gave direct orders like that. So, she took a deep breath and let it out slow, steeling herself for whatever was to come next.

"I'm fine," she whispered to Jack.

"What's the problem?" Terra asked, glancing over her shoulder again. "You forget it or something?"

"No," Brandi responded. "It's Freylin."

Terra's fingers hovered motionless over the keys before she turned around and looked at Brandi again, annoyance written across her face.

"Funny. Now, what's your actual code?"

"Freylin," Brandi repeated.

"That's impossible."

"I guarantee you it's not."

"Your access code should be a randomly generated sequence of letters and numbers," Terra countered. "That's the only way the ERIS works. The only way it functions," she explained. "If everyone had a familial code, the grid would malfunction with a flood of replicas in less than a year from the sheer number of people who access it," she said with a shake of her head. "So, the original architects took away that feature. No one but the queen has a familial code to access the grid and even then," Terra stressed, "it's integrated with numbers so that each monarch has a brand new code. So, either you're cracked," Terra said, narrowing her eyes, "or you're lying."

"Check it," Brandi challenged.

"There's no need," Terra said, shrugging. "You can't have that as your access code. If you did, it would break the grid," she shook her head, "it would mean that you're a direct descendant of the original architects. And going back that far in the data could crash the whole system!"

Brandi didn't say anything, she just held Terra's dark gaze with her green one. Terra raised her eyebrows and leaned forward in her chair, waiting for the punchline of whatever joke Brandi was telling her. But when it never came, she glanced over to Jack, who stood with his hands stuffed into the pockets of his borrowed shorts. He had the entirety of Rothe's knowledge now and stood back as Brandi waited to see what Terra would do.

"Alright," Terra said slowly, waving her fingers across the armrest to move her chair back to the holograms she'd been sitting in the center of before. "I'll bite," she said, allowing her own curiosity and the implications of what it would mean if Brandi were speaking the truth to drive her forward.

She stretched her fingers and took one last look at Brandi before waving the holograms back into place. Her fingers moved at a slower pace as she brought a single one into view. Unlike the codes she was accustomed to that were randomly generated, if she needed to access a familial code, she didn't need to search for the part of the system that housed that information. There was only one place where the ERIS would accept a curated code that contained less than ten letters and no numbers. They'd learned of the original network at the academy, but it had been taught to them as a myth.

Terra had found remnants of it when she'd gone rogue and began cracking into the ERIS, but seconds after she'd come across it, she'd been locked out. She'd tried circumventing the code requirement, even tried entering the familial code of every known monarch, but it had rejected her every time. Whatever the original architects had hidden, they'd made sure that it was unhackable. Without the proper code, no one would be able to access it.

As she typed in Brandi's code, her heart raced in her chest.

She couldn't remember the last time she'd been that excited — if she'd ever been that excited. But where she'd expected the numbers to spin and the holograms to react, instead, the power for the entire house surged. She gasped and looked around, her mind jumping to all the projects that required a constant flow of energy from the power grid she'd architected for the house.

"What's happening?" She shrieked.

Before she could respond, a green light filled the room and an image of Freya in all her glory filled the space of the holograph, and Terra's eyes widened. Her jaw fell open, and she moved her chair back to where the other two stood to get a good look at the goddess.

"I've been waiting for you, Brandi. Terra," Freya's image shifted to Brandi's right and smiled. "It is good to see you again, Jack. The time has come for a proper introduction and," she returned her gaze to Brandi's, "explanation of exactly who you are," she said as holographic images of the other gods took shape on either side of her, "and the truth of this realm we created."

"How is this possible?"

Terra whispered the question as she trembled in her chair. She pressed a hand into her short silver hair before pulling it across her face — as if closing and reopening her eyes would make the images in front of her any less real.

Brandi had no such hopes.

She'd met the gods before and knew them well — knew the forms they took and their mannerisms. Rothe stood on Freya's right, his fingers threaded through hers, and Lindl to the right of him. Carna and Asari stood on her left. And Freya smiled at Brandi, her holographic face glowing as she looked down at her.

Freya was as beautiful as she always was, her locs hanging freely down her back. But unlike most times when Brandi met her on her own in the god realm, she wore her crown now. It was a simple flower crown of maple blossoms that grew in her domain, but at its center was a skull. Brandi had never asked where the skull came from or who it had initially belonged to, but she knew that Freya only wore it when she appeared before mortals. It was the completion of her image, her reminder to the mortals that while she is the mother of the realm and the giver of life, she is also the taker of souls and the goddess of death.

Brandi was surprised to hear Freya speaking the natural tongue of the realm rather than the language of the gods, but she returned her smile and Jack, as expected, fell to his knees in prayer as he had done before in Rothe's realm.

"Calm yourself, child," Carna spoke, looking in Terra's direction. "We do not have time for your disbelief."

"I just..." Terra shook her head and glanced at Brandi. "Is this real?" Her head swiveled between the holograms of the gods and Brandi's cool demeanor. "How are you this calm?"

Terra's voice had raised several octaves, and Brandi reached out to place a gentle hand on her shoulder. Terra's head dipped to look at it, her eyes transfixed in one position as her mind spiraled around itself trying to make sense of what was happening — of what she had done.

"Your children aren't the brightest, are they?" Asari chuckled.

Carna shot a glare at him, and Brandi watched as he locked his jaw to hold back his words. Freya disliked it whenever the gods argued amongst each other, and it was well-known that arguing with Asari was a pointless endeavor. His fickle nature would lead him to rile up one of the gods just to lose interest halfway through the argument. He would then have the nerve to be curious as to why they were angry to begin with. The only consistent thing about Asari was his commitment to Freya. He worshipped the ground she walked on and never did anything that would draw her ire if he could help it.

"The child is fine," Rothe intervened, more than willing to argue with Asari despite the displeasure it caused Freya. "She's merely in shock. How would you expect a mortal to react?"

"Like yours I suppose?" Asari shrugged. "Bowing and muttering like a fool."

"Are you insinuating that I should be upset that my children worship me as they should?" Rothe's laughter shook the room as he chuckled. "It's alright to be jealous, Asari. I'm sure I would be too if my children only prayed to me out of need."

Lindl and Carna snickered, and Asari cut a glare to both of them before Freya raised her hands to stop them.

"Please," she said, her long green locs swishing across her back as she turned first to look at Rothe and then Asari, "we don't have time for your bickering." She looked to Brandi, the only one still standing in their presence. "We've come to speak with you," she waved her hand to Terra and Jack, "and your allies about what is to come. You will need them." She glanced around the room and noticed that not all the children she needed to speak with were present. "Where are your friends?"

"Upstairs," Brandi answered. "Do you need them?"

"Yes," Freya answered. "This program only allows us to connect with the mortal realm for a short time, but it's imperative they hear this information."

"How?" Terra asked, her engineering senses shifting into overdrive at the thought of understanding how the original network worked, nevermind the fact that she'd been rendered speechless by the presence of the gods moments before. "I've studied this network a million times and couldn't figure out the mechanics to make it work. So, how..." she trailed off.

Lindl smiled at her questions. "It would seem Carna's children are rather quick-minded," he quipped to Asari before walking over to Terra. Of the gods, he was the most upright. He wore a dark green turtleneck matching Freya's dress that clung to his toned arms and chest. His slacks were creased, and his light brown skin was flawless. Terra couldn't look away as he smiled down at her, his violet eyes welcoming as his short wavy tresses fell into his face.

"Come, child," he said, indicating the far end of the room where the locked door was located. "There are many things I can teach you in the brief time we have together, but we should leave them be for now," he said, indicating the others. "There is much to be discussed, but this is something that only you can understand."

Terra nodded and followed the holograph of Lindl through the door without looking back. Once they were gone, Freya looked to the remaining three.

"You should find your vessels and explain," she said softly.

"As you wish," they answered in unison.

Rothe turned to Jack and smirked. "Come, my son, stop all that praying now. I hear you. Lead us to where the others are so that we may speak with them."

"Of course," Jack said, rising to his feet and leading the holograms of the gods upstairs to where he'd left the others. Brandi watched them go and half expected their images to flicker out as they left the room, but when they didn't she chided herself for expecting them to be limited by mortal technology. They were gods. Mortal limitations meant nothing to them.

Once it was just Freya and Brandi, Freya descended to the floor in the same way she did whenever Brandi met with her in her temple. She copied the movement, sitting across from Freya close enough for their knees to touch, but this time she didn't feel her warmth. Brandi was surprised to realize she missed the feeling, but she didn't waste much thought on it. If Freya was projecting herself into the mortal realm, she had to have a good reason for it.

"As I told you, I don't have much time, so let's get right to the point this time, shall we?" Brandi nodded, and Freya waved her hand, transforming the room into one filled with the green light of her magic. It depicted what Brandi could only guess to be Carna's domain and her breath was taken away by the sight of it.

"Let's start at the part you already know," Freya said. "We created this realm centuries ago. Of our own blood and desires, we crafted everything you would ever come to know. And when we were done," she said, waving her hand again, "our children were born. Now," she said, pulling the images to her, and showing Brandi her own domain, "you know that all children are born of two lineages. Mine and one of the gods. Yes?"

"Yes," Brandi answered with a nod.

"Well, there's more," Freya whispered, with a smile on her face. "Mortals were not the only children born of our union," she explained. "We had many children before mortals were born of us, and our older children didn't care for them. So, Lindl created his Blind Sea," Freya said, showing Brandi a depiction of the entire realm being devoured by the sea until only the realm she was familiar with remained, "and separated them from you."

"There's more beyond the Blind Sea?" Brandi asked, amazed.

"Much more," Freya nodded. "But what you need to know is about your lineage," Freya said. "I'm sure you've noticed how the shaders respond to you?"

"It's your spirit in me they respond to."

"No," Freya corrected gently, "it is you, my dear child. You hear and communicate with them as I do because you are one of the few children who share no lineage with the other gods. You are mine."

"What..." Brandi frowned and tilted her head in confusion. "I don't understand."

"In the beginning, when we separated our lands into domains," Freya said, highlighting the dividing lines of each of the god's territories in the image she held, "there was a great fight over whose children would be allowed to live in mine. They each wanted their own children to be natives of my lands, but that would upset the delicate balance we had spent so much time creating," she explained. "So, like the shaders born solely of the darkness before the sun, there were a group of mortals, born solely of my own soul. They were called the clan of Freylin and they made a home in my domain, but they also traveled the realm, sharing stories of the gods and ensuring that the children worshipped us properly."

Brandi gasped and Freya smiled. "Do you understand now? It was not coincidence that I chose you as my vessel," she said. "Or that your soul resonated so powerfully with mine."

"I literally have your soul," Brandi whispered, struggling to comprehend the words as they took on a new meaning for her now. She'd accepted her connection to Freya from the beginning, but she'd always seen a clear divide between them, and Rothe had been thorough in teaching her that she was not the same as them. So, Freya's words contradicted everything that Brandi had accepted as fact.

"We are one and the same," Freya smiled. "You are as much the goddess as I am."

"But the gods…" Brandi shook her head, trying to unscramble her thoughts. "They're not in love with me."

Freya laughed. "Because they are in love with me. And I with them," she smiled. "Let me ask you this. Would your Jack fight Rothe for me? Or is that only for you?" Brandi's face grew hot under Freya's scrutiny as she thought back on Jack's words in the god realm. She broke her gaze away from Freya's and shook her head.

"No, I don't think so."

"The gods are no different. They love me because I am Freya," she explained, "not because I am the goddess."

"So," Brandi said, turning to meet Freya's holographic gaze once more, "why are you telling me all this now?"

"Because you will need the full extent of your power if you are to defeat Azinne."

"I don't know what we're supposed to do about him," Brandi admitted. "I don't..."

"It's fine," Freya soothed, reaching out her holographic hand to rest it on Brandi's knee. She didn't feel anything, but the simple act of the gesture soothed something inside Brandi she hadn't realized had grown so restless. "You don't have to have the answer right now. Even we gods don't have the answer, and we've been preparing for this for centuries."

Brandi nodded and searched Freya's face. The hologram of her flickered and Freya looked down at her body. It was beginning to glitch in and out, signaling the coming end to her time in the mortal realm.

"What do you need me to do?"

"Do what you feel is right," Freya said. "I do not have a path laid out for you anymore. You are the master of your own destiny from here on out."

"I don't think I like that."

Freya laughed, and the sound eased the anxious parts of Brandi. So much of what Freya was telling her was hard to believe, but she didn't have time to doubt her words. Freya had never lied to her and had never given Brandi a reason to distrust her. But hearing the creator of the realm and mother of all mortals tell her that they were equal in power... Brandi couldn't even begin to wrap her mind around that.

"You have always been displeased with the outcome of your life," Freya said gently. "You've always felt yourself to be nothing more than a pawn for the gods. A tool for the queendom. As helpless as the souls you send to us. I'm telling you now," she said, holding Brandi's green gaze with her own, "that you are not. You are more powerful than any being in either realm. You need only believe and choose for yourself which path you will lead us down."

"That's a lot of pressure."

"That is what it means to be a goddess," Freya chuckled. "It's more than power. You carry the burden of responsibility for every being who believes in you. It's no easy task," she warned, "but I believe you can handle it."

Freya's image flickered again, and she offered one last smile to Brandi.

"My time in this realm is up."

"I have more questions, though!"

"But I have no more answers for you," Freya said. "This is your journey now, Brandi, and you don't need me as you once did. You are not alone anymore. And the friends you've made need you just as much as you need them," she said, looking up as the other gods returned to the room, Jack, Noble, and Sarah trailing behind them. "Yes, you need them more than you realize," she whispered under her breath, standing to her feet.

She reached her hands out to the gods, and Rothe took her right hand while Lindl took her left. They smiled at her and then, one by one, they flickered out of the realm until only Freya was left. She held Brandi's gaze and winked at her.

"*You will be okay. After all*," Freya said, her voice lingering on the air, "*we have always been one and the same.*"

CHAPTER SEVENTEEN

It is in the depths of the night when the truths of our hearts become apparent. The anxieties and fears chased away by the light of the day engulf us and drag us under, captivating us with promises of an endless companionship. But their words ring hollow, for Asari's moon may rule the night, but Rothe's sun will always bring with it the dawn.

— Of Light and Love | Lindl's Second Holy Academy

CARNA'S SOUTHERN DOMAIN — PRESENT DAY

No one said anything once the gods left. They simply shared a look and went their separate ways.

Terra disappeared behind the door in the back of her workshop, Jack and Brandi slipped into the guest room across from Terra's, and Noble walked out the front door. Sarah stared after him, but she couldn't bring herself to wonder where he was going or what he was doing. Her mind was too exhausted from everything she'd experienced that day. She just dragged herself out of the workshop and to the living room where Russ stood at the bottom of the stairs, staring at the door Noble had slammed shut.

"Don't worry about him," Russ whispered, shaking his head. "He'll be alright."

Sarah nodded and followed Russ back upstairs. She hadn't thought about where she would sleep, but when Russ paused at the door to his room with a questioning look on his face, she realized she'd followed him without much thought.

"Oh," she sighed. "I'm sorry."

"No worries," Russ said. "Do you want to sleep in here with me tonight?"

Sarah thought about denying the offer — of walking across the hall to sink into the cold sheets of the last guest room to spend the night tossing and turning with nothing but her own thoughts to keep her company, wondering if Noble would slink back into Terra's bed whenever he returned. Or maybe into hers. She didn't have the energy to force herself away from Russ and face that kind of night, so instead she leaned forward and rested her forehead against Russ's chest and sighed as he rubbed her back in soothing circles.

"If you don't mind," Sarah whispered.

"Not at all," he said. "Come on in."

Brandi didn't speak a word to Jack until they stood inside the guest room Terra had lent them. It was across the hall from her own and, like the bathroom, the left side of the wall was nothing but glass. The moon was resilient in breaking through the clouds and its soft light sent raindrop shadows crawling across the queen-sized bed and hardwood floors.

"Why didn't you tell me?" Brandi demanded, the irony of repeating his words back to him not lost on her.

"Bee," Jack said gently, taking a step forward. "I did."

"No, you didn't," she huffed, wracking her memories for any conversation where he could have told her something that important. "I would've remembered that."

Jack looked away from her and sighed. "Back at Carol's Inn when I first woke up," he said, raising his gaze back to her. "It probably wasn't the best way to tell you since I was pissed and it was more accusatory than anything else, but..." Jack shrugged, letting his words die there and the memory struck Brandi with a force that knocked the wind out of her.

"So, when you said not to split hairs with you..."

"I already knew you were the goddess. It's part of the reason I was so angry that you kept telling me you weren't. But then I realized you didn't know. Freya hadn't told you yet."

Part of Brandi wanted to demand a better explanation from him, but she knew there was none. The truth was apparent to both of them. Even if he had told her the truth again, calmly and with patience, she still wouldn't have believed him. She would have rejected every attempt he made to tell her who she was and only believed it now because it had come from Freya herself. She knew that, but still, it somehow overwhelmed her even more to think that Jack had known the entire time.

"So, you're just cool with all of this?" She questioned. "Rothe tells you I'm a goddess and you just accept it as fact?"

"Of course," he said. "What else was I supposed to do? Argue with him?"

Brandi laughed under her breath at the idea of Jack trying to argue with Rothe about her true identity.

"I can't wrap my mind around any of this," she admitted. "I'm just a shadow, Jack. All I do is follow orders. I can't make decisions for the entire realm," she said, shaking her head. "I'm not fit to be anyone's goddess."

"You've never been 'just' anything, Bee," Jack said, stepping forward to pull her into his arms for a hug. "You are beautiful and strong, honest, loyal, thoughtful, the best shadow to have ever served the queendom and the culmination of all the best traits the gods have to offer. You have always been beyond extraordinary. Now, you have a title to prove it."

"What if the gods are wrong, though?" Brandi whispered into his chest. "What if they've put all this faith into me and I fail?"

"If the gods are wrong, then they have to be wrong about everything. Do you believe that?"

"No."

"Then you shouldn't believe they'd be wrong about this. About you," he said, a smirk slipping across his lips. "Besides, as many times as I've worshipped you on my knees, I have no doubt you're a real goddess."

Brandi laughed at that, her body melting into his at the memory. "You do have a point, I guess."

"You guess?" He scoffed. "I'm a devout believer, Bee. If you have doubts, I can always reaffirm my faith right now."

"I think that would be a good idea," Brandi said, leaning up to press a soft kiss to his lips.

"I'm a living sacrifice," Jack whispered against her lips, as she pulled him closer to the bed. "Take from me what you wish."

Brandi broke their kiss to pull his shirt over his head and feast her green eyes on his rich brown skin and sculpted abs. She never got tired of looking at him and always got a thrill out of seeing his reaction to her watching him. She reached out to trail a finger down his chest before pushing him lightly down on the bed and straddling his lap.

"Everything," she whispered, pulling her borrowed crop top over her head and tossing it to the floor. "From you, I want everything."

Jack didn't hesitate in pressing his lips to her skin, his tongue chasing after all the raindrop shadows cast over her, and Brandi let her desire push away any anxieties that lingered over Freya's words. There would be plenty of time for her to worry over what would come next, but if nothing else, Freya was right about Brandi not being alone. She had Jack, and that would always be enough for her.

"I hope shaders eat you and defecate on your mother's grave!"

The first rays of Rothe's sun had just begun to light the room when Terra's shouts startled Brandi awake. She bolted upright in bed, the knife she'd kept tucked beneath her pillow as she slept, gripped tight in her hand. Her eyes darted around the brightening room, searching for the problem, before her brain registered where the sounds were coming from.

"What in the gods' name..." Brandi whispered to herself, lowering her knife and rubbing her temples with her free hand as another voice joined Terra's in the hallway.

"Gods! Just do your job and we'll leave!"

Brandi's eyebrows shot up as she listened to the argument escalate and considered ignoring whatever was happening down the hall, but she knew it would be a worthless attempt. Jack was already gone and she knew he wouldn't be back until he finished his morning prayers to Rothe. Without him, she'd never be able to sleep through the noise. So, instead of sinking back into the warm sheets, she walked over to where she'd tossed her clothes from last night and put them back on. She didn't particularly care for the strapless crop top and denim shorts that Terra had lent her, but they were better than nothing.

Brandi moved down the hall to stand outside the door to Terra's workshop. Terra stood on the other side of the room shouting at three Rothian men who stood at her customer's entrance and Brandi recognized them immediately. Raymond, Ronald, and Roland were intel shadows who worked as a part of Sal's network. They were short and lean to be children of Rothe, but what they lacked in height, they made up for in intellect. Each of them had been enrolled in Lindl's School of Science, Technology, Mathematics, and Engineering until they'd been conscripted into Sal's service. Brandi had never asked why they'd left Lindl's domain to serve Sal as informants, but she recognized them from the basic training Jack and Noble had led three years ago.

They were triplets with identical faces and long locs down to their elbows. It had taken them less than a week to master the basic defensive techniques that Noble and Jack had taught, and the way they'd moved in sync with each other, they'd been almost impossible to forget and to tell apart. The only differences Brandi had ever noticed were the deeper notes in Raymond's voice, Ronald's slightly crooked smile, and the tiny mole beneath Roland's left eye.

Brandi had never had any problem with the triplets though, so she crossed her arms and listened to them speak with Terra. She wanted to understand why they were this far out in Carna's domain before she decided if she would intervene.

"I already told you," Terra snapped at the men, "I can't help you."

"Come on, T," Raymond, the triplet in the middle sighed. "You have to do this."

"I don't have to do anything but be a child of Carna and return to the gods," Terra shot back. "And if you don't want to meet them today, I suggest you get off my property."

"Just clear these names from the EREN and we'll go," Ronald, the triplet on the left pleaded. "We don't want to be here anymore than you want us to."

"I already told you," Terra said slowly. "I'm not doing it."

"But why?" Roland, the last triplet on the right, asked. "You've never said no before."

"That's really not any of your business, is it?"

"Terra," Raymond said, "please don't make us get rough with you," he warned. "Just clear the names so we can go."

"Eat. Carna's. Ass," Terra said, wrapping her fingers around the wrench on the workbench beside her.

At those words, Ronald and Roland lunged at her. Terra sidestepped the first triplet and swung her elbow back to drive it into the back of his neck. Roland regained his composure and moved to grab Terra, but as Brandi watched, it was obvious that he'd forgotten all of his defensive training because before he could get a hold on her, Terra swung her arm out with a scream of rage and smashed it into his throat. It would have been easy for him to avoid had he paid attention to her movements. Instead though, he'd been focused on reaching for her and lost his balance. Her blow sent him rolling over her worktable and gasping for air on the ground.

Raymond watched the exchange and pulled a knife from his side pocket. Brandi could see Terra heaving under the strain of defending herself and made her decision.

"*Bless me, for I am the wrath of the gods.*"

Before Raymond had a chance to attack Terra, Brandi's arrow pierced his forehead. His knife clattered to the ground as the light left his eyes and his knees gave way before sinking to the ground and collapsing backward into the cold cement outside.

"Raymond!"

Ronald was the first to scream his brother's name as he struggled to climb up from the floor. He scrambled to his feet, but Brandi released an arrow into the back of his neck, severing his spine. He dropped back to the floor, blood pooling around him as it gushed out of the open wound in his throat. Roland was the last to see the carnage and sank to his knees

316

in complete shock as his eyes landed on Brandi. He shook his head as tears ran freely down his dark face.

"Why?"

The question was barely more than a croak and was followed by coughs of blood that shook his whole body and doubled him over. Brandi glared at him as she approached his soon-to-be corpse.

"Because when a woman says no, she means it."

Brandi released her arrow then and he was returned to the gods with his brothers. When she was done, she let her bow dissipate and she turned to look back at Terra with a raised eyebrow.

"You okay?"

"Holy Carna," Terra whispered, shaking in her pink socks and staring at Brandi. "You are both terrifying and amazing. I..." she trailed off and shook her head. "I don't know if I want to run away or have you sit on my face."

Brandi barked out a laugh at that. She was used to people living in absolute terror of her whenever she sent someone to the gods. After training so many shadows over the years, she knew to expect it. So, it always caught her by surprise whenever someone's reaction was different. She definitely hadn't expected Terra to say something like that.

"Jack would send you to the gods if he heard you say that," Brandi warned, walking over to her, "but I appreciate the offer, I guess."

"He's one lucky man," Terra said, laughing. "I'm going to..." she dropped her wrench and pulled at her hair, "I'm going to step outside. I think... I'm not okay."

"Yeah," Brandi agreed, gripping the top of her arm and leading her outside. "Fresh air would probably do you some good."

Brandi led Terra outside and helped her to sit down on the brick steps. They were below the balcony she'd talked with Sarah and Noble on last night and Terra dropped her head between her knees to take steady breaths. Brandi stood beside her, waiting in silence for Terra to calm herself and catch her breath. When she finally looked up at Brandi, her dark eyes were wide and her face flushed.

"I guess I should thank you for that," Terra said, looking out over the valley. The sun was beginning to rise and the clouds that had been a dark blue during the night turned shades of pink and orange as the light stretched over the horizon and spilled over the hills.

"It's no problem," Brandi said, shrugging. "You've helped us out a lot, by getting me and Jack off the EREN and ERIS, and you even created an access code for Sarah to use when we get to Lindl's domain. The way I see it, we're even."

"Noble already paid me for that though."

"I want no parts of that," Brandi snorted. "What's between you and him is between you and him. And what's between me and you," she said, looking at Terra, "is between me and you."

Terra smiled. "I'm glad to hear that," she nodded. "Really glad. I thought…"

"What?" Brandi asked. "That you'd have to put up with Noble forever?"

"Something like that."

"I wouldn't," Brandi said flatly. "Not to be rude, but you're a child to believe affection isn't given freely, and you're a fool to believe you should ever be with someone who wanted you to earn it."

"Ouch," Terra winced. "You're about as soft as Carna's gaze, aren't you?"

"That gone be a problem?"

"No," Terra said, shaking her head as Noble came jogging back with Jack over the hill to the house. "It just gives me something to think about. But I should finish getting things ready for y'all."

She rose to her feet and paused when she looked back at her workshop. Brandi waved her away.

"We'll clean that up for you. Don't worry about it."

"Thanks," Terra whispered, disappearing down the steps and around to the front of the house. She watched Terra go and wondered if she'd be able to get everything prepared before they left, but Brandi was pleasantly surprised when she was ready to see them off in a modified pod a few hours later.

It was spherical and just big enough for the five of them to sit comfortably inside. It had been decided that Russ would be with them until they reached his brother's home in Lindl's domain. Terra had made it clear that even though she had gotten them off the EREN, they would still need to cash out their digital accounts for physical coins. They could convert the coins back to digital currency if they found someone willing to exchange it for them, but it wasn't something that could be done at one of the regular bank locations. When Brandi had questioned her about where they should go, Terra had suggested they go see her oldest brother, Shian.

Apparently, helping people disconnect from the EREN was Terra's job, she was the engineer with all the practical skills, but it was Shian's job to help people stay off of it. He lived just inside Lindl's inner ring, in fragment 20401. He was well known among the more unsavory types for running *The Unseen Horizon*, a nightclub that catered to the elite of Lindl's underbelly, where those looking to disappear off the grid could go to seek help.

His home wasn't an easy one to find. He was a man of the people, and without an exact location, every person in the fragment would lie through their teeth to protect him. Their only option was to be guided there by someone who knew him, so Russ had offered to show them the way. He'd claimed to need a ride back to his academy anyway, but Sarah was the only one who believed his lie. The others could tell from the way he watched her that his motives weren't as pure as he portrayed them to be.

Before they left, though, Terra had been sure to gift each of them a portable access point to the original network. She'd spent all night crafting them, using the instructions Lindl had given her. They were simple things, minuscule dark hoops that Terra wasted no time piercing through the top of their right ears.

The others had no reservations about it and had taken a seat in Terra's chair without hesitation. They hadn't even winced as the needle slid through their cartilage — Russ and Noble hadn't even bothered to take a break in their conversation. Sarah was the only one who had jumped at the needle and whined about the pain, and Russ had been the only one to care enough to offer her a small bag of ice to help soothe the sting it left behind. The others had simply rolled their eyes at her and continued on about their morning.

She wore deep bags under her eyes, but as she looked over their new piercings and the custom pod she'd created, her face glowed with pride. She'd hugged her brother as he climbed into the pod, and waved the rest of them off, but she'd stopped Noble in his tracks.

"You know I love you," she told him.

"Terra…"

"I'm not looking for a response," she said, holding up her hand to stop him from spilling whatever lies he thought she wanted to hear. "I'm just stating a fact. I've always been in love with you, and you've always known that. At one point I thought we might have had a chance at being together for real, but then you disappeared one day," she said sadly, "and when you came back, you were a different person. I didn't know you anymore. But I loved you enough that I thought I could bring back the boy who had been kind and gentle and my friend." She shook her head and laughed at herself. "So, I allowed you to drag me into this toxic cycle that always left me feeling like the bottom end of Carna's big toe. But I'm done, Noble."

"Okay," he said softly. "I'll leave you alone from now on."

"No," Terra said, taking a step forward to jab her forefinger into his chest. "I'm done with you," she emphasized. "Don't come back here, Noble."

"You serious?"

"As the gods' wrath," Terra said. "You come back here, and I'll make sure you meet them in their realm."

Noble searched her eyes and nodded his head when he realized she meant every word she said to him. He couldn't say that he hadn't expected her to get fed up with him at some point, but it surprised him that she was willing to draw a line in the sand so clearly with him now. It made him wonder what had changed.

"Understood," he said, backing away from her. "You deserve to be happy, Terra."

"And I will be," she said, turning on her heel and walking back towards the house. "You can trust that."

With those words, Noble climbed the steps of the pod, slid into his spot beside Brandi, closed the door behind him, and they'd taken off. The pod — that Terra had dubbed the *Ciel Noir* — shot through the domain with a speed Sarah had never experienced before. She'd been in awe when Terra had gathered them outside to show it off and explain its functions to them. It was more than Sarah could understand, but Jack had listened intently to her instructions as she explained how their pod was could access the EREN for navigation, but it couldn't be tracked on it and that it was based on schematics that Lindl had given her, so it could navigate the entire mortal realm without the need for the queendom's rail system. Once Jack had input their destination, the *Ciel Noir* had come to life, hovering a little less than three feet off the ground, and welcomed them aboard. Jack sat closest to the controls now, but he was relaxed with his arm draped around Brandi as they watched the scenery flash by.

The outside of the *Ciel Noir* was the same inky black shade of a shaders fur. It was dark enough to eat the morning sun, offering them privacy from any curious eyes, but the inside was transparent, and they could see all the hills and valleys of Carna's domain from where they sat.

Sarah's eyes had gone wide once they'd started moving, and it amazed her at how quickly Terra and the house disappeared from view. They were moving as fast as Brandi's shaders, but she felt none of the sudden motions that she had before. It was quiet, peaceful, and beautiful. It made Sarah want to live inside the pod forever, but she did her best to contain her excitement once she saw how unimpressed the others were.

Noble closed his eyes and dozed in his seat to her left, and Russ read a book to her right. She blushed and focused her eyes on anything but the other people in the pod and reached up to run a finger over her new piercing, wincing back from the light touch. Terra had assured her that it wouldn't get infected. The nature of the technology embedded in the accessory would work to deliver an antiseptic to prevent infections since it wasn't designed to be removed for at least a year, but Terra had warned that it would still hurt like a shader's bite if her pain tolerance was low. Sarah sighed, thinking about the backhanded insult, but didn't let it weigh her mind down.

"Your first one?"

The question came from Russ as he leaned his shoulder into hers. His book sat closed on his lap and he focused his dark eyes on her. When she looked at him with confusion, his eyes darted to her ear.

"Your piercing," he clarified. "Is it your first one?"

"Oh," she laughed. "Yeah. You ever get one?"

He held his tongue out and showed her the deep purple stud that rested in the center of it. She blinked a few times and laughed at herself as she stared at it.

"How did I not notice that before?"

He laughed too and leaned in closer to her. "I mean," he whispered, "you were naked the first time we met. Maybe your mind was on other things?"

"Don't tease me," Sarah giggled, shoving him lightly. "It's not my fault that your sister forgot about me."

"I honestly don't know how anyone could forget about you."

"Stop," Sarah smiled. "I'm no one special."

"You've met the gods," he said, his smile spreading wider. "Not once, but twice. And you're traveling with The Queen's Blade. You're more than special," he said, pushing his shoulder against hers again. "You're Sarah Rothens and you're incredible."

Before Sarah could make sense of what was happening, Jack and Brandi had Russ pinned to the bottom of the pod. The pod shook and veered off course with the force of their sudden movements, throwing Sarah into Noble's chest. When the pod righted itself on its path and Sarah managed to get her bearings, she saw Russ with his arms forced behind him and Jack's knee pressing into his back. Brandi stood in front of the controls with her boot pressed to Russ's throat and her knife in hand, but Noble remained still. He wrapped his arms around Sarah and pulled her body close to his chest, angling her away from the rest of them.

"What are you doing?" Sarah screamed. When no one responded, she tried to free herself from Noble's arms, but his grip remained firm, locking her in place.

"Let them handle this," he warned her, all traces of the lightheartedness she'd witnessed back at the house gone. It didn't seem to matter to him that the other two were pinning his best friend down or that Brandi was now forcing Russ to meet her gaze with the sharp end of her knife. Sarah tried to free herself from his grasp once more, but he pressed her closer to his body and she felt like he'd caught her in an iron trap.

"Don't you care that they're about to send him?"

"They have every right to, if they do," Noble responded, looking down at her. "Or were you planning to fight them?"

Sarah tensed when his eyes met hers and ceased her struggling.

When Noble sensed that the fight had left Sarah, he loosened his grip on her.

"Just watch, Blondie," he said. "She doesn't do anything without a reason."

"I don't see what her reason could be."

"Well," Noble said, focusing on the exchange in front of them. "She did promise to keep you alive."

"How do you know who she is?"

"What kind of question is that?" Russ asked, groaning under Jack's weight. "I know her the same way I know you two."

"I wouldn't recommend trying to talk your way around her questions," Jack warned. "She's not exactly the patient type."

"I'm telling the truth," Russ insisted. "I met her when I met you!"

Sarah started to interject on Russ's behalf, and Noble clapped a hand over her mouth. She turned angry blue eyes up to him but was met with a stony stare and a shake of his head. She didn't question Brandi's authority over the situation, but at the very least, she felt they should believe Russ if he was telling the truth. But as her eyes darted around the pod, at the seriousness in their eyes and stances, she remembered they were trained for this. Whatever she said would hold no weight with them.

All she could do was watch.

Brandi forced Russ's chin upward and a thin line of blood slid down the sharp blade of her knife. She squatted so that their eyes were level. They didn't exchange words, but there was a shift in the air around them as Russ sucked air into his lungs faster than he normally did.

"If you lie to me," Brandi said evenly, "I will not be swift in sending you to the gods. Do you understand?" Russ nodded slowly against the edge of her blade. "How did you know who she is?"

"I attend Lindl's Third Holy Academy," he answered. "We study the gifts of the gods. I knew who she was the second I saw her yellow hair and blue eyes."

"That would only make her touched by the gods," Brandi pointed out. "How did you know her family name?"

"Everyone knows about the missing princess."

"Do they?"

Brandi asked the question as she removed her knife from his neck. Before he had a chance at feeling relieved, she pressed a button on the controls behind her, opening the door to the speeding pod. Sarah yelped and clung to Noble, shutting her eyes against the sudden wind in the pod as she felt pulled toward the racing ground below them. She opened them when she heard Brandi speak the language of the gods, and in seconds Brandi's two shaders from before had surrounded the pod.

They matched the speed of the pod with little effort and howled in response to Brandi's words. Russ shook violently under Jack's weight, and he lost all the color in his sandy brown skin as Brandi walked back over to him.

"It's fine," Brandi said to Jack, hauling Russ to his feet with a strength that belied her smaller frame. "I can handle it from here."

Jack moved back from her with a nod, and they watched as she shoved Russ over to the open door of the pod where the shaders running next to them growled and snapped at him. Brandi held him over the door by the back of his hoodie with her knife aimed at the base of his spine.

"Now, I'm going to ask you once more how you know Sarah," Brandi told him, "and if you lie to me again, I'm going to let go."

The shaders below lunged at Russ and he whimpered before going completely limp in her hands and sinking to the ground in a lump of dead weight.

"He passed out," Brandi stated, dragging him back from the edge and allowing Jack to close the door. She raised her green eyes to Sarah and pointed her knife at her.

"Did you know that he knew who you were?"

Sarah started to shake her head, ready to deny the accusation, but stopped. Her thoughts drifted back to when they'd stood in the kitchen alone while everyone had been recuperating from the trek through Carna's storm. He'd mentioned her name then too, but she hadn't thought much of it past his explanation. She'd figured it was just another thing she'd been ignorant of growing up in Asari's domain. But as all three sets of eyes focused on her, she realized how wrong she'd been and nodded her head.

"He told me it was common knowledge."

"And you didn't think to tell one of us?" Brandi snapped. "Freya be merciful," she muttered under her breath, pulling her free hand through the neat rows of her braids. "If the shadows couldn't find you for almost fifteen years, Sarah, why did you think who you are would be common knowledge?"

Sarah hadn't thought of that, and blood rushed to her cheeks as she glanced around the pod. When she was met with no sympathy, she dropped her eyes and focused on the ground rushing by below them. She didn't have an answer, so she said nothing.

Brandi sighed and shook her head, turning to look outside at the shaders that ran beside them. She stared outside for a moment, before pointing to Russ's unconscious form.

"Get him up," she ordered. "I've got questions for him."

Noble set Sarah aside and he and Jack lifted Russ back into the empty seat of the pod. His head lulled, and Noble gave him two sharp taps on the cheek to wake him up. He groaned and rolled his neck as his mind came back to him. Noble and Jack flanked either side of him, and Brandi moved to stand in front. He rubbed his face as he opened his dark eyes, letting them grow wide as his mind caught up to the situation he was in.

"I want you to understand something," Brandi said, putting her knife back in her pocket as she stared at Russ. "The only reason you haven't been sent to the gods is because Noble is my brother and I like your sister." Brandi slid her hands into her pockets and shrugged. "But I won't hesitate to feed you to the shaders if you don't answer my questions," she warned. "So, I will ask you one more time — how did you know she was

Sarah Rothens?"

Russ's dark eyes danced between Brandi and the shaders she commanded outside, to Jack and Noble standing beside her, who were ready to enforce whatever decision Brandi made, even if that meant sending him to the gods. His face paled and his fingers began to shake as he released an uneven laugh.

"I guess I got careless," he admitted finally, raising his eyes to look at Noble. "I guess Terra was right. You're not the same goofy kid we knew from Carna's western domain."

"I haven't been in a long time," Noble said, nodding in Brandi's direction. "Answer her."

His dark eyes focused on Brandi, and the mistake he'd made was obvious as his face morphed from disappointment in his friend to one of frightened respect. He hadn't taken Brandi seriously. She'd let Jack take the lead while they were in Terra's home, but he'd failed to realize that she was the reason any of them were there. He'd fallen for the trap of believing her relaxed demeanor and casual conversation were signs of friendship.

Sarah could see it clear as day because she'd fallen for the same trap with Brandi as a child. Russ had seen himself as her equal — the same as the rest of them.

But he wasn't.

That much was apparent to everyone.

He adjusted the frames that sat on his nose and tried to regain what little dignity he had.

"I'll tell you," he said, "but if you send me to the gods, I won't be able to help you."

"Don't assume we would need you for anything," Jack said, the sharp edges of his voice in discordance with his casual stance.

"If you want the rebels to side with you, then you will."

"Rebels?" Brandi questioned with raised eyebrows. "They're just a rumor drifting on Carna's wind."

Russ shook his head. "It may seem that way in the queen's tower, but I assure you, we're real."

"We?" Noble questioned.

"You never did question why Terra went rogue or was so good at outsmarting the queendom," Russ said, shaking his head. "Or why she built a giant house in Carna's domain that the queendom couldn't touch."

"I thought it was unusual," Brandi admitted, "but I trust Noble. He said she was good enough, and she was," she said with a shrug. "That was enough for me."

Russ sighed. "I don't know how things were for you in the queen's tower, but outside of it, the queendom isn't as loved as Rothians would have you believe."

"Then enlighten us," Jack said.

"I'd be happy to," Russ offered. "But maybe we could have this conversation in a more comfortable atmosphere?"

"I'm comfortable here," Brandi stated, crossing her arms as the shaders outside howled around them.

Russ's eyes darted to the shaders outside, the pulse in his neck jumping at the sight of the monsters.

"The rebellion has been in the works for the last thirty years," Russ explained. "It started shortly before the last bid for the throne began, between the first princess Leia and the second princess Venetia. The second princess was the favored choice of the council, but Leia was the one who was hungry for the crown."

"I don't see how that's relevant information," Jack shrugged. "She lost her bid and was sent to the gods."

"It's relevant because, in order to win the bid, a princess must have the approval of the council and a consort from each domain in the realm," Russ said. "When both conditions are met, the current queen approves the princess as the next ruler. The other bids and princesses are discarded. Only the princesses who renounce their title and reject their right to the throne before the bid begins are allowed to live."

"That's common knowledge," Brandi said. "Get to the point."

"The point," Russ said, adjusting his glasses, "is that in order to seize the throne for herself, Leia organized the shadows. And their first order was to send Venetia's chosen consorts to the gods. Otherwise, she would have won within a week of placing her bid." He tilted his head to glance around Brandi to Sarah. "She was already pregnant with her first child by her favored consort when the bid began."

"And how would you know that?" Brandi questioned. "Why would someone like you have that information?"

Russ chuckled. "Does it upset you that I know something you don't?"

"You don't want to see me upset," Brandi warned.

Russ sucked in a sharp breath and cleared his throat as he averted his eyes from her. Russ had the upper hand in the conversation for the moment, but it wouldn't be wise for him to incite her more than he needed to. She'd already made it clear that his life was not guaranteed.

"Every rebel knows the truth of Glenn 'The Grim Reaper' MelForth. It's no secret to us," Russ shrugged. "It's the reason the rebels have grown so much in the past decade. Knowing that Leia was treacherous enough to sabotage her sister's bid for the throne and then hunt her down until she and her family were sent to the gods," Russ glared at the ground beneath them. "She's a disgrace to the gods and their realm. She doesn't deserve the throne she sits on."

"Tell me where you got that information," Brandi pressed.

Russ looked up and met her gaze again.

"From Glenn," he answered. "She's the leader of the rebellion."

"That's hard to believe," Brandi said with a shake of her head. "Glenn would never betray the queendom."

"Wouldn't she?" Russ asked. "Where do you think she's been for the past eleven years?"

Brandi didn't have an answer to his question, so she stared at him in silence. In all actuality, she hadn't considered where Glenn was or what she would be doing. She left the shadows, and that was that. She was free. And at the time, Brandi had been livid at her for not taking her with her. But even after her anger had subsided, she hadn't spent much thought on it. The shadows had become her home, and she lost her desire to leave. Her memories of Glenn became romanticized and, even though training under her had been a unique kind of torture she wouldn't wish for anyone to endure, she became grateful for it for shaping her into the person she became.

Brandi shook her head slightly as she mulled over Russ's information.

She didn't want to believe what he was saying was true because if it was, the queendom was facing a far bigger threat than that of any outlying blasphemers like Joyson Meys. But taking Russ's word for it wasn't enough for Brandi. She didn't think he'd lie to her at this point, but the implications behind his words wasn't something she could ignore.

Her loyalty wasn't to the queendom anymore, but its destruction would be far more inconvenient. If the gods expected them to fight a being of time that existed outside the reach of their power, giving free rein to the blasphemers and restructuring the politics of the realm would be less than ideal.

"What do you want to do, Green?"

Brandi glanced up at Noble and took a deep breath. This information didn't change what they needed to do. They still needed to find Glenn, revoke her blessing, find Lindl's vessel, and find a way to stop a being of time. The only thing that changed was how they would get those things done. But at least now, they had a lead on where to start.

"Nothing," Brandi finally said. "We keep with the plan and head to Shian in Lindl's domain. We'll regain access to our funds, I'll meet with my contacts, and you," she said, pointing to Russ who flinched back from her glare, "you're going to take us to Glenn."

"I can't do that."

"I wasn't asking you for a favor," Brandi clarified, shoving her boot into the seat between his legs. He jumped back again, and she snatched his hoodie to pull him forward as she leaned down to meet his gaze. "Either you do what I say, or you meet the gods," she warned, throwing him back into his seat. "I won't tolerate anyone who can't pull their own weight."

"Carna's ponytail!" Russ hissed as his head snapped back against the inner sphere of the *Ciel Noir*. "I get it already," he snapped, rubbing the back of his head. "I'll do what you ask. But it wouldn't send you to act a little more like Freya. Be a little nicer."

Brandi snorted and flopped back into the seat across from him, next to Sarah, as Jack readjusted the navigation on the *Ciel Noir* and the shaders dispersed to go their separate ways.

"You know nothing about the goddess," Brandi said with a sigh as the *Ciel Noir* shot forward again. "Freya is kind. Just. But she was never nice," she told him, meeting his gaze once more as everyone settled back into their seats. "And neither am I."

CHAPTER EIGHTEEN

Weak mortals search for power, wise ones know that it exists in everything that is known.

— Knowledge, Power, and Lindl: Three in One | Lindl's Third Holy

Academy

LINDL'S DOMAIN — PRESENT DAY

"I did what you asked me to do."

The words drifted over to Brandi from the other side of the stone gates surrounding the inner ring of Lindl's domain. She'd left Sarah with the boys less than an hour ago to make this meeting and gave a nod in greeting as she approached.

"I wasn't expecting anything less from you."

The guard who sat there barely looked up as Brandi entered her code into the access point and waited for it to register her ID. It took longer than usual, and a wave of apprehension crashed over her at the idea that Terra hadn't been successful in clearing her information from the EREN. She'd assured them that their codes made them look like nondescript

Rothians, but when the guard skimmed over the information that populated on his end, he paused to study Brandi's profile. She refused to look at him, and soon enough she heard him press a button on the dash to raise the short gate and allow her to walk through.

Brandi returned the half-hearted wave he gave her as she passed by him, making a note to herself to keep Terra in her back pocket for later if she ever needed her services again. As she exited the security checkpoint and continued deeper into the heart of fragment 20311, she noticed the warm body sidling up next to her as she navigated the crowds flooding the streets.

"A 'thank you' would be nice, you know," she said, flipping her dark wavy hair out of her face. "Just because I like you doesn't mean I have to cater to your every whim, raindrop."

Brandi glanced down at Pine and sighed.

"Thank you," she said, making a show of the words being forced.

Pine rolled her eyes but smiled anyway, falling into step beside Brandi as they made their way through the upper district towards Lindl's First Holy Academy. There were endless choices of clothing shops, restaurants, bookstores, furniture vendors, hotels, and attractions. Brandi let her eyes roam the streets, taking in all the splendor of Lindl's domain. Although she'd spent most of her time as a shadow in Rothe's domain, Lindl's had always been her favorite, since it was the heart of advancement for the entire realm.

Nearly every piece of technology they used originated in Lindl's inner ring where his academies were, from the transportation pods that darted all over the domain to the nanoscopic tech that allowed every individual to connect to the EREN with a single touch at the right access point. Brandi had always nurtured a love for books and learning and often wondered if she would have enrolled in one of Lindl's academies had her life not been so manipulated by the gods. She liked to think she would have, but she also didn't spend much time mulling it over. She couldn't change who she was any more than she could convince Rothe that the moon was the sun.

"Seriously though," Brandi said, breaking the silence that had settled between them while keeping her eyes focused on where they were headed, "thank you."

"Anything for you, raindrop," Pine said, linking her arm through Brandi's. "You know that."

Brandi jumped at the sudden close contact but didn't shrug it off. She understood that Pine was the touchy-feely type, so she did her best to suppress her urge to pull away as they navigated the streets. It didn't take long for the crowds to thin once they got further from the shopping district — and once they stood outside the gates of the First Holy Academy, they were alone.

Lindl's domain housed five academies in five disciplines, one in each fragment of his inner ring. The First Holy Academy was the most prestigious of them all, though. An institute dedicated to researching, understanding, and preserving the will of the gods — it held all the information ever known about the gods since the beginning of time. It stood above all other academies in terms of grandeur and notoriety, as well as in the dedication of its students. With the most rigorous entrance requirements in the realm, only the students of the First Holy Academy were allowed to enter the building. At its inception, Lindl had placed a barrier on the walls, blocking any outsiders from getting any closer to the hallowed halls than the garden.

Brandi was reminded of that as she approached the gate separating the public from the private gardens of the academy and the heat in her veins began to rise in protest. She carried Freya's soul within her, so she could enter the academies as she pleased, but the gods didn't hesitate in making their displeasure known. She would be granted entrance, but she had not been called to serve them as a scholar and would never know peace within its walls. It was something that had always annoyed her, but she let the thought slip away as she took a deep breath and pressed the button to call for an attendant. Within moments, a tall man with flawless light brown skin and deep violet eyes walked out of the frosted glass doors of the academy and stopped a few paces back from the other side of the gate. He wore brown slacks with a pressed white shirt and a dark green blazer and tie. His dark wavy hair was pulled back into a low ponytail that hung over his right shoulder and his eyes skimmed over Brandi's casual black outfit of cargo pants and a fitted high neck shirt before refocusing on her face.

A slight smile pulled at his lips as his soft voice drifted over to her through the gate.

"I believe I know what you're here for, but in case I'm mistaken," he said, clasping his hands behind his back, "how may I help you?"

"I'm here looking for someone."

"It seems my presumptions were correct then," he said, a wider smile pulling at his lips. "I will go and fetch her for you."

"I haven't given you a name yet," Brandi said, her eyebrows shooting up. "Mine or hers."

"You needn't to," he said. "You are the one known as 'Green', yes?" When Brandi said nothing and narrowed her eyes at him, he laughed lightly. "No need for hostility here. Your eyes tell me everything. And she has been waiting for you. Come," he said, pressing his palm to a biometrics scanner and stepping back to allow the gate to slide open. "I will take you to where she is."

Brandi glanced over her shoulder, and Pine followed them into the courtyard. The man walked with an easy grace and led them to a garden surrounded by ocean flowers. Their deep blue and purple petals offered up the light salty scent of Lindl's Blind Sea. Pine took deep breaths as they walked the paths towards the center of the garden, and Brandi was reminded of how often she forgot that Pine was a child of Lindl.

Before she'd met Brandi and started working for her, Pine had lived a life of luxury in Lindl's inner ring as the daughter of the district 02 guardians. She'd been the perfect, soft-spoken daughter who gave away her smiles with ease and listened attentively to whoever spoke to her. Even before Lindl blessed her with the gift of coercion, she had been beguiling in her own ways. And there were some things, like the scent of ocean flowers, that seemed to bring her mind back to those days.

"We are here," the man said, holding out his hand to show them the tiny courtyard tucked away in the garden. A small table sat beneath a gazebo with books scattered everywhere. He led them up the short walkway and touched the shoulder of the girl hunched over one of the tomes, her fingers flying in blurred motions across the digital display that housed her notes. She jumped at the man's touch, her curly brown hair shaking free of its loose bun as her eyes focused on him and the people behind him.

"Your guest has arrived," he said, clearing a few of the seats filled with books. "I'll take these back to our room for you."

"Thanks, Cedric."

He winked at her before turning back to Brandi and Pine. "May Lindl be kind to you this day," he said with a quick nod before disappearing back down the path. Once he was gone, Brandi and Pine took seats across from the girl and Brandi smirked at her.

"Who was that?"

"Ah," the girl blushed, "that was Cedric. He's here as a transfer from Lindl's Third Holy Academy. He's studying Lindl's influence on the originals and how that led to the eventual creation of the EREN and Lindl's academies as a whole." Her face brightened as she leaned forward, "And you know what? He even took a year away from the Holy Academy to study engineering so that he could better understand his research. How incredible is that? He's absolutely brilliant," she said, her voice soft.

"Seems you like a bit more than his mind," Pine pointed out.

"Oh! I –" the girl cleared her throat and averted her gaze from them and Brandi laughed under her breath.

"Seems you've been fitting in well here."

"Yeah," she said with a nod, her nose scrunching up as a wide smile stretched across her face.

"I'm glad that's working out for you," Brandi said, leaning back in her seat. "And have you found a way to make yourself useful to me?"

"Yes," she said with a solemn nod. "I finished my father's research. He was wrong about there being another god, but," she said, pulling up her display and scrolling through her notes, "there was someone else there. A being separate from the gods entirely. And," she said, shifting her display over to Brandi so that she could see, "I believe they will be making another appearance rather soon."

"That's why I'm here, Lena," Brandi said, glancing over the information. "Tell me everything you know."

ASARI'S DOMAIN — 6 MONTHS AGO

"I got your message," Brandi said, holding up a tiny sheet of folded notebook paper with bubbly script on it. "What do you want?"

The night Brandi sent Joyson Meys to the gods, she'd received a sloppy note — one with letters too big for the lines — that had been shoved beneath her door. At the time, she hadn't let her mind get distracted from the task at hand, but she asked the question now as she returned to the spot where she'd waited for Joyson. They were in the darkest part of Asari's night, and she was half surprised when she'd spotted a darting pair of eyes waiting for her. The girl was bundled in three layers against the cold of the winter night, but it was clear that she was determined. And Brandi had already decided that if whoever wrote

341

the note arrived at the designated time, she would hear them out.

Brandi stopped a few paces from the girl and watched as she took a deep breath.

"I want to go with you," she said.

The words seemed to burst out of her, spilling over each other as if they'd been caged in the pit of her belly for too long and she needed the release. Her cheeks flushed as silence descended around them and her chest heaved under her coat and scarf, creating puffs of mist in the night air that put her nerves on display.

"You do realize what I've just done, don't you?" Brandi questioned. She pointed to the clearing she'd just walked out from. "I've just sent your father to the gods. And you're saying you want me to take you with me?" Brandi shook her head and tossed the note in her hand at the girl's feet. "You sound cracked."

"I know how I sound," Lena whispered. "But I know what I want. I'm the one who told the queendom what he was doing."

"Did you?" Brandi asked, raising an eyebrow. Lena had her attention now. "Why would you do that?"

"Because he was ignorant," Lena snapped, her eyes narrowed toward the ground. "Ranting about another god." Lena shook her head. "He was dragging Ma and Kinley into it, and I couldn't allow that. If I hadn't said something, all of us would have been sent to the gods."

"I can't argue with that," Brandi shrugged, knowing she spoke the truth. The queendom didn't believe in leaving behind any remnants of a blasphemer's work. Brandi had already destroyed all of Joyson's research and burned down his offices. Jack, Noble, and Najé would be finishing up the same tasks with his colleagues and heading back to their meeting point at any moment.

"So, why have you convinced yourself I won't send you?"

"I haven't," Lena admitted, her voice shaking at Brandi's mention of having walked willingly into meeting the gods. "But I don't want to stay in these outskirts, and I don't want to inherit that inn. If gambling on you gets me sent to the gods, then so be it," she said, her voice firm. "At least I'll meet them without regrets."

Brandi chuckled under her breath as she studied Lena. If she was honest, she hadn't thought much of the girl when she'd arrived at the inn. She seemed like an average teenager of the outskirts — quiet, obedient, and primed to keep the family traditions running. But as Brandi witnessed the determination she clung to, she couldn't help but see the girl in a new light. She was clearly more than she led people to believe.

"Let's say I take you with me," Brandi said, sliding her hands into her pockets. "What do I get out of this deal?"

"My life," Lena offered.

"I can take that whenever I want." Brandi shrugged. "You got something better?"

Lena shook her head. "It's all I've got, but I promise you," she said, taking a step forward, "I'm worth far more to you on this side of the god's realm."

"That's what you're trying to convince me of," Brandi said, taking her knife out and spinning it around her finger.

"I'll be your personal informant," Lena offered. "No one ever pays attention to the poor girl from Asari's outskirts."

"I already have plenty of those," Brandi said, beginning to lose interest in the conversation.

"I can give you more information on the gods."

"Careful there, Lena," Brandi warned. "I just sent your father for claiming to be able to do the same thing."

Lena scoffed. "He was as bright as Asari's darkest night. He only wanted to be seen as a respected scholar. Nevermind the fact that he blasphemed against the gods he claimed to serve with every word that came out of his mouth. No," she shook her head. "I've done real research," she emphasized. "I'm just looking for an opportunity to continue it. And I'll do whatever you want if you'll give it to me."

Brandi mulled over Lena's words. She couldn't deny that there was a part of her that was curious as to what Lena knew. And it would be convenient to have an informant living inside Lindl's inner ring at one of his Holy Academies. Only the most qualified researchers were allowed to attend, and if she got in, there would be no parts of Lindl's domain that would deny her access. Her other informants were useful, but none of them would be able to accomplish getting into any of Lindl's academies.

And having someone outside of Sal's network was always a good idea.

"Alright," Brandi said slowly, eyeing the girl in front of her. "I'm considering it. But answer me this first." Lena sucked in a sharp breath and straightened her back, preparing herself for whatever question Brandi could ask her. "Why ask me? There are a dozen ways to get to Lindl's domain and one of his academies that are easier than asking a shadow," Brandi pointed out. "Why betray your father in order to do it?"

WE ARE THE ORIGIN

"Because I serve the gods," Lena answered. "And he was speaking against them publicly and putting all our lives in danger. Even if I didn't serve the gods as I do, I still would have ratted him out. If only to save Kinley."

"And will you do the same to me?" Brandi asked. "Dig a knife into my back if you disagree with my actions?"

"I doubt I even could," Lena said, laughing at the thought. "But I would never have a need to. You couldn't blaspheme the gods if you wanted to."

"You seem confident in that."

"I am," Lena said, meeting Brandi's gaze. "Your green eyes tell it all," she pointed out. "The only gift one can receive from Freya is her own soul."

Brandi's eyes widened at her words, and she spent another moment appraising Lena once more.

"How much do you know?"

"More than most, but not everything," Lena admitted. "It's why I want to leave. I want to do more than tell Kinley bedtime stories."

"You realize you may never see her again if I accept your offer?" Brandi asked. "You'll be dead to the queendom."

Lena nodded. "This life was never the one I wanted. I just hope she'll make her own choices one day and understand why I made mine."

"I respect your conviction," Brandi said, smirking. "Alright. You've talked yourself into a deal." Brandi held her hand out to her. "Give me your hand."

Lena did so and Brandi held onto her with an iron grip. Without warning her, Brandi poked the tip of her blade into Lena's skin between her thumb and index finger. Two round dots of fresh blood rose to the surface and Lena sunk her teeth into the fist of her free hand to stifle her yelp of pain, but she made no complaints. Brandi smiled beneath her mask at the girl's resilience and placed a bandage into her palm before releasing her.

"Get your affairs in order with your family and I'll send one of my corpses to get you."

"A corpse?" Lena asked, her body trembling in horror at the thought of someone undead coming in search of her. She knew Freya held power over souls, but Lena had never imagined it would be so literal.

"It's what I call my informants," Brandi clarified. "Like I said, you'll be dead to the queendom."

"I see," Lena whispered, looking down at her hands. "And what do I call you?"

"Green," Brandi answered. "I'll get everything in order for you to apply to the academy. When someone comes in to ask where you got that mark," Brandi said, pointing to where her knife would leave a scar on her hand, "tell them it came from a shader's bite. They'll handle the rest."

"I understand," Lena said, opening the bandage to wrap her hand. "I won't let you down."

Brandi smirked as she melted back into the shadows of the night.

"No, I don't expect you will."

LINDL'S DOMAIN — PRESENT DAY

Lena's eyes danced between Brandi's green gaze and Pine's hazel one. She recognized Pine as the corpse who had helped her get into Lindl's domain and his academy, but she hadn't expected to see her again. She'd made it clear that she took no personal interest in Lena, but when she made no moves to distance herself from the conversation, Lena understood she would be a part of it and cleared her throat.

"I began my research by retracing the steps my father had taken," Lena explained. "I wanted to know why he'd convinced himself there was another god when there was nothing to support that claim. What I found was this," she said, swiping through the display in front of Brandi by pulling her right hand through the air. "There's a brief period of unrecorded time between the creation of the realms and the first death in the mortal one," Lena pointed out to them. "At first, I thought it was strange. Lindl documented everything from the starting point of creation and kept the records until the mortals could do it themselves. So, what could have kept him from keeping a record before the first death? Did they simply not need that information? But then I realized," she said continuing to swipe through her notes until a timeline of the realm was displayed, "according to Lindl's observations, the first entry on the records would had to have been what we would perceive as hundreds of years after creation. But all the records say it was only the first day."

Lena looked up at them expectantly, and when Brandi quirked an

347

eyebrow at her, she continued.

"That means there had to have been a reason for the gap. So, after some digging, I found that every record has a specific date and time attached to it. There are hundreds of logs from dozens of different sources for every day that's ever existed in the mortal realm, but they were all meticulously kept, and every single one had a date. So, I thought," she said, swiping down and over to show them her personal notes on the display, "what if there was no record because there was no time? Evidence suggests mortals have been around longer than the three thousand years our date suggests, but there's no record of it."

"That tracks," Brandi said with a nod. "The gods don't control time."

"Exactly!" Lena shouted, leaning across the table. "So, if they don't control time, then they couldn't have started it. And without the passage of time, there was no way for the mortals to keep a record of anything."

"Wouldn't they have just noted whenever Rothe raised the sun and Asari the moon?" Pine interjected, annoyance written across her face for being left out of the conversation.

"That's a theory," Lena mused, "but I don't even think Rothe and Asari would have established their day and night cycles yet," Lena mumbled, her eyes drifting to stare into the distance. "I mean, it would've had to have been sporadic based on who was with Freya at the time, wouldn't it? And if it was neither of them, would it have been complete darkness?" Her voice trailed off and Brandi knocked against the table, bringing Lena back from her thoughts.

"Sorry! What I was trying to say is that what we see," she said, pointing to the timeline, "as years of time was just one long day for the originals. So, that means there had to be an outside force here," she said, pointing to the first point on the timeline, "to move things forward."

"The time being, Zareal."

"I didn't know that was its name," Lena said with wide eyes, "but yes. There's something even more interesting than that, though. May I?" She asked, indicating the display. Brandi nodded and swiped it back over to Lena, and she began scrolling through the documents she'd saved copies of. When Lena found what she was looking for, she widened the display and showed it to both Brandi and Pine.

"As I said, there are hundreds of records from dozens of sources for every day in the mortal realm. But I've noticed that the ones created within the last thirty years have discrepancies with each other."

"Is that not normal?" Pine asked.

"Not at all," Lena said with a shake of her head. "For nearly three thousand years, the records were in perfect alignment with each other. Albeit, there were some differences in the wording and speculations of the records about why certain things happened. It's really amazing how Rothian researchers did everything they could to write Rothe's lore into every one of their records, but still. Aside from their personal touches, the facts were always perfectly aligned. These, for instance," she said, showing two documents side by side, "have accounts of two different natural disasters on the same day and time that these," she swiped over to show a wide spread of at least twenty documents, "have no record of. Meaning —"

"Either they didn't happen at all or all of them are correct," Brandi said, her eyes focused on the table between them as her mind raced to piece together all the bits of information Lena had presented to her.

"Exactly," Lena said, leaning back in her seat. "But that's impossible. So, that's what I'm researching now."

"It's not impossible," Brandi said slowly. "Not if there was a being who could manipulate time at will. It would be a simple thing to shift the point where a natural disaster occurred on the timeline."

"But why would anyone bother doing that?" Pine asked.

"I'm sorry," Brandi said, rolling her eyes. "When Lindl blessed you, did you not play around with it to see what you could do?"

"I admit, I had far too much fun in the beginning," Pine said, giggling at the memory. "So, that's what you think is happening? Someone got blessed with the ability to manipulate time and they're just playing with it?"

"But how would anyone manage to get away with that unnoticed?" Lena wondered.

"It wouldn't be so difficult," Brandi shrugged, her mind thinking about how the council often ignored the more inconvenient aspects of ruling the realm. They often left all the real work up to the queen and her court. "As long as it didn't impact the inner ring of Rothe's domain or the flow of currency through it, the monarchy probably wouldn't have noticed."

"You put forth an interesting theory," Lena said slowly, her eyes widening as she leaned forward again and Brandi pulled the display back over to her. Lena and Pine watched as Brandi set the system to scour the documents for what she was looking for. When the search stopped and four documents populated on the screen, Brandi glanced over them before enlarging them and spinning the display around to face the other two.

"Incredible," Lena whispered.

"This is way out of my depth, raindrop," Pine said, shaking her head.

On the screen, each of the four documents displayed a record for the exact same natural disaster — a windstorm in the Scorched Desert, in the northernmost part of Rothe's domain. It destroyed fifteen homes and took the lives of nearly fifty people. The time was the exact same in each document, but the date was different for each one.

"How is this even possible?" Lena whispered, her fingers racing to keep pace with her mind as she pulled up other documents and checked other notable points in history that seemed to repeat. "I don't understand," she finally said, looking up from the display to look at Brandi.

"You've done well to get this far on your own," Brandi complimented. "But there's more to the story."

Brandi spent the next twenty minutes explaining what Freya had told her about the creation of time, the vessels of the gods, Zareal, and his apprentice. She answered most of Lena's questions as they arose, but it was Pine who asked the most direct one once Lena finally fell silent.

"So," she asked, resting her elbow on the table and letting her dark hair fall into her eyes, "how do you plan to stop this apprentice, raindrop?"

"I haven't figured that out yet," Brandi admitted. "That's why I'm here. I figured if anyone had information on the gods, it would be a student of Lindl's First Holy Academy."

"I wish I did," Lena said, fluttering her lashes in surprise, "but this is all brand new to me."

"And you said you'd found a way to be useful to me," Brandi sighed.

"I mean, I don't have any answers," Lena rushed out, "but I do have a theory."

"Then enlighten us," Pine demanded.

"Well, based on what you said, I have two," she said, holding up her fingers. "The first is that this apprentice must have a vessel of their own and that vessel has only had the power for thirty years," she said, pointing again to the timeline. "It would only make sense, given that the discrepancies we found don't happen any earlier than the year 2970. Assuming your theory is correct, Green, my guess is that they're coming from the vessel testing out the parameters of their new power."

"That sounds reasonable," Brandi said with a nod of her head. "And your second theory?"

"If my first theory is correct, and both the gods and this apprentice need a vessel, then that means their interactions with the mortal realm are limited. Their true powers can only go so far, which is why they can't interact with each other or the realm directly. They must have a mortal conduit. But," Lena said, holding up a finger, "and this is just pure speculation," she warned, "what if their interactions with mortals work both ways?"

Brandi considered Lena's words and her blood ran cold at the implication Lena seemed to be suggesting. Until now, it was always accepted as fact that the mortals do not influence the gods. It bordered on blasphemy to think such an idea was even possible. But if the gods were actually linking their souls to their vessels, and she could affect Freya in the same way she affected her, then the gods were taking a much bigger risk in choosing mortals to house their power than she'd thought.

"Are you suggesting," Brandi asked, leaning forward, "that the gods are making themselves mortal in order to share their power with their vessels?"

"At least in part," Lena said with a nod. "And if they're doing that, then that means that this apprentice —"

"Is making himself mortal as well," Brandi finished.

Lena nodded. "It's just a theory, but it's possible."

"So, why not just kill this apprentice's vessel?" Pine asked. "Uproot the source."

"Because the apprentice would just choose another one," Brandi answered. "They aren't bound to the souls they share power with in that way."

"So, how does this solve the problem?"

"It doesn't," Lena answered. "It just makes the problem solvable," she said with a shrug.

"Then I'm going to need one of you big-brained ladies to explain this to me like I have no idea what any of this means," Pine said, her hazel eyes darting between the two of them. "Because I, don't."

Brandi snickered and Pine smiled. "Alright, follow me," Brandi said. "You understand the issue of the time apprentice, right?"

"Yes. He's some being, not a god," she clarified, "trying to destroy the gods and the realm. That I understand."

"And you understand the idea that the gods don't control time?"

"Yes."

"Alright. So, assuming the gods and this apprentice make a part of themselves mortal when they link their souls with their vessels, then the apprentice can be destroyed if we find his," Brandi whispered, wrapping her mind around the idea. "I don't know how we're going to pull that off just yet, but," a small smile pulled at her lips at the thought of removing Azinne from her list of problems, "as long as his vessel is alive in the mortal realm, part of his soul is too." Her watch buzzed, reminding her of the time, and she looked up at both of them.

"We have to go," she said to Pine, who nodded and stood to her feet as Brandi turned her eyes back to Lena. "But I need you to do more research on this apprentice. Let me know anything you find."

"Of course," Lena said with a nod as Brandi rose from her seat.

"I'll be in touch," Brandi said with a wave.

"Be careful," Lena called after her. "If our theory is correct, then it's not just the apprentice," she warned. "The gods can be destroyed as well."

Once they left Lena and Lindl's First Holy Academy, Pine followed Brandi into a small boutique where Brandi greeted the owner, Flint, by name. They changed clothes there and slipped out the back entrance to melt into the budding nightlife crowding the streets.

They drew heads as Brandi navigated them through the streets. The dark skin clinging to the muscles of her exposed back and legs made more than her fair share of people stop and stare. Even Pine had a hard time looking away from her, and she knew there were plenty of eyes on her, too. She wore a dark green crop top with a matching high-waisted skirt and black platform heels with her wavy hair flowing freely around her shoulders.

Pine didn't ask any questions as she followed Brandi into the Lyserg building and up to the eighth floor. It wasn't until they had drinks in their hands and were sitting on the barstools by the windows, furthest from the bar and the music, that she broke the silence.

"Alright, raindrop," Pine said, sipping her pink cocktail, "why are we here?"

"I'm meeting someone," Brandi told her. "But we didn't get a chance to talk yet."

"No, we haven't," Pine giggled. "I was almost upset that you let that little Asarian bumpkin take up all my time with you."

"Well, I'm all yours right now," Brandi said with a slight smile. "Tell me what you found out."

"Well," Pine said, taking another sip, "you've missed a lot since you abandoned the queendom. But," Pine said, noticing how Brandi's green eyes kept darting to the walkway below, "I'll give you the highlights."

"That would be appreciated."

"Hm," Pine hummed, popping the olive from her drink into her mouth. "First of all, the queen is planning to open up the bidding soon."

"Already?" Brandi asked, pulling her gaze away from the streets below. "But Riné won't be of age for another seven months."

355

"It seems Leia is under pressure from the council to start the bidding early. Rumor has it that Asuna of Sentera and Cazie of Taren have already begun their search for consorts."

"I wouldn't be surprised," Brandi sighed. "They were always flirts."

"Ah, but here's where the surprise comes in," Pine said, leaning in with a bright glint in her hazel eyes. "Bert has a daughter he wants to enter into the bid."

"That's not possible," Brandi said. "Adam Bertanal doesn't have any heirs."

"But there's a girl he's got his eye on," Pine told her. "A Lindlian girl with red hair."

"Red hair?" Brandi repeated, her eyebrows rising as her thoughts strayed to Sarah and her blonde strands. "Which god gave her that?"

"No one knows," Pine shrugged. "She seems to have appeared out of nowhere, too. It's like she didn't exist before six months ago and I find it hard to believe that no one would remember a girl walking around looking like that."

"Do you have a name?"

"I can do you one better, raindrop," Pine said, slipping a microchip in a sealed plastic square from her cleavage. "Upload that to the EREN, or whatever it is you're connected to now," she said with a smirk, "and that'll give you all the information I found on her. Her name is Grace but I'm still working out how she's connected to Bert."

"Thanks," Brandi said, accepting the chip and slipping it into the hidden pocket sewn into her own dress. "And what has Bert been up to these days?"

"Nothing good, that's for sure," Pine said, rolling her eyes. "He's still holed up with his experiments and spreading discord among the council whenever he can. But," she said, perking up as she remembered something important, "this may interest you given what you told the Asarian bumpkin. I heard he's planning a trip to visit Freya's temple."

"What?" Brandi asked, snapping to attention. "When?"

"I don't know, raindrop," Pine said, leaning back from Brandi's sudden intensity. "But I can find out for you."

"Please do," Brandi said. "For someone so sacrilegious, it doesn't make sense for him to plan a visit to the most revered place in the entire realm."

"Consider it done."

"Thank you, Pine," Brandi said, reaching her fist out to the smaller woman as she caught sight of a blue hoodie below and stood to her feet. "I have to go, but if you need me," Brandi started.

"I know how to find you," Pine said with a grin, giving Brandi's fist a light bump before standing to melt into the crowd.

Brandi watched her disappear before making her own way back to the elevator. She rode down to the ground floor in silence, alone with her thoughts as she considered the implications of what both Lena and Pine had told her. It seemed that whatever plans this apprentice of time had in store for the realm would be set into motion soon. It made Brandi a little anxious, but she squashed the feeling before she let it build into anything serious.

Even if she wasn't sending souls to the gods for the queen anymore, she was still a shadow and the finest blade ever forged by the queendom.

A weapon.

And weapons didn't get anxious. They felt nothing. Glenn had taught her that, and there was no reason for her to forget it now. She took a deep breath when the elevator came to a stop and walked out of the building into the crowded streets below, her green eyes scanning for the out-of-place hoodie she'd spotted earlier.

"Well, aren't you as beautiful as ever?"

Brandi glanced to her right to see the person she was looking for leaning against the outer wall of the Lyserg building. She returned his smile as she walked over to him, happiness bubbling in her chest to see him still in the mortal realm. He wore a pair of loose-fitting jeans and a white shirt beneath an unzipped hoodie. His gray eyes were different from the dark ones she was used to, but the cropped silver hair and easy smile were the same as the ones she saw nearly every day of her life.

"Hi, Royal," she said, bumping her shoulder into his as she leaned against the wall next to him. "I heard you'd been looking for me."

CHAPTER NINETEEN

Use caution when drinking from the gods' cup, it will spill every secret kept by the lips that drink from it.

— Adage of the Gods | Lindl's Five Holy Academies Compilation

LINDL'S DOMAIN — PRESENT DAY

"This fire is like liquid," Sarah slurred, looking into her cup before shaking her head, sending her long hair swishing around her body. "No, wait," she giggled. "I meant this liquid is like fire!"

Sarah looked around at the lavish furnishings of *The Unseen Horizon* as she and Noble sat at their table by the expansive windows. She was overwhelmed in the best ways as she took in the dazzling chandeliers, the deep violet rugs covering dark wood floors, the shiny bar lined with an array of bottles behind them, and the breathtaking views of the skyline in Lindl's domain.

They were on the top floor of the Lyserg building in fragment 20401. *The Unseen Horizon* operated on the top five floors of the building, with the bottom two floors being an upstanding nightclub, the middle two floors a less-reputable bar, and the top floor being an exclusive meeting spot for the realm's most unsavory types. And though she knew she should be nervous with the kind of company she was in, she couldn't help but be impressed by the scale of the room. Five large tables were spread far apart and lining the enormous glass windows, with waiters moving silently between them. She'd never seen anything like it, had never imagined anything like it could ever exist.

The moment they'd crossed through the barrier into Lindl's domain, the tiny bubble she'd always lived in burst wide open, and she began to realize just how much she'd been missing in Asari's domain. Even the sheer number of people walking the streets below the *Ciel Noir* was something she'd never seen before. There wasn't a single horse or cart on the pristine roads. Instead, shiny pods of all different sizes and colors darted around far above the buildings reaching into the sky. They followed along some near invisible lines that crisscrossed through the clouds and when she'd asked, Russ explained they were part of what was called the rail system. From what she understood, they were weightless nanoparticles that were first conceptualized at one of Lindl's academies. They were strung together with lines of code that the transport pods could read and follow to any destination.

She'd been amazed by that alone, but when the *Ciel Noir* had risen to the skies to ride those lines alongside the other pods, Sarah had been unable to close her mouth at the breathtaking view. Rothe's sun was at the beginning of its descent and the entire fragment was lit up in warm hues, the shadows from the pods dancing across the people below. She hadn't been able to look away from it all the way to Shian's home.

The rest of her day was nothing but one surprise after another once they landed, from Shian being a taller, skinnier version of Russ with dark wavy hair, to the *Ciel Noir* shrinking to the size of a marble once they'd exited it and being slipped onto a chain that Russ hung around his neck.

She'd had a million questions, but she'd been silenced with pointed looks from Brandi and Noble. It became apparent to her that she was being too distracting and acting like a child when adults were trying to converse. That embarrassment alone had been enough for her to swallow the rest of her questions as they discussed doing their currency exchange at *The Unseen Horizon,* but she'd been unable to even look up from the ground once they'd gone into the shopping district to buy new clothes.

She'd followed Brandi into one of the smaller boutique stores and while she'd had a field day trying on the clothes, Sarah was convinced that there was no horror more mortifying than when the cashier asked if she was serious when she'd placed her Asarian coin on the counter to pay for her clothes. The woman behind the counter looked disgusted before bursting out in laughter and calling over every other employee to gawk at it. Sarah had tried to snatch it back, but the woman behind the counter was too quick and everyone in the store had enjoyed a hearty laugh at Sarah's expense. She'd learned the hard and fast lesson that not only were physical coins an antiquated form of payment most upstanding establishments didn't accept, but Asarian coins weren't accepted anywhere outside of Asari's domain.

Sarah rushed out of the store, her cheeks as red as the dress she'd picked out, and went straight to the first bank she could find to exchange her Asarian coins for Lindlian currency. She'd returned to the boutique fifteen minutes later to see Brandi walking out. She'd shoved one of the bags into Sarah's hands with a roll of her eyes before walking off to meet the boys. The red dress she'd wanted was inside along with the coin that had been snatched from her and the outfit she'd been instructed to wear to *The Unseen Horizon*.

She hadn't worked up the courage to thank Brandi before she had disappeared into the crowds. Now, Sarah sat alone with Noble, wearing the new black halter top and miniskirt Brandi picked out for her while Russ met with his academy friends, Jack converted their currency with Shian, and Brandi met with her contacts. They'd split up after returning from their shopping trip and had agreed to meet at the top floor of *The Unseen Horizon* where Shian had reserved a table for them.

Her heart raced inside her chest with nerves and excitement as she sipped from her cup and munched on the finger foods Noble ordered for them. She felt like she was seeing the realm the way the gods intended for the first time, and she couldn't wrap her mind around how she'd been so complacent in knowing nothing about the realm beyond Asari's barrier. She couldn't wait to learn everything there was to know about the realm and the thought made her chest swell with bubbles of laughter. She could feel the stupid grin plastered across her face, but she didn't try to hide it.

"Someone's a lightweight," Noble teased, leaning over to her.

"I am not!" Sarah laughed, her blue eyes bright and her face flushed as she looked up at him. "But I've never had anything like this before," she said, looking at the dark brown liquid in her cup. "What is it?"

"Actual liquor," Noble quipped. "Not that watered-down mess they sell in Asari's domain."

"This is definitely better than the best stuff we have there," Sarah murmured, thinking about the liquor she and Kyle had nicked from his mother's dresser when they were fifteen. They'd polished off the whole bottle in between clumsy kisses in his room and she didn't feel half as tipsy then, as she felt now off a single cup. "But why do you always have to be like that?" She asked, her voice rising as her emotions swung in an indecipherable direction. "Asari's domain isn't that bad!"

"Sure, it's not," Noble said, placating her, "but keep your voice down, Blondie. You're going to make people start looking."

"Let them look," Sarah snapped, downing the last of her cup. "I don't care if they watch."

"Famous last words," Noble chuckled, slipping her cup from her fingers. "I think you're done for the night."

"What? No," she complained. "I only had one cup."

"Clearly one cup too many," Noble said, shaking his head as he gave her a once over.

Her face was flushed and her blue eyes had lost whatever focus she'd once had. She swayed slightly in her seat and every bit of her exposed skin was pink, as if she'd spent the day baking under the heat of Rothe's sun. Her glossy lips were pulled into a pout and Noble's gaze got stuck on them.

"You're not the boss of me," Sarah stated, crossing her arms and turning her back to him. "And I won't listen to anything you say ever again!"

"That's a long time, you know?"

"I don't care!"

"Come on, Blondie," Noble coaxed, biting back his laughter as she swayed in her chair and he reached out to steady her. "You know you don't mean that. I'm just trying to keep you safe, like I agreed to."

"My name is Sarah!"

Noble raised his eyebrows at the sharp tone of her voice. "I'm aware."

"Then use it," Sarah snapped, turning back around, and stopping in her drunken tracks once she realized just how close he was to her. The heat from his palm on her waist burned through her shirt as he worked to keep her from spilling out of her chair.

"I'll think about it," Noble said, winking at her and laughing as her face turned a deep shade of red.

"Where are the others?" She huffed, looking away from him. "Weren't they supposed to meet us here?"

"They're fine," Noble said, accepting a refill of his own cup from the waiter who stopped by their table. He took a quick sip from it before leaning back and resting his arm on the back of Sarah's chair. "They'll find us when they're ready."

"I just don't see what could be taking them so long," Sarah whined.

"Is that your way of saying you don't want to be alone with me?" He asked, using a gentle finger to direct her gaze away from the window and back to him.

A shock of electricity shot through her, and she resorted to reciting all the ingredients she needed to cure food poisoning and where to find them in her head instead of letting herself get lost in his dark eyes. She knew if she did, it would be her complete undoing. So, instead, she brushed his hand away from her face and reached for the plate of nachos in front of them, focusing her attention on something concrete as she shrugged.

"I di-di-didn't say that," she said, cursing herself for stuttering.

"So, you like it," Noble teased, lowering his voice. "Being alone with me?"

"I didn't say that either!"

"Then which is it?"

"I'm going to the bathroom," Sarah announced, shooting up from her chair to avoid his questions and almost tumbling to the floor in the process. Noble's arm was quick in snaking around her waist to catch her before she fell. His arm rested on the bare skin between her top and miniskirt, and all of her good sense melted at the touch. She didn't really need to go to the bathroom, but her tipsy mind begged her to get some space between her and the man making her heart race unless she wanted to faint in the middle of the bar. She fixed her mouth to tell him exactly that, but when his gaze met hers again, she completely forgot how to form words.

"You can't even make a decent exit without me," he said, righting her on her feet, and grasping her upper arm in a gentle grip. "Come on. I'll take you there."

"Hm," she hummed under her breath.

It was a short walk through the dimly lit room to where the elevators waited. To their left were a set of stairs that would allow them to walk down the ten floors to the outside, and to the right was a single door that led to the restroom. Sarah saw it as her means of escape and freed herself from Noble's grasp as she reached for the handle.

"Thanks for your help, but —"

Before she could finish her rushed excuse, the heel of the strappy white sandals she'd worn caught on some imaginary object, and she went tilting forward again. She squeaked and Noble sucked his teeth as he reached out to catch her again, but she jerked away from him on instinct at the sudden heat that flashed through her when his palm came in contact with her exposed skin again. It pulled him off balance too, and they both slammed into the door.

Sarah had her eyes shut tight, braced for impact, but when none came, she opened them again. She was pressed into the door, but Noble's arm was wrapped around her shoulders, pulling her to him and protecting her head. She glanced up and realized that the sound of the slam had been the worst part of everything, and his forearm was braced against the door above her head.

"Gods, Blondie," he sighed. "Be more careful."

"It's not like I meant to trip," Sarah whispered, averting her gaze.

"Why do you keep looking away from me?" He asked, pulling her chin back to face him. "Am I that hard to look at?"

Sarah met his gaze and held it, studying his face. Now that she had permission to stare at him, she couldn't look away. Her eyes took in his symmetrical face, his short silver hair and eyebrows, his dark eyes and full lips.

His soft, smirking lips.

"No," Sarah responded, her brain struggling to give her mouth words. "But looking at you makes me want to kiss you."

A moment passed between them, with her words hanging in the air. They were both silent and Sarah's blue eyes turned to saucers as her own words registered in her brain. She tried to hide her face and look away again, but Noble smirked down at her as he lifted her chin.

"If that's what you wanted, you should've just said something sooner," he chuckled, dipping his head to meet her lips.

Sarah was in shock before her mind short-circuited and her instincts took control. Her eyes fluttered closed, and she reached up to wrap her arms around his neck. She thought she'd been kissed before — had spent her fair share of time sneaking around with Kyle — but what she felt now was like nothing she'd ever known. This wasn't the soft kiss of some Asarian boy who had no clue what to do with her. Noble's kiss was aggressive, cocky. His mouth took control of hers like he'd been waiting to show her what to do with it.

His fingers slid into her hair, and she let out a soft moan against his mouth. He released her lips to place feather-light kisses on her face under the guise of giving her a moment to catch her breath, but her alcohol-laced thoughts demanded she have more of him. So, when she was bold enough to search out his lips again, he grinned and gave into her unspoken request. He tightened his grip on her hair and gently pulled down on it, forcing her head further back. He eased her back against the door and placed hot kisses along her throat as his rigid body pressed into hers, releasing her hair to let his rough palms slide up her skirt.

"You know," he murmured against the base of her throat, "I'm really in the mood to eat something."

"I-I," Sarah's words stumbled over each other as she did her best to keep her voice down while his fingers trailed up her thighs. "I don't know what that means," she admitted, her mind unable to make sense of anything as her center burned with a heat that incinerated every coherent thought she might have had.

Noble's body shook lightly against hers as he laughed. He lifted his lips to hers once more, his thumbs tracing the crease of her thighs as he edged one of them just below the hem of her lace panties. A shiver traveled up her spine, and she almost whined in protest when his fingers slowed their exploration and his lips left hers.

"Would you like me to show you?" he asked, holding her gaze and licking his lips.

She was nothing more than a hot, jumbled mess of sensations and had no way to even guess at what his words meant. But she knew they'd be something she'd want to know. The heat melting in her core let her know that much, and she nodded her head.

"Yes," she breathed.

He leaned down to kiss her again, but before his hand could pull the handle on the bathroom door, he heard footsteps approaching from behind them and his name being called.

"Noble," Russ shouted, walking over to them. He must have recognized Noble's silver hair from the back. "You seen Sarah? Shian said he held a table for us, but she wasn't there."

Noble stopped his actions and braced his hand on the door behind them. He let out a deep breath before meeting Sarah's gaze and grinning at her.

"Sorry, Blondie. Maybe next time," he whispered before straightening up and leaving her leaning against the door with swollen lips, tousled hair, and wide blue eyes lost in a daze.

"She's all yours," Noble said, sliding his hands into his pockets and side-stepping Russ as his dark eyes landed on Sarah, righting herself.

"What happened to you?" He asked, reaching out to steady her as she wobbled on weak knees.

"Nothing," she said, pushing his hand away and starting towards the bar. "I just need another drink."

It was several hours later when Russ walked out of *The Unseen Horizon* struggling to keep a drunk Sarah on her feet. Brandi had called up to the bar when she'd finished with her business and Russ had stopped in his tracks when he saw her standing in a backless black dress. It stopped at the top of her thighs, had long, flowing sleeves, and was a far cry from her usual cargo pants and combat boots. She, somehow, managed to blend into Asari's night and draw every eye passing them on the street at the same time.

"Wow," he managed to get out. "You look amazing."

Brandi rolled her eyes at the compliment and glanced around him with raised eyebrows.

"Where's Jack and Noble?"

Russ shrugged awkwardly under Sarah's weight.

"Jack never showed up, so after a while, Noble went to look for him.

Neither of them came back."

"That's not like them," Brandi said, her green eyes searching the street as if her thoughts would summon them from the shadows.

It was far less crowded than during the day, but Lindl's domain never truly slept, not like Asari's or Carna's. There was always something open — some library hosting midnight readings or a nameless boutique catering to the outrageous fashion culture of the nightlife. There were still a fair amount of people milling about, and Brandi felt the eyes on their backs as Russ led the way down the street back to Shian's.

"How did your meeting go?"

Brandi glanced over at him with narrowed eyes as she kept pace beside him.

"I wasn't aware we'd become associates."

"Oh," Russ asked, lifting his eyebrows. "I figured it was at some point between you threatening to send me and going shopping together."

"Unfortunate that you misunderstood the situation," Brandi said with a shrug.

"Come on," Russ pushed. "You can trust me."

Brandi scoffed. "That's rarely true when it has to be announced."

"Fine," Russ sighed. "But I am serious. Noble is my friend, and Sarah is…" he hesitated as he glanced down at her stumbling along beside him, half asleep on his shoulder, "she's someone newly important to me. They wouldn't betray you, and I wouldn't betray them."

"Just say you have a crush on her," Brandi said, rolling her eyes. "It's obvious."

Russ chuckled. "I'm sure it is. I'm not as good with people as Noble and Terra."

"I doubt that many people are."

"Fair," Russ said with a smile. "But I don't know. She's the first person to ever make me think about wanting to kiss her."

"I did not need to know that," Brandi sighed. "But I hope Freya shows favor on your heart or whatever. Gods know hers is set on Noble."

"Yeah," Russ said, his eyes on Sarah. "But I haven't met a single person whose heart isn't." Brandi laughed at that, and Russ looked up at her. "What's so funny?"

"I've never once looked at Noble that way. Neither do most people I know either." Brandi shrugged. "Your world is just too small and Noble's too big in it. He's got options, sure. But he's far from perfect."

"I guess that's true."

"It is true," Brandi insisted, letting her eyes glance around the thinning foot traffic of the street. Her instincts were on high alert, and she could feel in her gut that something was wrong. She couldn't pinpoint from where, but she could feel that they were being watched.

"What if Noble likes Sarah back?"

Russ laughed. "Noble doesn't like anyone. Not really."

"But what if he does?" Brandi pushed. "You said you would never betray him, right? So, what happens if he decides he wants the girl you have your heart set on?"

"She could like both of us."

"She could," Brandi conceded, "but she might not want multiple lovers. You ever thought about that?"

"Not really," Russ admitted. "But I'll cross that bridge when I get to it. I don't make a habit of trying to solve problems before they become one. Right now," he said, glancing over at Brandi with a weak smile, "I doubt she realizes I'm doing more than just being nice to her."

"She's dense," Brandi laughed. "But that doesn't answer my question."

"Of what?" Russ clarified. "If I would betray Noble for my own selfish desires?"

"Yes."

"No," Russ said firmly. "My friendship with him means more to me than anything else."

"Good," Brandi said. "Then I'm going to choose to trust in that rather than your questionable actions," she said, slowing her steps in the near empty street and taking a few steps closer to them.

"What does that mean?"

"It means I need you to listen," Brandi said, keeping her voice light. "We're being followed. They're likely after me and Sarah. So," she said, glancing at him, "I'm going to tell you what I learned at my meeting and you're going to find Noble and report back to him. Can you handle that?"

"Of course," he said, matching her tone with a chuckle. "I am a rebel, after all."

"And I still have so many questions about that," Brandi admitted. "But for now, you need to know this," she said, slowing to a stop. "I have an idea on how to stop the time being's apprentice. His vessel is headed to Freya's domain, so we'll need to stop him before he reaches her temple."

"What about Lindl's vessel? Don't we need to find them?"

"That sounds like a great idea! Why don't you just pick them up on your way?" When Russ said nothing else, Brandi sighed. "It could take weeks to find whoever Lindl chose. We don't have that kind of time. Azinne's vessel will be at Freya's temple in the next day or two."

"I understand," he said with a nod.

"Then find Noble," Brandi said, moving to shift Sarah's weight onto her own shoulders. "And tell him to bring Jack when he comes to get us."

"Where are you going?" he asked, letting Sarah slip from his grasp.

"They've been closing in on us for a while," Brandi answered. "And since they haven't ambushed us, I'm guessing they want us alive. So, they're probably going to take us."

"What?" Russ whispered, taking a step closer to her. "Shouldn't we stay together, then?"

"You can't deliver the message if you get taken too," Brandi snapped, "and she's safer with me. Just do what I asked you to."

"Understood," Russ said, backing away. "May Carna's winds be at your back."

Once he'd turned on his heel to head back the way they'd come, Brandi turned to continue down the walkway. She pretended to struggle under Sarah's weight, but with the strength Rothe had given her, she weighed little more than a backpack. She pinched Sarah's side as they made their way down the street and she jolted awake from her dozing, her blue eyes wild as they glanced around.

"Where am I? What's happening?"

"You're with me," Brandi answered in a calm voice. "And we're going back to Shian's. You're wasted."

"Ugh," Sarah groaned, lifting a hand to her forehead. "I don't know why I drank that much."

"I couldn't tell you," Brandi answered, keeping her eyes on the passersby as they went. The further they got from the violet lights of the bars and restaurants, the darker the streets became and the more intense the gaze on her back grew. She did her best to locate where it was coming from, but whoever it was, knew how to obscure their presence, and that made Brandi uneasy.

"Sarah," Brandi whispered, "I need you to focus."

"What is it?" Sarah groaned. "You going to give me a hard time, too?"

"Listen," Brandi snapped.

"I am," Sarah whined. "What is it?"

"We're not going to make it back to Shian's," she warned. "I don't know when, but we're going to be attacked."

The blood drained from Sarah's face as her blue eyes danced around the shadows surrounding them as if she could decipher some clue from them that Brandi couldn't.

"Are we going to be okay?"

"We'll be fine," Brandi told her as they turned the corner, leaving the last of the stragglers on the main street for the abandoned one that led to Shian's home. "But you won't like it."

"Understatement of the century, isn't it, Green?"

Brandi shoved Sarah away from her at the sound of the voice behind them, but before she could even reach for the blade beneath her dress, she was pinned to the ground with her cheek pressed into the cold stone of the sidewalk. She glared up at the brown eyes towering over her.

"You know I'm not going to let you do that," Najé said, her voice cold. "I let you get away once. It's not happening again."

She pulled a small silver ball from her necklace and a transport pod grew next to her in seconds. She opened the door and nodded her head at whoever had Brandi pinned to the ground, moving over to the small patch of grass Brandi had pushed Sarah into.

"Get them inside. Glenn wants to speak with them."

CHAPTER TWENTY

A secret kept is a friend made.

— Adage of the Gods | Lindl's Five Holy Academies Compilation

---

LINDL'S DOMAIN — PRESENT DAY

Brandi and Sarah were thrown into the cramped pod with unceremonious thuds, and Sarah groaned from the sudden impact. The door to the pod was slammed shut before Brandi could see who was on the other side, and she cursed as Sarah tumbled into her while trying to right herself. She sent both of them sprawling to the floor and Brandi huffed as she got back to her knees.

Their hands were bound behind their backs, and Brandi prayed for patience under her breath as Sarah lost her footing twice more before managing to get into an upright position. The pod they were in was tiny, just big enough for the two of them. There were no seats for them to strap themselves into, and the inside walls were opaque and covered in work dust. Brandi sighed as she realized they weren't in a transport pod meant for people, but a supply pod meant for storage. Which meant that the ride was going to be rough, at best.

Brandi glanced over to Sarah with an annoyed type of concern. Brandi would be fine, being tossed around a supply pod was the least of her worries. However, she had no desire to be tossed around with Sarah while she was losing her stomach. So, she moved over to Sarah as she felt the transport pod begin to lift and nudged her back with her own.

"What are you doing?" Sarah asked, groaning as the pod jolted forward.

"Helping us," Brandi said, bracing her long legs against the edge of the pod. "Stretch your legs out," she commanded. "Brace them against the side of the pod and push back against me."

"Okay," Sarah said, moving slowly without her hands to help hold her steady. It took her a few attempts to get it right, but she managed to accomplish it before the supply pod reached the top of its ascent and jolted them forward again. It threw Sarah into Brandi's back, but with both of their legs braced against the edge of the pod, they weren't tossed around like a set of rag dolls.

"Ugh," Sarah groaned, leaning her head back into Brandi's shoulder. "Why is this happening to us?"

"Because you're a princess and I'm a shadow who abandoned the queendom," Brandi said. "There was no way we were going to be left alone to live our lives in peace."

"That's all I wanted, though," Sarah said. "To just be left alone in the woods. I would've been happy growing herbs and setting broken bones. I could have grown old and stayed with Jamie. That would've been enough," she sighed. "I didn't ask to be a princess."

Brandi snorted and rolled her eyes, leaning into Sarah as the pod took a sharp turn.

"Oh, woe is you," Brandi said, her voice void of any sympathy. "Your life is so hard. Whatever should we do?"

"You know," Sarah said, pressing her back into Brandi's, "you don't have to be so insensitive."

"Is that what you would call me?"

"Yeah," Sarah said. "I mean, I get your life wasn't easy either."

"You have no idea," Brandi agreed.

"That's because you've never told me," Sarah said, closing her eyes to whisper a healing prayer to Asari.

She didn't drink often, but part of that was because the effects never lasted for very long. With her blessing of healing, most toxins left her system before they had any time to affect her. It's part of the reason she was so surprised she'd felt anything at all — and why she couldn't stop, even once she knew better than to keep drinking. There were so many thoughts worrying her mind and so many emotions fighting each other in her chest on a near-constant basis, not having to worry about them for an hour or so had been bliss. But she recognized that letting herself stay this way wasn't the best decision. Right now, she needed the clarity of her own mind.

"What good would telling you do?" Brandi asked, shifting her heel-clad foot to the left as they jolted again. "I'm not looking for any sympathy."

"Aren't you though?" Sarah questioned. "You're annoyed with me for not knowing about your life, but how am I supposed to know anything you don't tell me?" Sarah glanced over her shoulder at Brandi as her mind became clearer. "Asari's power may entice me to follow you, but I'm still my own person outside of the gods, and I don't really know you."

"I'm not annoyed with you for not knowing about me," Brandi clarified. "I'm annoyed because you think your life deserves all the tears when you've always known who you were. You knew the queendom was looking for you and that one day, it would find you. But you chose to live your life as if that wasn't a possibility," Brandi pointed out. "You could have trained and gotten stronger. Learned how to protect yourself. Told Jamie the truth so he would be ready. But you didn't," Brandi snapped. "You lived your life as if pretending to be some poor girl from Asari's outskirts would turn you into that. And when it didn't, you wanted to cry about it. That," Brandi emphasized, pushing into her back, "is what annoys me."

"That I didn't prepare for this?"

"That you had a choice over your own life," Brandi said. "And you refused to make one."

"Is that what your problem with me is?" Sarah asked, pushing back into Brandi, finally catching the rhythm of the shifting pod now that she was sober. "That you somehow think I chose this life for myself?"

"The fact that you think you didn't," Brandi said with a shake of her head. "You're so spoiled you don't even see it."

"No," Sarah said, getting frustrated. "I don't. So, explain it to me," she demanded. "What happened to you that pissed you off so bad?"

"I'm not pissed off," Brandi stated. "I'm just tired of you acting like you have it so bad when all you did was play house with Kyle in Asari's domain. But I'll play this little game with you, Sarah," Brandi said, easing the tension in her legs as the pod settled into a smooth sailing motion. "You want to know what happened to me, I'll tell you."

"That's all I'm asking," Sarah said.

"I was born in Freya's domain with her soul inside of me," Brandi told her. "My parents were Freyan merchants. And if you know anything about the realm, then you'll know that Freyans do more than sell goods across the domains — they travel the realm telling stories of the gods and connecting other people with them. They rarely stay in one place for long, and that includes in Freya's domain."

"I'm aware," Sarah said with a nod, though Brandi couldn't see her.

"Then you should understand how strange it was that, once I was born, my parents never left Freya's domain again."

"What?" Sarah asked, raising her eyebrows in surprise as she locked her legs to keep the swaying pod from jolting them. "Why?"

"My mother was what most people would call frail," Brandi told her. "After she had me, her body couldn't handle the stress of traveling anymore. And since Freya's domain has the purest form of nature, it was good for her. My father built a house near Freya's temple and things were good. For a while at least."

"And then what happened?"

"What else?" Brandi snorted. "The queendom found us."

FREYA'S DOMAIN — 16 YEARS AGO

When the foundation of Brandi's life began to fall from beneath her, it was a sunny day. She'd spent the entire afternoon outside on the back porch, looking at books and listening to the stories her mother spun of all the different domains in the mortal realm and of all the places she and her father had been. Her voice had been as gentle as her hands as she parted and braided Brandi's hair into neat rows.

The sharp knocks on their door that day were unexpected and drew their attention back inside the house.

With one glance inside at her husband, Temari had taken Brandi by the hand and escorted her to her room. With a few firm words for her to not make any noise, she'd shut the door behind her.

Brandi hadn't wasted any time in pressing her face to the cracks separating the slats in her bedroom door. Her green eyes strained to see who was there and her breath caught in her throat the first time she laid eyes on Glenn MelForth. She was a tall, imposing woman who towered over her mother's slim figure and stood eye to eye with her father. Her complexion was several shades lighter than theirs, but what caught Brandi's eyes were the muscles straining against her form-fitting clothes. She'd never seen a woman look so strong, so healthy, and in an instant, Brandi decided she wanted to be just like her when she grew up.

She'd be healthy enough to live a full life like her mom had before she got sick.

"Ross..." Glenn said, pulling out the syllables of her father's name once he opened the door and met her gaze.

"I'm not going with you," her father stated, his fingers tightening around the frame of the door. "I don't care how many times you ask. I'm not going to abandon my wife and daughter."

"This is no longer a request," Glenn warned. "If you turn me away, the queen won't ask again. Do you understand what that means?" When Ross said nothing, Glenn narrowed her eyes at him. "I'll have to return as a shadow, Ross. Is that what you want?"

"Do what you must," he said, edging the door closed. "And I'll do the same."

Glenn left after that and Brandi thought that would be the end of things. But later that night, when her parents thought she'd been long asleep, their whispers drifted through her door. Brandi didn't pay much attention to them at first, but when her mother's sobs reached her, it seemed like they were rattling her own brain. It forced Brandi to sit up in her bed and strain her ears to make sense of their words.

"Please, Ross," her mother begged, hiccups breaking up her words, "I can't do this anymore."

"Do you realize what you're asking of me?" Her father snapped, tears thick in his own voice. "Do you?"

"It's cruel," her mother whispered back. "But I have to ask it of you. I don't want to hurt you," she cried. "Or Brandi. Anyone but Brandi. Please."

"And what is she going to do without you?" Ross questioned. "Did you not hear Glenn at the door? The queen is demanding I join her court now. And it wasn't a request this time, Temari."

"Then what are we going to do?" Temari asked, her voice broken and wet.

"I don't know," he whispered. "I don't know."

LINDL'S DOMAIN — PRESENT DAY

"So," Brandi said, "instead of being conscripted into the queen's court as one of her consorts and forced to leave us behind in Freya's domain, he sent my mother to the gods himself, told me to be strong and survive, then sent himself."

"Gods," Sarah whispered.

"Not even five minutes later, the shadows came bursting through the front door, looking for me. I locked myself in my room, climbed out the window, and never looked back." Brandi shrugged. "Which is why it annoys me that you act like you didn't have a choice in anything. You had more choices than I ever did."

"Where did you go?" Sarah asked after a moment of silence passed between them.

"Freya's temple," Brandi answered. "I knew that forest like the back of my own eyelids and I heard Freya's voice inside of me, guiding me there. But as small as I was, there was no way for me to outrun Patches, even with a head start." Brandi shrugged and looked up as the pod came to a stop. "I only got away because Tiki rescued me. It took me the rest of the way to Freya's temple. It protected me and raised me with the rest of its clan until that winter I got sick. Then, it took me to you."

"So, that thump on the door that day," Sarah said, her voice trailing off as her eyes got wider.

"Tiki throwing its paw against it," Brandi said with a nod, rising to her feet. "It's the only time Asari has ever allowed a shader through his barrier."

Sarah stood to her feet as well and looked at Brandi with a questioning look.

"But there's still something I don't understand," Sarah said, brushing the dirt from the bottom of her skirt as best she could with her wrists still bound. "Why would the shadows want to send your parents in the first place?"

"Because your aunt is a power-hungry blasphemer," said a voice from the other side of the door, "and she wanted a Freyan, specifically a Freylin, under the queendom's control."

Both Sarah and Brandi's attention snapped to the door as it opened. On the other side stood Glenn "The Grim Reaper" MelForth, in all her glory. Brandi's green eyes narrowed as she looked at her former teacher and guardian. She hadn't aged a day and looked the same as when she'd left, with her rich golden brown skin glowing, her muscles taut, her grin arrogant, and her long black locs pinned back into a bun.

"It's been a long time, Green."

"Hm," Brandi said, rolling her eyes.

"And here I thought you'd be happy to see me," Glenn chuckled. "Whispers on the wind say you've been looking for me."

"Aren't you the one who taught me not to believe everything I hear?"

"I did," she smirked. "I'm glad to know you haven't forgotten. But," she said, clapping her hands together, "this isn't the place for us to catch up. Follow me."

With those words, she turned on her heel to walk out down a narrow ramp and through a small tunnel that forced them to walk in a single file line. Brandi shot a quick glance at Sarah and followed behind Glenn, keeping as much distance between them as possible. They didn't walk for very long before the scent of Lindl's Blind Sea assaulted their senses, and the dim light of Asari's moon glinting off the water greeted them.

Sarah's steps faltered as she took in the grandeur of the ocean and her blue eyes were as big as the moon itself as she looked at it and Brandi slowed her steps to give Sarah more time to take it all in. Whatever books she might have read about the Blind Sea, seeing it for the first time was its own experience. Just looking at it was enough to make anyone understand just how vast the realm was. There was nothing but inky blue water for as far as the eye could see, meeting the sky in the distance. She heard Sarah taking deep breaths of the salty air and could almost sense her muscles relaxing with every exhale she released.

The warm sand snuck its way into Brandi's heels as her feet sunk into it and she paused to kick them off rather than try to walk on the beach with them. Under normal circumstances, she would have loved being at the beach. Aside from Freya's temple, it was one of her favorite places to be in the realm. And, if she let herself, she could almost imagine coming back with Jack and Noble — maybe even Sarah, and letting her run around in the rolling waves. But it was a fleeting thought and she let it go as she moved to stand by one of the chairs situated around a fire pit burning in the sand.

"Have a seat," Glenn directed, falling into one of the low-sitting chairs herself.

"So, you're not going to untie us?"

"Of course not," Glenn said with a raised eyebrow. "I know how you were trained. The princess might not be any real threat, but I know better than to underestimate you, Green. So," she said, pointing to the chair, "sit."

Brandi sighed and sank to her knees before falling back in the chair. Sarah copied her movements, but still yelped in surprise when the unbalanced flopping of her weight nearly sent her sprawling into the sand, face first. Once she was situated, Glenn turned to face Brandi, a smile breaking across her face.

"You really turned out alright," she said.

"All things considered."

"Well," Glenn said, leaning forward to rest her elbows on her knees. "I know you have questions for me, so I'll let you go first. Ask me anything."

"Are you going to answer anything?"

"No," she said plainly. "But you knew that already."

"Why did you leave?" Brandi asked.

The question was direct, and her gaze held Glenn's as she waited for an answer. Brandi didn't really care what the answer was at this point, she'd given up on trying to understand Glenn a long time ago. She just wanted to see how much Glenn would be willing to share with her, and starting with why she left seemed like a good place to begin.

"I had other callings to attend to," Glenn answered. "You were strong enough to take care of yourself, so my job of protecting you was done."

"So, you just assumed I wouldn't need you anymore because I could send someone to the gods?"

"No," Glenn shrugged, "I just didn't care if you did."

The words stung Brandi to her core, but she kept her face and breathing even as she processed the words. She'd known all along that Glenn wasn't her mother, that she didn't truly care for her, and she wasn't the person who was going to love her in Temari's absence. But Glenn had been the only person she'd been left with. And for three years, she was the one who had cared for her, protected her from taking on the crushing responsibilities of the queendom before she was ready, taught her how to survive in a world where being sent to the gods was commonplace.

She'd known better, but a small, childish part of her heart had hoped that Glenn would say something different.

"What other callings were more important than leading the shadows for Queen Leia?"

Glenn laughed. "Come on, Brandi," she coaxed. "You're old enough to understand that there's more to this realm than being loyal to some self-serving monarchy."

"Do I know that?"

"You should," Glenn shrugged. "Otherwise, why aren't you serving it now?"

"I have my reasons."

"And I have mine," Glenn told her. "But if you want me to spell it out for you, then I will." She clasped her hands together as they hung between her knees. "I left to support the rebellion against the queendom."

"Why would you betray the queen?"

"After learning who she really is, why would anyone stay loyal to her?" Glenn shot back, her voice becoming hard as she thought about it. "You have no idea what orders I carried out under the guise of serving the queendom."

"Then tell me," Brandi said, using the same words Sarah had thrown at her. "How am I expected to know what you've been through if you've told me nothing?"

"I never expected you to know," Glenn said. "It's not something that concerns you. All you need to know is that I left, and I have no plans of coming back. I never had any reason to explain myself beyond that."

"But I don't understand," Brandi said, pulling her eyebrows together and shaking her head. "What would make you want to tear down the same queendom you helped to build?"

"Let me ask you this," Glenn countered. "Why didn't you leave the shadows, Brandi? I may have forced you into her service, but you stayed once I left. Why was that?"

"I made a deal and —"

"And I wasn't there to keep it anymore," Glenn interrupted. "You knew I wouldn't go after some unknown princess. If you truly thought I would, you would've started trying to protect her a long time ago," Glenn pointed out. "Try again."

Brandi's face grew hot under Glenn's intense glare and she felt less like the hardened shadow she was, and more like the eight-year-old child she used to be, faltering under Glenn's gaze. She huffed and coached herself back to calmness. Glenn was trying to get a rise out of her, make her emotional to coax her into giving away things she wanted to keep to herself. So, instead, Brandi didn't say anything, and Glenn smirked.

"I'll tell you why," she said. "You found people you didn't want sent to the gods. So, you stayed. And when you realized the queendom didn't care about who you wanted to protect, you left."

"Don't speak as if you know me."

"You think you're the only one?" Glenn laughed. "It's why we all leave eventually. We get an order we can't complete. Mine was when I got the order to kill your father. He was a good man and a close friend."

"Well, you didn't send him," Brandi said, turning her gaze to the waves. "He made sure of that."

"It doesn't make me feel any less guilty about it," Glenn responded.

"So, why didn't you leave then? Why stay for years after that and force me to join you?"

"You already know why. Or did Rothe not tell you?"

"Enlighten me," Brandi said, feigning ignorance.

"The job with your father was meant to be our last," Glenn told her. "I couldn't disobey the queendom, but I knew I could make sure I never received another order from them. So, once we sent you and your parents back to the gods, Patches and I were going to disappear. But when I got there," she shrugged, "your parents were gone, and you were running away. Patches chased after you, but Rothe pulled me into his realm of the gods. Told me who you were."

"So, you knew? Even then?"

"Did you never wonder why we never came back to send you?" Glenn asked her. "You may have made it to Freya's temple that night, but you know for yourself how simple a task it would have been for us to send a child. No," she said, shaking her head. "We didn't come back because I refused to allow the order to be carried out. I made it known that anyone who wanted to send you would have to send me first."

"Then why did you force me to join the shadows?"

"Because you left Freya's domain."

"I had to."

"Yes. But I'm only a single person, Green," Glenn said with a smirk. "You might think I'm all-powerful, but even I have my limits. Keeping shadows out of Freya's domain was one thing, no one wanted to go there anyway. But if you could've been anywhere in the realm, then I couldn't protect you. You know for yourself how many shadows lurk through the domains, unnoticed. I couldn't stop all of them."

"So, you made me join you."

"Rothe instructed me to protect you, and the safest place for you was by my side."

Brandi shook her head, trying to make sense of everything Glenn was telling her. If her words were to be trusted, then she'd never wanted to be a shadow any of the time Brandi had known her. She'd always planned to work with the rebellion and had worked for the queendom only to keep Brandi safe. And, in the beginning, Brandi had only listened to Glenn in order to keep Sarah safe. Her head ached at all of the opportunities she'd given up in order to be a shadow and she ground her teeth thinking of how things could have been so different had Glenn made her decision a single day sooner.

If she'd never gone after her father, he wouldn't have sent himself and her mother to the gods. Brandi wouldn't have lost her family to be raised by shaders, and Glenn wouldn't have pressed her into the service of the queendom under the guise of protecting her. She would have been able to listen to all the stories her parents had to tell her. She might have traveled like they had — fallen in love with Jack in a more honest way and attended one of Lindl's academies with him.

Her life could have been simple.

Ordinary.

Uneventful.

And a part of her soul burned with rage that those opportunities had been denied her. She knew there was nothing she could do about it now, she couldn't bring back the people she'd sent to the gods, and she couldn't unlive all the experiences that shaped her into who she was. But still, she was angry, and it wasn't something she could just shake off.

"Do you understand now? The queendom is more corrupt than you think. Shadows are expected to be weapons," she said, looking away from Brandi into the fire she'd nearly forgotten was burning in front of them. "Tools of destruction meant to carry out the orders of the queendom without question. And because of that, good people get sent to the gods without ever having the chance to plead their case." Glenn shook her head and met Brandi's gaze. "I didn't want to be a part of it anymore, so I left. I fight with the rebellion now to make sure no one else has to be either."

"Why didn't you take me with you?" Brandi asked. "I would have gone anywhere with you."

"Because you needed a home, and I couldn't give you that." Glenn paused as Brandi took a deep breath and processed the words. "At least," she said after a moment, "I couldn't give it to you then."

"And what's that supposed to mean?"

"Join the rebellion," Glenn stated. "There's a war brewing in the queendom, Green. And everyone's going to have to pick a side."

"And you want me to side with you?"

"Of course I do," Glenn chuckled. "I trained you myself. I know better than anyone what you're capable of."

"And I'd prefer to not have to fight my own sister again, if you don't mind."

Brandi's gaze snapped up to Najé's at the sound of her voice. She grinned and waved as she strolled through the sand with Russ and Noble behind her. Brandi started to smile at the thought of them truly coming to rescue them, but she stopped once she realized that Jack wasn't with them. Her heart pounded with a painful force as she searched Noble's face and he refused to make eye contact with her.

He was looking more disheveled than he usually did. The sleeves of the black dress shirt he'd bought were ripped off and dark bruises littered his arms. Russ didn't look any worse for wear, but like Noble, he refused to meet her gaze.

"Where's Jack?" Brandi asked, jumping to her feet.

"No 'hello' for me, I guess," Najé scoffed.

"Where is he?" Brandi demanded, her pulse rising in her throat as her mind began to spiral through all the worst possibilities.

"I've never seen you this worked up, Green," Glenn said, surprise lacing her voice. "Who is this Jack person?" Glenn asked, looking at Najé.

"Her lover," Najé said. "Since she was around thirteen. They basically share the same brain at this point. He left the shadows the second she did. And he," Najé said, jabbing her thumb over her shoulder towards Noble, "wasn't too far behind."

"You left too?" Glenn asked with raised eyebrows.

"I go where she goes," Noble answered evenly.

"I'm not surprised. You always were her little bodyguard."

"I swear to Freya, if someone doesn't answer me…" Brandi said, her voice shaking with rage as the wind swirled around her, picking up sand and sparks as she began to lose the grip she had on her spiritual power.

"I'm sorry, Green," Noble said softly.

"For what?" Brandi demanded. "Where's Jack? Why isn't he with you?" She turned a sharp glare onto Russ and took two menacing steps forward. "You said he went to find Jack."

Russ stumbled backward, away from her, and nodded his head.

"He did."

"Then where is he?"

"Shian turned him over to some kid who works for Bert named Saya," Noble told her. "I tried to stop him, but he used some weird power to turn all of my hits back on to me," he said, holding up his arms. "I'm sorry."

"Why would Shian do that?" She turned her gaze back to Russ and shook in her restraints at the pure rage and fear that coursed through her. "Why would Shian do that, Russ?"

"He's part of the rebellion, too," Russ answered carefully, angling his body behind Noble's as he looked at Brandi. "We had orders to contact the queendom if we came across any of you."

"Why?" Brandi said, whipping around to face Glenn. "Liar," she accused, raising her voice. "You gods forsaken liar!" Brandi screamed. "Why are you working for the queendom if you're trying to destroy them?"

"Because some of us are still working inside the queendom," Najé interjected, stepping in front of Glenn. "And we've got orders we can't just ignore. You know how it is."

"No," Brandi said, shaking her head. "I don't. I left because I got orders I couldn't accept!"

"This wasn't an order I couldn't accept," Najé said with a shrug. "I swore to always protect you," she said. "That never applied to anyone else."

Brandi gasped as her chest heaved and her mind worked to understand what was happening. Saya had found them. Jack was taken by him. He was likely wielding the time apprentice's power.

Jack was in danger of being sent to the gods.

"Whose side are you on?" Brandi whispered, looking at the sand. "Glenn. Tell me."

"I'm going to destroy the crown," Glenn said with confidence.

"I came here to revoke the power Rothe gave you," Brandi told her, raising her head to meet her gaze. "And I've got other priorities than the silly politics of the queendom," Brandi said, taking a step towards her. "But if you would help me save Jack, I will destroy whatever you want me to," Brandi bargained. "I'll become the weapon you trained me to be."

Brandi snapped the restraints that bound her with ease to hold out her hand towards Glenn. "Do we have a deal?"

"Yeah," Glenn said, standing to her feet with a smile and shaking Brandi's hand. "We have a deal."

"Then tell me where Saya is," Brandi said, looking at Najé.

"You can't fight him, Brandi," Najé said softly, shaking her head. "He's got some weird power, and your blessing won't work on him."

"Did I ask you for your assessment of the situation?" Brandi snapped. "Tell me where he is."

"Freya's temple," Najé answered, shocked by the hostility in Brandi's voice. "He's gone with Bert and about ten other shadows under his command. He plans to make an offering to the goddess before the bidding starts."

"We can leave at first light, then," Glenn said. "There's enough people at our base to put up a good fight. I'll get them ready and we'll be there in two days."

"Too slow," Brandi said with a shake of her head. "I'm leaving now."

"You can't," Najé said. "Even you can't handle ten shadows on your own."

"If it was Sal, would you wait?" Brandi snapped. When Najé said nothing, she scoffed. "That's what I thought."

"Green…"

"I swear on all of Freya's lovers, if you say one more word to me…" Brandi screamed, shoving her finger into Najé's face. "You knew! You knew they were going to try and take him from me, and you did nothing!" Brandi shouted. "I would've never let Sal be taken. Never," she spat. "So, don't put my name in your mouth if this is how you plan to treat me."

"I'm sorry," Najé whispered.

"Shove your apology up Rothe's ass," Brandi shot back at her, stomping over to Russ. "You'd better pray that Jack is still on this side of the gods' realm when I find him," she warned, snatching the black marble of the *Ciel Noir* from Russ's neck and tossing it into the air for it to expand. "Because if he's not, all of you will meet the gods on unfavorable terms."

"That's a big threat, Green," Glenn pointed out.

"It's a promise," Brandi shot back, climbing into the pod. "Because if you think for even one second that I wouldn't destroy the gods and betray this entire realm for Jack, then you have no idea what kind of weapon you created."

CHAPTER TWENTY-ONE

Do not fall in love with the goddess for who you wish her to be — for she will love you in the same breath that she denies you mercy.

— Freya and the Power of Incarnation | Lindl's First Holy Academy

FREYA'S DOMAIN — PRESENT DAY

The moment Brandi exited Lindl's barrier and entered Freya's domain, Tiki was already waiting for her. She'd discarded her dress and changed back into her standard outfit of cargo pants and a high-necked shirt, so she wasted no time jumping out of the *Ciel Noir* and shrinking it back down to its marble size.

I have seen your mate, Tiki whispered into her mind. *He does not look well.*

"I'm here to get him," Brandi told it, swinging herself up onto its back. "We'll need all the help we can get, too."

They wait only for your call.

"Good," Brandi said, urging Tiki forward. "Then take me home."

Tiki wasted no time taking off through the forest, its giant paws thundering against the ground as it navigated the thick trunks of the trees as if it were Carna's wind flowing through them. Brandi's chest swelled with emotion as Tiki raced them towards Freya's temple in the center of her domain.

The thick branches growing together above them blocked out all light except for the little pinholes that managed to sneak their way through. Brandi looked up, reminded of the stars she'd seen in Asari's domain on clear nights, and took a deep breath, forcing down every fear, anxiety, and distraction that bubbled up inside of her.

Her heart wouldn't be able to handle losing Jack to the gods.

She accepted that as fact. And if she didn't want to face that reality, she needed to dismiss her emotions and focus on what was ahead of her. She was a shadow, a weapon forged by the queendom. And weapons didn't need emotions to send men to the gods.

She repeated those words in her head and closed off her heart until she felt nothing.

There are men up ahead, Tiki whispered into her mind. **What do you want to do?**

"*Let me off,*" Brandi whispered, jumping to the ground. "*Flank them. I'll take the ones here.*"

May I devour them?

Brandi nodded and pet Tiki's fur. "*To your heart's content.*"

Tiki huffed warm air into Brandi's face and sped off into the distance, a blur of black fur that slipped through the shadows. Once she was alone, Brandi closed her eyes, focusing on the blessing pulsing in her veins. It had been a long time since she'd used her power in Freya's domain and had nearly forgotten how much stronger it was there. She smiled at the heat that pooled in her belly as she took deep breaths, focusing on it as it spread through her body until a light sheen of sweat broke out along her skin.

When she opened her eyes, she focused until she sensed Bert's first shadow. He stood balanced in one of the lower branches, prepared to ambush any unsuspecting targets from above.

Brandi rolled her shoulders back as she whispered her prayer.

"Bless me, for I am the wrath of the gods."

Her bow and arrow were in her hands in seconds, and she grinned at the thrill of power that raced through her fingers. Focusing her thoughts, she honed her senses in on her target once more, her eyes narrowing as she worked to tamper down the rage boiling inside her chest. She could feel the tight grip she normally had on her emotions loosening at the rise of her blessing.

"May the wrath of the gods have no mercy on your soul."

She released her arrow, and it flew through the air, straight and true, until it embedded itself in her target's chest, pinning him to the tree until it dissipated and he fell to the ground.

"That's one," Brandi whispered, as she turned to take aim once more. "Four more to go."

"Five," Brandi whispered to herself, stepping over the last body in her path as she approached the clearing. She stood a few paces back, lingering in the shadows as her green eyes raked over the scene before her.

Saya stood next to Bert, his features plain in the light of day. He was less impressive now that Brandi could see him clearly, but she didn't let that ease her tension. The last time they'd fought, she couldn't say for certain that she would have walked away unscathed had Najé not intervened. With that in mind, she wouldn't underestimate him again.

Bert stood with his back to her as he spoke with Saya outside the temple, but what made her heart race was Jack's body lying bloodied on the bottom of a clear transport pod.

Everything in the realm went dark, and for a solid minute, Brandi could do nothing but stare at him as her heart thundered in her chest, threatening to break through her ribs. She heard nothing but the sound of her own blood rushing, and the heat that bloomed within her, singed her clothes and sent steam rolling off her in waves. She didn't blink until she saw his chest heave. When she did, she refocused on the souls she planned to harvest.

Without thinking, she summoned three arrows for her bow and released them at once into Bert's back.

Saya noticed and managed to block two of them, but the last one wedged itself deep into Bert's right shoulder, and he screamed in pain as green flames licked at his clothes and blood spilled from the fresh wound. He fell to the ground, flailing and pulling at the edges of his suit that were melting onto his skin, but Brandi didn't hesitate as she walked into the clearing. Her steps were silent, but green flames rose from beneath her feet as she walked, and her shots were relentless.

She rained fiery arrows down on them until Saya was forced to deploy their transport pod and shove Bert inside it. Her arrows dissipated against the reinforced exterior that was no doubt coated in whatever godforsaken magic the time being used and Brandi's rage grew. The flames beneath her feet rose higher until she felt as if she were walking out from the core of Rothe's sun.

"Did you do this?" She questioned.

"You gone have to be a bit clearer than that," Saya drawled, tightening the bands for his projectiles around his wrist.

"It doesn't matter," Brandi said, firing more shots at him that dissipated before hitting him as they had before. "I'll send you to the gods and they can drag the truth out of you themselves."

"You sure about that, sweetness?" Saya grinned, flashing his pearly whites at her. "Cause it seems like you still can't hit me."

"I don't need to," Brandi said, stopping in her tracks as she reached the center of the clearing.

"*Hear me, children of Freya,*" she shouted in the god tongue, holding Saya's gaze as his brown eyes grew wide in surprise. "*I am the incarnation of your goddess. The child of Temari who grew beside you as one of your own. I have returned home and am in need of your help. Would you hear my request?*"

The forest around them shook with the thundering stomps and growls of dozens of shaders. The very ground beneath them vibrated and Saya's eyes whipped to the forest line, his eyes desperately searching the trees for the source of the sound. He took a trembling step back as growling shaders began stepping into the clearing, just enough for him to see that he was surrounded.

Tiki, the largest one and leader of the pack, stepped from behind Brandi. It walked in measured paces through the clearing with a regal air. When it stood at Brandi's side, her flames parted to allow it through. The mangled corpse of one of Bert's shadows was still clenched in its jaws, and it tossed the body into the air, catching it again between its sharp teeth. A sickening crunch echoed through the clearing as Tiki ripped through the bones and flesh of the corpse, cleaving its head from the rest of the body. It ate the lower half as the head of the boy rolled over to Saya to look up at him with lifeless brown eyes.

Saya took another step back, his knees giving out as he watched Tiki bend its front legs to bow to Brandi out of respect.

We would hear you, Tiki whispered into her mind while the other shaders stomped their feet in unison, anticipation thrumming through the forest.

"*This man,*" Brandi said, pointing to Saya who sat shaking and wide-eyed on the ground, "*would defile your goddess and her temple. Undermine her power and destroy my beloved in the process. We cannot allow that.*" She said, waiting as the shader's roars and growls shook the trees at the clearing's edge, sending every other living creature skittering away from them.

We cannot, Tiki agreed. *What would you have us do?*

Brandi let her eyes lock onto Saya's and, without missing a beat, she raised her head and spoke in the common tongue.

"Feast," she commanded.

With those words, Tiki stood and roared into the skies. The other shaders added their own voices to Tiki's and rushed into the clearing. Before he could even scream for help, Lia, who led the charge, pounced on him. She bit into his left arm, ripping it whole from his socket. The other shaders were no better as they fell over each other, using their paws to pin him down and their sharp teeth to rip into his flesh, bit by bit. His screams were silenced in seconds, and they ate until there was nothing left but the stained ground beneath where his body had once been.

"Gods."

Brandi whipped her head over to the clear transport pod that Jack was in and nearly screamed as she saw Bert standing by it. He must have snuck over to it while her attention was focused on Saya, but she saw that he now held a canister in his right hand. Bert's chest heaved and his left hand held tight to the wound in his shoulder, but his eyes were determined.

"You truly are the wrath of the gods, aren't you?" Brandi raised her bow at him, but before she could release her shot, he'd popped the top of the canister and thrown it into the pod with Jack.

"*NO!*" Brandi screamed, racing towards the pod.

"You'll meet the gods like the dogs you are," Bert spat, hobbling away from the pod as fast as he could and up the steps of Freya's temple.

Brandi paid no attention to him as she slammed into the pod, pulling at the door Bert had just opened, only to find it locked. She could see Jack's weakened body trying to crawl away from the black smoke spilling into the pod, but it was a small space and it filled up fast. His fist was only able to beat against the inside of the glass twice before his body went limp again and he fell back into the smoke.

Brandi screamed wordlessly as she threw her fists against the pod, tears streaming down her cheeks as every shader in the vicinity turned toward Bert. Before they could charge him though, he disappeared inside the temple, and shaders with malicious intent toward mortals weren't allowed inside. It was an antiquated edict from the time of the originals, when Freylins lived in the domain alongside shaders. The temple was meant to be a peaceful place for mortals and shaders to come together, so Freya withheld entry to any who would attempt to do harm.

Brandi slammed her fists into the clear transport pod, screaming for Jack, but she could no longer see him through the smoke. It wasn't until Tiki and Lia arrived at her sides and began smashing against the transport pod together that it finally shattered under their weight. Brandi lunged for Jack as his body fell to the ground, but Lia held her back, and Tiki blocked her path until the smoke cleared. Once it had, she rushed to Jack's body and held onto it.

"Jack," she cried, searching and failing to find a pulse. "Stay with me," she whispered, pressing into his chest. "Don't leave me here."

His eyes were closed, and his face was badly swollen, with dried blood caked along his cheeks. His arms had been broken in multiple places and he looked nothing like the man she'd fallen in love with. She wailed as she pushed against his chest, trying to force life back into his body.

"What is happening here?"

Brandi looked up to see Glenn and the other rebels entering the clearing. Najé stood with them, and Brandi screamed wordlessly at her, all of her sorrow and rage coalescing into unspoken commands. Two shaders raced towards her with their teeth bared as the others swarmed around her. They only stopped when Noble pulled her behind his back, unable to harm a vessel of the gods.

"You don't want to send her, Green," he said.

"*Don't tell me what I want!*" Brandi wailed in the god's tongue. "*This is her fault,*" she cried. "*Hers!*"

"What's going on?" Sarah asked, pushing to the front of the crowd and looking around the scene. "Dear gods," she whispered once she saw Jack and Brandi sitting in the middle of a ring of almost thirty shaders. All of them were tensed and pacing, with low growls rumbling through the clearing over to the newcomers.

"Let me through Brandi!" Sarah called over to her. "Let me help him."

Brandi nodded her head as she pleaded with Jack, begging him to open his eyes. To look at her. To say anything. To stay with her. Tiki stomped and the other shaders made a way for Sarah, who sprinted over to Brandi, her chest heaving at seeing her so heartbroken. She fell to the ground beside her and brushed Brandi's hands aside as she prayed to Asari.

"*Hear me, Asari, the plea of your chosen. Light the way for the wounded. Guide them out of their darkest nights.*"

Tiny Human, Lia called to Brandi, pulling her thoughts away from Sarah and the blue light emanating from her. *There are more humans coming. They do not seem to come with pure intentions.*

"What did you do?" Brandi asked, raising her wet face to pin Najé with a death glare.

"Bert sent out a distress call," Najé admitted. "There are at least two dozen shadows and at least fifty soldiers headed here now to aid him."

Brandi's eyes grew wide as she finally understood the full implications of Najé's words.

Freya's temple was about to become a battleground. All because of Bert and his selfish decisions. Brandi dragged herself to her feet and looked down at Sarah.

"Can you save him?"

"He's not with the gods yet, but he's flirting with them. I'll do everything I can," she said, sweat already dripping down her face.

"Please," Brandi whispered, her voice cracking. "Please bring him back."

Sarah nodded, tears slipping down her own cheeks at the pain in Brandi's voice. She'd never heard anything so heart-wrenching and the sound alone was like needles in her chest. She never thought the fearless woman who navigated dangerous situations with ease could be broken — especially not to the point of having her weakness put on display. It made Sarah wonder exactly who Jack was and how he was able to hold so much power over her. Sarah trembled at the thought of loving anyone that much.

Brandi straightened her back and wiped her face before turning her green eyes on the rebels. There would be time for tears later, but they wouldn't save Jack. She'd have to put his soul in Sarah's hands and keep her mind on the tasks in front of her. She climbed onto Tiki's back and rode it over to where the rebels stood looking up at her in awe. But Brandi only had eyes for one person, and that was Najé MelForth.

"*Move,*" she demanded, and Noble backed out of her way, the rest of the rebels following his lead until Brandi and Najé were left with a wide berth. Najé stood in front of Tiki's towering bulk without wavering, her eyes locked with Brandi's green ones. "It's time for you to pick a side."

"I don't know what you mean, Green."

"Don't," Brandi snapped, closing her eyes and shaking her head. "Don't play games with me, Najé. I don't have the patience for it," she warned. "You cannot be loyal to me, the rebels, and the queendom. So, choose," Brandi demanded.

Najé hesitated, her fists clenching and unclenching as she broke her eyes away from Brandi's to stare at the ground. Najé had never been a hard person for Brandi to read, and the frustration was clear on her face as her plans came crashing down around her. Brandi didn't know how long Najé had been working for both the rebellion and the shadows, and in this moment, she didn't truly care. But the fact remained that she'd been ignorant of her involvement and that showed that Najé had done an immaculate job of crafting the perfect cover to fool everyone.

Including her.

Brandi wasn't ready to try and process that yet, but it weighed on her. Najé was her sister — they had chosen to be family. And Brandi couldn't fathom how they'd gotten to this point, but it didn't matter. Najé had made her choices.

Either she would live with them, or Brandi would send her to the gods to account for them.

"Answer me," Brandi said.

"I've always got your back," Najé finally relented.

"Then prove it," Brandi told her. "Decimate the soldiers of the queendom."

"Okay," Najé said with a nod. "And what are you going to do?"

"I'm going to go have a nice long chat with Bert."

Are you sure about this? It is reckless, taking him to gods.

The question came from Tiki as Brandi slid from its back and walked alongside it over the wooden floors of Freya's temple. The door behind her altar was open, and Brandi sighed.

"*No,*" she answered truthfully, "*but what other choices have been left to me?*"

Tiki didn't respond as it followed Brandi into Freya's throne room. Shadows danced across the floor as Bert pulled a small doll out of his pocket. It was a simple thing that was obviously handmade, and Brandi was surprised. For all of his advances with technology, he appeared to be more than clumsy when it came to a needle and thread. But seeing him kneel there with a doll in hand left Brandi devoid of any emotion she could name.

She loathed Bert with every fiber of her being, but offering a doll to the goddess was an ancient tradition that most people had forgotten. It was done just before the winter snows began in the realm when people were preparing to hunker down inside with their loved ones to wait out the cold weather. The doll was to symbolize the wish for a daughter, and by offering it to the goddess, it was meant to represent the promise to raise that daughter to serve Freya.

A cold rage burned in Brandi's chest as she watched Bert pray over the doll. If he was praying for a daughter who would serve Freya, then Pine's intel had been right. His visit to Freya's domain was nothing as nefarious as Brandi had feared. Nevertheless, knowing that didn't stoop Brandi from marching forward and grabbing Bert's wounded shoulder with her iron grip.

"What do you think you're doing?" Brandi hissed.

Bert winced in pain, but before he could twist away from her grasp, she called out to the gods.

"Hear me, Freya, mother of this realm. You are me and I am you. We have always been one and I seek you now. Allow me to bring this man into your presence."

With a burst of light blooming from where she held onto Bert, she felt the heat rise beneath her skin as they were pulled into the realm of the gods. They both shielded their eyes and when they opened, Freya sat upon her throne. She wore a long flowing gown of dark green lace with her crown sitting delicately on top of her locs. She smiled at them as the other gods appeared, one by one, to stand around her.

"It is rare for you to seek an audience with me," Freya said, raising her hand to rest beneath her chin. *"What can I do for you?"*

Brandi stood to her feet, shoving Bert away from her as she approached the gods.

"This man is working for your time apprentice. I request that his soul be judged with the utmost prejudice."

"*Oh?*" Freya shifted her gaze to Bert, who sat kneeling on the floor. His head was bowed in silence as he huddled over his doll. "*And what say you, Lindl, dear? Does your child carry the stench of that apprentice on him?*"

Lindl glanced over to the man huddling over the poorly crafted doll and shook his head.

"*I'm afraid not,*" he said. "*Though it does appear he's spent ample amounts of time with someone who does.*"

"*That's impossible,*" Brandi said, shaking her head. "*He's the one who tried to have Sarah sent to you,*" she said, looking at Asari. "*And the one who's been creating tools to undermine your power. And spreading blasphemous rhetoric throughout the queendom. How can it not be him?*"

"*He's bitter,*" Freya said softly. "*He withers under the punishment for his previous transgressions and beseeches us now for mercy and favor,*" she told Brandi. "*But he is not the vessel of Azinne.*"

"*Then why would he try to send Jack?*" Brandi asked, confused.

"*I told you that being the goddess is about more than power,*" Freya said. "*That also means understanding the burden of loving another beyond reason.*"

"*What?*"

"*He has known a loss like you have never imagined,*" Freya said, indicating Bert still bowed on the ground. "*He is unable to give his lover a child, and it drives him to love his queen in a way no other can. So, her wishes are absolute to him. He desired to be rid*" *of Jack because Leia desires to be rid of you. And those who have met you both understand that one cannot exist without the other."* Freya shook her head. *"His intentions were nothing but cruel, and you,"* she said to Lindl, *"should keep a closer eye on your children."*

"My apologies," Lindl said, bowing low. *"I will seek to correct my mistakes."*

"But then…" Brandi sighed, sinking to the floor. *"What am I supposed to do?"*

A chuckle she'd never heard before broke through the barrier of the realm, and even Freya stood from her throne as cracks began emerging by the door to Freya's throne room. She motioned for Brandi to come to her, and she did so, hiding behind the gods as they moved to stand alongside Freya.

With a quick motion of his hand, Lindl sent Bert back to the mortal realm, and the cracks began expanding as the realm pulsed under the new pressure. Freya looked around and motioned to the others.

"I think it would be best to summon your vessels here," she said. *"I believe the time has come for this apprentice to make himself known to us."*

"Well, aren't you the astute one?"

The cracks grew until they met in the center and the realm shattered, revealing an empty void on the other side. A young man with dark gray skin and eyes like the void he walked out of stood before them in a black monochrome suit. His grin was cocky as he sealed up his entrance point and leaned against the wall. He was the spitting image of the one called Zareal that Freya had shown Brandi in her memories, but this man was younger. He moved with a litheness that age hadn't yet begun to slow down.

"*Go ahead and summon your vessels,*" he said, waving one ringed hand through the air. "*I'll wait. I've got nothing but time,*" he said, laughing at his own joke.

The gods shared a look, and one by one, the other vessels began to appear before them. Noble was first, his eyes wide as he met Brandi's gaze and spun around to take in the situation in the room. When his eyes landed on Azinne, he backed away to stand by Brandi and gripped her hand in his own. Sarah was next, followed by Glenn, and then by Cedric, the boy who had opened the gate for them at Lindl's First Holy Academy.

He nodded at Brandi but said nothing as he moved to join their ranks.

"*Pay attention,*" Rothe told them, keeping his eyes focused on Azinne. "*You'll not want to miss this.*"

"*You're a rather dramatic bunch, aren't you?*" Azinne asked.

"*Why don't we skip the banter and move straight to the point,*" Freya asked, taking a slight step forward. "*Why are you here?*"

"*You said it yourself,*" he said, shrugging. "*It was time I introduced myself. I am Azinne Nighseniall, an apprentice of time,*" he said with a slight bow. "*But you knew that already.*"

"*Indeed,*" Freya said. "*And I'm sure you're more than aware of who we are since you decided to let yourself into our realm, uninvited.*"

Azinne laughed at that and the sound of it grated against Brandi's nerves.

"*I am.*"

"*So, why show yourself now,*" Asari asked, "*when you've been more than content to hide amongst the mortals up until this point?*"

"*Because this game of ours was getting boring,*" Azinne said with a straight face.

"*Game?*" Rothe repeated. "*I wasn't aware that we were playing one.*"

"*You wouldn't,*" Azinne smirked. "*But all of time is nothing but one big puzzle. One big game. And I grew tired of waiting for you to make your move.*"

"*So, you've arrived here in a poor attempt to force our hand?*" Lindl asked.

"*Poor attempt?*" Azinne scoffed, pushing off the wall. "*It's a magnificent attempt,*" he shouted, holding his arms out from his sides like some sick kind of circus ringmaster. "*Have you not all gathered here with your vessels? Have you not been scouring the realm for some sign of me?*" He tsked his tongue and shook his head. "*You underestimate the value of moves in this game.*"

"*So, what's the objective of this game you wish to have us play?*" Freya asked. "*Or are you simply a little boy too lonely to know how to ask for proper company,*" she teased. "*Because there are simpler ways to remedy that.*"

Azinne laughed and flashed a smile at Freya that made the other gods bristle, the heat in the room rising to unbearable temperatures.

"*I have lived more lifetimes than you gods ever will,*" he shot back. *"And I do not enjoy the anonymity that is relegated to me simply because I am not one of you. So,"* he said, sliding his hands into his pocket with a smirk, *"I decided to take over your little realm and have the mortals you created worship me instead. And I'll show the Galaxiers that we beings of time deserve recognition as well."*

"That is a rather entitled way to throw a temper tantrum, is it not?" Lindl asked.

"Mock me as you wish," Azinne said, unbothered by Lindl's goading, *"but it doesn't change anything for you."*

"Let's pretend for a moment that we'll play along with your silly game," Rothe said, crossing his arms. *"What are the rules and how do we win?"*

"Simple," Azinne chuckled. *"The winner is whoever destroys the other first. If I win, I get to keep your realm. If you win, you fulfill my master's request and save your little mortals from impending doom."* He grinned again. *"Fun, right?"*

"And what assurances do we have that you'll keep your word?" Freya asked. *"You don't believe us simple-minded enough to trust your word, do you? A being of time could easily reset the clock were something to not go in his favor."*

"I do like you," Azinne said, grinning. *"And the way you think. So, this is what we'll do,"* he said, waving his hand through the air until a black piece of parchment appeared before them with glittering white ink written on it. *"I propose a deal."*

"And?" Carna asked, pulling Freya back, away from the glowing

parchment.

"*We'll put everything on the line,*" Azinne said. "*This is a contract supervised by the Galaxiers. Breaking it is outside of even my control,*" he pointed out. "*We'll both sign, agreeing that the Galaxiers will have the final say on the winner of this bet and abide by whatever verdict they agree to.*"

"*Fine,*" Freya said, stepping forward again. "*But I propose an amendment.*"

"*Freya,*" Rothe shouted, reaching for her. "*You can't just agree to this!*"

"*We have no other choice,*" she told him softly. "*A game with rules is better than fighting him without limitations.*"

"*But —*"

"*Trust me,*" she said, placing her hand over his. "*And trust them,*" she said, nodding to their vessels, who were huddled around Brandi. Rothe glanced in their direction and released her, and she returned her attention to a patiently waiting Azinne.

"*That amendment you wanted?*"

"*You have to make it possible for your soul to be destroyed.*"

"*Thought of that, have you?*" Azinne chuckled. "*Alright then. I'm game,*" he nodded. "*But the same rules would have to apply to you. If my soul must forfeit its immortality, then so must yours.*"

"*I understand.*"

Azinne grinned and snapped his fingers again, and a new parchment appeared before them with glowing inkwells. He signed his name first with a flourish before snapping and having the document move in front

417

of Freya. With a deep breath, she signed her name to the document. The moment she finished, the contract disappeared and a deafening pulse beat twice throughout the realm, sending all the gods staggering back. Azinne laughed as they struggled to right themselves.

"Don't worry," he said, *"that's just the weight of your impending doom on your shoulders. It'll pass."* He threw his fist into the wall beside him, creating another void that he sauntered into with a slight wave over his shoulder. *"Enjoy the time you have left in this realm,"* he said. *"It won't be long,"* he laughed.

With that, the void sealed behind him, and he was gone. The room was silent as the gods turned to face their vessels.

"Well," Freya huffed with a gentle smile. *"It seems that you all have a fair bit of work ahead of you."*

Before Freya had another moment to say anything else, the ground below them shook. The stone walls of her temple began to crack, and the birds that had been frozen in mid-flight began to regain their motion.

The god realm was beginning to crumble.

"I think it would be best if we spoke to our vessels alone," Lindl suggested, moving over to Cedric. *"We'll meet again, I'm sure,"* he said with a quick nod to the others before disappearing.

"Come child," Asari called to Sarah. *"We have much to discuss."*

"C-c-can you —"

"Yes, yes," Asari snapped, interrupting her. *"I've heard your incessant prayers and will heal the incarnation's beloved. Now move yourself."*

With a quick glance over to Noble and Brandi, she let go of Brandi's hand and moved to Asari, disappearing in an instant as Lindl had. Carna said nothing, but Noble walked to him anyway, and they were gone without a word. Only Rothe, Freya, Glenn, and Brandi remained, and he smirked over at them.

"I think a change of scenery is in order."

With a flick of his wrist, they were back in his realm in all its burning hot glory. He sank into his throne and grinned in Brandi's direction.

"Well, vessel of Freya. You've done well to keep your word and bring my vessel to me."

"I've done nothing."

"You haven't," Rothe agreed, making Brandi's shoulder sag, *"but still, you've done a great deal. And there is much more to come."*

"Why am I here?" Glenn asked.

Rothe frowned at her and pulled his hand forward, dragging her to his throne and forcing her to her knees as he looked down on her. Her brown eyes stared, unblinking, at the clouds below them, and Brandi realized she had never seen Glenn look afraid before.

"Sixteen years ago, I shared my power with you," Rothe's voice boomed. *"I directed you to protect the vessel of my beloved and instead you chose to spend the last decade using my power as you see fit to assuage the whims of mere mortals,"* he said, narrowing his eyes. *"Do you hold no regard for your own soul to go about displeasing me as flagrantly as you have?"*

Glenn shook as she waited on her knees and Rothe turned his bright, burning eyes onto Brandi.

"Vessel of Freya! What would you have me do with her?"

Brandi bowed her head and spoke gently. *"Please give Jack the pleasure of being your vessel instead."*

"You were bold in asking for punishment for the soul of Lindl's child. Would you have me keep her soul in this realm to do the same?"

"That is not her decision to make, my love," Freya said, walking forward. *"It is mine."*

"Do with her as you wish," Rothe said, twisting his hand through the air to spin Glenn around to face Freya.

"You silly child of Rothe," Freya said, her voice cold and her words sharp. *"You would defile the power of my beloved and reject the love of my own incarnation to serve the very mortals we created. You misunderstand us and overestimate our grace,"* she told her.

"I'm sorry," Glenn whispered, pressing her forehead into the ground.

"As you should be," Freya snapped. *"But do you believe that an apology will right the wrongs you've committed? I should send your soul into Rothe's sun to endure its burning for all of eternity."*

Glenn whimpered as tears slid down her cheeks and Brandi looked away. She'd known the truth of the goddess her whole life, and she wasn't surprised by the darker nature she was witnessing now. Most people only wanted to remember Freya for her gentle parts, but they often forgot that she created the shaders from darkness, that she is the gatekeeper of souls and the executioner of the gods. She is kind, but she is also just.

"But," Freya said, stopping in front of Glenn, *"your work within*

the mortal realm is not done yet. So, I withhold judgment of your soul."

"Thank you," Glenn whispered.

"However, your punishment will not be light," Freya retorted. *"As penance for serving the mortals instead of the gods, you will never again know rest. You will travel the realm doing only good deeds for the less fortunate and working to undo the blasphemy you helped spread while obeying the orders of the crown. Should you stumble in your purpose even once,"* she warned, *"your soul will receive the harshest of punishments. Do you understand?"*

"Yes."

"Good," she said, turning her eyes away from Glenn and over to Rothe. *"I'll leave her to you."*

"As you wish, my love."

"Come, Brandi," Freya called to her, reaching her hand out. *"We'll leave them to their business."*

Brandi accepted the hand Freya held out to her and was pulled back to Freya's temple. This time, though, Brandi could hear the yelling and clash of battle happening outside the temple doors. The walls that had once separated the throne room from the altar were gone, and the stones beyond it were crumbling and falling to the ground one after another. Freya's throne room never had a ceiling to begin with, but Brandi's heart ached as she watched the temple fall to ruin.

"This was your home," Freya said gently, turning to look at the growing rubble. *"I'm sorry it's being destroyed."*

"What's happening?"

421

"*The time has come for you to choose a path,*" Freya said, turning to face Brandi.

"*What does that mean?*"

"*It means that for centuries, I have guided my vessels through every step of their journey until their souls returned to me. But you are different,*" she smiled. "*You must decide for yourself if you will rise to the occasion and defeat Azinne to save the realm,*" Freya explained, "*or let it fall into his hands and be destroyed.*"

"*Why do you keep putting this on me?*" Brandi asked. "*I can't do anything without you.*"

"*Did you not see what happened with Azinne?*" Freya asked. "*We, the gods, are no longer immortal. And you, our vessels,*" she said, placing one long finger against the center of Brandi's chest, "*now embody our power. Or have you not noticed it growing stronger with every passing moment?*" Freya smiled gently at Brandi. "*You must move forward without us now. Because without our immortality, we are subjected to the whims of time and our power fades. We can no longer protect you as we once have.*"

"*Are you...*" Brandi said, gulping down air, taking a step back in shock, "*trying to tell me...*"

"*You are the sole goddess of this realm now,*" Freya said. "*I told you once before, and now the words ring true more than ever.*"

"*I can't,*" Brandi said, shaking her head. "*I don't know how to be you.*"

"*This is not the expectation, Brandi,*" she said, pulling Brandi into her arms for a hug. "*You have always been you. Now, you are simply you with free rein of my power."*

"And your responsibilities," Brandi muttered, burying her face into Freya's soft form, trying to calm her anxious thoughts.

"That too," Freya chuckled, resting her head on top of Brandi's. *"But I'm not leaving you,"* Freya said. *"My soul is yours, so I will always be with you. But my time of guiding you is over. Now, it's up to you and your friends to decide the fate of the realm."*

"You really expect us to defeat a being of time?"

"And save the entirety of the realm while you're at it," Freya agreed with a wink. *"But I have complete faith in you. You are my incarnation, after all."*

"I don't think I can do this," Brandi whispered.

"You don't have to," Freya said. *"You can choose to live a simple life with Jack. It will be a short life, but you have already done so much for the gods and this realm, none of us would fault you if you chose not to fight anymore. The realm will fall, and we would perish, but that is our failure as gods. Not yours."*

"I don't think I would ever know peace if I sat by to watch the realm be destroyed."

"Then fight to protect it," Freya said softly. *"Or don't,"* she shrugged. *"As I said, my dearest Brandi, this choice is yours, and yours alone, to make. Because no one else can be Brandi Freylin, the Queen's Blade and fiercest shadow in the realm. Commander of shaders. Incarnation of the first goddess."* Freya guided Brandi to her throne and placed a kiss on her head, imbuing her with the last of her power before removing her crown and placing it on Brandi's head.

"*You have always been the wrath of the gods,*" Freya whispered, her form disappearing as Brandi looked on in shock, barely catching her last words as she faded away.

Once Freya was gone, the others returned from the god realm, one by one. They looked up at Brandi, sitting in Freya's throne, with expectation in their eyes and she realized just how big of a seat Freya had left for her to fill. She looked around at Noble, Sarah, Cedric, and a freshly healed Jack with apprehension and gratitude in her heart.

"They tell you the same thing?" Jack asked, walking over to her to sit on the edge of the throne as Rothe did in the tapestry with Freya.

"Yeah," Brandi whispered as she pulled Freya's crown of maple flowers and skulls from her head to look at it. She had no idea what it would mean for her to be the goddess. To sit upon her throne and fulfill Freya's role as mother of the realm and judger of souls. Just the thought of it was overwhelming, but as she looked out at the others staring back at her, she felt her anxiety ease.

She wasn't facing any of this alone.

She had Freya's soul inside of her, her friends standing by her side, and the gods' support at their backs.

That would simply have to be enough for now. So, she smirked at them as she leaned back in the throne that was now hers.

"Apparently," she said, looping Freya's crown around her wrist and watching as it shifted form to fit snugly around it, "we are the origin of a new era of gods."

TO BE CONTINUED...

ACKNOWLEDGMENTS

So, I'm going to keep this short and get straight to the point.

This book absolutely could not and would not exist without two people.

Benjamin Lockhart. My husband and absolute favorite person to ever exist in this universe, bar none. He is my biggest supporter in this fever dream we call life and I would fight all the gods for him, without question.

Amanda Ross. The friend and critique partner I needed. She pushed me forward, encouraged me, and did many a late-night writing sprint with me. I adore her so much and I encourage you to read her books because her creativity inspires mine in so many ways.

There are a slew of other people who are such a huge impact on my life and therefore this book:

My mama, daddy, and brother. Without them, I wouldn't be myself.

Audra Russell. My friend and co-host on the Melanin Chat who always gives her honest opinion and supports me like no one else. I love her to pieces.

My patreon supporters. Without them, I would have lost the courage to do any of this a long time ago.

The Melanin Network. I say it all the time, and I will continue to say it — community is everything and I am so grateful for mine. Having a safe space to be both Black and creative is everything I've always wanted.

My beta readers: Akuwa, Ashleigh, Ashley, Ayo, Celeste, Jessica, Katrina, Rafael, Aran, Daja, and Kizza. They truly helped shape this book.

My editor. This book would be a complete mess without his input.

I am also, so, so grateful to whoever chooses to read this book. Thank you for trusting me with your time and imagination. I hope you enjoyed it.

 Chelsea

ABOUT C. M. LOCKHART

C. M. Lockhart (also known as Chelsea) is a Black writer of fantasy because she loves creating worlds, exploring relationships, and writing stories about Black girls who aren't all that nice. She is the founder of Written in Melanin LLC — which encompasses the Melanin Chat, and a weekly podcast and YouTube channel of the same name — and the Melanin Library, an online database of books written by Black authors.

She is also a lover of video games and anime, so whenever she isn't reading and writing — or talking about reading and writing — she's watching anime, playing her Switch, and dreaming about the day her books get animated.

Find her on social media @CLockhartWrite, @WrittenNMelanin, & @Melanin_Library

CPSIA information can be obtained
at www.ICGtesting.com
Printed in the USA
BVHW080816090623
665686BV00020B/1344

9 781952 978050